I0762956

The NIGHT KING'S COURT

The Night King's Court

ELISA A. BONNIN

HARPER
An Imprint of HarperCollins*Publishers*

HarperCollins Children's Books,
a division of HarperCollins Publishers,
195 Broadway, New York, NY 10007

HarperCollins Publishers,
Macken House, 39/40 Mayor Street Upper,
Dublin 1, D01 C9W8, Ireland

The Night King's Court

harpercollins.com

Library of Congress Control Number: 2025940303
ISBN 978-0-06346301-1
Typography by Catherine Lee
26 27 28 29 30 LBC 5 4 3 2 1

First Edition

To Dante, my sunshine.

PART ONE

REVELS

By the year 826 in our common reckoning, in the twelfth year of Aurel IV's reign, the king had ceased to be seen in the daylight hours entirely, and rarely left the grounds of his southern castle, Asteria. The Whitestone Palace of his ancestors languished in Trissaire, its esteemed halls home to only the king's least favored relatives, his heirs. It was well known among the peerage that the true court of King Aurel could not be found in the palace's gilded halls or in the overflowing sophistication of the capital, but in the mountains. A court not of gold and fire, but of moonlight and air.

—Herbert Ardinger, *The King of Moonlight: A Comprehensive History of Aurel IV*

Chapter 1

CASTLE OF STARS

When Ida ran away from home, she left her mother not a note, but a memory written into a candle. She'd mixed the lavender and mint scents of her grandmother's garden into the wax with a captured song, and had dyed the entire construct the deep, sunset orange of the rug that had once decorated their flat in Trissaire. The rug itself—a bright, tropical creation that her father told her had come from his homeland—had been sold or thrown away when her mother had taken Ida away from the city, but she knew the color would evoke a memory. She'd weaved that memory into her candle's design so that when her mother burned it, she would smell the scents of home and hear Ida's voice humming the tune her father once used to sing her to sleep, and she would know where Ida had gone.

Ida hoped she would understand. But even if her mother did, she knew that her other relatives, her grandmother, grandfather, aunts, and horde of perfect, blond cousins, would not.

She sat bundled into the back of a cart as it inched its way up rocky mountain roads, her back pressed against the wooden siding. The rocking motion of the cart was making her ill. The back of the cart was filled with boxes of fruit from the valley, giving the air a sweet smell, but even that could hardly counter the overwhelming odor of horse. She pressed her lips tightly together and gave up, resting her head on her knees.

She wasn't sure if the sudden churning in her gut had come from motion sickness, or from nerves now that her journey was finally coming to an end. Whatever it was, she took slow breaths, trying to ignore the way her stomach lurched with each jolt of the cart, the stiffness in her limbs from the long climb. Her solitary piece of luggage, the cracked, hard-leather case that her father had once carried with him over the ocean, was wedged uncomfortably at her side. The tools tucked inside that suitcase, packed in among her spare clothes and the trinkets she had grabbed from home, had saved her at the train station in Feld. The cart driver almost hadn't wanted to take her up the roads into Asteria, not believing when she said that she was here to answer the king's invitation to become the new luminaire.

Without her candles, she would have been lost. Ida had inherited enough of her mother's classic Arreden features to not seem out of place in the country, but although her skin was several shades paler than her father's, it was still dark enough to make her seem permanently tanned, and she had inherited her father's thick brown hair. She didn't look foreign, not at first glance, but—as her grandmother often told her—she gave off an air of disreputability, as if she had gotten this way by spending all her time running wild in the hills.

Reputable, to her grandmother, meant *Arreden*.

One breath. Another.

Magic came from stillness. Ida let her thoughts roll off her like water from a stone, sinking into that place where she could become a conduit for power. If she held herself there, she could forget the rocking of the cart, the nausea and fear and guilt that pooled deep in her gut. She could forget for a moment— A knock on the wooden wall separating her from the driver's bench startled her, and Ida looked up.

"We're coming up on the castle," the driver said, as toneless as if he brought young girls up to King Aurel's court every day. "You can see it now."

Ida scrambled up onto her knees, thrusting her head out through the canvas flap. The mountains spread out in front of her, a jaw-dropping landscape of emerald meadows and yellow flowers and snowcapped peaks. Air so wide it felt like she could drown in it. Endless, blue, blue sky. Nestled into that beauty, like a jewel in a crown, Ida caught her first sight of Asteria, the home of the Night King.

Her first thought was that it did not look real. Walls of sheer white stone cradled the mountainside as if the castle had simply formed there, as if a winter wind had swept in and formed it out of frost. Delicate towers like spun sugar reached grasping fingers up from the stones, terraces flung themselves wide into the bracing mountain air.

But for all its beauty, it was empty, bereft in the light of day. She saw no sign of anyone around the castle aside from them, no guards on the walls or carts moving along the dirt road on their way to pay tribute aside from hers. No flags or banners waved in the breeze, nothing declared that this place was the seat of the Arreden king.

A castle of ghosts.

Her anxiety returned, sharper now. She looked up at Asteria as the cart drew closer, at its empty walls and shadowed windows, and remembered why she had come.

Because this was the last place anyone had seen her father alive.

The cart pulled into a delivery tunnel so cleverly concealed that Ida wouldn't have spotted it if she had been walking past it and unceremoniously unloaded her in the kitchen along with the crates of supplies. If she could think straight, Ida might feel offended, but she was still coming to terms with the gravity of what she had done.

She had come to Asteria, to the court of the Night King.

It lived up to its name. At the moment, the kitchens were cold and bare, despite the noontime warmth, and the entire castle had a hush to it, as if it were still asleep. She might have believed it was abandoned, if not for the murmur of voices in the air, words spoken so softly that she could barely make them out.

The cart driver, discussing what to do with her.

When he reappeared a few moments later, Ida straightened up and tried not to look so much like she was waiting outside the head teacher's office to be scolded. He glanced in her direction, gave her a curt nod, and slipped his cap back onto his head as he marched back to his cart. Ida opened her mouth, the question of what she should do now already on her lips, but before she could say anything, a new figure loomed in the kitchen doorway, clearing his throat.

It was an older man, his thin gray hair cut short. He was dressed in a severe black suit, a design emblazoned in silver on the front of it—the king's chalice and crossed spears. He wore white gloves and carried a polished black cane. His skin was pale, his eyes a washed-out green, so that it seemed like there was barely any color left in him. But she felt the sharpness of his gaze as it settled on her, and she resisted the urge to smooth out her skirt, now hopelessly rumpled and smelling of horse.

When he spoke, even his voice was colorless. Dry, like the rasp of old paper.

"*You* are the luminaire?"

Ida cleared her throat, picking up her case with one hand as she dropped into a passable curtsy. "My name is Ida Rosales. I work in candles."

"Hmph."

The man snorted in disdain, and Ida wasn't sure whether it was for her personally. He seemed like the sort of man who was displeased about everything. He couldn't have failed to notice her surname, very un-Arreden, but he made no comment on it. Instead, he said, "You realize, the position advertised isn't for any mere candlemaker."

"I'm no mere candlemaker." Ida was grateful that propriety allowed her to keep her head down, and her voice at a murmur, so that this man wouldn't hear how it wavered. Her fingers gripped the handles of her case tighter, and she willed them not to shake as the silence pulled taut between them.

"We'll see about that," the man finally said, stepping away from the door. "Follow me."

He led her through the empty kitchen, down a cavernous hallway with wide, open arches along one side. The corridor was awash with bright sunlight and bracing mountain air. Ida's footfalls echoed eerily on the white stone floor. To her right, all she could see was the blue of the infinite sky, the jagged peaks of the mountains cradling a clear lake below. There was no sign of anyone else. It was as if the two of them were the only ones in the world.

She'd been staring, and almost didn't notice that her companion had halted. Ida jerked to a stop, narrowly avoiding bumping into the man. His brows arched in disdain, and she took a step back, embarrassed.

He was facing a heavy wooden door, a ring of keys of all different sizes in one hand. As she watched, his fingers moved through the keys with the ease of long practice, selecting a heavy metal key, stained black as if by char. He inserted it into the lock, and Ida heard something equally heavy shift on the other side of the door before he pulled it open.

The room inside was pitch black.

A puff of cold air flooded out into the hallway from the room, chasing away the warmth of the sun and making Ida's skin prickle with gooseflesh. She bit back a gasp. The darkness of the room was more than paint, more than shadow. It was something elemental and primordial, as if darkness itself had been distilled into the air and stones.

The man was watching her, waiting for any sign of weakness. Ida swallowed her nervousness, peering into the heart of the room.

"This is the court of moon and starlight," the man said, his voice as dry as dust, as bones, "but it's also the court of midnight and shadow. If you claim to be able to bring light, Miss Luminaire, then this room should not intimidate you at all."

She was intimidated. How could she not be? But his words were flint to kindle inside her, and she felt the warmth of the resulting fire flooding her bones. Ida should have been used to people underestimating her. Her whole life, people looked at her and lamented about what she was not, all the ways she wasn't *enough*. After seventeen years of this, the words shouldn't have affected her anymore.

But they did. The barbs stung each time, digging into her skin like burrs, and each time, she felt this fire. This urge to prove all of them wrong.

She stepped into the room.

Inside, though the darkness wasn't solid, Ida thought she could feel it. A hungry void, robbing the light and warmth from her, threatening to take away even the light of her life. She couldn't see anything, not even her hands in front of her face. When she turned, she could see the open door, the white hallway and sunlight streaming in through the arches, but it was like looking at a painting. Sunlight didn't shine into this room.

The servant was staring into the room, unimpressed. He wasn't looking at her, and Ida realized that it was because he couldn't *see* her, that when she had walked into the room, she had been swallowed up by that ravenous void.

He *wouldn't* be able to see her, unless she accomplished what even the sun couldn't do.

Bring light into the dark.

Ida reached into her pocket, pulling out a heavy metal firestrike. Her finger rubbed over the words engraved on its casing for warmth. The firestrike was commemorative, and the symbol engraved on the front of it, the emblem of the university her father had attended once, had no particular meaning to her. But it was one of the few things Ida still had from her father.

She flicked the firestrike's cap open and ran her thumb over the grooved wheel inside. Flame flickered to life at the motion, but although she could hear the sizzle as it came up, could feel the heat against her skin, she couldn't see the fire. Ida flicked the firestrike shut, extinguishing the flame. Well, fair enough. She hadn't truly expected that to work to begin with.

Ida dropped into a crouch, placing her suitcase on the ground. She popped open the latches, lifting the lid. Navigating entirely by feel, Ida reached for her candle kit. She didn't have time to make an entirely new candle for this task, but she had expected an audition, and had prepared a selection of candles in advance.

The question was, which one would best bring light?

She ran her fingers over the tapers, all arrayed in a row and strapped to the upper wall of her suitcase. They quivered beneath her fingertips, each of them ringing with the sensations that Ida had woven into their making, but they weren't quite right. Until her fingers came to rest on one, the third from the last.

She'd almost forgotten she'd made this candle.

Carefully, Ida extracted the taper from the set. She left her case where it lay, rising to her feet. And once again, she flicked open her firestrike, this time holding the flame to the wick.

Ida held her breath, uncertain. Hopeful.

The flame sputtered as it caught, pushed back at first by the darkness. But then it changed, stretching into a golden orb that hung just over the candle's tip. Ida exhaled, holding the taper out in front of her as the magic she wove into the wax came to life.

The orb expanded, and as it did, gold veins flared into life along the sides of the candle, flooding the room with the light and warmth of a midsummer day. The air became hot and sticky, redolent with the scent of flowers, the buzzing of bees. The light cast shadows on the walls of the room, forming the illusion of hedges and leaves. A carpet of green appeared at her feet, lush grass spreading until it touched the edges of the room. From somewhere off in the distance, Ida caught the mouthwatering scent of baking bread, of honey and the fragrant tea her grandmother favored. For a second, the effect was so disorienting that Ida almost felt like she was home again, that all of this was a dream.

But then she looked back over her shoulder and saw the man standing in the door, watching her with an expression of astonishment. When he caught her looking, he quickly composed his expression, though he couldn't quite take his eyes away from the candle in her hand.

At length, he placed his hand to his heart and dropped into a courtly bow.

"My name is Heinrich Dallenbach," he said. "Day Steward to His Majesty, King Aurel IV. On his behalf, allow me to be the first to formally welcome you to Asteria."

Chapter 2

EYES OF ICE

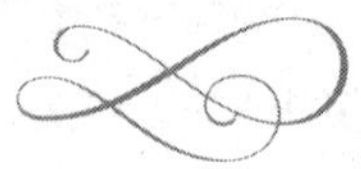

Steward Dallenbach led Ida to a bedroom on the upper level of the servants' quarters. It was well-equipped but sparsely decorated, with a sturdy wooden bed tucked up against one of the whitewashed walls, a wardrobe for her things, and a trunk at the foot of the bed. Heavy curtains hung over the room's one window, blocking out sunlight—a necessity, Ida thought, in a court that conducted most of its activities at night. There was a mirror and a basin for her to wash with, a writing desk, and a rug that softened the stone floor, but there were no personal touches, nothing to indicate that anyone had stayed in this room before her.

"These quarters are for the use of the Court Luminaire," the steward explained, gesturing to a wooden door on the left side of the room, beside the armoire. "That door leads to the luminaire's workshop. If His Majesty approves of your appointment, you will gain access to it soon. For now, I suggest you rest. Tonight, you will be summoned to an audience with His Majesty."

Steward Dallenbach paused, his gaze flicking disdainfully over her appearance. "Something suitable will be brought for you to wear. Should you need to relieve yourself, the servants' privy is on the right of the hall. It's equipped with baths, which I suggest you make use of. If you pass this trial, you will be granted access to the Knights' Bath. Someone will come to fetch you at sunset. Have a good day."

With a stiff bow, Dallenbach left, the door shutting heavily in his wake. He hadn't given her the key.

Ida didn't bother unpacking. She hadn't brought much, nothing suitable for an audience with the king. And Dallenbach had been very clear—her stay in this room and her status in this court were temporary. If King Aurel didn't approve her appointment, she would be on her way home by sunrise.

Instead, she took Dallenbach's advice and tried to sleep. It was difficult. Even with the heavy curtains blocking out the sunlight, Ida's body couldn't forget that it was still the middle of the day. And as she stretched out on the bed, looking up at the room's ceiling, her mind wandered to the inhabitants of this room before her. To her father, who may have resided here during his tenure with King Aurel. If he had been here, she saw no sign of him.

At length, she gave up on sleep and paced the room, looking for any trace of the previous luminaires. There wasn't much. The writing desk and wardrobe had both been cleared out, and only a symbol, scratched into the inside of the wardrobe door, told her that this room had ever been occupied before her. She ran her thumb over the engraving, feeling a prickle of energy bursting across her skin. It was obviously a ward of some kind, possibly against moths, but neither Ida nor her father had ever worked with glyphs as a medium.

Memories burst into her mind, the scent of incense heavy in the air, scenes of childhood fairy tales playing out on her ceiling as she fell asleep. It had been her father who showed her how scent could carry magic, but for once, she wished that he had chosen something more tangible.

Because now it seemed like he was gone without a trace.

The last time she had seen her father, she'd been nine. He'd gone to Asteria, as its Court Luminaire. And then he simply never returned. She and her mother received no explanation, no acknowledgment that he had ever served as the Court Luminaire. One day, his letters stopped coming. A few months later, an article in the broadsheets described the Court Luminaire as an Arreden man named Maxwell Mueller who worked using carvings as his medium. There had been no mention of the Niresso man who wrought illusions out of smoke and light.

Ida had wanted to demand an explanation. She had wanted to march down to the king's main palace at Trissaire, ten years old and full of rage and fury, and not leave until *someone* told her where her father was and what happened to him. Her mother stopped her. Girls *like her* didn't make demands of the royal family. Girls like her didn't dare raise their voices within an inch of aristocracy. Didn't step into palaces unless they were invited, or unless they were the maid.

By "girls like her," Ida already knew her mother meant girls who weren't Arreden.

"So what?" Ida remembered screaming at her mother. Because how could her mother, who was part of this world, who fit so *neatly* into it, understand how much Ida's heart was breaking? *"So what, we just leave him? That's that?"*

"Yes, Ida." Gisela Rosales had tears in her eyes, but her words were as harsh as blades. They were always unforgiving as steel when

she began one of those speeches and started to tell Ida how the world was less fair for *girls like her*. *"That's that."*

A month later, her mother stopped waiting for word. Another month, and she packed up the apartment in Trissaire, gave up their life in the heart of Arred's largest city to drag Ida to the mountains to be with her grandmother and her horde of cousins. She'd taken Ida from a place where mages were loved, welcomed even, to the type of small village that still called magic witchcraft, that thought of its popularity as another symptom of the nation's moral decay. A village where the only thing worse than a mage was a foreigner.

Ida had never quite forgiven her for it.

A year later, Gisela Rosales had gone back to being Gisela Wenderoth, and Ida's father was hardly mentioned again. It felt like the whole world was ready to forget him, but Ida remembered. Her father had gone to Asteria. He would never simply leave them. Something had happened to him there.

Seven years later, seven years after her father vanished, Maxwell Mueller retired, and the news came that the king in Asteria was looking for a new luminaire.

It was the only way a girl like her would ever get into Asteria. Ida saw her chance, took it, and ran.

She stopped her explorations, popping her thumb into her mouth to soothe away the lingering buzz of magic. Ida left the wardrobe and set her suitcase on the desk, taking out her selection of candles. Without access to the luminaire's workshop, and without much time left, she wouldn't be able to create any new spells for her audience with the king. And she would have only one chance to impress him, to show him that she *could* do this job.

She pulled one slender taper out of the box, a bright sunshine yellow. Ida lit it, setting it in a candleholder on the desktop, and let the room fill with a bright, citrusy scent that instantly made her feel wide awake. With that settled, she pulled her hair back from her face and got to work.

At sunset, someone knocked on her door. Ida pulled the door open wide, half expecting to see Steward Dallenbach, and found two women waiting on the other side. One was only a little older than her, the other could have been the first woman's mother. Both were dressed in clean white uniforms with King Aurel's crest embroidered over their hearts. The younger one held up a shimmering golden gown. The other carried a box in her hands.

"Mistress Ida?" the woman with the box asked, her tone curt as she looked over Ida's rumpled dress, her messy hair, the bare feet that she was suddenly self-conscious of. "We're here to prepare you for your audience."

Two hours later, Ida was washed, scrubbed, dressed, and painted, and she could no longer recognize herself in the mirror. Glittering gold eye shadow accentuated her skin's natural light brown, and her dress sparkled as she moved, catching the light in a way that made Ida feel as if she were glowing. The baubles the maids had woven into her hair tinkled and caught the light with every movement.

She barely had a moment to admire herself, though, before she was being hustled out of the room, her candlemaking kit heavy in her hands. The worn black briefcase was at odds with the rest of her outfit, and Ida caught the older of the two maids staring at it with disdain. When she offered to carry it for her, Ida didn't refuse, although handing it over felt like she was handing over a piece of her heart. The news reports all said that King Aurel was vain, and the last thing Ida wanted to do was lose her chances by somehow offending his sensibilities.

Besides, with the way her stomach was roiling and her hands shaking, she wasn't confident that she wouldn't drop it.

The maids led her up a narrow spiral staircase. Then they emerged through a heavy wooden door at the top and into—

—light.

Ida's breath caught as the full splendor of King Aurel's court struck her. From the road, Asteria seemed a statue, all sharp white lines and bare planes, but now that the sun had set, the court was *alive*.

They were in a stone courtyard, ringed with trees, awash in color. Light hung on every available surface, iridescent lights gilding the trees in multiple colors and bright, fluttering lights drifting this way and that. Music, quick and joyful, sounded from the corner to Ida's left; to her right, an acrobat in silks whirled, flipped, and contorted herself along the rampart to adoring applause, heedless, apparently, of the sheer drop just inches from her. And then there were the courtiers themselves. Ida thought that she was dressed in finery, but *they* were resplendent, in gem-colored gowns and fine suits, in jewels and feathers and masks. Some of the most powerful people in Arred were here waiting on the king's word.

One of the little lights flitted past Ida's eye as she walked, and she was surprised to see a human form in it, small, barely larger than her thumb, with wings like dragonflies.

Fairies, Ida realized, and she had to stop herself from standing there open-mouthed. As one of her escorts cleared her throat, Ida hurried to follow them, trying not to trip over the hem of her gown.

A few people watched curiously as Ida walked past, but most

paid her no heed. It seemed like new arrivals were common at King Aurel's court, and amid everything that was going on, no one would look at her unless she did something worthy of attention.

Unless she performed. Like she was going to have to do, in front of the king.

Anxiety churned her stomach, making Ida feel vaguely nauseous again.

Her escorts led her up a set of stairs, to a landing that overlooked the courtyard below. The landing was also decked in lights, multicolored globes of glass strung from one of the central trees to bathe the area in a soft glow. They left her with instructions to wait, and headed up another flight of stairs, toward a third tier of the courtyard.

The maids had taken her kit with them, leaving her with no idea what to do with her hands. After a moment of twisting her fingers into knots, she smoothed out her skirt and decided to walk. She had too much nervous energy in her to be able to stand still for long, and as long as she stayed on the same landing, she was sure her escorts would be able to find her.

She needed something to eat. Food would settle her stomach, and make her feel a little less like she was about to faint. She plucked a pastry from the tray of a passing waitron, the plainest on the tray to avoid getting jam and sugar and cream down the front of her dress. The treat still looked more delicate than the ones sold at her village bakery. Ida was reminded of the stories she had heard as a child, of people who wandered from one world into another. Once they ate the food there, they were trapped forever.

But this wasn't some fey land, or a witch's house in the dark woods. This was the court of her own king.

Ida raised the treat to her lips and took a bite. Buttery, flaky pastry broke between her teeth and flavors exploded onto her tongue, her eyes widening in surprise at the complexity of them. She tasted something tart and citrusy and for a moment, she thought she could feel warmth on her face and smell salt in the air, like she was standing on the beach by the sea. She recognized magic, woven carefully into the food, and closed her eyes to savor the illusion.

When she opened them, she was not alone.

A boy stood in front of her, staring at her with an intensity that took her by surprise. She stepped back, startled, but he didn't move, and in that moment she thought he was still part of the illusion. In the whirlwind of color, he was dressed in black, a suit the same midnight shade as his hair. His features were sharp, almost aquiline, and his eyes—

Ida had never seen eyes that shade of blue before. A blue like winter, like ice, a blue so sharp that it cut.

She looked into his eyes and felt her heart speed up with something that felt at first like attraction, but upon closer inspection was recognition, something in her calling out to something in him. Some latent magical sense telling her—screaming at her, really—that this was no ordinary boy.

Ida cleared her throat and brushed flecks of pastry from her lips. "Can . . ." Her first word came out softly. She frowned, annoyed with herself, and forced more strength into her throat. "Can I *help* you?"

The boy looked at her, unmoving, and for a second, Ida had the disconcerting sense that she was speaking to a statue, that at any moment someone else in the crowd would laugh at the new girl for talking to an art installation. But then he spoke, his words lightly accented with something that reminded her of snow and rain.

"You seem . . . familiar."

There were moments that felt significant. Moments where the world shifted on its axis. Moments like this one, standing on a balcony in a palace courtyard in a gown finer than she had ever worn in her life, staring at a boy with winter eyes.

She said, truthfully, "I've never met you before in my life."

The boy didn't dispute that, but his eyes narrowed slightly. He studied her carefully, as if Ida were a puzzle he was trying to solve. He said, "It's true, you're different. But your soul is . . . warm. Full of light. You remind me of someone."

Someone.

The shift stopped, the floating, moving pieces of Ida's world jolting painfully back into shape. She'd only been here for a moment. Less than a day. And her father had been missing for years. She hadn't expected to find any trace of him so soon, but was it possible—?

"Was it a man?" Ida asked, speaking quickly. "A luminaire? Did he work in scents? Was he foreign? Was his name—"

She swallowed. The name "Tomas Rosales" was on the tip of her tongue, but movement out of the corner of her eye stopped her. Someone shouted in her direction, and Ida spun to see that her escorts were walking toward her at pace, moving as quickly as they could without shoving their way through the crowd.

"What are you doing?" the older maid asked as she reached Ida. She swatted the half-eaten pastry out of Ida's hand and started brushing the crumbs off her dress, her movements brisk enough to hurt. "Clean yourself up, girl! You're not here to eat pastries, you're here to see the king!"

The other maid took Ida firmly by the arm, tugging her away from the balcony. Before she could fully understand what was happening, the two of them were marching her forward, like she was a prisoner between them.

"Talking with *that* boy too—of all the things—" the older maid muttered under her breath.

Ida's head whirled to face her, the prospect of information momentarily overcoming her indignation at being treated like a puppet on strings.

"You know him?"

"Know him?" the maid replied, glaring at Ida. "Of course we know him. He's one of the King's Collection."

"Collection?"

The younger maid shuddered. Ida could feel the tremor through her grip on Ida's arm.

"That boy isn't human."

Ida absorbed this and found it curious that it didn't bother her as much as she would have thought. She had known before embarking on this trip that King Aurel was rumored to collect magical things. And the boy hadn't seemed dangerous.

He'd seemed . . . almost sad.

"What is he, then?"

"Never you mind about Vegard," the older maid said, tightening her grip on Ida's arm hard enough to pinch. "If I were you, I'd focus on His Majesty, or this is the last night you'll ever spend at this court."

Ida knew she was right. King Aurel was known to be temperamental, and this audience with him would be everything. All her plans would be meaningless if she couldn't impress King Aurel enough to convince him to let her stay.

But as they led her up the stairs, toward the man who would decide her fate, the last man who had employed her father before his disappearance, her mind kept spinning, latching on to one thing.

The boy, with eyes like ice, the way magic curled and rippled around him as if it were woven into his skin.

And his name, now humming in her head, the syllables of it ringing together like a clarion call.

Vegard.

Chapter 3

THE NIGHT KING

Ida's first feeling as she stood before her monarch was disappointment. She had always imagined that King Aurel would be special. He was the Arreden king, the most powerful man on the continent, and he had built a castle of magic and wonder. But surrounded by splendor, seated beneath an embroidered awning on the highest tier of the courtyard's five levels where he could watch the revelry, the king himself looked so very ordinary.

An Arreden man at the end of his middle years, hair more gray than red thinning at the top of his head, skin beginning to sag with age. He was dressed in fine clothes and wore a royal circlet, was neatly groomed and dressed in finery, but—

—but the world didn't ripple around him the way it had for Vegard.

She was aware that her thoughts were insolent and did her best to keep them from her face. This was still the king, after all, and if Ida wanted to stay in Asteria, she would need to impress him.

"So," King Aurel said, and even his voice was unimpressive. Wispy and uneven, like a flame in danger of being snuffed out by the wind. "What do we have here?"

"A candlemaker from the north, Your Majesty," one of the maids said, head bowed. The younger one. "She's here to fill the post of luminaire."

Ida shot her a surprised glance. She hadn't truly expected help from the maids, not after the disdain they showed her. Beside her, the maid who had spoken didn't look her way.

King Aurel caressed his chin with one hand, thoughtful. He looked back at her. "What do they call you?"

"Ida Rosales, Your Majesty," Ida said. She wished she could watch the king's face, could see if there was any spark of recognition at her name. With her head down, she could only see a vague outline of him.

When the maid next to her cleared her throat, Ida lifted her head. She did so a little too quickly. Titters of amusement rose from the gathered courtiers. Ida felt the heat rise to her face. King Aurel did not look amused. His brows drew together in thought, watery eyes fixed on her. His fingers laced together, forming a cradle below his chin.

"Rosales," he said, rolling the name around in his mouth like it was a foreign delicacy. "You are from Callania?"

Ida had expected this question, but it still pinched. Callania was Arred's neighbor to the south, and it *was* true that her surname originated from there. But it had come to her by a roundabout route. Her father had been born in the Niressians, a longtime Callish colony. The relationship between Callania and its colonies was strained, built upon centuries of blood and pain.

That didn't stop her grandmother and her mother's relatives from telling everyone that she was Callish. In Arred, that was far more respectable.

But she refused to lie. Not about this.

"No, Majesty," she said. "I am Arreden. But my father was from the Niressians."

Murmurs rose in the crowd, and Ida could feel them reevaluating her, her dark hair, her tan skin, her brown eyes. She tried to not let it bother her, but it was hard when the sharp intake of breath from one of the maids beside her made her wonder whether she should have said nothing.

King Aurel, however, didn't look disturbed. He merely watched her, with vacant eyes. If he had ever had a Niresso in his court before her, if he had ever met another Rosales, there was nothing in his expression to suggest that.

It made her want to scream, to demand to know what had happened to her father. But she choked it back. That would be a good way to get thrown out of the court. She had come this far. She could wait, see this through, and secure her place.

King Aurel studied her a beat longer before nodding.

"Very well," he said. "You must know, girl, that I am seeking more than a mere candlemaker." He gestured expansively at the world around him. The warmth, the bright lights, the soft sounds of merrymaking from the balconies below. "I am seeking a luminaire who can bring light to this court. Wonders such as my guests have never seen. Is this who you are?"

Ida knew the right answer. She had lived in Trissaire long enough to know that there were those before whom she could assert herself, and those who would judge her regardless of what she said or did.

"That," she murmured softly, "depends entirely on Your Majesty."

King Aurel settled back into his seat.

"Very well," he said, extending a hand toward her. The gesture was small and dismissive, as if she was meant to take it as a sign of exceptional generosity. "Dazzle us."

Ida accepted her kit from the maid who had taken it from her. Now that the moment of anger had passed, she was nervous again, her stomach threatening to reject even the small bit of pastry she had eaten. She stepped forward carefully, willing her face to be a mask. Showmanship was part of a luminaire's craft, and Ida had practiced enough to know that hers wasn't lacking.

She swept her gown out in front of her with a hand, orange silk billowing around her as she dropped down to her knees on the floor. With a flourish, she set the kit down in front of her, popping it open.

Her candles waited inside, lined up in rows like soldiers. For the test that had gotten her this audience, Ida had used a simple creation, one that would bring light to the darkness. But for this, she sensed that that wouldn't be enough. She would need a grand illusion, on par with the court's splendor, to convince the king of her worthiness to stay.

She'd known from the start that she would have to prove herself, though, and she had come prepared.

Ida selected the last candle in the line. A long, slender taper, stained a deep blue violet. Silver designs were traced into its surface, elegant filigree patterns. She lifted it from the box, holding it up in her hand to show the audience. A wide sweep, from left to right, making sure that everyone around had a chance to look at the candle before she presented it to the king.

When he didn't stop her, she reached for her father's firestrike with her other hand, coaxing a flame to life.

To make this candle, she had carved out the pattern herself with her smallest, sharpest knife, and had painted over the lines to make them stand out. It had been hours of work, and she still remembered the way her fingers had been stained blue at the end of it, the way her hands trembled as she wrapped the finished candle and set it back in its case. But the work had been worth it, because as Ida had drawn her knife over the candle, as she carved ornamentation into the wax, she had also been imbuing it with an illusion.

When she touched the flame to the wick, the illusion burst into life. It pulled itself out of her like a breath, a wisp of her essence drawn into the candle and expelled like smoke through the flame. The air filled with a sharp, clear scent first: of mountain air, snow, pine, and winter secrets. Then the darker scent of cherries, a brief hint of liquor. A laugh, like bells. A sound, like galloping horses.

The wind changed. The scent shifted to something floral and soft, a lady's perfume, and Ida heard the gasps in the crowd as the illusion took hold.

She had never been to a ball in the royal court, but she could imagine one. From the sketches in the broadsheets, or the porcelain music box her mother had brought with her from Trissaire, the one of the man and woman dancing, round and round in an endless waltz. The illusion was given life by Ida's imagination, and it tore through the crowd now.

It swept over the watchers, enveloping each of them in finery. They had all been dressed in their best silks, but now the ladies wore billowing gowns of a fabric that glittered and gleamed like starlight. The gentlemen's cloaks rippled like the midnight sky, their outfits decorated in intricate brocade. But the centerpiece were the masks.

Elaborate masks rested on each of the onlookers' faces, beaded and feathered and dripping with jewels, each one unique to the wearer. Ida felt the same change come over her, and as she rose to her feet now draped in a gown of gleaming silver, her mask trailing crystal beads down her cheek, she knew that they could see what she saw.

Through the eyeholes of her mask, the whole world had changed. They were no longer standing on a balcony; a ballroom spread out before them, tiled marble floors and chandeliers dripping with lights. Music played from an orchestra off to her right, each of the members wearing identical black masks. And the room was full of dancers, arm in arm, twirling around her, each wearing the elaborate masks of her masquerade.

The illusion held for a moment, swelled.

And then, with a soft sound like tinkling glass, it faded, leaving Ida and the courtiers standing on the balcony once more.

Ida blinked at the sudden change. The transition often left her disoriented and wanting. All around her, others remained, staring at the illusion with rapt attention. Her illusions never lasted as long for her as they did for others.

She held the lit candle up to her mouth and gently blew it out.

A murmur rose around her as the illusion faded for the others, the candle's scent lingering in her nose as a coil of smoke rose from the wick. Then, once it became clear what had happened, her audience rewarded her with applause.

Her heart was pounding. She could tell she had excited them—the whispers around her could mean nothing else. But it was not them who would decide her fate. It was the king.

She raised her head to him as King Aurel lifted a hand, and everyone around them quieted.

He studied her for a long time, long enough that Ida fidgeted and wondered whether she should bow again.

At length, he said, "Where did you learn your skills?"

"My father taught me," Ida said, watching his face carefully. It never changed, not a flicker of recognition. "He worked in scents—perfumes and incense. My mother taught me candlemaking."

"Do these illusions require your presence?" King Aurel asked. "Or is it simply enough for you to make the candle?"

"The candle will produce an illusion for whoever lights it. But for the more complicated workings, complex illusions such as this one, it helps if I am present. I can anchor the illusion, guiding it."

"And if I were to light this candle?" King Aurel asked. "Without you?"

"You would see the ball," Ida said. "Everyone would view the illusion separately, at their own pace. The effect would not be harmonized, and I worry that people would quickly be confused."

"How long does the effect last?"

"Until the candle is extinguished, Your Majesty."

King Aurel extended a hand toward her, palm up. Ida didn't immediately understand what he was asking for, until the footman at his side walked over to her and reached for the candle. She handed it over and watched, trying not to fidget with her gown, as the king took it from the footman's hand. He held it up in front of him, making a show of examining the workmanship, turning it this way and that and running his fingertips along the carved exterior.

At length, he handed it back to the footman and rested his hands on his armrests. He eyed her critically, and it was all Ida could do not to squirm. She tried to read his thoughts from his expression, but it was unreadable. A royal mask of its own.

"Are you affiliated with a guild?"

"No, Your Majesty."

"You've signed no contracts? You have no other master?"

"None, Your Majesty."

The king hummed thoughtfully. "I am willing to offer you a provisional appointment to the post of Court Luminaire."

Ida's heart leaped into her throat. "Provisional" was not the same as "full," but an appointment was still an appointment, still a chance. She kept her eyes on the king, hanging on to his every word.

"You will occupy this post for a trial period of one year. If you perform to our satisfaction, your appointment may be extended. During this year, you will be afforded all the privileges of Court Luminaire, including access to the luminaire's workshop. You will be expected to keep court hours. Your assignments will be given to you. While you are resident in Asteria, if you require anything to perform your duties, you may request it from my staff. You must not leave my service or take up regular employment until your year is complete, though you may take commissions from members of my court if you wish, so long as they do not interfere with your duty to me. Do you find these terms acceptable?"

A year.

A year was enough. It had to be. If she couldn't find any trace of her father in a year, she doubted she ever would. Ida dropped into a curtsy and managed, somehow, not to tremble.

"Yes, Your Majesty."

King Aurel extended a hand toward her, and this time Ida approached the throne. She dropped to a knee, the stone floor of the balcony cool through the fabric of her gown, and kissed his signet ring.

She felt a sudden shock as her lips touched the cold metal of the ring, a pinprick of pain like the ring had bitten her. Ida flinched back—too quickly, she realized, because when she looked up, she could see the displeasure in the king's eyes. They were shadowed, hooded beneath the weight of the crown.

There was ice in her veins, her blood suddenly rushing through her ears.

That had been—that had been magic, hadn't it?

A spell in the ring. A spell like—

Her mouth tasted like blood.

She stood and stepped back a little too quickly, keeping her head bowed, and resisting the urge to scrub at her mouth. She was overreacting, she told herself. Of course there was magic. It was an oath made to a king.

But what would the magic do to her should she fail?

She clasped her hands in front of her, waiting, her heart thudding in her ears. At a curt gesture from King Aurel, the footman returned her candle. The king dismissed her with a wave of his hand, already moving on to his next diversion, and the crowd of courtiers closed ranks around him as Ida and her maids stepped away from the throne.

It was only when they were a balcony below the king, once more immersed in the crowd, that the enormity of what had just happened hit her. Ida leaned against the stone wall that bordered this tier, letting out a long sigh as the maids fluttered around her.

"—ruined these gloves, silly girl," the older one was saying, tugging them off her hands. Looking down now, Ida saw they were wax-stained. "What *are* we going to do with you?"

"She simply mustn't wear gloves, Petra," said the other maid—the younger one. Sabine, Ida thought, the name coming to her.

"She'll only ruin them working with wax and fire."

"A lady without gloves." Petra snorted, as if the bare state of Ida's hands was proof that the world was coming to an end. "I suppose we could talk to the tailor." She turned her gaze onto Ida, still disapproving. "Well. I suppose you must be pleased."

"Yes," Ida said, "very."

"Now that the king has taken your oath, you have the freedom of the castle," Sabine said. "So this is where we take our leave of you."

"Yes, the freedom of the castle," Petra echoed, with a haughty sniff. "As if that wouldn't give any young girl ideas. I suppose you'll want to stay at the party?"

Ida didn't have an answer for that. She had come to Asteria to search for her father, not to attend the Revels. But she hadn't expected King Aurel to act as though he had never met her father at all. Would the other courtiers know anything about him? It had been seven years since his disappearance—had any of them remained at court for that long?

She'd never know unless she tried. And she still had to play the part of the Court Luminaire. She'd have to get to know the court in order to fill that role, and—

—and the night was young and glittering. There was so much left to see.

"Yes," she said. "Yes, I'd like that."

Petra made a dismissive gesture, one that seemed to decry youth everywhere in the world. But she took Ida's soiled gloves and her kit with her, and after a moment, Ida handed her candle to Sabine so that she could do the same. Sabine took the candle, then paused as Petra walked away. Her expression was strangely somber, and Ida wondered if there was something she wanted to say, but Sabine only said, “I’ll be working on the lower balcony during the Revel. Come find me when you’re ready to retire. Asteria can be confusing, for those who don’t know the way.”

The two of them disappeared into the crowd, leaving Ida alone.

Chapter 4

RECKLESS NIGHTS

With Sabine and Petra gone, Ida was free to explore the Revel.

She didn't know where to start. From her place by the railing, the entire world felt spread out beneath her, glorious and gleaming. In the sea of people, she felt like an invisible observer. Conversations washed over her like rain, and although a few people tittered excitedly as they passed her, likely other members of the king's audience, most left her alone. This was a far cry from the village fetes Ida had been to at home. She didn't know where to begin.

A rumbling in her stomach gave her all the direction she needed. In the confusion, it was easy to forget that she hadn't eaten since arriving, the couple of bites she had stolen before attending the king notwithstanding. Ida glanced around, searching for something a bit more substantial than pastries.

"Might I assist you, miss?" a voice asked, making her jump.

Ida spun around, but there was only a shimmer of air off to her left, like motes of faintly glowing dust spinning themselves together. Her skin prickled with magic, with the sense that someone was watching her. Mouth dry, Ida asked, "Did you say something?"

The dust motes swirled as if a wind was passing through them, and a voice spoke again. "You seem to be looking for something," they said, in a pleasantly neutral register that was neither masculine nor feminine. "Might I assist you?"

"Oh—" The castle was bursting with magic. She supposed invisible servants weren't out of place. "I was just . . . a little hungry. Do you know where I can get something to eat? Something other than desserts?"

The motes bobbed helpfully. "That can be arranged, miss. Please follow me."

The dust motes funneled themselves into a stream, a faintly glowing ribbon that wove its way deftly through the crowd. Ida followed, moving carefully past courtiers and other guests, as the ribbon led her down the steps and onto the lower tier. Her first thought was that her guide would take her to the lowest level, the one where the fairy lights played, but the stream of light banked away from those revels, leading her around the curve of a stone wall.

It was awkward to follow behind someone, even someone unseen, and not make conversation. "Are you a fairy?" Ida ventured.

The voice made a sound very much like a sniff. "Hardly. Although I suppose I seem similar to you."

"I didn't mean any offense."

"None taken, miss," the voice said, their neutral tone never changing. It was difficult for Ida to tell whether the voice meant it, or whether they were only trying to be polite. She opened her mouth to ask more, when the stream of lights led her up a narrow staircase, and she had to focus on ascending the steps without tripping over her own skirt.

She smelled the food before she saw it, the rich odors of roasted meats, freshly baked bread, and herbs. Her stomach came to life with an embarrassing whine, and Ida placed one hand over it, looking around.

The spirit had led her to a small balcony overlooking the forest below, the air above glittering with fairy lights. Now that she could see the entire Revel, Ida realized that this balcony was one of several set a little farther away from the others, each one slightly darker than the main balconies and hosting only a handful of tables. Quiet spaces, Ida realized, where Revelers could go to be alone or to have a private conversation. The balcony she was on hosted three small round tables, each lit by glass globes in the same hues as the fairy lights. The smell of food emanated from a fourth table resting by the balcony railing, laden with delicacies. Ida's mouth watered.

"Please feel free to help yourself," her guide said. "If you require assistance, you only need to give the word. If you'll excuse me."

"Wait—" Ida said. She'd been meaning to ask if the guide had a name, something she could call them, but with a sound like a rush of wind, they were gone. She pressed her lips tightly together, smoothing down a flutter of nervousness as she made her way toward the food.

The table bore a wide selection of options, smaller samplings from what Ida now saw was a larger dining table near the forest below. With so many choices, it was difficult to know where to start, but Ida worked her way across the table, piling her plate with a cut of roast pork glistening with juices, potatoes, a bread roll still warm from the oven with a slab of soft white cheese, and a glass of something dark that smelled like berries and that she hoped wasn't *too* alcoholic. She would need her wits about her if she wanted to ask anyone about her father tonight.

She turned, about to head over to one of the tables on the balcony, and froze, because she wasn't alone.

A girl stood behind her. Unlike the other Revelers, who seemed draped in every gleaming, glittering thing they could get their hands on, this girl was dressed relatively simply, in a gown of earthen colors, with strands of silver cord sparkling like stars in her auburn hair. Ida stared at her, arrested.

There was something familiar about her. The way her expression sharpened as she caught sight of Ida, as if she was seeing right through her. Her green eyes, the way they met Ida's with so much force that Ida could never have looked away.

The magic hit a second later.

Ida was still so unused to feeling magic other than her own. It took her a moment to recognize it for what it was: the sensation that she was standing in the heart of an ancient forest, surrounded on all sides by reaching, grasping, *growing* things. The scent of sap and petrichor in the air, the taste of rich soil at the back of her throat, the awareness that everything around her was *alive*, craning desperately toward the sun. It was nothing like Vegard's magic, which hit like a battering ram and left her breathless. This was subtle and slow and syrupy sweet, the kind of magic you could get drunk on.

Ida swallowed, forced breath back into her throat. Her skin was buzzing with the weight of the girl's magic, a languid heat that dragged its fingers down her spine and left goose bumps in its wake. She pressed her lips tightly together and had the embarrassing sense that she had just been staring, open-mouthed, at the girl.

"I—um—" Ida said. "I—I'm sorry—I hope it's okay if I sit here—"

"You're the new Court Luminaire," the girl said, saving Ida from embarrassing herself further. Ida let her mouth snap shut, warmth rising to her cheeks. "I saw your audition. It was very impressive."

Ida tried to remember if she had seen this girl anywhere in the crowd that surrounded the king. It seemed impossible that she might not have noticed, that this girl could have been in that crowd and Ida had had no idea. Some of the confusion must have shown on her face, because the girl smiled slightly and tipped her head toward the balcony railing. The smile pulled at the corner of her lips, showing off a flash of teeth.

"These Revels often contain many secret vantage points, for those who want an uninterrupted view of the proceedings. If you know where to look."

Ida worked her way past the knot in her throat, finding her voice. "I'm very glad you enjoyed the performance, Lady . . . ?"

"Lenore," the girl supplied. The fact that she didn't correct Ida's use of the title told Ida she was right in assuming the girl was highborn. She'd known that most of the people attending the Revels had titles of nobility, but she never thought she would be here, casually speaking to them. "Please don't stand on ceremony. Most people would rather I didn't have the title. Call me Lenore."

"I'm Ida." Should she curtsy? It felt odd—Lenore had just told her not to stand on ceremony. Ida had been feeling confident in herself since her audience with the king, but Lenore made her feel like she was on display again. She had the sense that Lenore's sharp eyes didn't miss anything, and she suddenly wasn't sure what to do with her hands. "Sorry, I was just looking for a place to—" She gestured sheepishly at the plate of food she was still holding.

"To eat," Lenore said, nodding. "I know. Gloam told me."

"Gloam?"

"Your guide," said Lenore. "The spirit you met? I asked them to give us a moment to speak. I hope you don't mind."

Ida stared at her in astonishment, the plate of food nearly forgotten. "You wanted to speak to me?"

"Yes," said Lenore. "We get very few mages coming through Asteria." She gestured at the tables behind her. When Ida didn't move, a look of uncertainty crossed Lenore's face. "Unless . . . you have other plans."

"No—no, not at all!" Ida said quickly. She willed her legs into motion, internally scolding herself. She wasn't going to waste this opportunity by standing here and gaping like a fish. She walked over to the table before she could change her mind. "Yes, of course I'd love to sit with you."

Lenore returned a few moments later with a plate of food of her own. It was much lighter than Ida's, consisting of a small selection of appetizers. Possibly sensing Ida's rising embarrassment, Lenore quickly set her at ease. "I've been eating small bites all evening," she said. "A common hazard of these Revels. Please, go ahead."

She nodded at Ida's plate. Before Ida could let herself feel self-conscious again, she quickly started to eat. She wanted to play it cool, to wait for Lenore to speak first, but her mind was racing. There were too many questions running through her mind.

"Have you been in the court long?" Ida asked. Lenore looked like she couldn't be much older than Ida herself. And it was hard to imagine anyone Ida's age having been here for long.

"Long enough," Lenore said. "Years ago, my father—well, that hardly matters." She lifted her eyes, looking up at Ida. There was something about those eyes—Ida couldn't quite place her finger on it. Her gaze had its own gravity—Ida's mouth went dry. "I'd rather hear more about you."

The moment dragged. Ida realized abruptly that she had been sitting there, not responding. She cleared her throat, scrambled for words.

"There's . . . nothing much to say about me," she said. "Except—"

Here she hesitated. Lenore had clearly been at court for a while, was clearly interested in magic and in magical goings-on. In other words: she was exactly the kind of courtier who might know more about Ida's father. Ida couldn't let this opportunity pass her by without asking.

Yet a part of her didn't want to, the same part that couldn't pull her eyes away from Lenore's slender fingers delicately brushing sugar off a pastry, that felt lulled by the soft cadence of their voices together.

She scolded herself for her hesitation. Wasn't this what she had come all this way *for*?

"I was wondering if he might have met my father."

"Your father, who taught you your magic?" Lenore asked, and Ida was startled until she remembered that she had said as much to the king.

"Yes," Ida said. She paused, taking a sip of the juice in her goblet. The taste of berries left a pleasant tang on her tongue, the scent making her think of dark forests and hidden secrets. Warmth ran down her throat as she swallowed, taking some of her nerves with it. Nothing for it but to jump. "He was here—before Maxwell Mueller. He was the Court Luminaire."

Lenore frowned at her, studying her for a moment. Then a look of pain crossed her face, a brief wince, like she had bitten down on something hard.

"How many people have you told about this?" Lenore asked.

"No one yet," Ida said. "Just you. Why? Do you know something?"

"Maxwell Mueller joined the court seven years ago," said Lenore. "Are you saying you haven't seen your father for seven years?"

Ida nodded, breathless with hope. Lenore hadn't said anything definitive, but she wasn't dismissing Ida outright. That *had* to mean something. But when Lenore looked up at Ida, Ida felt some of the hope she carried in her begin to crack. Lenore's expression was one of grief. Of pain.

There was an abyss somewhere in Ida's mind, a cold, dark heart that she couldn't bring herself to look directly at. At the expression on Lenore's face, she could feel it yawning open behind her, cold air like fingers dragging down her spine. It was a chasm born out of a single possibility, an irreversible reason why her father had been gone for so long, without word. A possibility Ida would never allow herself to entertain.

She pulled herself away from it, forced it down to the depths of her consciousness. Forced herself back into this moment, seated across the table from Lenore.

"If you know something," Ida said, "you have to tell me."

"I don't know anything right now," Lenore said. "But I do know that these questions are dangerous. Tell no one else about this."

"Why?"

Lenore's response was to look off the side of the balcony, toward the scene below. At the Revelers, dancing and laughing. At the tight knot of courtiers, still surrounding the king on his platform.

"This isn't the place to discuss it. I need to do some thinking. Look into it, if you have to, but be cautious. I would be careful what you say out loud."

"I don't understand," Ida asked. "Are you saying I should lie?"

Lenore shook her head. "Just be careful," she said. "There aren't a lot of people in Asteria that remember that time, and those that do may react . . . oddly to questioning. Never ask the king."

Ida shook her head. She already knew she couldn't ask the king what had happened directly. It wasn't safe for girls like her.

"I have to go," said Lenore, sliding out of her seat. "When you're finished, you should rejoin the celebration. I'm sure everyone will want to meet the new Court Luminaire."

"Wait," Ida said, as Lenore started for the stairs. Lenore paused, looking back at Ida, those eyes seizing hers once more. "You said we couldn't talk here. Can we talk later?"

Lenore considered for a moment, but nodded. "I'll find you," she said. "I promise."

She left the balcony, making her way quickly down the steps, skirts in hand and hair shimmering behind her like a banner. Ida watched her go, feeling oddly adrift, like she had been tossed into a whirlpool. She wasn't sure what to make of that conversation at all. It felt almost too strange, too bewildering to be called a lead.

Except . . . Lenore wanted to see her again.

Ida could live with that.

Ida finished the rest of her food in a daze, not even noticing the other Revelers beginning to fill the platform until one of them approached her table, clearing his throat. It was a boy about her age, wearing a white ruffled shirt, a matching doublet, and breeches the same blue gray as his eyes. His hair was a blond the color of honey, his features classically Arreden. Self-consciously, Ida brushed breadcrumbs off of her fingers.

"Can I help you?"

"My friends and I . . ." Here, he gestured at a group of youths behind him, similarly attired. " . . . were, uh . . . wondering if you would like to join us for the evening. We would love to meet the new Court Luminaire."

Ida blinked in surprise, looking over him again, the clothes he was wearing, the jewel that gleamed casually at his throat. Unlike Lenore, who had dressed down, this boy was obviously noble, or at least extremely rich. People like him didn't talk to people like her.

And yet, he looked almost shy as he stood in front of her, like he thought *she* might say no.

"Of . . . course," she said. "I'd love to."

His face broke into a smile, a grin stretching from ear to ear. He looked almost relieved, which only served to confuse Ida further as he extended a hand. "Lukas von Hayner, son of Baron Karl von Hayner of Erelbech."

Ida took his hand. "Ida Rosales. As you know, I'm the new Court Luminaire."

"Pleasure to make your acquaintance," said Lukas, dropping into a courtly bow. He grinned, releasing her hand so that he could step back and gesture at his friends. "Shall we go? The evening awaits."

Ida nodded, getting to her feet to follow them. It was only later that night, as she fell into a breathless heap on the soft grass of the fairy forest, warm from racing through a maze filled with fairy lights and laughter, that she remembered something. She froze in place, her mind racing as Arred's young nobility proceeded to get even drunker behind her, downing small glasses of a golden drink that tasted like honey.

It was something she should have considered before, a truth lost in the splendor of the evening, in the light and the warmth and the glow of having found another mage to talk to, of being *recognized* as a force all on her own. But now that she had found the memory again, she couldn't help herself from running the entire conversation with Lenore through her head, examining every word in a different light.

Because she remembered that King Aurel had an illegitimate daughter, and that *her* name was Lenore.

Chapter 5

ROUGH MORNINGS

When Ida opened her eyes the next day, it was to a pounding in her head and the sweetness of honey clinging to her tongue. She groaned, dragging her pillow over her face to blot out the light and burrowing deeper into her blankets.

Someone reached out, grabbing the pillow from her, and she shrieked in surprise, throwing her hand up to cover her eyes.

"Very impressive, mistress," a dry voice said. "I take it you had fun at the Revel?"

Revel.

At once, the memory of last night came rushing back. The king, Lenore, dancing in the fairy forest, drinking sundrops on the ledge overlooking the palace grounds. She was in Asteria. She was at the Night King's Court. She was—

—she was Arred's Court Luminaire.

Ida's eyes flew open, and she sat up in bed. Too fast. The world spun alarmingly in her wake. A hand reached out to grab her shoulder, steadying her, and Ida turned to see a familiar woman standing beside her. One of the maids from the night before. The name came to her, floating to the top of her memories. Sabine.

"Are you going to be sick?" Sabine asked. "Should I fetch you a bucket?"

Ida turned her thoughts inward, feeling things out. She had a headache, yes, but she didn't feel like last night's dinner was about to come up her throat. She had had worse—at the summer festival last year, Ida's mother had allowed her to go out alone, and Ida had spent her night of freedom getting roaringly drunk on cheap beer.

She needed water, and something to get the taste of honey out of her mouth, but she thought she would be all right.

"I'm fine," Ida said, pressing the heels of her hands over her closed eyes. "What time is it?"

"An hour before sunset," Sabine said. "Early, as far as things go for the court, but I thought you would appreciate the chance to bathe."

Ida winced. She glanced down at herself, pleased to find that she had at least remembered to take off her gown before falling into bed. She hadn't, however, taken off her shift, and the thin white fabric was dusted with something that looked suspiciously like . . . pine needles?

How many drinks had she had last night?

"Yes," Ida said, clearing her throat and trying to sound like an adult—a proper court artisan. "I'd love a bath."

"The Knights' Bath is open for artisans and other honored commons in the hour before sunset," Sabine said. "If you hurry, you can have a decent soak. I'll have your clothes sent up after you."

Ida paused in the middle of getting out of bed to consider just why Sabine was in her room. She blinked blearily at the maid. "*You* will?"

"Of course," said Sabine. "I've been assigned to be your maid. I believe I told you this last night." She squinted suspiciously at Ida. "How much *did* you drink?"

"Um . . ."

Sabine sighed. "You're not the first youth to be overtaken by the court's excesses, and you won't be the last. But a word of warning—the drinks served at the Revels go down smoothly, but lead to rough mornings, as I'm sure you're now aware. And you'd do best to keep your position in mind."

It was very far, Ida thought, from morning, but she supposed that was just how things were in the Night King's Court. She stumbled to her feet, searching for her shoes.

"My position?" Ida asked.

"As a royal artisan," Sabine said, handing Ida's shoes to her, along with a robe she could pull on over her clothes. "His Majesty expects perfection. You're young for the position, but the king won't take your youth as an excuse if you fail him."

A bite of poison against her lips, a feeling like ice running through her blood. She shivered at the memory of her oath.

But of course the king would be demanding. He was the King of Arred. Ida knew that when she had come to Asteria.

She shook the thoughts from her mind. "I'll keep that in mind," she promised, as she made for the door.

"The Knights' Bath is on the castle's third floor," Sabine called after her. "Turn left out of your room, take the spiral staircase up three flights. When you reach the third floor, walk to the end of the hall and it should be there."

Ida nodded in thanks. She felt like a husk of her usual self, but those directions were clear enough. She stepped out of her room, heading for the staircase. As Ida climbed, she was gratified to see she wasn't the only shambling mess in Asteria that morning. People rushed past her up and down the stairwell, bright-eyed servants heading to their duties and disheveled souls alike. They traded looks of commiseration with her as they passed each other on the landings.

On the third floor, Ida stepped out onto a wide stone hallway, bordered on all sides by high glass windows. The hallway was wide enough to march an army through, but empty, and Ida stood there by the stairs for a moment, blinking the light out of her eyes.

A breeze brushed past her ear, carrying a familiar voice. Gloam, Lenore's invisible guide from the night before, sounded almost amused as they settled into the space in front of her.

"Miss Ida," they said. "I can see you're a little worse for wear."

"I've been better," Ida said. "Did Lenore send you to find me?" A note of hope crept into her voice, despite herself.

In the light of day, it was harder to see the servant than at night. If Ida squinted, she could only make out the faintest glowing traces of their presence, could see them bob up and down, almost apologetically. "I'm afraid not," they said. "But I could convey a message to Lady Lenore, if you wished—"

"No, no, that's okay!" said Ida quickly, feeling the heat rise to her face. "I'm just—I'm looking for the Knights' Bath. If you have time . . ."

"Of course." Gloam dropped into a conciliatory swirl. "Please follow me."

Gloam led her through a set of open doors at the end of the hallway. The air on the other side was humid, heavy with steam and the scent of soap.

"The baths, miss," Gloam said. In the shade of this new chamber, it was easier to see them dip into something like a bow. "I'll leave you now."

They rushed over her shoulder, streaming out the doors and leaving Ida blinking in the marble antechamber. After taking a second to collect her thoughts, Ida followed the instructions of a tiled mosaic on the wall, advertising single-gendered bathing rooms to the right. She climbed a set of stairs, followed further signs pointing her to a women's bath, and stepped around a tasteful divider to find herself in heaven.

The bath in front of her was a heated pool, tiled in white and cut into the shape of a half-moon. The arch followed the curve of windows thrown open to overlook the valley. Dark mountains and snowcapped peaks, clouds golden in the sunset and scented with clean mountain air. Despite being open to the outside, the room wasn't cold, and Ida felt the hum of magic in the walls as she stripped off her clothes and placed them in a cubby before stepping into the water.

Warmth embraced her, chasing away the excesses of last night. Ida closed her eyes in bliss, swimming to the other side of the bath so that she could take in the view from the windows. She folded her arms on the cool marble floor and sighed.

She hadn't forgotten why she was here: to search for her father. But it was hard to believe that a place like this could exist, and hard to believe that she was allowed to use it. It was hard to believe that only a few days ago, Ida had been lying in the dark in her attic room, bags packed under her bed, waiting for the right moment to slip away.

As she floated, she considered her next move, trying to prod her mind into motion. It felt a little like thinking through molasses, but she managed. The Revel had been . . . informative. If Lenore was right, she couldn't just ask people about her father at random. She had to be a bit more circumspect.

The other artisans, maybe?

Once she could think straight, there was a lot she could do with her day. Or—well, her night.

Ida stayed in the bath until the sun sank beneath the mountain peaks and a bell rang, spurring the other bathers into motion. She dressed quickly in clothes that had appeared for her in the changing room—black working clothes, decorated with the king's livery—and followed the others down to breakfast.

The dining hall was a massive affair, with high, vaulted ceilings and rows and rows of wooden tables. As she stepped in, the stone tiles at her feet lit up, a golden path leading her to a table tucked into the far left corner of the room, beneath high windows. There were already others seated there, and she could feel their eyes on her as she took a seat. The woman next to her didn't waste any time in addressing her.

"I don't mean to ambush you, but are *you* the new Court Luminaire? We've all been dying to know."

She was older than Ida, but still relatively young. Ida thought she must have been in her twenties. Her hair was long and dark, running down her back in thick waves, and her eyes were a striking mixture of brown and green. She spoke Arreden with an accent, making Ida wonder if she had come from the west. Her style of clothing was similar to Ida's, but green where Ida's was black and missing the king's livery. Her own clothes, Ida realized. The sort of things Ida would assemble in time if she was allowed to remain at the court.

"Yes . . ." Ida said, realizing that she had left the question too long.

The woman smiled. "The court can be quite overwhelming, especially on the first night," she said. She picked up the menu card that rested on the plate in front of her, glancing over it once. "A honey pastry, fresh fruit, a cup of yogurt, some raspberry jam, a glass of sparkling water, and a coffee with milk and sugar."

The menu card disintegrated from between her fingers, dissolving into sparkling dust. As the last motes faded away, food appeared on her plate, arranging itself into the spaces around her. Ida gaped, and the woman winked.

"I've never gotten used to coffee at sunset," she said, taking a bite of her pastry. "It's so very Arreden, no? Make your own selections."

Ida glanced at the menu card in front of her and skimmed the list, looking for something familiar. "Um . . . a bowl of fresh fruit and . . . the assorted bread, cheese, jam, and sausage plate? And a coffee with milk and sugar, please."

Her own card started to vanish, sparks fleeing across its surface like it was being burned. Ida jumped as the sparks touched her skin, but they only left a tingling sensation behind. At once, food appeared in front of her, a small basket carrying a handful of assorted bread rolls, a plate with several appetizing-looking jams in delicate glass containers, and another plate with a mixture of sliced cheeses and sausages. A cup of coffee appeared to her right, the rich scent rising into the air.

Her seatmate clucked her tongue. "Very traditional."

"A little taste of home," Ida said, although from the looks of the spread, this was a far cry from breakfast at her grandmother's. She chose one of the bread rolls at random, beginning to cut into it. "Thank you for the help. I'm—"

"Ida Rosales," the woman said. "We know. I'm Celeste Valois, Court Painter."

Ida jumped, nearly spilling food all over the place. Even *she*, who lived in the middle of nowhere, knew about Celeste Valois. Her paintings were supposed to be so real, they were the barest step from life.

"I—um—" she said. "It's nice to meet you, Madame—"

Celeste raised a hand, letting out a musical laugh. "Oh, let's not stand on formality," she said. "We're all artisans here. And speaking of which, look lively, I think your first commission may be here."

She nodded at something just behind Ida, over her shoulder. Ida twisted around in her seat to see a servant walking toward her, carrying an envelope on a silver tray. When he reached her, he gave her a polite bow, holding the tray out toward her, and Ida saw that the letter was sealed with the royal crest.

Conversation at the artisans' table drew to a standstill. Ida picked the letter up off the tray, handling it carefully. As she set it aside, the servant rose, clearly waiting for some word from her. Feeling a little awkward, Ida said, "Thank you."

He bowed and left. Ida wiped her hands on a cloth napkin before breaking the envelope's seal. Inside was a sheet of cream-colored paper, heavy and expensive. She unfolded it, aware that everyone was watching her, and held it closer to read.

His Majesty, King Aurel IV, Ruler of Arred, requests an illusion for a Revel to be held in the Grotto, seven nights hence.

The illusion will complement an evening of entertainment,

featuring music from the King's own Collection.

His Majesty requests that the illusion give the impression of being underwater.

Below, the letter was stamped with the king's seal, and signed in a heavy, looping hand. Ida felt a swell of excitement, tempered with uncertainty. Her mind was already racing, coming up with ideas, things she could try to get the illusion to stick, but *seven nights*? Could she really come up with something so intricate in only seven nights?

And her father—when was she going to have time to search for him?

"Well?" asked Celeste, watching her.

Ida could feel the eyes of the other artisans on her and had the sense that she was being tested somehow, like they were weighing her up to see if she was worthy. Worthy of being one of them. She pressed her lips tightly together and summoned up every ounce of her professionalism.

"It seems like I have a lot to do," she said. "Where is the Grotto?"

"On the fourth floor, just beneath the king's own chambers," said Celeste. "It's a lovely space, difficult to describe. You'll need to see it for yourself. It houses several sirens, members of the Collection."

The King's Collection. Inhuman beings.

She was thinking about Vegard's magic again. The howl of a wintry wind contained in a single glance. She shuddered and pushed the thought from her mind.

"I need to get to work," Ida said, setting the letter aside and attacking her breakfast. If she was going to do this, she would need to familiarize herself with her workshop, request supplies. And she would need to do research. Research King Aurel's expectations, research the venue, the theme. The other artisans could prove invaluable there.

And she could also—

A thought struck her, and she glanced at Celeste. "Celeste . . ." The name felt too familiar. It hung oddly on her tongue. "You've been here long enough to remember the previous luminaire, haven't you?"

"Of course I have," Celeste said. "Good old Maxwell. He was a delight."

"And the luminaire before him?" Ida asked.

Celeste laughed. "How old do you think I am?"

She supposed that was too much to hope for. There had been no word about her father for years. Nothing sent back to her and her mother. She had been very open about her last name, her Niresso identity. If anyone remembered her father, wouldn't someone have asked her about it by now?

There was something else happening here. Perhaps her father had worked in the castle under a different name. She'd *thought* the broadsheets at the time had used his real name, Tomas Rosales, but she had been very young then, barely reading at the time of her father's disappearance.

Maybe she was misremembering.

"I'd love to find out more about my predecessors' work," she said instead. "Do you know where I could find information about past luminaires?"

"Well, I suppose you might try the library," Celeste said, returning to her meal. "It's unlikely you'll find any samples of their spells.

Your line of work is so . . . ephemeral, after all. But there's nothing that goes on in this castle that isn't recorded somewhere."

Recorded.

That was what Ida was hoping for.

She nodded, and though her stomach roiled with anxiety at the thought, she took another bite of food, washed it down with a sip of fine coffee.

Ida had not come here to fail. She would find her father. No matter what.

Chapter 6

A STITCH IN TIME

"I'm sorry," Ida said, looking up from the stack of paper that had been placed in front of her. "I'm looking for information on all the previous luminaires, not just Maxwell Mueller."

The librarian, a plump woman with dark brown hair and tan skin, gave her an apologetic smile. "These are all the records we have, child. Sadly, most of our records were lost in the fire that took the old library."

Ida pressed her lips tightly together, trying not to let her disappointment show. The castle library was a bibliophile's dream, with two levels of high walls lined with shelves from floor to ceiling, connected by a set of wrought-iron staircases. Its floors were polished to a gleam, while arching glass windows let in illusory sunlight just bright enough to light the space, but not bright enough to be overwhelming. Overhead, an enormous astrolabe hung from the ceiling, its concentric rings tracking the movements of the stars and planets in a mesmerizing dance.

It was a place that looked like it could have housed all the information in the world, which was why it was particularly disappointing that it could give her no more than a handful of pages describing the work of Master Maxwell Mueller, Court Luminaire, and nothing of her father.

Ida glanced up at the librarian and decided to try again.

"Surely there has to be something. Even their names would help."

"Well . . ." The librarian frowned, pausing in the middle of sorting through the pile of books in front of her. Her nose wrinkled, brow furrowing as she grew deep in thought. "Now that you mention it . . . it is a bit odd." As soon as it had come, the frown vanished, leaving a cheery expression behind. "But many things in Asteria's beginnings weren't recorded so diligently as they are today. And such mystery is the way of things in the Night King's Court. You'll get used to it in time, dear."

Frustration simmered just under Ida's skin. She glanced down at the sheet of paper. For a second, she thought about just *mentioning* her father's name, to see if it provoked any reaction. Lenore's warning gave her pause. If something *had* happened to him, maybe it wouldn't be a good idea to ask around so openly.

She didn't want to guess at what the consequences would be if people thought a girl like her was questioning the King of Arred.

Ida hesitated, and then ventured, "Have you been in the king's service long, ma'am?"

"Oh, over twelve years at this point." The librarian laughed. "I'm quite an old hand at this."

"Well, then, you *must* remember the luminaire before Master Mueller." Ida gestured at the records in front of her, which began just over seven years ago. "Please, I just need his name."

A peculiar thing happened. The librarian stared at her, eyes fixed intently on Ida. The shine in her light brown eyes vanished, the levity fleeing from her expression. The woman stared at her like she was seeing right through her, and all the sound of the palace seemed to vanish, leaving an impenetrable hush in its place. Ida's skin prickled in goose bumps, in warning, in the sensation of magic.

And then the world started moving again, as if it had let out a breath. The first thing Ida heard was the sound of a ticking clock, and then the great rings of the astrolabe, spinning overhead.

"I'm sorry, dear, it's the funniest thing. I really can't remember."

Ida jumped, turning toward the librarian. But the uncanny expression was gone from her face, the same cheerful expression she had been wearing throughout this interaction returning.

Had . . . had everything *stopped* for a second?

"What?"

"The previous luminaire," the librarian said. "Whoever he was, he must not have come often to the library, or else I never took notice. I was so overwhelmed in those early days. I suppose you can relate."

"I—um—yes, of course."

Ida took the notes with her, hurrying out the door. The click of the library doors behind her made her breathe out a sigh of relief. She clutched the notes tightly to herself.

The look in the librarian's eye—that frozen moment—

—that hadn't been normal.

"Where to next, miss?"

Ida's skin prickled with the familiar sense of magic. She felt a rush of air brush past her shoulders and looked to see Gloam hovering in the hallway. She had called the spirit right after breakfast, asking for directions to the library. Gloam had been eager to oblige.

"I . . ." Ida hesitated, glancing at the notes she was holding. The papers had been bound, but even though they weren't exactly what she was looking for, she still didn't like the idea of walking around with them, possibly letting them be lost or damaged. Besides, if anyone was watching, she intended to look like a studious young luminaire. "I need to drop these off at my rooms. I think I know the way. But after that . . . I would really like to take a look at the Grotto."

"His Majesty's Grotto is open to the court between the hours of nine in the evening and three in the morning," Gloam said. "I'd be happy to show you the way. You have just over an hour, if you'd like to retire to your room. Please feel free to summon me again when you are ready."

"Yes, Gloam," Ida said, a little stiffly. "Thank you."

"My pleasure." Gloam dipped into a bow, beginning to stream off down the hallway.

Ida couldn't help it. She blurted out, "Gloam?"

"Yes, miss?"

"Has . . . the castle's time ever . . . stopped?"

Gloam went silent for a moment. A beat, long enough that Ida wondered whether she should have spoken at all. Her mouth opened, words flooding out in her rush to fill the space. "It's only that I'm looking for information about someone. And today, in the library—"

"What a curious question," Gloam said, interrupting her. "I would say only in an illusion. Perhaps you ate or drank something potent last night. But you should take care, miss, what questions you ask. The castle's delights ensnare the unwary."

A wave of cold fear washed over Ida.

The castle's delights ensnare the unwary.

She swallowed, opening her dry mouth to ask Gloam another question, but the feeling of magic had left her. The hallway was empty. Gloam was gone.

It took Ida longer than she expected to leave her room a second time.

When she arrived, she found that Sabine had cleaned up most of the mess from the night before, and that the door to her workshop was open. The workshop, a large, roomy chamber that was almost double the size of her bedroom, with multiple furnaces and worktables, seemed like entirely too much trouble for a few candles, especially since Ida was used to working at her desk at home or at the well-worn corner of her family shop that her mother had set aside for her. But it was also, concerningly, empty. That shouldn't have come as a surprise to Ida—luminaires rarely worked in the same media, and there was no guarantee that her predecessor's supplies would have been compatible with her magic anyway, but it left her with a worrying sense of unease. She didn't realize until then just how reliant she had become on her mother's candlemaking supplies always being available for her use.

Thankfully, on the desk, there were requisition forms, with a note from Sabine that she could request anything she required. The forms included a box she could tick if her request was urgent—and Ida thought her first royal commission, due within a week, counted. She set the notes on Maxwell Mueller aside and filled out two forms, one urgently requesting several blocks of wax, dyes, and wicks, and everything she would need to get started immediately, and the other with all the things she would eventually want in her workshop.

There were other ingredients that she needed—scented oils beyond the basics, herbs and flowers and all of the things that she could use to imbue her illusions onto, but until she could see the Grotto for herself, she wouldn't know what they were. The basics would have to do for now. She didn't know how long it would take the palace to get her the rest of her ingredients, but if she could requisition them by the end of the night—

"Mistress Ida?" The door to her bedroom opened, making Ida jump. It was only Sabine, coming to stand in the workshop door. The maid took one look at Ida, hunched protectively over her desk, one hand tangled in her hair, and let out a breath.

"Is there something you need?" Sabine asked.

"I just received my first commission," Ida said. "Do you know how long it will take these materials to get here?"

Sabine came over to glance at Ida's forms, her eyes flicking over the text. "Wax and dyes? You'll have them by the end of the night. Why do you ask?"

A knot of tension between her shoulders uncoiled. She sagged in relief. "I have seven nights to come up with something suitable for a Revel."

"The Sirensong Revel?" Sabine's eyes lit up. "Do you know what you'll create?"

"I have some ideas . . ." Ida glanced down at the forms and added a few water-themed items—sea salt, seaweed, and, remembering her bath, lotus-scented oil. The fine details of the illusion would come later, but the king had given her a theme. She could work with that. "I need to visit the Grotto and see the space. Would you like to come?"

Sabine gave Ida a tight smile. "Unfortunately, I can't, but I hope you enjoy yourself. I've just come in to drop off your correspondence."

"My . . . ?" Ida trailed off, looking past Sabine into the bedroom. A pile of brightly colored envelopes rested on her desk, each one seeming to try to outcompete the others, all wax seals and ribbons, filigree and ornamentation. There were so many of them she worried they would start falling to the floor. She looked back at Sabine, eyes wide. "What *is* all that?"

"Your mail," Sabine said. "Invitations, mostly, I think. People want to meet the new luminaire."

People wanted to meet *her*? Ida found that difficult to believe. In her home village, most had avoided her, or grudgingly invited her to parties only when it was clear that they couldn't get around it politely.

She approached the stack of letters warily, as if they were a mirage that might vanish if viewed from the wrong angle, and thumbed through them. Up close, she could tell that each letter was written using only the highest quality paper. Many were decorated with ribbons and frills and artfully folded paper roses. A few of them were scented, the smells tickling her nose. She wasn't sure which one to open first.

That was, until she felt the tug of magic and caught the scent of the world before the rain. She sifted through the pile until she found a deep green envelope. Ida's name was written on the front of it in silver, in a looping hand. She broke open the seal, quickly pulling the letter out.

Dear Ida,

Our conversation last night was illuminating.

I've heard from a mutual friend that you may be encountering difficulties. Perhaps I can help?

I find myself needing to attend tonight's Revel, as the king will be presenting his starborn horses. There will be races and other performances. It may prove to be diverting.

If you can attend, I would love to see you there.

Many regards,

Lenore

Ida's breath caught in her throat. Lenore *had* said that she would reach out to her, but Ida hadn't believed it until that moment. And Lenore wanted to see her? Tonight?

A flutter began in her stomach, and her eyes drifted from the mess on her desk to the letter, making calculations. Three hours between nine in the evening and midnight. Enough time to go to the Grotto, make her measurements, and make herself ready for the Revel?

She glanced up at Sabine, startled to find that she had been reading over her shoulder.

"What would I have to wear to the Revel?"

Sabine's brows furrowed. For a moment, Ida thought she saw a look of disapproval on her face, but it was gone as soon as it had come, shuttered behind her eyes.

"I can find you something suitable. Do you plan on going?"

The smart thing to do would be to stay and work on her commission. But . . . if she thought about it, there wasn't much she could do *tonight*. She had no ingredients yet. If she couldn't do any work, she might as well attend the Revel. There could be people there who had met her father. Maybe she would find a lead.

She could make up for it later. Being a member of the court was a once-in-a-lifetime experience. Surely there was nothing wrong with enjoying it a little?

A small, traitorous part of her mind whispered the true reason: it meant she could spend more time with Lenore.

"How long would I need to get ready?"

"An hour, to be safe," Sabine said. "But the commission—your work? Are you sure—?"

"I have plenty of time," Ida said. She got to her feet and packed a satchel with supplies from her desk drawer. Her predecessor had left her a selection of pens, scraps of paper, and measuring supplies. "I'll be back with an hour to spare. Please submit those requisition forms in the meantime."

Sabine looked unconvinced, but Ida tried to exude confidence as she slung the satchel over her shoulder, hurrying for the door.

She had enough time. She would do it all.

Soon, no one would have any reason to doubt her again.

As soon as she shut the door behind her, she called Gloam's name.

Chapter 7

REVELRY IN STARLIGHT

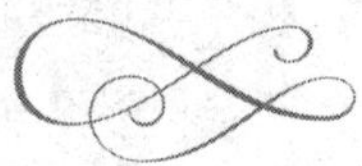

Gloam led her to a marvel.

No doors led into the Grotto. It stood at the end of a long, winding hallway, whose tiled floors and high stone walls morphed by inches into natural stone. Before Ida knew it, she was walking not in a hall, but in a cavern, surrounded by stone walls. The light had changed as well, shifting from the golden orbs favored by the king to a ghostly, bluish green. As she walked along the tunnel, Ida understood why the king wanted her to give the illusion of being underwater—the space already felt halfway there.

The tunnel opened into a chamber that had been painstakingly constructed to appear natural. The ceiling stretched endlessly above, lined with glittering stalactites. Looking closer, Ida saw that the light came from the stones themselves. Veins of quartz glowing in faint whites and blues and greens threaded through the stone, giving the room an unearthly glow. When she walked, her footsteps echoed, and she could almost imagine the din of a hundred people in this space, all here to partake in the Revel.

The Grotto's walls were striking. Stone arches protruded from them at regular intervals, shaped to look like windows. They temporarily broke the illusion that she was in a cave, but they added something more tantalizing: between the arches, there appeared to be water. A whole world of water on the other side, filled with seaweed, colorful fish, and . . .

And shapes, lingering in the dark.

A humanoid shadow hovered in one of the water-windows, just outside Ida's field of vision. She turned her head toward it, but it swam away, leaving a trail of bubbles behind. Ida walked up to the window, cautiously reaching out with one hand. She expected to feel glass, to find that this was a cleverly constructed aquarium.

Instead, her fingers sank straight into the surface, cold water brushing her skin. Ida's eyes widened. She made to pull her hand away, but before she could, a shape popped up from below the window.

It looked like a young girl, about her age. But her skin was a bluish gray, her eyes with gold irises and black sclera. Dark green scales were sprinkled across her skin, concentrated along her arms, the backs of her hands, her sides. They dotted her cheeks, disappearing into the tangle of her darker green hair. There was webbing between her fingers and her toes. She blinked at Ida, curiously, and then one of her hands reached up, her fingers brushing across Ida's own.

Ida gasped and pulled her hand away. The girl shrank back immediately, looking embarrassed. After a moment, she instead pressed her hand, her whole palm, to the surface of the barrier between them. Ida stared at her.

Realization dawned slowly.

Ida could stick her hand into the water. She could probably climb into the tank if she wanted. But . . .

“You can’t come out?” Ida asked.

“The members of the King’s Collection are not allowed to leave.”

Ida spun around, startled. Behind her, she heard a splash and saw a flurry of movement, the girl swimming away as quick as an arrow. But as surprising as the girl’s appearance had been, Ida couldn’t spare a second thought for her. Because, standing in the archway that led to the Grotto, was Vegard.

It was just like before, at the beginning of last night’s Revel.

Vegard’s eyes pinned her in place, bringing with them the intensity of a winter storm. Goose bumps erupted in ripples up and down her skin, the air around him so charged with magic it was like breathing in static. He took a step toward her, another, and it was all Ida could do to stand there, even though a part of her mind was ringing in alarm, telling her that Vegard wasn’t human. That he was dangerous.

He came to a stop a few feet away from her, his eyes on hers.

“You . . . look familiar. Why?”

It was a testament to the presence he carried, the way the air seemed to ripple and curve around him, that at first Ida didn’t hear what he said. And then the import of his words dropped.

Did Vegard . . . Did Vegard know her father?

She wasn’t sure it was safe to ask him. But Ida was running out of options. No one else in the castle knew of Tomas Rosales. And when she’d asked, odd things had happened in the library. Gloam’s warning still echoed in her ears. *The castle’s delights . . .*

She said, “My father was once a luminaire here. Maybe you remember him.”

Vegard’s brow furrowed. He looked troubled, his aura of magic diminishing for a second as he took a step back. He shook his head, and looking at him, Ida felt a pang of sympathy. In that moment, he didn't look dangerous. He only looked lost. As lost as she was.

"I don't . . . I feel like I should . . ."

And then his eyes snapped up, meeting hers, and the sympathy was gone, burned away by the intensity of his gaze. In spite of herself, Ida recoiled.

"You might be the key to that night. You could help me."

He took a step toward her. Ida stepped back. She was aware of how alone she was, in the Grotto with no one else around her. If anything happened to her now, no one would know.

The castle's delights ensnare the unwary.

"I—I have to work. I'm sorry, I can't help you."

"But—" Vegard said. Power surged around him, a snap of winter air, so cold that it hurt to breathe. His expression had gone from confused to desperate. "But you *can* help me."

"I can't." Frost spread across the ground between her and Vegard, would have spread over her feet if she hadn't taken a quick two steps away. The magic in the air was so potent that it hurt to breathe. It moved past an ache and began to *burn*. "I'm sorry!"

Vegard took another step toward her, hand outstretched.

"Go away!" Ida said, the words echoing in the stone chamber. Vegard's eyes widened at the sound, and then—

He shattered. Falling to pieces like glass, like ice on a warm day. The pieces dissolved into motes of light, and the frost on the ground melted into nothing, but Ida still felt cold. She exhaled and was surprised when her breath didn't mist in front of her face. Ida pulled her arms close around herself, shivering.

"Gloam?"

"Here, miss," said a voice next to her left ear.

"What—what just happened?"

"You drove him away. Vegard is bound to the king's command, and the king has commanded that he obey the members of his court. Vegard couldn't break that enchantment, even if he wished."

"Who is he?"

"He's . . . a winter spirit, miss. A young one, from the far north. He's . . . troubled."

"I didn't hurt him?" Vegard had scared her, but there had been something so human about his desperation. She hadn't wanted to hurt him.

"I don't think you *could* hurt him, miss. But he won't be able to approach you again tonight. If he finds you in the future, you can always drive him away again."

Ida swallowed, unsure what to do with that information. Vegard might know something about her father, but she didn't know if she wanted to speak to him again. His magic was so strong. She didn't think she could stand against the force of his power and survive. It would swallow her whole.

She breathed deep, steeling her courage. The smell of ice had faded, leaving her with a cavern smelling of water and stone.

Vegard aside, she had a job to do.

She reached into her satchel and got to work.

Ida measured every inch of the main floor of the Grotto, sketching out its dimensions and taking note of the places where the castle's magic hung heaviest, pooling into the cracks and crevices in ways that might interfere with her illusion. A good illusion was as much working with her surroundings as it was creating something entirely new. She marked the water-windows into her sketch, the stalactites and their lights, and made some notes about the ambient color. This took her more than an hour. By the time she finished, it was nearly time for her to meet Sabine, and she had to race back through the castle to her chambers.

Sabine was ready for her.

As soon as she burst through the door, Sabine took her by the arm and dragged her to her wardrobe to get dressed. Ida had no idea where Sabine had found clothes that fit her so perfectly, but the next thing she knew, she was standing in front of the mirror dressed in an elegant, deep red riding habit, with ruffles across the collar of her jacket and a lace veil added to her cap.

Sabine looked rather proud of herself. "What do you think?"

"It's beautiful, Sabine, but I don't think I'll be riding." Lenore's letter had mentioned something about starborn horses, but Ida had assumed she would only be a spectator. Sabine shrugged as if that was a mere technicality.

"It's the look of the thing. The others will be dressed for riding, even though they'll never come within an inch of the starborn."

It felt a bit silly to be wearing riding clothes to watch other people ride horses, but if that was the fashion here . . .

Ida exhaled, smoothing out her skirts.

"It's lovely," she said. And despite the voluminous fabrics, it was much easier to move in than her gown from the night before. A gown that Ida hadn't seen since she had draped it over her desk chair last night. "Thank you, Sabine. I'll try not to make a mess of it this time."

"Don't bother," Sabine said. That bitter note was back in her voice, giving Ida pause as she made for the door. "You'll only wear it once."

Only once.

Ida pondered Sabine's words as she made her way into the night air, following the crowd toward the Revel. It seemed like a waste. But if the dress itself was made from magic, it wasn't much different from the other magical pieces that built up the king's court.

It was an illusion. A beautiful, pointless illusion.

The layout of Asteria was still somewhat confusing to Ida, but thankfully, there were always other Revelers to follow. She joined a crowd of people in riding clothes, following the stream, and stepped out into a massive courtyard, the scenery dominated by a large fountain at its center. Streamers and lights strung around the space lent it a festive air. To one side, rows of seats had been placed, like the ones that Ida imagined lined ordinary racetracks, but there was no track in sight. No horses even. It should have been comical, a parade of people in fine riding clothes without a single horse, but the discrepancy was so very like Asteria, and Ida found it difficult to dislike.

Difficult to feel anything at all, she admitted to herself, except the mingled nervousness and anticipation in her gut as she scanned the crowd for Lenore.

Lenore hadn't told Ida where to meet her, and Ida was wondering if she should ask someone when she caught sight of the top row of seats. There, several boxes had been set aside, curtained and decorated in different colors, likely for distinguished guests. The smallest box was wreathed in black cloth, the curtain drawn over the front of it. She remembered the high balcony Lenore had chosen to lead her to during the previous Revel. If Lenore really was the king's daughter, she would have a private box of her own.

Fighting down her nerves, Ida climbed the seating scaffold,

making her way toward the smallest box. Already rehearsing her apology in case she was wrong and about to intrude on some random high-ranking courtier, she twitched the curtain aside, and let out a breath of relief when she saw Lenore looking back at her.

Like before, Lenore's clothes were just on the edge of practical: a riding habit in earth tones that would have seemed almost somber and utilitarian if not for the vines embroidered in gold snaking their way across her shoulders and trimming the edges of her sleeves. Unlike some of the other costumes Ida had seen, it looked like something Lenore could actually wear riding. Perhaps she even had. Lenore looked like someone who might know how to ride. She wore her hair pulled back in a braid, secured in place by another golden bangle, and wore riding gloves and boots in soft leather. Her eyes moved up to the gap in the curtain as Ida entered, and Ida thought she saw Lenore exhale, some of the tension leaving her shoulders.

Was she imagining it, or did Lenore look equally relieved to see her there?

"You made it," Lenore said. "I wasn't sure—you didn't send a response."

Ida felt her face flush in embarrassment, because it had never even occurred to her to send a response. It was only now, face-to-face with Lenore, that she realized that given the *volume* of invitations she had received, surely most people at the court would assume she would not attend their functions unless she said otherwise? Sabine had never said anything about it, but then again, Sabine had hardly seemed to approve of Ida's association with Lenore.

"I—uh—didn't know I was supposed to. Sorry. I'll remember for next time."

"It's all right," said Lenore. She gestured at the seat beside her, a plush armchair upholstered in the same shade of black as the booth. It was the only piece of furniture inside the box aside from a single small table, in silver, that stood between the two chairs, bearing a bottle of wine and a selection of pastries. Ida realized that Lenore must have *asked* for her box to be prepared for two, felt the heat rise to her face again. In this small space, away from prying eyes, their meeting felt oddly intimate.

She let the curtain fall back into place behind her, and took a seat next to Lenore. Seated, she realized she had a good view of the courtyard. Although the box had seemed to be curtained off from the outside, from the inside she could see the courtyard almost without obstruction.

Ida worked in illusions, so she could appreciate a particularly good one. She weighed that feeling with the sudden, *urgent* knowledge that although she could see out, no one outside of the box would be able to see in.

Lenore cleared her throat, and this time, Ida was not sure she was imagining the dusting of rose across her cheeks. Was her hand trembling as she started pouring wine, or was that wishful thinking on Ida's part?

"I hope you'll forgive the theatrics," said Lenore. "I'm not . . . well-liked in Asteria. I prefer my privacy when I do attend the Revels." By the time she finished speaking, she had mastered herself, her expression so calm that Ida wondered if she had only imagined seeing her flustered a moment ago.

She handed Ida the wineglass. Ida took it by the stem, but didn't drink. She kept her eyes on Lenore.

Lenore did not look like a princess. If Ida didn't know, she would never have guessed that Lenore was King Aurel's daughter. But now she could see the similarities. It was in the color of their eyes, in some facial features. She knew why Lenore had seemed so familiar to her before.

"I'm sorry about last time," Ida said. "I didn't realize who you were until much later."

Lenore snorted. "I'm honestly relieved," she said, then took a long sip of her wine. "If I had my way, you would go forever without figuring out who my father was."

"Why?" Ida asked. She blurted it out without thinking, scrambled for an explanation. "I mean, surely—if your father is the king—?"

"I would be well-liked?" Lenore asked, brows raising. "My *siblings* are well-liked. I'm tolerated. Arred's one embarrassment. I wouldn't even be attending these Revels if my father didn't demand I accompany him to whichever Revel *he* makes an appearance at as well." She took another long sip of wine. "I'd prefer you treated me like you had no idea who my father was. That would be easier for all of us, I think."

Ida thought it might be best to change the subject, if only to stop Lenore from downing the entire glass in one go.

"I do appreciate the invitation," she said. "Although I'm still not clear what the starborn are. All I've heard so far is that they're horses."

"They're flying horses," said Lenore with a shrug, as if flying horses were something so ordinary that they barely required her attention. "Beautiful creatures, with pure white coats. My father acquired them from a mountaintop on some range or another. The court loves them, so he regularly schedules Revels that feature them. Tonight will be a series of races. You can place bets on them, if you'd like."

"Oh, I don't have any money . . ." Supposedly, Ida was drawing some sort of salary from her work as a luminaire, but it hadn't occurred to her to ask how she could access that money, not when everything she required was taken care of in the castle. But she trailed off at the look of mischief in Lenore's eye at Ida's words, the smirk that pulled at the corner of her lips.

"Oh, you don't gamble with *money* in Asteria. You bet time. Secrets. *Favors*. For example . . ."

She tugged on a velvet rope that hung from the ceiling of the tent, leading to a sound like tinkling bells. Ida felt the prickle of magic work its way across her skin, stealing her breath. Into the silence, Lenore spoke.

"I'll wager a secret that the winner of the first race is a starborn bearing an even number." The magic seemed to hang in the air of the box, expectant, as Lenore turned toward Ida. "What do you say? There are six horses racing in the first race, so your odds are one in two. Care to meet my bet?"

Lenore's smile was pure mischief, intoxicating. Ida found herself rising to meet the challenge.

"Done," she said. "A secret on odd."

The magic swelled to a crescendo, and sparks of silver light rained down from the top of the box, brilliant and captivating. As they settled, a card materialized on the table in front of them, made of heavy white paper. On the back was a silver star. On the front, black ink outlined the terms of their wager, inscribed with both of their names—Ida Rosales, and Lady Lenore of Arred.

"Now what?" Ida asked.

"Now," said Lenore, "we wait." She turned her gaze toward the stands, which had filled up in the time since Ida had entered

Lenore's booth. There were more people seated now, and it was only a moment before the music that had been playing since Ida arrived stopped, and a young man dressed in silver and black stepped up onto the small stage at the foot of the stands.

"Revelers," he said, "welcome to the Starborn Revel!"

The crowd roared in response.

"The king isn't going to address the crowd himself?" Ida asked Lenore, sipping at her wine.

Lenore shook her head. "My father rarely addresses the crowd himself. I suppose he used to, in the past, but these days he prefers to observe. Watch, he's about to introduce the first race."

Ida turned back to the stage as the announcer accepted a white banner from someone in the audience, a noblewoman in an emerald-green riding habit who looked thrilled to have been given the privilege. He made a show of holding the banner in both hands, of carefully unfurling it. And then he raised the banner high and Ida heard a trumpet blast. The crowd cheered, and Ida's eyes were drawn skyward as horses appeared out of the corner of her vision.

Lenore had described the starborn as flying horses with pure white coats, but Ida thought Lenore had undersold them. They weren't simply white horses. They *shone*. It was like moonlight had been woven into their manes and tails, sparkling across their elegant forms. Their saddles and bridles seemed to be made of pure silver, and they were so stunning that the riders on their backs—each dressed in a differing color of riding gear—seemed perfectly extraneous. They raced across the sky as if it were solid ground, heads down as they charged forward. And as they ran, the racetrack seemed to form itself underneath their hooves, motes of golden light forming a path with lines delineating the portion of the track given to each horse. There were numbers on their flanks, one through six, and it took Ida a moment to remember that this was still a race, that she had made a wager with Lenore.

The horses raced over their heads, and Ida cheered with the rest of the crowd as she felt the wind of their passing. They neared the end of the track, drawing close to a banner that had suddenly appeared in the sky, formed out of the same insubstantial golden motes that made up the track, and Ida realized with bated breath that two of them had pulled ahead of the group. One of them was number six, a strong-looking horse with a splash of silver across the front of its face. The other, sprinkled with faint spots of silvery gray like stars, was number three.

Lenore had bet on even, Ida on odd. They were only trading in secrets but still—Ida wanted to win.

The horses rounded the last corner of the track, bearing down on the finish line. Numbers three and six were neck and neck, so close that it was difficult to tell who was ahead. They brushed past the finish line, so in tune that Ida couldn't see which of them had won.

For one breathless moment, everything slowed to a stop. And then the crier made the announcement, his voice booming out across the stands.

"And the winner is number three!" he said. "Moonlit Serene! Number three!"

A roar of sound washed over the stands as people exclaimed in either triumph or dismay, clutching their betting cards. On the table between them, Ida and Lenore's own betting card began to glow with a faint golden light. The light flowed toward the center of the card, outlining the letters of Ida's name and her wager in bright, molten gold. Those same gold motes settled on Lenore's shoulders, forming a chain of gold dust around her neck. She swatted them away with one hand, turning to face Ida.

"I won," Ida said, grinning at her. "You have to give me a secret."

"A secret . . ." Lenore repeated. She tipped her head back, and although she had lost their contest, she didn't look disappointed. A part of Ida wondered if this was what Lenore had wanted all along. To lose. "What sort of secret should I give you?"

Ida paused, her breath catching in her throat.

There was something *here*. Lenore had been so distracting, so delightful, that it was only now that Ida was starting to think that perhaps Lenore had plans of her own.

"What—what sort of secrets are normally traded in Asteria?"

"By official definition, a secret is something that no one else knows," said Lenore. "But of course, it's very hard to think of something that *no one* knows at all. So we settle for secrets that no other court member is aware of. Such as this one. I have no memory of my mother."

"What?" Ida asked, blinking in surprise as she turned to Lenore. "Not at all?"

Lenore shook her head. "I remember some things. Basic things. That I had a mother. That we lived in a cottage in Callania. That she was sometimes stern, and when I misbehaved, I was sent to bed without supper. But I don't remember her face, the sound of her voice, her scent. I don't remember a single exact word she said. I couldn't even tell you her name."

"That's—" Ida wasn't sure she had the words. For all she didn't get along with her mother, at least Ida had some mental picture of her. "That's *horrible.* Is it because you were so young when you came to Asteria?"

"I was eight when I came to Asteria," said Lenore. "That's certainly old enough to remember one's mother. At least, so you would think. But when I try to think of my mother, all I see in my memory is darkness. If I try to think about her as hard as I can, it only hurts."

Lenore looked up at Ida then, the intensity in her eyes seeming to trap Ida in place. Ida felt it again, that fluttering of concern that she had miscalculated. That Lenore had *other* reasons for inviting her here.

"Tell me, Ida," said Lenore. "How much do you remember of your father?"

"I . . ." Ida hesitated. What sort of a question was that? "I guess I remember most things? I probably don't remember everything as clearly as I should, but the last time I saw him was a long time ago."

"And does everyone in your life remember him the same way?" Lenore asked.

Ida frowned at Lenore in confusion. It seemed like such a nonsense question. Of *course* those around her remembered her father. Every time Ida made a mistake, her grandmother always had words about that "Niresso troublemaker your mother married, whatever-his-name-was." And her mother . . .

Come to think of it, she couldn't remember the last time she had talked about her father with her mother.

"Why are you asking me about this?" Ida asked.

"Because there's something I'm trying to understand," said Lenore. "You mentioned your father went missing. Do you know what could have happened to him?"

Ida could feel the abyss opening again, the chasm in her mind she refused to touch. Words came to her tongue before she could even consider them. That was Ida's talent—the show must go on.

"I don't. We simply lost contact with him. Whatever it was . . . it must have been enough to stop him from coming back to us, from sending word. Maybe he had to flee over the border, for some reason, or was sent back to the Niressians. Maybe an accident happened with his magic and he's trapped somewhere ordinary people can't reach. Maybe . . ." She was getting too close to the abyss. She pulled back. "Maybe he's in hiding. I have no idea why he would be, but maybe it has something to do with why no one in this court will acknowledge him."

"It's not that people don't *want* to acknowledge him," Lenore said. "It's that they *can't.*"

"What do you mean?"

Lenore hesitated, her gaze moving from Ida to the stage below, where the crier was already facing the crowd, drumming up excitement for the next race. Only a thin curtain separated them from the nearest seats. Ida could see the back of people's heads in her periphery.

"This is . . . not the place for this discussion," Lenore said. "But I promise, we *will* have it. I'm sorry."

Ida fought down her frustration. It was a wave, rising inside of her, making her want to lash out, but she pushed it back down. She could be patient, she told herself. She had a lot of practice.

She startled as a hand touched hers, and looked up to see Lenore looking at her, something gently understanding in her eyes, before she pulled her hand back.

Ida leaned forward, seized with the vague compulsion to reach for Lenore's hand again, but was interrupted by someone making themselves known on the other side of the entrance to the box, an apologetic twitch of the curtain. She thought for a moment it would be Gloam, but a human servant poked his head into the box, looking sheepish.

"Lady Lenore," he said. "My apologies, but His Majesty wants to see you."

Lenore sighed, and just like that, the spell was broken, the two of them no longer the only ones in the world. She got to her feet, smoothing out her clothes.

"It seems we're out of time," she told Ida. "Please feel free to stay as long as you like. Enjoy the refreshments. There will be more races."

She started to walk, heading for the entrance.

There were moments that felt encased in amber, frozen moments, perfectly preserved in a breath, that Ida knew would stay with her for a long time, possibly forever. This was one of those moments because Ida knew she did not want Lenore to leave. She wanted to stop her, to ask her more questions, to talk all night. She told herself that it was because she was trying to unearth the secrets of the castle, to find out what had happened so long ago, but even in her own thoughts, Ida could hear the lie.

She didn't want Lenore to go. Not yet.

"Wait," she said, "don't I get a second secret? Since we both wagered one?"

Lenore stopped walking.

"You do get two secrets," she said, looking back over her shoulder. Her smile was muted, not the sharp, delightfully wicked smile she had shown Ida earlier, but something more subdued. Ida was aware suddenly of the servant's presence, that like herself, Lenore always knew where her audience was. "The second is your own, which you get to keep. But I'll give you one for free."

Her expression grew distant, her eyes sliding away from Ida to fix on the tent walls. On something else. Another place and another time.

"I'm also part of the Collection. Which means I can't leave Asteria either."

Chapter 8

POINTLESS ILLUSIONS

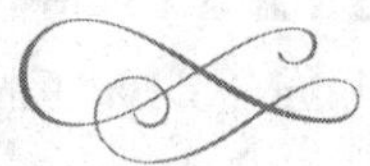

Ida waited on tenterhooks for Lenore to send for her, but no message came the next day, or the day after, or the day after that. Her heart sank, and by the third day, she was forced to face an inconvenient truth.

She wanted to see Lenore again. The wanting made a butterfly out of her breath. It was caught in her throat, and she could feel every beat of its wings. Eventually, Ida found herself questioning if the Revel had been a dream. She asked some of the younger members of the court about Lenore, but they had very little to say, only that she existed, lived in Asteria, and supposedly wasn't fully human. That her mother had been a witch of Callania, and that was why King Aurel kept her here, far from her siblings in Trissaire, where she couldn't be any trouble. They confirmed that she was part of the King's Collection.

She gathered that very few people in Asteria had good opinions about Lenore. She was something of a specter that haunted the Revels. Depending on who Ida asked, people either thought that she was a frightening witch who could curse you with a glance, or an arrogant bore who pretended to be higher than her station.

Neither of those had been Ida's impression of Lenore, and the words of the other court members sat heavily in her gut as she drifted through her daily life at the castle.

She didn't have much time to think about it, though. Work on her first commission occupied all her thoughts, and Ida practically shut herself in her workshop until it was done.

The candle she made was a beautiful thing, deep blue and dusted with flecks of sparkling gold like sunlight playing on a high mountain lake. Ida had built the candle in layers of wax, carving the surface to look like fish scales. Hints of green and silver and gold peeked out through the carvings, catching the light. The candle itself had been shaped to look like a fish, its sinuous body curved as if it were leaping out of the water, its mouth open wide to catch invisible prey.

The candle had taken her days to create, and she had the bags under her eyes—cleverly hidden by Sabine's makeup skills—to prove it. Her fingers still ached from the carving, and she thought that the tips of her fingers might have permanently been stained blue, if not for the miraculous lotion Sabine had given her.

Sabine had dressed her very similarly to her candle, in a shimmering bluish-green gown with a wide skirt, the fabric giving the impression of scales. It was gaudier than anything Ida had worn before, even to the Revels, but it was worth it, because it matched the candle, and the candle was the best work she had ever done. She knew that because an appreciative murmur rose up from the crowd at the Revel, long before Ida even lit the flame. She turned to face the crowd, half-shadowed in the Grotto's blue light, and although she knew she should have been looking at King Aurel, seated in an alcove far above the chamber floor, she was scanning the crowd for Lenore. Lenore, who should have been there, since she attended every Revel the king did. But if Lenore was watching her, Ida couldn't find her, so she forced aside her disappointment and began her performance.

By now, Ida had seen enough artisans perform at the Revels to know how it was done. When it was her turn to perform, she wasn't to speak unless it was necessary. Instead, she was to let her work speak for itself.

She rose from her bow, and when she stood, she had her father's firestrike in her hand. Ida flicked it open, relishing in the heavy feel of the lid hanging off the hinge, and produced a flame. As the crowd watched, rapt, Ida touched the flame to the wick hanging out of the fish's mouth.

This was always the most terrifying part, the moment before the flame caught, before the illusion took. Ida had fine-tuned her recipe before working on the candle, and tested it as many times as she could, but there was no telling whether one candle with the same recipe would be the same as another, whether two tapers dipped from the same pot of wax would produce the same effects.

She sucked in a breath. She prayed. And she let her magic sweep out of her and into the fire.

The flame caught with a hiss, flaring brightly.

And then immediately, it turned blue. A haunting melody rose from the fish's mouth, a lament that echoed in the Grotto's high ceilings. Ida felt herself uncoil.

This was perfect. This was magic.

This was what she lived for.

The singer's voice rose in strength, going from a soft whisper to a cry that stirred Ida's soul. She'd gone to the Conservatory to capture that tone, laid blocks of wax carefully around the stage where the royal musicians practiced and left them there for a night and a day until the music was imbued in the wax itself, in its structure and chemistry.

Scents rose from the candle, hovering in the wind. Salt and flowers and palms, and beneath it all, the tang of the sea. Ida had been to the coast only a handful of times in her life, those rare summers when her mother closed the shop and Ida and her cousins went north to the coast, but her father had told her so many stories about the ocean.

The music swelled and then plunged, as if the listener had dived into the water. And then the room went dark, the sound becoming warped and distorted.

Once, Ida had heard a sad story. A young woman, looking for her lost love, had climbed up to a cliff above a river and fallen to her death. If Ida had her way, she would bring that story to a happier end. She'd whispered that story to the wax as she shaped it, letting it come to life under her hands. The light dimmed, and when it rose again, it carried the illusion with it.

It was the illusion of being underwater, the air filled with a shimmering, distorted haze. There were no longer any walls in the cavern, any division between the cave floor and the water that waited behind the windows. Brightly colored fish swam throughout the air, darting among the crowd. Above them, sunlight dappled the ceiling, repeating the patterns of the sun on the surface of the ocean. Below them, the floor had vanished, turning into a sandy bottom far beneath, dappled with sunlight and interspersed with rocks. The air turned cool, faintly damp.

The crowd gasped in wonder at the display. Around them, the

song swelled, gaining a new quality from being underwater.

Ida caught sight of movement out of the corner of her eye and turned her head, surprised to see the sirens there too. The girl she had spotted a few days before had come to the front of the barrier separating them, her eyes on Ida, drawn to the song.

Her eyes were so sad. Ida swallowed, looking away. She couldn't afford any distractions now, not while she had an illusion to guide.

She could see the threads of the illusion in her mind, brilliant and golden, and she wove them together, pulling them taut and wrapping them tight around her fingers. The song changed, going from a diffuse melody to something firmer, something with a direction and a body. It came from her right, and Ida knew she had done it properly when the audience's heads turned to follow the sound.

A girl appeared, swimming through the air over her head. Long blond hair, spilling out around her. A billowing white dress, the fabric like a sail. Her skin was so pale it was almost translucent, reflecting the light of the false sun above. To create her, Ida had asked Celeste Valois for a single strand of hair. Celeste was one of the most eye-catching women in the court, and Ida had wanted to capture that mystique. She'd tossed the hair into the mix with a dusting of gold.

Ida met Celeste's eyes over the crowd as the girl swam over them, cutting through the water. She was still singing, her mouth opening with the song's melody, as if she didn't need to breathe. The song gained an edge of desperation, the woman's voice losing some of its refinement. It became a call, projected across the lonely expanse.

And it was answered.

A second voice joined the first, coming from the left. A man's voice, deep and edged with longing and regret. Underwater, the words were difficult to understand, but the voice didn't need words. It needed only the sensation of feeling. Ida knew she had captured that emotion when a shadowed figure broke through the shallows to her left, speeding across the expanse as he rushed toward the woman.

In the story, the woman drowned without ever finding her lost love.

Here, Ida made the drowned man out of sand and salt, and powder carefully scraped from a seashell. She transformed him from something dead into something alive, a figure of power and vitality. A thing of the sea, like the sirens themselves, with grayish-green skin and green eyes the color of the ocean, seaweed woven into his long dark hair.

The lovers met. They embraced, and he spun the woman in a circle over the audience's heads. The song came to a crescendo, washing over the watchers like the ocean waves. And then it vanished into bubbles and foam.

The flame guttered and blinked out, leaving only the burnt wick and a coil of smoke behind. All around Ida, people blinked as they found themselves standing on a stone floor once more. The song still echoed in her ears.

Ida glanced down at her candle. Her wax fish's mouth was slightly melted, but not so much as to break the structure. She exhaled, trying not to twist her fingers into the fabric of her gown out of nerves. The audience held its breath too.

Then the room broke out in wild applause, and Ida took her bow.

The evening at the Grotto was breathless, and Ida felt like she had been pulled into the center of a hive. It was her first real performance as luminaire, and everyone in Asteria wanted to know who she was, where she came from, how she had learned her craft, and what else she intended to make. To those questions, Ida always answered that she had learned her craft from her father, hoping to open a conversation about him, but never received more than a few polite inquiries or puzzled looks in response. Before she knew it, the conversation always turned back to her, to how delightful her performance had been, and Ida found herself floating on the praise. It had been a long time since anyone had looked at her magic as something that brought joy, and Ida could not remember anyone ever looking at her with stars in her eyes, as if she were one of the wonders of the castle.

For the rest of that evening, Ida flitted from table to table, making a full circuit of the room. She danced and drank and ate and laughed and felt happier than she had in a long time. As she twirled around the room, wrapped in the light and life and warmth of Asteria, she realized that this was what she wanted. To be where things happened, to be a part of them. To feel connected to the rhythm of humanity, to the beating heart of the world.

She knew in that moment that she would never want to live in a small town again.

The Revel ended almost too soon, leaving Ida bereft. A few others, Lukas von Hayner and his friends included, had invited her to various after-parties, but the emptying of the room and the slow raising of the lights had reminded Ida of the absolute state she had left her workshop in, the wax cooling in puddles on the countertop and the herbs and tinctures which would lose their potency if they were still out when the sun rose. She excused herself to go back and clean up, and wandered the halls still wrapped in the spotlight's afterglow.

In that moment, the castle had never seemed more beautiful. Ida was filled with a rush of affection for everyone and everything in it, a sudden understanding of why her father had worked as hard as he had, why he devoted his life to bringing such beauty to the world. The faces of her audience were still with her, their rapt expressions as they watched her illusion play out, and so it took her a moment before she noticed that everything was going wrong.

It was when she took a step and it echoed that she stopped, looking up and taking in her surroundings. The path she had been on a moment ago had been carpeted stone, the fabric soft beneath her feet as it ran down a long, well-lit hallway, surrounded on all sides by paintings and tapestries that displayed fantastical things. The path she was on now, that seemed to stretch into infinity in front of her, was one she had never been on before.

The hallway around her was dark, lined with shattered glass from the orbs of light that had once hung on the walls. Torches in their sconces had guttered, burned down to nothing, the only light coming from a sliver of moonlight outside. Threadbare curtains hung over the windows, fluttering in a breeze. The air became frigid. Ida was suddenly aware that it was the middle of the night in the mountains at the turn of the season, and the shadows seemed to be pressing in on her, formless and hungry.

Her breath turned to ice in her throat, her heart skipping in her chest. The gripping cold of magic pressed against her, all around her. And while that wasn't unusual in Asteria, while that was something Ida had felt many times before, this magic *hated* her. This magic wanted to *destroy* her.

Shapes burst out of the darkness at the end of the hall. Ida had scarcely glimpsed them before she turned and ran.

The darkened hallway stretched as far ahead of her as it had behind her. Ida fled, her feet kicking up dust as she raced through shadowed halls and along corridors ravaged by time and decay. Behind her, she could swear that the darkness had taken form, could hear the sounds of pounding feet, heavy breaths, infernal snarls, as if the darkness had summoned its own hounds to run her down.

Everything was wrong. She raced down a spiral staircase, stumbled at the landing, and nearly fell over as her foot caught the gap of a missing tile. Her heart was pounding, blood rushing in her ears—

She leaped over the mess, brushing spiderwebs off of her face as she charged out of the hall and into a courtyard—the first courtyard inside Asteria's gates, she thought, except it couldn't have been. Because Asteria's courtyard was always full of life, and this was empty, overgrown, with roots spilling out of planters and pulling up paving stones, like an Asteria a hundred years in the future when every member of the court was dead and dust.

Ida didn't understand it. She didn't have *time* to understand. Footfalls rang out from behind her, and Ida had only a moment to freeze like a startled rabbit, a moment to look back over her shoulder and catch sight of black fur and gleaming eyes and slavering fangs before she was running again. Out the courtyard, past the rusted gates, throwing herself down the gravel path like a girl possessed.

They pursued her. Her heart was in her throat, her lungs screaming for air. Ida was a child of the hills. She was used to running, racing her way across rough paths and taking shortcuts through shadowy woods, but even she had her limits.

She could feel the hounds snapping at her heels. Could smell their fetid breath. The outer gates of Asteria were ahead of her, impossibly far. She put on a burst of speed. The portcullis was raised, but if she could get to the other side—if she could lower it somehow, or if the outpost was manned—

Her vision wavered. She was close, so close.

She lowered her head to charge through the gates and slammed into an invisible wall.

Ida struck it so hard that she bounced off of it, so hard that it knocked the wind out of her. There was a flash of light, a sensation racing across her skin like lightning. She hit the gravel, out of breath, rolled over to see what she had struck and saw nothing but empty air. Her entire body hurt from the fall, her mind ringing like a struck bell. She turned, vision wavering, and saw her pursuers rushing toward her—three hounds, each as large as she was, trailing smoke and shadow.

The first hound leaped, mouth gaping, fangs flashing as it charged for her. Ida stumbled back, threw her arm out in front of her face, and screamed.

The creature was an inch from her, close enough for her to feel its warmth, when it yelped, jerking back into the air. Ida opened her eyes and had enough time to see what looked like a giant vine wrapped around its belly before the vine reared back and slammed the hound into the ground. It vanished in a puff of shadow, and the vine shot forward again, spearing through the body of the second hound before wrapping around the neck of the third and yanking it to the ground.

Shadow rolled across the ground like a storm as the last of the hounds vanished. Ida felt something like spider silk brush across her skin, as if she were passing through a very thin curtain. When she lifted her eyes, Asteria once again shone before her, glowing with a thousand lights like it had before she'd found herself on that dark path. And standing in the middle of the road, breathing hard, her hands raised in front of her with the tips of her fingers touching, was Lenore.

The vine coiled at her feet, making a rustling noise as it sank into the earth. It was the only sign that anything had really happened, besides Ida's shaking limbs, the sweat soaking her dress, and her racing heart.

She didn't feel like herself. Lenore came to stand in front of her, holding a hand out toward her, and Ida stared at that hand like she had never seen one before.

Lenore waited for a moment, and when Ida didn't move, said, "Are you all right?"

Ida thought if she spoke, she would throw up, but she had enough strength to reach up and take Lenore's hand. Lenore pulled her to her feet, surprisingly strong as she steadied Ida against her, eyes dark. "I think it's best we had that discussion now."

Chapter 9

LADY LENORE

Lenore's rooms were on the western side of the castle, hidden along little-used corridors. Ida had been so stunned by the ordeal that Lenore had had to take her, shivering, by the hand down those winding halls, away from the paths Revelers were most likely to take. Away from prying eyes. Ida would be grateful for that later. Lenore's touch was warm, her hand the only thing grounding her in reality. It was enough to keep her going, to help her take one step in front of another, trailing behind Lenore like a shadow trailing the light.

The night was wearing thin, a bluish tinge lining the horizon by the time they arrived at Lenore's door.

At first glance, it appeared to be an unmarked stretch of wall, but when Lenore placed her hand on it, Ida felt magic stir, a gust of wind that rippled through the space around her and made her hair stand on end. From the place she had touched, glowing vines radiated out across the door, curling in intricate, golden patterns. Leaves and flowers unfurled from them, blooming into place on the polished wooden surface. They spread until the door was covered with them from floor to archway.

On the other side of the door, Ida heard something heavy and metal turn, and then the door swung open.

It opened onto a carpeted sitting room, with fine wooden furniture and a cushion-lined alcove beneath a large glass window. To the right, another door led into a bedroom that, from what Ida could see, was almost twice the size of her workshop.

Lenore ushered her inside, the door closing behind her. From this side, it looked like an ordinary wooden door, but Ida could feel the magic settling into place, concealing the room from view.

For a moment, they stood there, Ida too numb to offer much conversation, Lenore unusually hesitant. The awkward silence stretched a beat, another, and then Lenore shook her head as if she were rousing from sleep and said, "You're probably frozen. I have a bath."

Ida wanted to say that she didn't need one, wanted to instead demand an explanation from Lenore then and there, but her gown was still covered in dust and cobwebs, clinging to her oddly from her mad dash, and the feel of the sweat-soaked fabric made her skin crawl. She sucked in a breath and nodded.

Lenore led her to a bath chamber adjoining her bedroom, and offered her a nightdress and a dressing gown to wear. The bath was the size of Ida's bedroom, and the water in the pool was already hot, as if the castle had assumed someone would need it. A shiver ran through her at the thought of using Lenore's bath, something that felt oddly ordinary after the events of the night. But she was cold, and exhausted down to the bone, and the water was inviting. Ida stripped off her clothes, sank into the tub, and let the water warm her for a long time. As she sat, she studied the slowly forming bruises on her arms, and thought about the barrier that had stopped her from leaving the castle grounds.

She thought about magic, about the way it had ripped through her in that moment like a bolt of lightning, about the way empty air had coalesced into a solid, impenetrable barrier. She thought about hounds, fangs snapping, tongues lolling, prepared to rip and tear into her flesh. And she thought about a siren girl, the way her hand had come up to press against the surface of water as if it were glass. Stronger than that. A compulsion.

"I'm part of the Collection too, aren't I?" Ida asked, when she made her way back to Lenore's sitting room, dressed and mostly dry, to find that Lenore had procured tea and pastries from thin air.

Lenore didn't look surprised by Ida's question.

"Yes."

"How?"

"When you took the oath of fealty. The king doesn't let his magical things simply leave."

The bite of metal on her lips, poison in her veins. Ida sank into an armchair across from Lenore, the weight of the revelation settling down on her. She said, "All the luminaires have been part of the Collection?"

"I don't know about all the luminaires. But Maxwell Mueller certainly was."

"He retired," Ida said numbly. "He left."

"He left," Lenore agreed. "His magic didn't."

Lenore slid a cup of tea across the table to her. Steam rolled gently across its surface. Ida stared at it, unable to even think about picking it up and taking a sip.

"But I have a provisional appointment. My oath is up in a year."

"And if you weren't so obviously good at your job, that might not be a problem." Lenore poured honey into her tea, golden strands pooling at the bottom of her cup. "In any case, you'll be free to leave in a year. You could leave now, if you resign. But not with your magic."

Who was she without her magic? Ida thought back to the night she had sworn fealty, the oath she had made. It had seemed so simple then.

"Why didn't anyone warn me?"

Lenore's smile was sad. "We couldn't get to you in time. Vegard wanted to catch you, but he grew distracted, as he often does. And I couldn't get away."

Vegard.

Eyes like winter ice. The taste of snow on her tongue, frost creeping up her veins.

She didn't realize she had frozen until Lenore set her cup down. The clink of her cup on her saucer startled Ida awake, as if from sleep.

"You . . . know him?" Ida asked, and immediately felt foolish for asking. Of course they would know each other. They were both members of the Collection. They were *all three* members of the Collection.

"Yes. We've been friends for a long time. He apologizes for scaring you, by the way. He never intended to do it, but sometimes, during periods of high emotion, his magic is out of his control." Lenore's eyes rose to study Ida, and Ida felt pinned in place by their gaze. "What happened to you today, Ida?"

Ida stared down at her hands. After the bath, they were scrubbed clean, fingers wrinkled from the length of time she had spent in the water. But she could still feel herself running down that dark corridor. Could still hear the hounds—

"I was just on my way back to my room," she said. The voice that spoke didn't sound like her. It was far too calm, too monotone. As if she were only reciting the facts of her life. As if she hadn't lived them. "The castle changed, somehow, between one step and the next. The people vanished, and the place looked . . ."

"Yes?" Lenore asked, when she trailed off. Ida looked up and saw that Lenore was leaning forward in her seat, watching her with interest. "It looked?"

"Old . . ." Ida said. "Worn down. Like a ruin."

"Then those dogs found you?"

Ida nodded. Saying it out loud made her feel embarrassed, the situation ludicrous. Even though she had the bruises to prove it. Even though Lenore had seen them too. "They came out of the darkness. I . . . felt something happen. And then I ran. And you found me."

Ida lifted her eyes to Lenore. She hadn't asked Lenore what she had been doing that far away from Asteria, at the edge of the outer wall. She studied Lenore carefully now. "How did you know where to look?"

"Do you think I had something to do with what happened to you?" Lenore asked, surprisingly calm.

She didn't want to. She really didn't. But after everything that had happened, she couldn't rule it out.

"Wouldn't you?"

Lenore exhaled, relaxing a fraction. "Fair point. But I didn't have anything to do with that. I came to look for you for another reason." She met Ida's eyes. "I wanted to talk to you about your father."

Ida sat up, startled. Her thoughts came all in a rush. Had her father been part of the Collection too? Had *he* tried to leave? But no—her father had come and gone from Asteria several times before he finally disappeared, and he'd retained his magic.

Whatever was going on with the luminaires, it had come after his time. Or maybe . . . maybe it was the reason he had disappeared.

Maybe this was all connected. Maybe this was what she had been searching for from the start. She spoke, and tried not to sound too quick, too breathless. "What do you know about him?"

"Nothing," Lenore said. "Which is odd, isn't it? I haven't been able to stop thinking about it, not since we first met and you asked me about him. You said he was a luminaire here. We *should* know him. But we don't."

Ida nodded. She remembered the confused look in the librarian's eye when Ida asked about other luminaires, remembered how she had scoured the workshop for traces of her father and never found anything, remembered how King Aurel had looked at her without even an ounce of recognition in his gaze, as if he had never met another person with Niresso blood in his life.

"Vegard and I are searching for the same thing," Lenore continued. "Our memories. There is a night missing from both our recollections. We believe you might hold the key."

"Why?"

"Because you remember your father. And no one else does."

"And you think that has something to do with the night you can't remember?"

"It was seven years ago," Lenore said, and Ida perked up. Seven years ago was the last time she could remember hearing from her father. "I was new to Asteria. My father had brought me here from

Callania less than a year before. My mother . . ." Lenore looked pained and shook her head.

"My memories of that day are . . . confused. In that time, my father spoke to me very little, and I spent most of my time in my room. In this room. That day should have been like all the others, except . . . except I remember Father was agitated that morning. He always invited me to have breakfast with him. In those days, it was something that he did to . . . I suppose, try to force a bond between us. I was lonely and happy to oblige. On that day, though, he seemed distracted. Jittery. He barely cared about what I had to say. As soon as I was finished eating, he dismissed me before I could set my fork down. And that night . . ."

She paused, glancing off out the window. Ida found that she was hanging on to Lenore's every word.

"Can you remember anything at all?"

"It's difficult to describe." Lenore glanced at Ida, taking her hand over the table. Her touch was warm. Ida could feel her heartbeat rising, breath catching in her throat at the feel of Lenore's hand on hers. Lenore was half leaning over the table, staring at her, and the look in her eye, so intent, warmed Ida from the crown of her head to the tip of her toes.

She felt her throat tighten.

"Lenore?"

"Can you feel this?" Lenore asked, and at first Ida thought that she was talking about her hand. She could feel it, the warmth of Lenore's skin, the storm churning in her blood. Or perhaps the flutters in her heart that had turned hummingbird-quick at the touch.

But then she felt it: a slow, rolling pulse against her arm. Subtle and strong, like growing things. The scent of soil filled her nostrils, of a forest in the light of day, powerful and alive. It was the same magic she had felt from Lenore in the garden.

Ida's mouth was dry. She nodded.

Lenore nodded back, slowly removing her hand from Ida's wrist. If she was as affected as Ida was, Ida couldn't tell from her face. There was only the slightest tremble at the tips of her fingers.

"Magic knows magic," Lenore said. "You can *feel* magic at work, the same way I can, the same way Vegard can. Otherwise, Vegard's meltdown in the Grotto wouldn't have affected you the way it did."

Ida trailed her fingers around the skin of her wrist, the place where Lenore had touched her. Outside the castle, where magic was rare, she'd rarely felt another person's magic. The last breath of magic she remembered sensing was her father's. It was like the sun, golden and warm, the way she imagined the air in the Niressians must feel.

"And what you felt that night . . ." Ida said, now that her racing heart had calmed enough to allow herself to speak. "That was magic?"

Lenore nodded. "I can't remember the details, but whatever it was, it was powerful. It felt like . . . like the foundations of the world were coming unmoored. Like something was shattering. I ran to my window—that window"—she nodded at it—"to see better. But I can't remember what I saw. Only a bright light, and then it was the next day. And life in the castle went on."

Ida got to her feet, facing the window. She had taken two steps forward before she remembered her manners and looked back at Lenore. She cleared her throat—it was still thick, her body still buzzing from what Lenore had done, and asked, "May I?"

"Be my guest."

To peer out of the window, Ida had to kneel on the bench of cushions that had been arranged nearby. Outside, the horizon was starting to glow with the coming dawn, the castle's windows jewels of light in the dark. Lenore's window looked out onto the mountainside, but she could see some of the castle to her left. A bank of windows, and above it, nothing but open sky.

Ida tried to angle her head upward, changing her vantage point to that of a child, but the view was still completely ordinary.

"Do you remember where the light came from?" Ida asked.

"It came from everywhere."

"But was it centered around any specific point? Was the whole castle glowing?"

"I can't remember." Lenore paused for a moment, then added, "I suppose . . . it might have been coming from somewhere high. The sky above the castle, perhaps."

Mysterious lights in the sky. A night that both Lenore and Vegard could only vaguely remember.

The glass was cool beneath Ida's fingertips. She drew in a shaky breath, aware that this was the first thing she had found since arriving at Asteria that might be called a lead.

"You think that what happened to my father . . . happened on that night?"

"It would explain why none of us can remember him." Lenore winced, covering up the motion by taking another sip of tea. "When I try to think about that night, it hurts. And just now, when I tried to remember the name of the luminaire before Master Mueller, it hurt in the exact same way. The two must be connected."

"And your other reasons?"

"The way you feel. Like summer. Like warmth, and blue skies, and golden sunlight." Lenore glanced at Ida, looking a little self-conscious. "Your magic feels . . . remarkably familiar to me. But I am certain I've never met you before in my life. I would remember you."

I would remember you.

It was as if Lenore had reached into Ida's mind and echoed the thought she'd had the first night she met Lenore:

I would have noticed you.

Ida looked back out the window quickly, not wanting Lenore to see the blush on her face. She pressed her palm firmly against the cool glass, focusing her mind. She had never felt her own magic, but Lenore's description reminded her of her father. If Lenore had memories of Ida's father, Vegard likely had those same memories.

"What does Vegard remember?" she asked.

"You'll have to ask him yourself," Lenore said. "I'm not sure I could explain it. He agrees with me about what we both felt, about the burst of magic. But as for the rest of it . . ." She shook her head. "What he remembers doesn't make sense to me. I don't think it makes sense to him."

Ida wasn't sure how she felt about meeting Vegard again. There was a danger to him that made her hesitate. And yet . . .

She remembered Vegard in the Grotto. He'd looked so confused, so lost. And she'd ordered him to go.

If Vegard and Lenore could help her get her father back . . .

Ida stepped away from the window, turning to face Lenore. "Does this have to do with what you told me at the Revel? That you don't remember your mother?"

"I think so," Lenore said. She glanced down at her lap, smoothing out a wrinkle in her dress. "It isn't just my mother. I remember very little of my life before coming to Asteria. I believe that that night could be the cause. Vegard believes the same. And while he does remember his past before Asteria, time doesn't flow for him the same way it does for us. It likely hurts him, that there are moments gone from his memory."

Lenore pinned Ida in place with her gaze, sharp and green and vibrant. "We've told you why we want your help. Will you help us? In return, we'll do whatever we can to help you find your father. And if there's a way to break the castle's hold on you, we'll try to find that too."

A chance to find her father and be free of the castle. A chance to leave Asteria with her magic.

There were wise choices. But there was only one choice Ida would ever have made.

"Yes. I'll help you."

Chapter 10

CREATIVE SOULS

By the time Ida made it back to her room, the halls of Asteria were empty, stark and clinical in the harsh light of day. She'd returned to find her bed turned down, and fallen into a dreamless, exhausted sleep. The next evening, she'd been forced to answer Sabine's concerned inquiries about where she had been the night before, and what had caused her to stay out until well past dawn. Ida managed to direct Sabine's curiosity with some vague answer about celebrating too much, and while Sabine watched with concern as she ate the cold breakfast she had set aside for her, she didn't say much more about it, instead bringing Ida her correspondence.

The stack of letters had only grown since her first successful commission, but Ida found that looking at them didn't bring her the same joy it once had. The letters seemed frivolous, happy invitations written by people who didn't see the chains that had been tied around Ida's limbs, that settled heavy on her shoulders and bound her to the castle. There were only two she opened.

One was another royal commission—the king had wasted no time in setting her another task. This one was to create a candle for an autumn banquet held in something called the Orangerie in ten nights. The candle needed to complement music, and the theme was the changing seasons. It seemed simpler than her previous task, with a longer deadline, which was good, because Ida struggled to muster a spark of inspiration with her mind still on the Collection.

The second, which came in a heavy violet envelope that smelled faintly floral, was an invitation to visit Celeste Valois's workshop at Ida's earliest convenience.

What Ida wanted to do was to ignore all her correspondence and while away the nights in her room, waiting with bated breath for Lenore to summon her again. But even with everything that had happened, even with the knowledge that she was tied to the castle, it was hard to make herself refuse an invitation from Celeste. Hard to fight the curiosity to see a master at work.

She found herself sitting, two nights later, at one of Celeste's tables, taking care not to accidentally set her arm in wet paint. From this angle, she could see Celeste's canvas. The artist was working on a ballroom scene, a Revel lit with a thousand floating lights. For one breathtaking second, Ida thought that the girl occupying center stage in the painting was Lenore, but upon closer inspection, Ida thought it was meant to be King Aurel's oldest daughter, the Crown Princess Maria Sophia, who had not actually been present at the Revel. She was still beautiful, but her eyes didn't have the same fire as Lenore's. They didn't make Ida's stomach do flips, or make her feel like she was being drawn in. There wasn't any magic in her smile.

She looked perfect in the painting, but it was a fake, flat sort of perfection, and Ida was so tired of it. It made her think of her own commission, the candle she would make for the autumn banquet. She hadn't been able to bring herself to do more than basic work. Some leaves changing colors, a few scents that mimicked the seasons. What she had done so far was passable, but could she really be proud of it? Did she want to be? "How can you stand it?" Ida asked. "Painting *them* all the time."

"It pays for my other work," Celeste said, with a wink. She dabbed a bit of paint onto Her Royal Highness's gown, glancing back at Ida. "Do you want to see?"

Ida would have given anything to not have to think about royalty for another second.

"Please," she said, sliding off her stool.

Celeste grinned, setting her palette and brush aside. She stood, wiping her hands off on a nearby towel, and ushered Ida toward the back of her workshop, where a door led to a small storage room. She snapped her fingers, and a soft glow spread throughout the room, illuminating the space. With the light, a riot of color came to life, making Ida stop in her tracks.

Inside the room, several easels had been set up, displaying paintings in varied states of progress. But unlike the staid realism of Celeste's portrait work, the paintings in this room depicted a world that Ida had only ever seen in her dreams. Bright, vibrant colors created scenes of wonder and magic: castles floating in the sky; birds in all the colors of the rainbow flocking around a woman in a red, ruffled dress; an army of mythical creatures escorting a young girl with a lantern through a dark forest. Ida worked in magic, in illusions, but it was Celeste's art that seemed to want to jump off the page, to come to life and dance around the room.

"These are *beautiful*, Celeste."

Celeste gave Ida a half-joking bow, drawing herself up to her full height. Praise seemed to roll right off her, as if she considered it her due. Ida wished for an ounce of her confidence. She felt like a mouse in comparison.

"These paintings are my real work," Celeste said, as Ida stepped closer to get a better look at a painting of a young child seated primly at the center of a lily pad. "The work I do for His Majesty and the other members of the royal family allows me to use palace resources to create these works in my spare time. It's one of the benefits we have as royal artisans, the opportunity to let our work *breathe*."

Ida faltered. She admired the passion in Celeste's voice, the certainty. But her mind flashed back to her own workshop, her desk empty, her storage cupboards full of test versions of the candles she had made for the last Revel, and her countertops littered only with the ingredients she had requisitioned for the next one. With everything going on, when was the last time she had actually *created* anything for the art of it?

"I haven't done anything like this," Ida said. "I haven't worked on anything for myself since . . ."

Since coming to the palace. Since she had first seen that advertisement in the broadsheet, asking for a Court Luminaire. When was the last time Ida had sat at her bench and *created*, without trying to meet another person's specifications or needs? She wanted to tell herself it was because she had been busy, because she had come here to search for her father and *that* was her great work, the work she did on the side of the king's commissions. But that wasn't entirely the truth either. There was so much wrapped up in her thoughts, in her feelings, but from the sympathetic look on Celeste's face, Ida knew that Celeste was only thinking of art.

"It's a trap we get into, Ida. The money is nice, and the

recognition, and the *challenges.* For a while, it's enough simply to follow. But we are artists, you and I. We are creative souls, and if we don't feed that part of ourselves, that spirit dies. What do *you* want to make for yourself?"

For herself?

Ida looked around her at the paintings, at the scenes on display, the worlds Celeste had created.

Who was Ida when she wasn't thinking about other people?

"I want to bring these to life. I want to make people experience something that doesn't exist, that can't exist."

She wanted to set people free. From rules, from *reality.* But the words felt pretentious in her mind, and she couldn't bring herself to say them.

"Then why don't you?" Celeste asked.

"Because I'm busy." The excuse came so easy to her. A lie, spring-loaded, ready at the tip of her tongue. "I have a royal commission to work on, and only eight nights left until the banquet."

Celeste rested one arm across her chest, tapping her chin with a finger. She stood in the doorway like this for a while, thinking. She seemed to take great delight in leaving Ida to squirm.

At length, she nodded, as if coming to a decision. "Take one."

Ida stared at her, shocked. "Excuse me?"

Celeste beamed broadly. She spread her arms wide, to either side of her, encompassing the entirety of the storage room. "Any piece you want. It's yours. Take one."

Ida's mind spun at the enormity of what was being offered to her. An *original* Celeste Valois? She couldn't even begin to calculate how much that was worth. "I can't possibly—"

"You can," Celeste said, interrupting her. "And this is what you will do for me. You will make me an original candle, anything you want, and I will display it here. And when you are famous, I will tell everyone that this candle is an Ida Rosales original. And you will stop with this moping around. It's unbecoming. You are a rising star, Ida. One day, everyone in this castle will brag about the fact that they knew you as you are now."

It was hard not to imagine it.

Even though Celeste's vision of the future seemed so unlikely, with the oath of fealty hanging over her head and this constant feeling as if the shadows of Asteria were closing in on her, trying to swallow her, Celeste had a way of drawing her in, of making her believe it.

Did she dare?

The future Celeste spoke of wasn't one her mother would have called appropriate for girls like her. But in that moment, Ida wanted it. She wanted it, and hated herself for wanting it at the same time, because it was so impossible.

It was easy for Celeste to speak like that, Ida thought. She had everything Ida wanted, with none of the drawbacks, none of the pain. *She* wasn't part of the King's damned Collection. Her paintings were spun only out of pigment and brush; the magic in them came solely from her talent. Celeste's fate wasn't tied to Asteria or the King of Arred. And she didn't have to deal with this fear, this *shame* that she wasn't enough. That she was no closer to finding her father, and that part of her still wanted to turn around and go home.

Her father had said to her once when she was young that to the Niressos, family was everything. And every time Ida faltered, she felt like she was betraying that. Betraying him.

Because she had to be Niresso. She had to be. Even if she had never been there. Even if her father was the only Niresso she had ever met. Because if she wasn't Niresso then she wasn't anything.

"I'm not even Arreden," Ida said. Celeste blinked, and Ida froze, her breaths coming hard in her chest.

Why had she said that out loud?

That wasn't at all what she had intended to say. What this conversation was about.

Celeste watched her, and something in her gaze sharpened. When she spoke, her voice was flat, devoid of its usual teasing lilt.

"Aren't you?" Celeste asked. "Certainly, you're more Arreden than me. You're a citizen of this country, a subject of King Aurel. Born and raised in Trissaire."

"I . . ." Ida faltered.

"What makes someone Arreden?"

History. Culture. Language. *Blood.* All the things her grandmother—the villagers—insisted she lacked, but Ida couldn't answer. Celeste's eyes narrowed at her.

"And why is it so important to *be* Arreden?"

Ida couldn't answer that either. In her mind, she saw her grandmother looking at her, pointing at her with her bony fingers and telling her mother, as if Ida wasn't in the room, as if Ida could not understand—"*That child has too much of her father in her. She will never be Arreden.*"

"How am I supposed to belong here if I'm not?" Ida asked.

"*I'm* not Arreden," Celeste reminded her, her voice sharp. "Do *I* not belong here?"

"I'm sorry!" Ida said. "I didn't mean—"

"It's fine," Celeste said, placing both hands on Ida's arms to cut her off. The touch was meant to be comforting, presumably, but it felt to Ida that Celeste was one wrong word away from shaking her. "You're still so young, Ida. There's so much you don't understand about this world. You *are* Arreden, but you don't need that to be great."

Ida knew that Celeste was right. Her words were exactly what she would have said, if she had ever met anyone who felt the way she did now. But somehow, Ida couldn't make herself believe them.

She took in a breath. Let it out.

"I really want to see what you see, Celeste."

Celeste smiled, as if Ida had just conceded a victory. "It's often difficult to see yourself the way others see you," she said. "That's why it helps to have others who can serve as your mirror. Please, take a painting. Any one of your choice. And have courage."

Courage.

Celeste couldn't possibly know what was on Ida's mind, couldn't and shouldn't know about everything that was happening to her.

But she was right that Ida needed to be brave.

She couldn't wait for the world to change for her. She had to take things into her own hands.

That night, as dawn painted the horizon in shades of light blue and gold, Ida hung Celeste's painting up on her workshop wall. She'd chosen the girl with the lantern in the dark forest, her figure a sole focus of light and warmth in the cold world around her. Ida stared at it for a long moment, gathering that courage.

She turned to face her countertops, studying the materials she had assembled, the trial candles she had made and the hasty designs she had sketched for her next commission. In that moment, Ida made two choices.

The first was that her work was her own, *not* the king's. He might be keeping her in the Collection, but he didn't own her mind, and if she was going to be forced to work on these commissions, she was going to do it her own way. No more half measures.

The second was that if she truly wanted to find her father, she couldn't keep being afraid. Now was not the time for hesitation. She pulled a piece of paper out from her desk and began to write.

Lenore, she wrote. *I'm ready to meet Vegard.*

PART TWO
SECRETS

It's hard to name the very moment that Aurel IV's reign fell apart, in part because of the fog of mystery that shrouds the king and his activities to this day. Some say that his acknowledgment of his bastard daughter, Lenore, was his undoing, although critics are quick to point out that Lady Lenore was brought to Arred in 824, two years before King Aurel's seclusion. The years that followed were some of His Majesty's most prosperous, and their influence in the culture of Arred and beyond will likely carry on for centuries. Indeed, we cannot say with any true feeling that this is the moment when King Aurel's star began to fall—after all, in the face of miracles, wonder, and yes, wealth, what 820s Arreden noble would quibble over the existence of a single bastard child?

—Herbert Ardinger, *The King of Moonlight: A Comprehensive History of Aurel IV*

Chapter 11

THE PRINCE OF WINTER

"I see you decided to rejoin the land of the living, mistress."

Ida groaned as she pushed herself up into a sitting position, blinking in the late-afternoon sunlight. She'd gone to bed shortly after sending her letter to Lenore, but her mind had been too active for her to sleep. Unable to do anything with her energy, she'd gone into the workshop to start on the king's commission, and had ended up working well into the morning, trying to capture a few dollops of autumn sun to make her candles that much more memorable. She'd gotten a lot of work done, but it had been a while before sleep came for her, and Ida felt tired and groggy.

With a start, she remembered why. Her eyes drifted to her writing desk, where her post appeared in the evenings. Instead of the usual collection of letters and invitations, there was a box, wrapped in dark paper. She almost reached for it, but then she remembered Sabine, who had no doubt spotted it as well. Sabine, who Ida hoped would assume it was just a trinket or some other souvenir from the Revels, and not ask about it further.

Ida swung her legs over the side of the bed and stood, facing

Sabine. "I got up after you left and decided to get started on the candles." It wasn't *entirely* a lie. "I made a lot of progress, but I think I stayed up too late."

Sabine cocked her head to the side, one hand on her hip. The stare she gave Ida was startlingly familiar, reminding her of her mother.

"Well, you've definitely overslept. You'll have to run if you want to use the Knights' Bath."

Ida winced, glancing at the position of the sun. She thought about jogging up the steps that led into that wide hallway and gave Sabine a pained look. "Could I . . . possibly use the servants' bath today?"

Sabine sighed. "I suppose. You'll have to wait until after everyone's had their turn. I hope you weren't planning on being anywhere tonight."

Ida's eyes darted toward her desk. She quickly looked away, but from the suspicious look Sabine gave her, she hadn't been quick enough.

"No. I'm not attending the Revel tonight. I'll just be here, working on my candles." She winced at the sound of her own voice. If Sabine *had* been her mother, she would have known immediately that Ida was planning something.

But Sabine only nodded. Once she left, Ida dug her hairbrush out of one of her drawers, frantically trying to comb her hair into something presentable before breakfast. Then, she reached for the box and carefully removed the wrapping paper.

The box inside was made of dark wood, polished until it was almost black. A scrap of fabric lay neatly folded on top of it. Ida opened it and read:

I received your note. Vegard will meet you tonight at midnight.

Unfortunately, I've been summoned to meet with my father, but we shouldn't delay.

Gloam will show you the way.

Vegard asked me to give this to you, with his apologies.

It will shield you from his power when you meet with him.

As long as you wear it, he won't be able to hurt you, even unintentionally.

—L

Ida opened the box. Silver glittered, gleaming coldly in the fading sunlight. A heavy pendant rested on a bed of cloth, a thin silver chain coiled next to it. As she reached for it, she could feel the biting snap of winter just beyond her fingertips. Her heart raced. Bracing for the cold, she took hold of the chain. It felt like ice as she drew it out of the box. She shuddered at the thought of how it would feel around her neck, against her skin.

Nothing for it. It was like leaping into a cold lake—the only thing she could do was take the plunge.

She slipped it on quickly, hiding the chain under the fall of her hair. As soon as it touched her, Ida gasped and drew herself inward, arms folding tight across her waist. For a second, it was like walking naked into a blizzard, into the kind of cold that punched all the air out from her body, that made her feel like she had slammed straight into a wall.

But then it faded, the sensation of magic receding. She uncoiled slowly, straightening up and taking slow breaths to get the air back into her lungs. A few moments more, and she felt completely normal, as if the cold had never come. The pendant was still cool to the touch, but it was a comforting chill, like ice on a summer day. She held it in her hand and raised it so that she could see it better.

It was round and silver, with unfamiliar, angular characters carved onto its outer edge. At the heart of it was a design like a great tree, its roots spreading as wide as its branches. It was a locket, and when Ida opened the clasp, she found a piece of cloth hidden behind glass, with a drop of something silver and shimmering at its heart. The glass, when she pressed her thumb against it, felt unbearably cold.

Ida closed the locket, slipping it under her shirt so that it settled against her skin. It rested there, and though she could still feel its power if she thought about it, it no longer felt like ice and death. She'd have to work to hide it from Sabine, especially in the baths, but for now . . .

For now, Ida fixed her hair and went to breakfast. She had work to do.

At midnight, when Ida's test candles were cooling, just after she had sent Sabine away, Gloam came to her. She felt their presence as a prickle across her back and shoulders, Gloam curling and twisting in the air over her head.

"It's time, miss."

Gloam's voice was quiet in her ear. Ida straightened up, stepping away from her work. Her heart sank into her stomach with nerves, and she reached up, feeling the outline of the locket through the fabric of her shirt.

"Lead on."

Gloam led her out of her rooms and into the night. Like the

night before, Asteria's halls were hushed, most of its residents at the Revel or meeting in private. The Revel tonight was an indoor affair, though, and the sound of distant conversation followed Ida as she tracked Gloam across the stones. Ida felt very much like a child who was supposed to be in bed, sneaking around the periphery of adult socialization.

She prayed they wouldn't run into anyone tonight.

In minutes, Gloam had led Ida through deserted corridors, up staircases she had never noticed before, until before she knew it, she was standing in front of a heavy wooden door.

"In here, miss," Gloam said, their voice soft in her ear. "I'll wait outside, and let you know if anyone comes."

"Thank you, Gloam."

Ida pushed the door open. Unlike Lenore's chambers, there was no magic at play here. It was an ordinary door, sliding open on well-oiled hinges to reveal a small room. A single globe of light hung over the hallway so that Ida could see it was a theater of some kind. Plush couches stood in rows before an empty stage.

Here, Asteria lost some of its polish. The upholstery on the couches was faded, the wooden stage scuffed and worn. A thin veneer of dust coated the surfaces, and Ida knew why this location had been chosen. It was not likely to be used for a Revel any time soon.

"It's a remnant of before," a voice from behind her said.

Ida spun around to face the speaker.

Vegard stood in the aisle between seats, wreathed in an aura of silver. She hadn't heard him enter, but he didn't look powerful, or terrifying. He looked hesitant, as if he was afraid to approach her. She braced herself for the bite of his power, but it never came, although the amulet around her neck hummed in resonance.

Ida found her voice. "Before?"

"Before Asteria became what it is." Vegard gestured at the room. "This was built for intimate gatherings. The king and a handful of others he chose to honor. There haven't been any small gatherings like that since the Revels began."

"And when was that?"

"Not long after I came."

He raised his eyes to hers for the first time that night. Now that the weight of his aura had been lifted, she could see them clearly. They were not merely gray, but silver, almost white, as if all the color had been leached from them. Even without her magic, it would be hard to mistake Vegard for human.

But there was pain in those eyes, and that was very human. He said, "You're wearing my amulet. I'm glad. I'm sorry for scaring you last time."

Ida nodded. She could still feel the fear, but it was locked up somewhere in the back of her mind. Without the sting of magic, it was difficult to remain afraid of Vegard. "I was told you couldn't help it. It's fine."

Vegard nodded sharply. He looked guilty, and awkward, as if he didn't know how to continue. Ida realized this must not happen very often, him speaking so casually to another. Did he have any other friends besides Lenore? She hadn't asked, hadn't thought to ask in the middle of everything she had learned about the Collection.

"Why don't we sit down?" she asked, inclining her head toward the chairs. "We can have a more natural conversation that way."

The two of them sat next to each other at the edge of the stage, looking out at the theater. The chairs had been dusty, and neither of them had wanted to sit with their backs to the door.

Vegard didn't say anything. He was clearly struggling, unsure how to begin. Ida waited a few moments before she spoke up.

"Lenore told me about the night you lost your memories. Could you tell me what happened to you?"

He closed his eyes, letting out a shaky exhale. It was such a human motion that Ida had to fight the urge to place her hand on his shoulder. She didn't know how he would react to her touch. When he opened his eyes, his expression was distant, his eyes fixed on something far away.

"I came from the north. From a land where winter never ceases. King Aurel found me, asked me to return with him to Asteria. I had no desire to remain, so I agreed. I wanted to see the rest of the world."

"And he trapped you here?" Ida asked.

Vegard looked confused. He shook his head, looking down at his hands. "No . . . I . . . don't think . . . not at first. I can't remember—"

He began to look distressed. Ida reached out, tugging at the fabric of his sleeve. A cold sensation sparked up her fingertips at the touch, but there was no pain.

"It's okay," she said soothingly, when he looked at her. "Tell me what you do remember."

Vegard stared at her, his breathing ragged. His eyes were wide, pupils shrunk to points. He looked like a stray cat Ida had found once, like he wasn't sure whether to come to her or run away.

The cat had chosen to run. Vegard mastered himself, taking slow breaths until the panic dissipated.

"There's a hole in my memories. Not only that night that Lenore refers to, although that's the worst of it. But much of what came before, and . . . and some of what comes after. I'm not . . . what I was."

"Because of what your memories mean to you?"

"I was born from the magic of the world," Vegard said. "Memory is all I have. My memories, to me, are flesh and blood to you."

Ida was still holding his sleeve. It didn't take much effort to move her hand upward, to rest it gently on his shoulder to comfort him. He flinched—she felt the ripple of motion underneath the cloth—but he didn't pull away. Beneath, he was surprisingly solid. His shoulder felt no different from any other, except that it was much colder.

She could feel cold radiating through the fabric, could taste frost on her tongue, but once more she was relieved to find it didn't hurt. She could still feel his magic, but it was like a storm raging on the other side of a glass window. Its ferocity couldn't touch her.

From this remove, she could evaluate him critically. He'd said he was a spirit, and she had seen him vanish into thin air, but to her eyes, to her hands, to all her human senses, he looked only like a boy her age. He had presence and weight. He seemed solid enough to her.

But he wasn't. Because now that the storm had been pushed away, Ida could feel the cracks in him. Magically, he was like . . .

Like torn fabric.

Like someone had taken a sheet of silk and slashed through it with a knife. There were holes, frayed and ragged edges in him. She and Lenore were body and soul, their magic encased in a cage of humanity, but Vegard just—was.

A being of magic and memory, and he was broken.

She pulled her hand away, letting out a shaky breath. Vegard shuddered at the loss of her touch.

"So warm . . ." he said, as Ida cradled her chilled fingers in her lap.

Ida remembered what Lenore had said about her magic. That it felt like summer.

"Please tell me what you remember," she said gently. "Focus on that night if you can. Stop if it causes you distress."

Vegard nodded. As he spoke, he started to get himself under control, his cadence becoming smoother and more elegant until it felt to Ida like he was telling her a fairy story, something that had happened a long time ago, far away.

"I remember coming here of my own accord. Asteria was still being constructed. King Aurel asked me to lend his power to the stones, so that they could support the type of place he dreamed of. There were others with us then, drawn in by the king's vision. Human mages, other spirits, and . . ."

He paused, looking pained. His brows furrowed, and Ida felt his magic flare, a ripple of power that crackled like lightning. The hair on her arms stood on end.

"What year was this? How long ago? Can you remember?"

Vegard frowned. "Ten . . . no, fifteen years ago. I can't be sure."

Fifteen years ago.

Ida's heart was thumping. Fifteen years ago, she would have been two. Asteria would still have been under construction. She and her mother would have lived in Trissaire, and her father—

She had so few memories of that time in her childhood, those early stages of her life. But she thought, although she couldn't be sure if it was just wishful thinking or reality, that her father had already been working as King Aurel's Court Luminaire.

"Did you feel any magic like mine, back then?"

Vegard's aura spiked worryingly. He looked away, expression

contorting in pain. Ida quickly changed tactics. "Never mind. Sorry I asked. Please continue."

He breathed deep and went on. "We gave our power willingly to the court, and for a while, it was beautiful. People came from all over to admire our work. But King Aurel wanted more. He would go on long expeditions, collecting magic from all over the world. Magical artifacts, and magical beings like myself. Not all of them came willingly. There were . . . arguments . . ."

Vegard faltered again.

Ida held her breath. It took everything in her not to interrupt, not to ask: arguments with *whom*?

Because the father she had known would not support what Vegard described. But . . . the last time she'd seen him, she had been nine. With a twist of uncertainty in her gut, she wondered if maybe she was remembering him as someone better than he was. If she was wrong about the man he had been.

". . . The air at the time was . . . unpleasant," Vegard said. "And then Lenore came to Asteria."

Lenore.

Ida thought about the way Lenore had spoken the day before, about her transition to Asteria. About her mother and the things she could no longer remember. And almost unwillingly, her thoughts drifted to the warmth of her touch and the feel of her magic and the light in her bright green eyes.

"It was not an event in and of itself," Vegard was saying. "Lenore was not . . . yet significant. She was politically important, and her arrival caused a stir among the humans in residence, but she was only a child. But after Lenore's arrival, the king began to change. He became . . ."

Vegard trailed off, shaking his head. One of his hands rubbed at his other arm as if soothing a wound, but the wound was inside of him. Buried deep. A cut straight to the bone.

"I don't remember much else. Nothing before that night. There was a lot of confusion. A fight—there was shouting. A struggle. There was a lot of noise, and then a lot of pain. Nothing has felt real since." He turned to look at her then, silver eyes boring into her own. Even with the amulet's protection, Ida felt the weight of his stare, heavy on her shoulders as he said, "Nothing until you."

Ida's throat was dry. It took a moment to find the words, because Vegard was still staring at her. His eyes burned a path straight into her soul.

"Me?"

He nodded.

"When I first saw you at the Revel, it felt like . . . a beacon. For the first time, I felt like myself. I felt . . . almost whole. I think—I *believe* that you're the key to understanding what happened that night. That if I have any hope of gaining my memories back, of fixing what's been broken, it's through you."

Vegard shifted, turning to face her. He caught her hand, holding it tight between his own. Ida jumped at the touch, the storm on the other side of the glass growing closer.

"Will you help us?"

Lenore had asked her the same question. And Ida had answered, because it would bring her closer to finding her father, because she had no other way of getting her freedom back, and because she couldn't believe that her father had not been somehow involved in whatever had happened that night.

But she answered Vegard for a different reason.

She answered because he had been hurt, and because no one had ever looked at her like that before. Like she was important and significant. Like she *meant* something.

"I'll do whatever I can."

Chapter 12
LOST IN MEMORY

"Are you planning on attending tonight's Revel, mistress?"

Ida frowned from her seat at the vanity, glancing at Sabine in the reflection of her mirror. There was a letter burning for her attention in her desk drawer, a letter Ida had snatched from the sunset post and stashed away like she had something to hide. She was sure Sabine had seen it, though.

The letter was a cream-colored envelope from Lenore. At the thought of it, Ida felt her heart flutter. "I might," Ida said. "If I can finish work in time."

Sabine frowned at Ida's answer, concern clear on her face. Ida pretended not to notice.

With the autumn banquet approaching, Ida didn't have many nights to waste, but it was worth it if she could see Lenore. She told herself it was simply because Lenore would have more information about the mystery of the castle, and nearly made herself believe it.

Once Sabine had left her, Ida took the letter out from her drawer and tore it open.

Ida—

I know that you are working on a commission for my father, for the autumn banquet.

I also know that you have already visited the Orangerie.

If you are willing to indulge me, please meet me there again tonight.

The oranges are ripe, and I believe they may be of interest to you.

Yours,

Lenore

Yours.

Ida swallowed, staring at the end of the letter, the sweep and curve of Lenore's handwriting, carving out the channels of her name. She shouldn't read into it, she told herself as her fingertips grazed lightly over the letter. It was a perfectly normal way to sign off. And yet . . .

She swallowed past the knot in her throat, forcing her eyes upward to take in the rest of the words. Ida doubted that Lenore only wanted to talk about the commission. She, Ida, and Vegard had agreed that they wouldn't talk about the missing memories where anyone could hear them, nor write anything in letters. If Lenore wanted to speak to Ida about a new development, this was how she would do it.

Ida tucked the letter away, locking it back in her drawer, and headed to the Orangerie.

The Orangerie was a greenhouse, an improbable narrow hall with its outward-facing side entirely made up of high glass windows through which artificial sunlight filtered in. Trees lined the hall on both sides, each one heavy with oranges. The citrusy smell of the fruit filled Ida's lungs the second she pushed open the frosted glass doors. In her whole life, Ida had never seen so many.

Arred's climate didn't lend itself well to the growing of oranges. They preferred the warmer climate of the south, and even in cosmopolitan Trissaire, cost an eye. That the king had them where anyone could reach out and take one was a clear sign of his wealth, but—Ida thought—otherwise perfectly ordinary. Ida wasn't sure why Lenore wanted to meet her here, of all places.

But Lenore stood among the trees, an orange in her hand.

She was dressed casually today, in a white blouse and skirts in layers of brown and deep red. She wore soft leather boots, as if she were planning to go walking in the garden. Was it Ida's imagination, or did Lenore's eyes linger on her as she approached? Her mouth went dry.

"Are you attending the Revel tonight?" Lenore asked.

"I might," Ida said. It was a normal thing to do in Asteria, to attend the Revels, but something about the way Lenore looked at her made her feel flustered. She lowered her head to hide the flush and said, "If—if there's time after this. Is there something wrong with that?"

"No," Lenore said. "I just thought you might want to avoid the Revels for a time. After . . ."

She trailed off, and Ida remembered the night Lenore had found her, shivering and bruised on the path outside of the castle. In spite of herself, she felt a chill and forced it back. She would be strong.

"It's fine. I want— I need to prove to myself . . ." *That I'm stronger than them. That my magic is still my own.* She shook her head.

What was she even saying? "Never mind. It doesn't make much sense."

It sounded so hollow when she tried to put it into words. A boring, petty motivation. She could almost *hear* her mother's voice in her ear, telling her that if she really was fine, she wouldn't need to prove it. But Lenore only looked Ida in the eye, and said, "It makes perfect sense to me."

That did odd things to Ida's breath, made her heart race in a way that sent a flutter through her belly. She cleared her throat, fought back the heat rising to her face, and tried to change the subject.

"You said you had something to show me? Now that the oranges are ripe?"

Lenore nodded. She held up the orange in her hand for Ida to see.

"You must have realized by now that nothing in this castle is what it seems to be," Lenore began.

Ida nodded.

"The oranges in the Orangerie aren't simple fruit. They're enchanted. Meant to help bring out a person's memories."

Ida remembered Lenore's words on the night of the Starborn Revel, the two of them seated together inside Lenore's private box, wagering secrets in the dark. Lenore admitting she had no memory of her mother.

"But I thought—" Ida began.

"I've tried them many times," said Lenore. Ida could see the pain in her eyes. "But the memories I lost are still gone. I can remember things *around* those memories quite clearly, but the things I've forgotten are lost. You, on the other hand . . ."

Lenore stepped closer and pressed the orange into her hands. It was heavier than Ida expected. She closed her hand around it, felt Lenore's fingers brush and curl against hers as Ida took its weight. Lenore was so close—Ida's eyes dropped to their hands before they could linger on the soft curve of her lips.

"You remember your father," Lenore went on, dropping her hands from Ida's. "So there's nothing blocking your memory of him. You weren't in Asteria that night. You weren't affected the way Vegard and I were. Maybe it will help you."

"But you said I have all my memories," Ida said. The loss of Lenore's touch left cold in its wake. Ida took a step back, fought back the sense that she was somehow bereft. She cleared her throat, working past a sudden knot as she turned the orange over in her hands. "I don't understand. How will this help me?"

"Memories fade. With time, the way we remember things changes. We don't remember any one event exactly as it was. And the farther back we go, the harder it is to remember." Lenore gestured at the fruit in Ida's hands. "That can pull back the fog of time, help you remember the truth of an event. It will be as if the thing you want to remember is happening again. Try it."

Ida broke the skin with her thumb, releasing the fruit's sharp scent. It hit her nose, and as she breathed it in, she caught a hint of something oddly familiar, a note of cologne that rang like a chord in the back of her mind. She dug her fingernail under the peel quickly, extracting a sliver of orange, popped it into her mouth, and bit down. Juice burst through the thin outer layer, the taste bright and citrusy. The second it hit her tongue, her mind was pushed back, back, back—

She was sitting on a deep orange carpet, the bristles rough against her hands. Around her was a small living room, a couch with a fuzzy plaid blanket, wooden furniture scuffed with age and wear, framed sketches and a single black-and-white photograph on the wall. Sunlight filtered in through a thick glass window above her, dust motes swimming in her vision. The air was filled with music, a cheap phonograph crooning a waltz. Just over the music, through a door that led into the flat's single bedroom, Ida could hear voices.

"I don't understand why you have to go with him. Surely it's enough that he works you to the bone here in Trissaire. Why do you have to join in him in this madness too?"

"He's the *king*, Gisela. What am I supposed to say?"

"He is not *your* king."

"But he is *yours*. Can't you see? Everything I do, I do for you and Ida."

"Tomas—"

Hands grasped her by the waist, lifting her up into the air. Ida screamed with delight and understood—in the memory, she was happy. The person holding her swung her around, pressing a scratchy kiss to her cheek. There was that scent again, the sharp bite of cologne, and then Ida was looking into dark eyes so much like her own, dark hair, a warm smile, a thin black mustache, all the features of the father she could barely remember.

"There she is," Tomas Rosales said, nuzzling her face until she laughed. "There's my girl."

The memory stuttered and stopped, fractured in time. How old had she been here? Old enough to be lifted into her father's arms. Young enough to not understand. Younger Ida was still laughing, but older Ida was looking out from behind the child's eyes. Older Ida saw her mother standing in the door to the bedroom, face flushed and eyes bloodshot, as if she had been crying.

The memory faded like the sun behind the horizon, leaving Ida standing in the center of the Orangerie. The taste of orange lingered on her tongue, laced with salt, and she realized there were tears running down her cheeks. The rest of the orange was still in her hand, and Ida felt torn between the desire to eat more and a full-body revulsion that made her want to throw it away and never see it again.

"Ida . . . ?" Lenore's voice was laced with concern, and when Ida looked up, she realized that Lenore was standing right in front of her, hand hovering awkwardly in the air between them, as if she wanted to reach for her but didn't know how. "Are you okay?"

Ida practically shoved the rest of the orange at Lenore, reaching up to scrub at her eyes. The memory had been so potent. Like she was there. Lenore waited, eyes on her, until Ida's breathing had steadied into something that might have been calm.

"Sorry," Ida said. "I just . . ."

"There's no need to explain."

Lenore cradled what was left of the memory orange as if it was something precious. Ida felt a pang in her heart. If anyone understood, if anyone knew what this felt like—this grief and this longing—it would be Lenore.

"Did you remember anything useful?" Lenore gently asked.

The memory of her father was still strong in her mind, crisp and clear as if she had just seen him yesterday. If Lenore was right, the memories were accurate—more accurate, even, than the way she remembered them. She didn't remember her parents arguing, but it must have happened. She must have just forgotten it.

If she were a toddler, her father would have just been appointed as Court Luminaire.

"It must have been just before Asteria was completed. My father and mother were arguing. She didn't want him to leave, to join the king. The king wanted him to come to Asteria."

Lenore nodded. "That would make sense. Those early days are when my father first began gathering the magically inclined. He needed them to construct the castle."

"I didn't see anything else. But . . ." Her eyes drifted to the orange in Lenore's hand. She wasn't sure she could handle taking another bite. But if it helped her find her father, she would do anything. ". . . Maybe a different memory. From when I'm a bit older?"

Lenore nodded. "If you focus on what you want to see, you can trigger specific memories. I'll have some oranges sent to your workshop, with my compliments."

Ida thought about her workshop, the barren rooms that still didn't feel like her own. She thought about coming back from such memories to those four walls, to a world where her father was missing. She didn't know what she would see, but she knew she didn't want to be alone.

Ida looked up at Lenore. Did she have a right to ask this? Would Lenore think she was being childish?

Nothing ventured, nothing gained.

She took a deep breath.

"Would you . . . come with me?" she asked. "So I'm not alone?"

Chapter 13

NEW PERSPECTIVES

"What's that, Dad?"

The memory smelled of incense and smoke, a haze of magic in the air as seven-year-old Ida climbed into her father's lap. From her child's perspective, Ida had only been happy to see him home, seated at the table tucked beside the kitchen window, next to the remnants of his breakfast, a half-drunk mug of coffee, and the broadsheet folded up beside his plate. But the older Ida, the one that looked out from behind her child self's eyes, took in everything.

The weary sigh her father made as he wrapped an arm around her waist so that she wouldn't fall. The wrinkles on the backs of his hands. The way he looked gaunt, his fingers trembling as he pushed the broadsheet away. The stutter in his aura, like clouds passing over the sun on a summer day.

Her father was tired. So very tired.

And his breakfast—burnt eggs, burnt toast, coffee darker than Ida remembered—told her that he had fixed it himself, because her mother would never have served them anything less than perfect.

Increasingly, in these memories, her mother was nowhere to be seen.

Child Ida made a grasp for the paper with both hands. Her father casually pushed it away, but not before she caught a glimpse of the front page. There was a sketch there, a castle rising up from the mountains. The castle looked enchanting. The headline was a bit more damning.

KING AUREL'S NEW FOLLY?

"Nothing you need to worry about, princess," Tomas Rosales said, bouncing her a little on his lap. "When did you get so big?"

"I've been growing," Ida said, with a gap-toothed smile. "Mama says I'll be wearing her clothes before she knows it."

It was something she was proud of, Ida felt. The fact that she was growing up. But as she tilted her head back up to look at her father's face, older Ida only saw that he looked sad.

She was growing up without him.

"Say . . . Ida," her father said. "Would you like to live in a castle someday?"

"A castle?" Ida frowned, probing the gap where her top tooth should be with her tongue. She pointed at the sketch. "Like that one?"

"Yes . . ." Tomas looked pained. "Like that one."

"Is that the castle where you work with the king?"

Ida was old enough by now to know that her father worked for the king, old enough to feel pride in it. Not yet old enough to wonder why her mother wasn't pleased, nor why her mother was often unhappy when her father was home, and unhappier when he was gone.

Too young to wonder why the mention of King Aurel caused her father pain. Why he hesitated before he said, "Yes, Ida. It is."

"I thought only princesses lived in castles."

"Well, you're my princess. You can live in a castle if I say so."

Ida laughed, aware that her father was teasing her. But she reached out, toying idly with a piece of half-eaten toast, and said, with all the tentativeness of a child who saw more than anyone expected, "Does . . . Mama want to come live in a castle?"

Tomas sighed, and older Ida was painfully aware of the empty kitchen, the silence in the rest of the apartment, as if the two of them were the only ones in the world. Wherever her mother was during this memory, it wasn't here.

"Don't worry about your mother," Tomas said, placing a hand over hers. "We'll figure this out, Ida, you and I."

Coming back to the present was like surfacing from drowning.

Ida felt heavy, drained, like she couldn't breathe. She sat up, gasping for air, knocking a few of Lenore's cushions to the ground in her wake.

"Shh—" Hands, on her arms, steadying her. The rustle of autumn leaves, the rich scent of the forest, the touch of Lenore's hands and her warmth by Ida's side. It brought Ida back to the present, holding her there as she remembered where she was. In Lenore's room, her mouth tasting of oranges as Lenore held on to her. "Shh, Ida. You're all right. We're here."

Vegard's face came into view across from them, concerned. His silver eyes met hers. "Are you well?"

Ida sagged in Lenore's grip, taking in a few labored breaths. Her mind was still adjusting, the past and the present overlaid in her mind. Vegard's eyes left hers, looking past her at Lenore. "I thought you said the oranges were safe."

"They are," Lenore said, "normally. People don't usually react this violently."

"The same block on her memories as on ours?"

"Likely. Weakened by distance, but the same. Ida, can you hear us?"

Ida breathed, slow and deep. Her throat felt sticky, her mouth waxy like she had tried to eat one of her candles. She nodded.

"I'm all right. Just . . . needed a minute."

They waited as she got herself under control, as the past faded and crashed headlong into the present. That memory couldn't have been long before her father's disappearance. It had been during a time in their lives when her father had alternated between their apartment in Trissaire and his time at the court, which by then had moved to Asteria. That much was clear in Ida's memories. But she couldn't shake the nagging thought that there was something she had missed.

Lenore pressed a silver cup into her hand. It was filled with water, cool and clear, and Ida drank until it was gone. She handed the cup back to Lenore and said, "He wanted me to come live with him in Asteria."

Thinking about it, there had been something strange about that broadsheet sketch of Asteria.

Something . . . different.

Ida tried to remember, but her mind wouldn't focus on the broadsheet. That was strange. Every other piece of the memory was as bright as if it had happened seconds ago.

Her eyes flicked toward the remnants of the orange, resting on a silver plate between her and Vegard. If she tried again . . .

Vegard followed her gaze and picked up the tray, setting the orange just out of her reach. "It's not safe. It's been getting harder and harder for you to come back. Who knows what could happen if you keep at this."

"I almost have something."

Vegard stared her down. Appealing to him felt like having an argument with a glacier: frigid and pointless. When he had heard what they were planning to do, he insisted on attending in case anything went wrong, and neither of them could convince him otherwise.

Not that Ida minded having the extra company, truly. Not after the memories took hold of her, thrusting her into the past and leaving her bereft in the present. Having them both there to talk to her, to help her return to herself . . . it had been invaluable, in the end.

Ida sighed, tucking her feet up onto the couch and wrapping her arms around her knees. She rested her head back against the plush fabric, trying to settle the pounding in her skull.

"I really feel like I'm getting close," she said. "It's like . . . dreaming."

"How so?"

"When I'm in the dream, everything makes sense. I understand everything that's happened. I have all the answers. But as soon as I wake up . . . it's like things fade. I always feel like I'm forgetting something important. Is it like that with you?"

"Sometimes," Lenore said. Though she was no longer holding on to Ida directly, she was seated close enough to hover, her eyes never leaving Ida's. "When I'm trying to reach for memories I know have been taken."

Ida glanced at Vegard, but he shook his head.

"The oranges don't work on me. Some things, I suppose, you have to be human for."

She bit her lip. They were so close. Something about that sketch—

"Is there any way I can find an old broadsheet? Maybe I can compare it to the one in my dream."

"We have the best library in Arred," Lenore said. "We may have it in our archives. Do you remember the date?" She was already moving, reaching for the notebook on the table in front of them. Lenore flipped the notebook open to a blank page, watching Ida expectantly.

The date jumped out to Ida, as clearly as all the other unimportant details in her memory. She gave it to Lenore, who frowned, writing it down.

"What's wrong?" Ida asked.

"It's not long before I was summoned to the court," Lenore said, idly doodling flowers into the margins of the page. She did that when she was thinking, Ida had noticed, when she needed something to do with her hands. Since the three of them started, their notebook had become a garden. "A little over a month, actually, after my mother—"

The quill skated across the page, drawing a jagged line through the flower. Ida watched in sympathy. Lenore's mind seemed to skip when she touched on a missing thought, like a broken phonograph.

Especially thoughts that had to do with her mother.

"You think there's a connection?" Ida asked after another moment.

"Who knows?" Lenore responded. Without being able to remember the night in question, they were all grasping at straws, trying to fill in the gap by understanding the spaces around it.

Her father's exhaustion and sudden insistence that Ida move to

Asteria with him. Lenore being taken away from her mother. King Aurel's mood swings. They all happened around the same time. That was clear enough from all their memories. But were they connected? That was much harder to determine.

"I'd like to see that broadsheet," Ida said. "I want to know if there's any difference between it and the one I saw in my dreams."

"The library's archives would be the first place I'd look," said Lenore.

Ida remembered her last futile attempt to get information from the library, the way the librarian's face had gone blank for a moment. She hadn't gone back to the library since, but she was free to look up whatever she wanted. No one would fault her for taking a visit to the library, as long as it didn't interfere with her work.

The autumn banquet was coming up. She would take tomorrow night to add the finishing touches to the candles she was making for it. But if all went well, she would have a night or two free after, before she needed to be on stage for the king.

"I'll look into it," Ida promised.

Chapter 14

A TRICK OF MEMORY

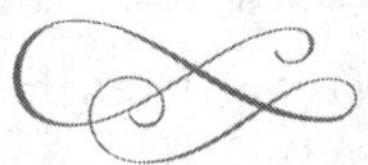

Despite Ida's best attempts at finishing the candles for her commission quickly, it was only on the night before the autumn banquet that Ida was able to carve out time to go to the library. She tried not to look too impatient as she brushed past the courtiers heading to that evening's Revel—the library was not usually a place people in Asteria traveled to with any real urgency. Still, it was only when she stepped into the brightness of its artificial sunlight and closed the heavy doors behind her that she felt herself relax, some of the tension leaving her body. She hadn't realized until then that she had been bracing herself for another incident like the one with the hounds, or for something to prevent her from coming here.

The library wasn't empty, but neither was it crowded. That evening's Revel would be beginning soon, and while very few courtiers attended *every* Revel, it seemed that only a select group of courtiers considered the library a good activity for an evening off. The library's current crowd was far quieter than the Revelers Ida was used to. They were content to read alone or in pairs, occupying the reading nooks and alcoves, sipping at coffee or tea or wine. Ida had never been particularly bookish, and had always felt more enraptured by the noise and the crowds that came with a Revel, but she could appreciate this too. There was comfort in it, a soft unraveling that made her think that in another life, or under other circumstances, this was something she would be able to enjoy as well.

Or with the right company . . .

She shook her head, fighting off the flush that threatened to overtake her face as she walked past a couple seated in one of the reading nooks, leaning against each other in companionable silence, and made her way to the front desk, where the librarian waited.

Ida had worried that the librarian would remember their last conversation—and the way she had frozen in place at the end of that conversation—but the librarian only looked up at Ida and offered her a welcoming smile, as if Ida were any other visitor.

"Welcome," she said. "Can I help you with something?"

She'd rehearsed her story beforehand, wanting to make sure the request seemed natural. She was sure it would seem odd if she just asked to see the broadsheet outright, and while the librarian *would* probably comply, she would likely remember, and Ida wanted to avoid being associated with strange requests or questions, lest it lead to future trouble.

"I've been doing some research into the history of the castle," Ida said. "The more I understand about a place, the more natural I can make my illusions."

That, at least, was a verifiable truth. Ida had no idea how Maxwell Mueller had conducted his work, but she had always felt more comfortable working in a location she knew well. There were so many tiny factors that went into a successful illusion, and not all of them could be quantified or written down. The more she knew, the easier it was for her to smooth those rough edges, to mold her illusion to the space it occupied.

The librarian's eyes lit up at the prospect of a research project. "We have an extensive collection devoted to the history of Asteria," she said. "Is there anything in particular you're looking for?"

"Do you have any old broadsheets from when the castle was being built?" she asked. "I'd like to see what people outside Asteria thought about it."

The librarian led her through the lobby, past the reading area and the stacks and toward an archway with the words "Records Room" inscribed over the top. Inside was a large room, its walls lined with file cabinets and drawers. At the center was a heavy wooden table, surrounded by a handful of chairs. The room's high ceilings led up to a false skylight, bathing the space in the warm glow of the artificial sun above.

"Brilliant, isn't it?" the librarian asked Ida, beaming. "An ordinary archive room usually doesn't have any windows. Sunlight does awful things to paper and ink over time. But we don't have to worry about that here in Asteria. I *will* have you wear these, though."

She handed Ida a pair of gloves, white trimmed in gold. They reminded Ida more of the gloves she had worn to her first Revel than any kind of craftsman's gloves. She slipped them on, marveling at the soft feel of them.

"I don't need to tell you to be careful, I'm sure," the librarian said. "No food or water in here, and don't take any materials out of this room. The rules are enforced by magic, so you won't be able to leave the room with anything anyway, but I'd really prefer you didn't try it. If you need any help, you can ring that bell on the desk to call me. It's enchanted, so I'll hear it even if I'm not at my desk—no need to ring it more than once." She gestured at a call bell resting on the surface of the table, its domed silver surface engraved with intricate designs. The librarian beamed at Ida. "Feel free to stay for as long as the library's open, but remember, we close at dawn."

With that, she left Ida to her own devices. Ida stepped into the room. There was magic here too, but it was a far subtler magic than Ida was used to feeling in Asteria. It was the magic of preservation, a low hum instead of a roar, the careful controlling of the humidity in the air, the amount of light in the room, the temperature. It was pleasant to walk into, like stepping into a cool room on a hot summer day. Ida breathed out some tension she wasn't fully aware she was carrying, letting the magic wash over her as she studied the wall of cabinets in front of her.

After a cursory inspection, she realized that the cabinets were arranged first according to publication and second according to date. Armed with that knowledge, it didn't take her long to find the section dedicated to the *Trissaire Herald*, to narrow it down to the appropriate drawer. Within the drawer were several file folders, each labeled with a date. As carefully as she could, Ida extricated the folder she wanted, taking it over to the table.

She set it down and opened it, holding her breath. And there it was: the broadsheet she wanted, pressed between two clear sheets.

It was a weekend edition, preserved magically so that it was as crisp and new as the one Ida had seen in her dream. She could still see the sketch on the front page. Asteria among the mountains, spires gleaming, beneath the headline:

KING AUREL'S NEW FOLLY?

Ida skimmed the article, waiting for something to catch her attention, but it wasn't particularly interesting. The other members of the aristocracy and the royal council were worried about the amount of money King Aurel was sinking into Asteria. Some thought he should retire, that he was unfit for the throne. The crown princess had been unreachable for comment.

She felt a growing sense of frustration. There was nothing here that pointed to her father, nothing that spoke to Asteria being anything other than what it was. A king's dream. Her eyes drifted back to the top.

And yet—

And yet there was something about the sketch of the castle. Something Ida couldn't ignore. She let her eyes trace the lines of the castle's spires, its walls and turrets, the way it hugged the mountainside. It was a faithful rendition of Asteria.

And yet—

Something was *wrong*.

Ida's gaze traced over the top of the castle, counting spires, counting towers.

One. Two. Three.

This sketch of Asteria had three towers. But the one in her memory . . .

She traced the lines of the other castle in her mind. She'd been a child then, only glimpsed it for a moment, but Lenore insisted the memory oranges only showed the truth.

And if she was right . . .

Then the castle in her memory, the one in the broadsheet that her father had brought home, didn't have three towers.

It had *four*.

Four towers.

The image in her head was so clear, so vibrant, and it clashed so obviously with the sketch she saw in front of her. It felt like a bell, ringing inside her head. The odd sensation swept through her, and it was only when Ida felt the change in the air around her, in the carefully woven spells that protected the Records Room, that she realized it wasn't all in her head, that something had changed in the world around her.

In the quiet of the Records Room, it was difficult to tell exactly what. At first glance, the room looked exactly the same, but the change was stifling. Smothering. It was as if the air itself had gone still. It took her only a moment more to realize that the magic that protected the room, that careful, subtle weave that Ida had so admired earlier, had vanished.

She held her breath, waiting, but whatever was happening now was not like the incident with the hounds. The room around her didn't suddenly dissolve into ruin and decay, nor did the broadsheet crumble to bits at her touch. It felt remarkably like it had the first time Ida had visited the library, when the world had frozen for an instant.

Except this time, it didn't unfreeze.

Ida stood up, and the sound of her chair scraping against the stone rang uncommonly loud in the stagnant air. There was so much *work* in Asteria dedicated to the little things. To the smoothing of life's little annoyances. Cutlery didn't screech against plates, doors were never slammed shut by the wind, sparkling wine didn't lose its fizz when left out on a table. Wool didn't itch, and furniture glided noiselessly over the floor. Ida ran her hand across the table, the pads of her fingers picking up the whorls and cracks in its surface, the rough spots. She felt the first prickle of fear as she stepped carefully around the table, heading for the door.

Ida peeked her head out into the hallway. Everything was exactly as she had left it, and yet not, as if a thin cloth had been drawn over the entire room, and only Ida was trapped beneath it. She was the only thing that moved, the only thing that breathed. The other courtiers who had been enjoying the library were nowhere to be seen. It was as if the world was frozen, as if Ida lingered in the space between two breaths.

And in that space, she was not alone.

There was something *else* in the library with her. Ida became aware of its presence in the same way a mouse was aware of a tiger. It wasn't simply the sensation of magic that alerted her, but something deeper. Something more primal, more human.

It wasn't a danger to her in the same way the hounds were, but that was because the hounds had only wanted to destroy her.

The thing in the library was larger than she was, so much so that it had no regard for her at all. That would have been terrifying enough on its own, but there was also the fact that it was *watching* her.

She could feel its eyes on her as she crept through the library stacks, trying to move as quietly as possible despite the fact that everything seemed so impossibly *loud.* Her breath, the rustle of her clothing, even the sound of her own heartbeat. All while it was watching her, *studying* her, as she crept around the corner, past the reading nooks that looked like they had never been used by a single soul, past desolate alcoves and abandoned cubbies. The sensation of wrongness only increased when Ida made her way back to the lobby and found it empty.

Ida swallowed, working moisture into a throat that felt suddenly dry. She had no idea what had happened, but she was sure it had to do with the broadsheet, with her uncovering yet another contradiction of Asteria.

Wherever she was now, she had to get out.

But how? Ida reached out with her senses, looking for a crack in the space around her, something she could slip through, but there was nothing. Hardly any sensation of magic at all, even, aside from the oppressive weight of the thing that watched her. It still hadn't moved, but Ida had the feeling that if it moved toward her, it would already be too late.

She was sure now that she was in the space she had glimpsed when speaking to the librarian for the first time, back before Ida knew not to ask outright questions about her father.

But that time—the dream had simply dissolved around her.

And why was that?

Was it perhaps because she hadn't been alone?

Ida spun frantically around, as if she might turn up somebody else who was trapped in the same space, someone who might be able to help her, but once again she was alone.

"Gloam?" she ventured, speaking the name out loud.

She felt a stirring from the air around her, some faint movement, but nothing so definitive as Gloam's usual presence. That was at least *something*. It proved that part of Ida was still on the same physical plane as the rest of Asteria, that Gloam could hear her and was trying to reach her. And better yet, Ida thought she felt the dimension around her buckle underneath the weight of her words, stretching and cracking. Suddenly, it no longer felt so solid, instead seeming like a gap that Ida could step through.

Unfortunately, Ida's triumph was short-lived, because the second she had spoken, she felt the presence home in on her, its gaze sharpening. It stole the breath from her lungs.

She tried the only thing she could think of as it began to move toward her.

"Gloam!" she called again, her voice growing increasingly more desperate. "Gloam! *Gloam! GLOAM!*"

The stirring ceased for a moment, and then returned with a vengeance. Ida felt the wind around her pick up, the air growing less stagnant as Gloam threw themselves into the weak point between the two of them, over and over again. The air began to smell of ink and paper. She heard the low hum of concentration, felt the warmth of false sunlight against her skin.

The presence surged toward her. It was no longer content to observe her. Now it wasn't just moving toward her, it was *running*.

Ida stepped backward, fear closing her throat. She had only the sense of something massive bearing down on her, something that bore its own mind. Something both ancient and terribly young, curious and hungry. She took another step backward just as Gloam surged forward, just as the thing reached forward to swallow her whole.

The world *shattered*.

The strange, still world she had been standing in vanished, the presence's frustration echoing in the ether as its grasp closed around empty air. Ida was once more standing in the library's lobby, reeling beneath the vaulted ceilings, the astrolabe that tracked the movements of the heavens.

Everything was moving again. Colors were brighter, people moved all around her. Magic once again flowed through the empty space, and Gloam was speaking in her ear.

"Miss Ida," they said. "Miss Ida, where did you go?"

Ida's heart was crashing painfully in her chest, and she had no idea how to answer that. Her hands trembled, and she swallowed hard against her own fear, trying to calm her racing pulse.

"Miss Ida?" Gloam asked again, and Ida raised her head. She was about to speak, to at least try to explain what had happened, but the words froze in her throat. Because standing across from her in the library's lobby, looking right at her, was the king.

It shouldn't have been a surprise to Ida to see him there, but with the exception of an occasional meal, Ida had never seen King Aurel outside of a Revel. She had not spoken to him directly since her first night in Asteria, on the day she had sworn fealty to him. A part of her had begun to believe that the king never wandered the halls, never left his chambers unless it was to attend a Revel. For a fraught moment she was sure that if he was standing in the library, now, it was because of *her*.

Aurel's gaze pinned Ida in place, and for half a second, she was reminded of that terrible presence. The thing in the library, watching her, rushing toward her. And then the moment passed and there was once again nothing special in King Aurel's eyes at all, nothing particularly worthy of honor or of fear. He was just an older man again, the disappointingly unimpressive King of Arred.

Ida remembered belatedly to bow her head, to dip into a curtsy.

"Your Majesty," she said. "Good evening."

"Mistress Luminaire," King Aurel replied. "Was the Revel this evening not to your taste?"

Ida honestly had no idea what Revel had been scheduled for that evening. She had been focused entirely on this, on coming to the library. But she could hardly tell the king that she, his Court

Luminaire, wasn't paying attention to the Revels he hosted. That she would rather spend her time asking questions, looking into something else.

She swallowed, grasped for a response.

"I needed to do some research, Your Majesty," Ida said. "For my work. There are some techniques I've been wanting to try."

"Not for tomorrow evening's Revel, I hope," Aurel said.

The words made Ida freeze, but the king was watching her expectantly. A joke? They had been said so mildly, so neutrally, that Ida couldn't honestly tell.

"Of course not, Your Majesty," she said carefully. "The candles for tomorrow are ready. I meant for future work."

"Future work." Something tugged at the corner of King Aurel's lip. A smile, or a sneer? "It's good to see you're so diligent, Mistress Luminaire. But since you *are* here, it would be good to discuss your next commission."

Next commission.

The words frustrated her when they should have excited her. She had been looking forward to a gap between projects, where she could speak to Lenore and Vegard, tell them what she had found in the library and work on her next lead. Another commission would take away from that time.

But there was nothing she could do. She couldn't refuse the king.

"I'm at your service, Your Majesty," Ida said.

"I enjoy walking through my library," King Aurel said. "And yet, I rarely have the time to do so. Which appears to also be the case for the members of my court. So I would like to host a Revel in the library, perhaps in two weeks. What would you say to making candles out of fairy tales?"

There were two streams of thought running through Ida's mind, enough at odds with each other to threaten a headache. The first was already thinking of how she could do it, the tales she would bring to life, the way she would set up stations throughout the library, each with a different candle, a different story. She could choose fables from all over Arred, highlighting its different regions. Perhaps even fables from all over the world?

The second was a constant refrain, ringing over and over again.

No time, no time, no time, no time.

She couldn't refuse the king.

The smile on her face felt wooden, completely at odds with what Ida really wanted, which was to run out the door, forget the king's request entirely, and track down Vegard and Lenore to tell them everything.

But it must have been a passable illusion, because King Aurel didn't react at all as she said, "Your Majesty, I would be delighted."

Chapter 15

BEAUTIFUL LIES

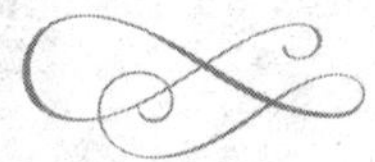

The guests at the autumn banquet the following night showered Ida with applause and admiration at the end of her performance, but this time, Ida's eyes were fixed only on the king. He sat at the head of the long table that had been laid out in the Orangerie, laden nearly to collapse under the weight of the fruits of the season, and had watched her performance with stern, focused eyes. Ida was not certain he had even blinked. At the end, as the last notes of the musicians' melody faded away and her illusion like smoke with it, he'd offered her only a brief nod. It was as much as he was expected to give an artisan that pleased him, Ida knew that, but after her meeting with him in the library, she felt unsettled. She bowed low and tried to hide her uncertainty from her face.

When she raised her head, she saw that Lenore, seated next to him, had offered her an encouraging smile. Ida smiled back, trying to look reassuring. As much as Ida was desperate to update Lenore on what she had found, now was not the right time. She took her last bow toward the crowd and made her way to the middle of the table, where space had been made for her and for the other performers.

Each step felt like a monumental effort. Ida had been nearly unable to sleep, her mind circling the picture of Asteria in the broadsheet, and the thing she had encountered in the library. She tried not to dwell on it too much, afraid that to even think of it would trigger another episode, but whatever had happened the night before seemed to have been tied to her discovery of the broadsheet. For better or for worse, Ida thought she was still safe in her own mind.

She accepted the greetings of the musicians with a smile, letting herself be enfolded into their midst as she took her seat at the table and accepted a glass of wine.

Yet as she sat there, surrounded by Revelers and admirers eager to praise her performance, trying to muster up some enthusiasm for the autumn banquet, she could only come to the same thought. It chilled her to the bone, and made her wish she *could* just stand up, walk to the head of the table, and blurt it out in front of Lenore. Because Lenore had lived in the castle longer. Because Lenore would know what to do.

Asteria is haunted, she wanted to say, to tell anyone who would listen. *And whatever is haunting it doesn't much like me.*

In the end, it was a day and a night before Ida could get Lenore and Vegard together. A day and a night of shutting herself in her workshop under the pretense of working on her library commission, jumping at shadows and peering around corners as if the furniture in her room might come to life. Of pacing like a caged tiger, her mind turning over everything she had learned, going over the facts again and again.

Three towers from the sketch in Trissaire. Four in the one from her dreams. The castle turning on her when she tried to reconcile the differences.

When the knock came at her door, Ida almost jumped out of her skin.

"Come in," she said.

She had been expecting Sabine, sure that Lenore would send Gloam to her when she was ready. When her door opened, revealing both Vegard and Lenore on the other side, Ida could only stare at them in surprise. They stepped into her small room like they owned the place, and the sight of them together, larger than life, brimming with magic, within the room she now called home, stole the breath from her lungs.

"Uh . . ." said Ida, suddenly conscious of her unmade bed, the crumb-filled plate on her desk from the pastry she had brought with her from breakfast, and the absolute horror that was her dresser. She attempted to kick a stray stocking under her bed and failed miserably. "I—uh—wasn't expecting company."

"We thought we'd drop by," Lenore said, carefully picking her way over a woolen shirt that had ended up between the trunk and the door. She was kindly not looking at the mess. Ida wanted to shrivel up and die. "I hope you don't mind."

"Mind—no—of course not." She didn't even have any places to sit down. Between the three of them, someone—more than one someone—would have to sit on her bed. The thought of Lenore on her bed sent a rush of heat through her, immediately followed by mortification. She straightened up sharply, a solution coming to her at once. "But this room is a bit small for the three of us. Plus, Sabine could come in at any time. Do you mind if we talk in the workshop?"

Her workshop, twice the size of her bedroom, had seemed like an inordinate amount of space when Ida first arrived. Now, with a handful of commissions under her belt, it felt almost like home. She cleared some space at one of the worktables and offered Lenore one of her high stools. She left a second seat open for Vegard, but he was content to pace the room, pausing in front of the painting Celeste had given her to study it intently.

Lenore seemed fascinated too, albeit with Ida's work. She had picked up one of the half-carved candles, turning it over in her hands. It had been meant to be a ship on the waves, but Ida had abandoned the design when it became clear that the illusion was uneven. The magic hadn't taken.

Lenore looked at the piece with wonder, reverence. Ida's eyes were drawn to her hands, the way they ran lightly over the grooves, the places where Ida had pulled wax away to reveal the layers of color underneath.

"Incredible," Lenore breathed, and Ida's heart skipped a little beat. "Is this for your next commission?"

Ida shook her head. She had barely had time to work out the recipe for her next commission. "That's the candle I first made for the Sirensong Revel, but it didn't work out. The illusion didn't take as well as I wanted. Look, you can feel it here and here—" She tapped the lump that was meant to be the ship's mast with one finger, then the crest of a blue wave. Lenore nodded, following along.

"It does seem a little uneven. Unsettled?"

"Exactly," Ida said. "Because I work through a medium, I'm bound to the limitations of the material. The slightest imperfection in the wax and the magic bounces right off it."

"Like mineral inclusions. Pockets where the magic won't take."

"Something like that. I try to select the right blocks, but you never know how magic will anchor to the material until you start."

Lenore hummed in thought, pressing her finger down on the spots Ida had identified. She turned the candle over in her hands, fingers roving, searching for more gaps. Ida could sense Lenore's magic intertwining with hers, Lenore's awareness gently moving over the network she had made for her spell. She spoke without thinking.

"You can have it," Ida said, "if you want. It won't work properly, but it's still—still a pretty candle."

The smile Lenore gave her nearly made her forget the dangers of the castle, a flash of teeth, there and gone, leaving Ida warmer for their presence. "I'd be honored."

Vegard cleared his throat. During her conversation with Lenore, he had stopped looking around the office and had come over to approach the table. Ida looked up sharply, embarrassed. She'd almost forgotten he was there.

"How do you select the ingredients for your work?" he asked.

"I . . . um, mostly go by feel," Ida said. "I try to create a link between the illusion I want and something real, something to ground the mind to. So, for an ocean illusion, I'll use sea salt, or for a countryside scene, fresh grass, or water from a spring for a scene from the mountains. For my next commission, I'm thinking of using ashes, from pages."

"Ashes?"

Ida nodded. "The king asked me to make candles depicting fairy tales. I asked the library to make copies for me I could destroy. My plan is to read the tales aloud while I mix the ashes in, maybe work at different times so I can capture day and night across all the stories."

Of course, she was never really sure how something would turn out. Creating a recipe for a new illusion was a balancing act, involving a surprising amount of trial and error. While each individual candle might not take long to make, the recipes themselves took time to develop. It was frustrating sometimes, but to Ida, teasing out the various ingredients that would bring an illusion together was a fascinating puzzle, and even when she thought she was tired of a project, she couldn't stop her mind from coming up with a hundred new things to try.

It was one of the skills she was most proud of, but it wouldn't bring her any closer to finding her father. Unlike the memory oranges, which could show her the truth, all Ida's magic did was create beautiful lies.

She slumped over the table with a sigh, tugging at a lock of her hair. "Anyway, as much as I like talking about this, it's not bringing us any closer to finding out anything real."

Lenore exchanged a glance with Vegard. "About that," she said. "You mentioned you had something to talk to us about? Did you find something in the library?"

Ida gave them a quick summary of what had happened, beginning with her looking at the broadsheet and ending with the strange events that had happened in the library. And then she told them what she feared most.

"It almost feels like there's something in the castle that has a will of its own," she said. "And it doesn't like me very much."

Lenore frowned, looking down at her hands folded neatly in her lap. "I have always wondered whether Asteria has a will of its own, but I've never seen anything like what's happened to you. Something so . . . targeted."

Ida nodded. "It's like it wants to stop me from figuring this out," she said, feeling uneasy. "Like the castle itself doesn't want me to know what happened that night."

Doesn't want me to know what happened to my father.

Lenore looked concerned. She leaned forward, her gaze fixed solemnly on Ida.

"I'll give you something to protect you," she said. "I promise, it won't happen again."

The offer made Ida feel warm all over. Her instinct was to refuse, but there was so much concern in Lenore's gaze that she caught herself. The castle had put her in danger twice.

"I'd appreciate that," Ida said, giving in. "What do you think about the tower?"

"If you're sure about the fourth tower, then it makes sense that the tower must have been lost the same night that's missing from our memories," Lenore said. "Which means they're related somehow. You must have considered that."

Ida nodded. A night that nobody could remember, a luminaire lost in time, a missing tower. They were too connected to merely be coincidental events.

"It would help if we knew where the fourth tower was," said Vegard. "Can you make an illusion of what you saw in your memory?"

Ida shook her head. "I've thought about it, but every time I think about it for too long, it feels like my head is going to split open. I don't know what trying to make that kind of illusion will do to me . . . or what kind of attention I'll attract if I try. But I was able to draw it. Here."

She walked back into her bedroom and took the notebook from her desk, laying it open between them. On the left side of a two-page spread, Ida had drawn the castle as it was now, in the sketch from the library. On the right, she'd drawn, as best as possible, the castle from her memories. She would never be as good of an artist as Celeste, but her drawing skills were passable, honed by the carving and sculpting she often did for her candles.

Vegard frowned down at the drawings. "Can I have a glass of water?" he asked.

It was nice to have friends who were also magical, Ida thought, as she slid out from her stool to pour some water for Vegard from her workshop's tap. It meant that she wasn't the only one making odd requests of people. She walked back over to him, handing him the full glass, and let out a sharp exhale when he promptly dumped it all over her notebook.

Ida opened her mouth to shriek at him, but a prickle of magic washed over her skin and she looked down to see that her notebook wasn't wet. The water had never even made it to the surface. Instead, it had crystallized in the air, forming two castles.

The first showed Asteria as it was now. The second, the Asteria from her memory. They rotated slowly in the air, every facet rendered in perfect detail.

Ida stared in awe. Vegard set down the glass, and though his expression was normally impassive, Ida thought he looked a little smug.

"This seemed easier for visualization."

Lenore huffed. "Ask next time. You nearly gave Ida a heart attack." She reached out, touching the castle on the right, the one with four towers. It spun a little faster from the pressure of her finger. Like this, the subtle differences between the two castles were easier to see. Lenore studied the place where the tower jutted out from the castle's body, lips pursing in thought.

"You're sure about the placement?" Lenore asked Ida after a while.

"It's my memory of a sketch," Ida said. "I couldn't tell you the exact floor, or hallway. But yes, it was in that general area."

"Hmm . . ." Lenore frowned. She ran her finger lightly along the spine of the missing tower, her nail catching in the grooves of ice. Ida followed Lenore's touch with her gaze, tracking each movement closely. Lenore stopped the ice castle's spin with another jab, holding it in place, then trailed her finger down from the tower onto the exterior of the castle. She stopped on the curve of an outer wall.

"This is my room."

Lenore had witnessed something from her room that night. From that angle, the tower would have been visible. Ida's eyes widened.

"You think that whatever happened, happened there?"

"I think so," Lenore said, tracing a line from her window to the top of the tower.

Ida grabbed for her notebook, excitedly flipping to a blank page. "We need to find the base of that tower. What else is on that floor, in that part of the castle?"

"The theater," Vegard said. "The main one, not the smaller one we spoke in. A few ballrooms. A secret garden. Some unused rooms. And . . . other things. It depends what floor you want to start at."

Ida's brow furrowed. Asteria was enormous. Even with the right general area, the tower's entrance could be anywhere.

"This is going to take us forever."

"Maybe not," Lenore said, surprising her.

Ida glanced at her. "What do you mean?"

"Do you have the schedule of the Revels? The ones for next week."

"Sure. Why?"

Lenore's smile was wicked. "Because I have an idea."

Chapter 16

LUCID DREAM

If it hadn't been for Lenore, Ida would have skipped right past this Revel on the schedule. She was particularly busy these days with her commission for the upcoming Mythic Revel in the library, and while most Revels came with a paragraph or more of explanation, telling prospective attendees about the wonders they would experience, this Revel had only a single sentence.

The Dreaming Revel–Midnight–The Subterrane
Dress comfortably. Masquerade. Dark colors preferred.

Telling Sabine that she was planning on attending this one had gotten her some raised eyebrows, but Sabine had walked off to find Ida something to wear with only the briefest of complaints about the hedonistic youth of today. Ida felt an odd mixture of curiosity and embarrassment as she let Gloam lead her through the halls, dressed almost entirely in black. Her floor-length black gown might have looked funereal, if it wasn't for the embellishments that had been worked into the off-shoulder design, glittering silver patterns that made it look like moonlight played off the surface of her dress.

Her mask, a silver-and-white construct that sat on her nose and only covered her eyes, was doing very little to hide her identity. And her hair was down, black and white flowers braided into the strands.

"You'll want to be able to lie down," Sabine said, when Ida studied the simpler hairstyle curiously. At Ida's confused look, Sabine's brows rose. "Don't tell me you don't know what you signed up for."

"No. I was just curious." Anxiety fluttered in her stomach like a bird shaking water off its wings. "Why? Is it something bad?"

"No . . ." Sabine said, after a moment. "Not bad. Just . . . well, you'll see when you get there. It's hard to explain. You'll be able to choose how the night goes."

She still looked suspicious, shooting Ida glances as she packed the cosmetics away. Ida pretended to be very busy examining her earrings. She hadn't told Sabine anything about what she was doing or who she was spending her time with, but her friendship with Lenore and Vegard was an open secret. The time they spent together was impossible to hide. As far as she knew, though, she wasn't doing anything *wrong* by enjoying their company.

There was no rule against being friends with members of the Collection. Even if Sabine didn't know that Ida was one of them.

Now, though, as Gloam led her through twisting corridors lit with pale blue light that barely did anything to illuminate the space, Ida wished she had asked Lenore for more information. She had never been to the Subterrane before, the twisting knot of tunnels beneath Asteria. And though she'd never thought of herself as claustrophobic, the narrow pathways and eerie lighting weren't doing much to calm her down. She fought the urge to tug at her braid.

When the tunnel opened up into a wide room, Ida exhaled in wonder.

The floor beneath her was completely black, polished to so great a shine that it reflected the ceiling enchanted to look like a night sky, lit with thousands of shimmering stars. A few discreet orbs hung in the sky, illuminating the hall in shades of silver. Just enough to see by, not enough to break the illusion of walking in the night sky itself. Of being surrounded by infinity.

There were others milling around the room, which looked like an antechamber. Gloam led her toward Vegard and Lenore, who were waiting in the corner.

It was rare to see both Vegard and Lenore at the same Revel. They had taken the prompt in different ways, Vegard dressing all in shades of white and silver in a way that set off the dark of his hair and made him seem otherworldly, and Lenore in a dark, dark red gown that seemed almost black, made of a fabric that seemed to flow with her every movement, like a river in the night. She had painted her lips to match, drawn thicker eyeliner around her eyes. The contrast between how she normally looked and how she looked now was doing funny things to Ida's insides.

"Ah, good," Lenore said. "You made it."

"What on earth have you signed us up for?" Ida asked.

Lenore and Vegard exchanged a quick glance, Lenore smug, Vegard amused.

"You'll see." Lenore took Ida by the arm, threading their arms together. Ida's heart jumped as Lenore pulled her close to her side, bodies flush against each other, breaths mingling as she led Ida toward a silver door on the other side of the hall. She could smell perfume rising off Lenore's skin, a subtle floral scent that made her dizzy.

The door opened onto a narrow hallway that stretched on for a long time, a maze of corridors crisscrossing it so there seemed an infinite number of passageways. Up and down the hallways, there were doors. Doors with symbols painted on them, some easy to recognize, some obscure. All the doors were different shapes and sizes, different shades on the spectrum between white and black. Some weren't doors at all, but only curtains. Some seemed to be completely open archways, but try as she might, Ida couldn't see through to their interiors.

"What is this place?" Ida asked.

"The Dreaming Rooms of the Subterrane," Lenore said. "They're only used between the autumn and spring equinoxes, when night is longer than day. Each of these rooms can give you a dream of your choosing."

"A dream?" Ida frowned at the symbol engraved on the nearest door, one that resembled a horse reared up on its hind legs, the wind whipping through its mane and tail. "Like an illusion?"

"Of sorts," said Vegard. "Your illusions play on the waking mind. In the Dreaming Rooms, Revelers sleep, and as long as their wishes match the theme of the room, they have some measure of control over their dreams."

"The dreams can be shared," Lenore said. "So, the three of us could share a single dream." She paused to move aside as a group of courtiers in elaborate black gowns, coats, and masks moved past, holding each other's hands and giggling. "We could get a better picture of the castle you saw, without putting much strain on your mind. With the three of us together, generating a shared dream, we could perhaps spread the effects around, so that no single one of us bears the pain."

Ida thought about shared dreams, Sabine's disapproving comments, and felt her cheeks heat up at the implications. "Um . . . so you and Vegard would be in my dream?"

Vegard nodded. "That's correct. We only need to stay in your memory long enough to see the sketch of the castle you saw. With the actual image in front of us, we might be better able to find the base of the tower."

Ida tugged on the end of her braid. Sabine's reservations aside, she had to admit, it was a good plan. Her eyes roved over the multitude of doors ahead of them. It would be a lot of work, creating bespoke dreams for this many people.

The symbols carved into the wood of the doors made Ida suspect that this had been created by her predecessor, Maxwell Mueller, who worked in glyphs. If Ida had to guess, the reason the rooms were themed was that illusory spells were anchored to each door, providing the general feel and theme of the dream. The subject's mind would provide the rest.

If they wanted this to work, they'd have to find a door with a theme closest to Ida's memories. "There have to be hundreds of doors here. How do we find the right one?"

"You'll need to lead us to it," said Lenore. "It's your memory. You remember the details far better than either of us ever could. Choose a door with the closest feel."

Easier said than done. Ida normally had a good sense for magic, but this part of Asteria was so steeped in it that it was like trying to detect a single scent in a perfumery. She turned down one of the hallways, leading Lenore beside her. People parted as they passed, and Ida knew how she and Lenore must look.

Like a pair of lovers, searching for a shared dream.

In Asteria, even the presence of Vegard trailing along beside them wouldn't have anyone batting their eyes. It was the Dreaming

Revel, and Ida had noticed from the beginning that people were freer with their affections here.

The thought made her wish she had worn something cooler. She focused on the doors.

There were doors upon doors upon doors. A few tempted Ida, with depictions of feasts, of castles, of knights and dragons and ships across the sea. A few gave Lenore pause, depicting forests, and cabins, and a child in the arms of their mother. There was one door that they practically had to drag Vegard away from, a door depicting swirls of light above high mountains, that Vegard had stared at with such melancholy it nearly broke her heart. And there were other doors as well, promising darker, sweeter temptations.

The hallway they were walking along ended abruptly, continuing on toward the right and the left. But in front of them were two red doors, garlands of roses strung along each one. The door on the right was open a crack, and a scent like perfume wafted from it into the hallway, along with a lurid pink mist that pooled at their ankles.

The door on the left depicted a man. The door on the right a woman. Ida was glad for the dark, because she was sure her face was as red as a beacon. It wasn't hard to guess what dreams these doors offered.

"Are you all right, Ida?" Lenore asked, looking from her to the doors. "We don't really have time to dally."

"I'm fine," Ida squeaked out, because she was *not* going to get embarrassed over this here and now. "Just wondering which way to go."

Lenore, damn her, smiled wickedly beneath her mask. Her eyes shimmered, green and vibrant and fey. "To be honest, either way is fine with me."

That mental image sent all the blood rushing to her face. Ida's breath caught. Was Lenore just teasing her? Or was she—?

Her gaze was fixed on Lenore's lips, on the curve of her smile. Ida's mouth, suddenly dry, fell open. She swallowed, working moisture back into her throat. A thousand words she wanted to say crashed together in her mind, so that all that left her was a breath.

Vegard's oblivious "Women, personally, although rarely" snapped Ida back to the moment at hand.

"That is *not* what we are talking about!" she said.

"Isn't it?" asked Lenore.

Ida's heart jumped. If she stood here any longer, she was going to explode. "We're in a hurry," she said, taking Vegard by the wrist with her free hand and pulling them down the hallway to the left, for no other reason than to get away.

"We have until sunrise, Ida." Lenore was practically laughing. "And you never answered the question."

"Because I never asked about the doors in the first place," Ida blustered.

She was *not* going to tell Lenore, here and now, that her answer to that question was all of the above and everything in between. Not when the very thought of that conversation made her feel set aflame.

Thankfully, she was saved by the sight of another door.

This one was an innocuous gray door, set into one of the black corridors. The symbol engraved into it wouldn't have looked like much to an outside eye. It was a simple representation of a window, a square divided into four panes, curtains hanging on either side of it.

But Ida was an illusionist, skilled at deriving meaning from fragments, from small pieces that made up a greater whole. Windows were ways of looking past a barrier, of peeking through a divide.

She walked up to the door, placing her hand on its cool surface.

"This one," she told Lenore and Vegard, pushing it open before she could lose her nerve.

The door swung open weightlessly, as if all it had needed was her intention. Inside was a small room, empty except for a servant dressed all in black, face obscured with a full white mask. They held a silver tray, on which were three small glasses. The floor of the room was soft black carpet, and just behind the servant, it dipped into a recessed pit full of cushions.

She stepped into the room. Lenore and Vegard followed behind her, and the door swung shut.

The servant turned to face them. They spoke with a musical voice, one that, like Gloam's, seemed to defy any expectations of accent or gender. Ida's skin prickled with warning—the servant wasn't human. Yet if a member of the King's Collection was surprised to see Vegard and Lenore with the Court Luminaire, they didn't show it. They simply turned their head to regard the three of them in turn before speaking.

"Three, this evening?"

"Yes," said Lenore. Ida was grateful that she took charge, because she was starting to feel a little out of her depth. "A shared dream, if you will."

The servant nodded, moving a white-gloved hand over the cups. When they held the tray out to the three of them, Ida noticed that the liquid in the cups sparkled and shone like liquid silver. It looked uncomfortably like mercury, and when Lenore and Vegard each reached past her to grab one glass, Ida hesitated.

"What is this?" she asked.

Vegard answered. The cup in his hand was already beginning to freeze, a thin film of frost coating the metal. "An elixir. One to help with dreams. It's perfectly safe."

"We need to take it at the same time," added Lenore. "Together."

In for a penny, in for a pound. Ida picked up the glass, bracing for the feeling of unfamiliar magic. It rolled over her, a wave of blackness like deep sleep. Like nightfall, midnight, shadows, and all the world's secret things.

"Sweet dreams," the servant said ominously.

They stepped away from Ida, moving to stand with their back to the door. Ida kept the cup in her hand, walking over to join Lenore and Vegard. They had already stepped into the center of the pit, and as Ida joined them, they sank down, lowering themselves among the cushions. Ida braced herself against the pit's padded wall, pillows surrounding her. She looked at Lenore, at Vegard. Neither of them looked afraid or uncertain. Ida swallowed her own fear.

"Bottoms up," she said, raising her glass.

Vegard and Lenore mimicked her.

"On the count of three," said Lenore. "One . . ."

Vegard continued. "Two . . ."

"Three," Ida said, and drank.

It felt like falling.

Ida tumbled backward through a silver sky, wind whipping at her hair. Clouds streaked past her as she fell and her stomach lurched, but the sky was endless and aside from the dizzying sensation, Ida felt no sense of danger. It took a moment for her senses to reorient themselves, for her to realize that this was, essentially, an unformed illusion, a dream waiting for one of them to give it shape.

And for this to work, it would have to be her.

She looked to her left and found Lenore. To her right, Vegard.

They were too far away for her to reach with her hands. But if this was her dream, she knew how she could manipulate it.

She pictured that morning, her child self seated on her father's lap, the smell of coffee and burnt toast in the air, the broadsheet on the table. And she envisioned tearing a small hole into that memory, a gap that the three of them could slip through.

Below her, a cloud loomed, white and endless. Ida looked at the cloud and imagined that behind it was a window. A glimpse into that world.

They fell into the cloud with a sound like shattering glass, punching through into the world beyond.

"Ida, what would you say to living in a castle someday?"

Her apartment's kitchen was oddly gray, as if the color had been leached from it. Ida—the older Ida—stood in the center of the room, watching her younger self curled up with her father. Behind her stood Vegard and Lenore. It should have felt crowded, five people in this small kitchen, but the dimensions of the room hardly seemed to matter. At a thought, all motion ceased, young Ida and her father holding perfectly still as if this were a painting. Her father, setting aside the broadsheet. Ida, turning to look at him with a perplexed expression on her face. A stray breeze, catching a lock of her younger self's hair, left it hanging suspended in the space between them.

That space consisted only of the kitchen. When Ida looked

behind her, the door that led into the living room yawned open into a black void. The windows were gray panes that looked out onto nothing. It gave her the odd, claustrophobic feeling that this small patch of floor was a raft, the only thing keeping them afloat on a dark ocean.

Lenore appeared on her left, Vegard on her right. Ida swallowed down the flutter of embarrassment she felt at her friends seeing where she had come from, a small apartment in Trissaire with a kitchen and dining room smaller than Lenore's private bath. But neither of them were looking at the furnishings, at the faded paint, or the dust that had gathered on the windowsill.

They had eyes only for the broadsheet.

Lenore reached for it, but her hand passed straight through, the table fading to static as it swallowed her hand up to the wrist. When she pulled it back, the details came together as if she had merely disturbed the surface of water.

"I can't pick it up."

"I don't . . . think we can touch anything here," said Ida. To test that theory, she stepped forward, placing her hand on the table. It passed straight through, giving Ida the disconcerting impression that the room was made of smoke. She pulled her hand back. "This isn't normal for one of these dreams, is it?"

"There's nothing normal about any of these dreams," Lenore said. "But not being able to touch anything is new." She looked at her hand, contemplating, then reached out and rested it on Ida's shoulder. Ida jumped. Lenore's hand was solid and warm, and the touch brought to mind uncomfortably lurid doors that promised shared dreams.

Lenore pulled her hand away from Ida and poked Vegard in the cheek. He reacted with much more composure than Ida had. He only blinked at her.

"We can touch each other," Lenore said. "So perhaps it's more that we exist on a different plane from the dream."

"It's a window," Vegard said, as if that were obvious. "We're standing on one side. This scene, Ida's memory, is on the other."

Lenore nodded. She glanced at Ida, who was still struggling to maintain her focus because this was, after all, her dream, and the last thing she wanted was for it to go somewhere unexpected while Lenore and Vegard were present in it.

"How well does this match up to what you saw using the memory orange?" Lenore asked.

"It's a perfect match, I think."

"Then can you guide us to a part of the memory with a good view of the broadsheet?"

Earlier, Ida thought. Before the talk of castles. Before the talk of kings. When her father had been reading the broadsheet, and Ida had only been sitting with him.

At the thought, the memory blurred into motion, moving in reverse. The young Ida and her father shuffled backward through the routine, coming to a stop at the scene she envisioned. Her father had the broadsheet open, obscuring the view of the child sitting on his lap. The front page faced outward, in full view of the interlopers in the kitchen.

Ida froze the memory there, before her father could talk. She didn't want to hear his voice now, not while she wasn't alone, not when she might lose her composure. In the silence, she joined Lenore and Vegard in crowding around the sketch on the front.

This one was straight out of Ida's memories. Four towers. Beside her, Ida heard Lenore let out a shaky breath.

Vegard reached between them with a hand, his fingers framing the fourth tower. The broadsheet vibrated where his fingertips sank into the surface, but Vegard's eyes were fixed on the tower. He had traced it to its base, which Ida now saw was connected to one of the castle's sloping walls, the tower protruding from what was otherwise the third floor.

Vegard let out a breath that froze the air and stepped back so rapidly that he caught Ida in the shoulder and nearly knocked her over. Lenore grabbed her by the forearm to steady her, stopping Ida from a heart-pounding fall, but Vegard didn't seem to notice. He looked from Lenore to Ida, his eyes wide, expression frantic. Even in the dream, the ground at his feet was turning to ice, and only the cold metal of the locket resting against her chest stopped Ida from feeling the bitter cold.

"Vegard?" Ida said. "What's wrong?"

For a second, she thought he wouldn't answer. He didn't, sometimes, when he got like this, when his eyes darted so quickly from one of them to another that he looked like a scared animal, his hands clenched into fists at his sides. But then he looked at Ida, and he looked at Lenore, and said in sharp, staccato bursts like an ice floe cracking, "I know—where this is—"

"Where?" Ida asked.

He looked straight at her, eyes wide in terror.

"My room."

Chapter 17

ABODE

From the second Ida crashed back into her body and found herself sprawled onto the mass of cushions on the floor of the Dreaming Room, she was moving. She had only a second to register Lenore leaping to her feet before she felt the ice-cold sensation of the floor freezing beneath her, a telltale sign of Vegard losing control. She sprang up off the floor, her mouth still tasting oddly of berries, and helped Lenore grab Vegard by the other arm. The amulet hanging from her neck flared into a frigid knot against her skin as she pulled herself close to Vegard's left side, but she was grateful for its presence, because with it, touching Vegard like this felt only like leaning against cool glass on a hot summer day.

"Where are we taking him?" she asked Lenore. Vegard was gritting his teeth, his eyes so bright they almost hurt to look at, his brow furrowed as if it was taking all his energy to not drown them in white, so she figured it was best not to break his concentration.

"His room," Lenore said breathlessly. "I know the way."

Ida didn't protest, following Lenore out the door. She was worried they would get stopped on the way out of the Revel, but aside from a few people who looked at them curiously as they swept past, the hallways were clear, most guests happily ensconced in their dreams.

If someone held her at knifepoint after this, she wouldn't be able to tell them the way to Vegard's quarters, or the twisting hallways that Lenore led them down. Her attention was fixed on Vegard, sagging at her side, on the frost skimming across the fabric of his white suit and over her skin, on how pale he had gotten. Vegard was the palest of the three of them, but she was sure he was not supposed to look blue. She looked at Lenore in alarm.

"Lenore—"

"Almost there," Lenore said.

She rounded a corner, coming to a stop in front of a white door.

Unlike Lenore's door, which had been decorated to look like a forest, this one was covered in a mountainscape, the engraved outlines of icy peaks tearing into the air. That wasn't what gave Ida pause. What stopped her was that the door had no handle, no keyhole, nothing except the relief of an enormous serpent coiling down the slope of the mountain.

Its mouth hung exactly where a handle should have been, and its fangs were wickedly sharp.

"It needs blood," Lenore said, as they shuffled closer to the door. "Yours. It won't let you through without it."

"And you?"

"It's already tasted mine."

Not for the first time, Ida wondered about the closeness between Vegard and Lenore, if it truly had been nothing more than friendship. But there wasn't any time to think about it. Not while Vegard was growing colder and weaker between them, not while his magic pulsed and his aura frayed.

Ida studied the serpent's head. Up close, she saw that both it and the door were made of stone, and its head looked heavy enough to crush her hand between its jaws. But Vegard's magical aura was now coruscating across his skin like the buildup to an explosion, so she shoved her hand into the snake's mouth and hoped for the best.

She braced herself for pain and was surprised when the snake's jaws closed lightly, with only enough pressure to graze the back of her hand. Its fangs drew a drop of blood, and the snake's eyes flashed red.

"Release," Vegard gasped, and the snake uncoiled, the stone door swinging open.

Lenore wasted no time ushering Vegard inside, practically dragging Ida along with her. The antechamber of Vegard's rooms was tiled with white stone, empty except for a steaming pool tucked on the other side of the door, near a staircase that led to a loft. It was to this pool that Lenore dragged Vegard. She lay him down beside it and began to paw at the white suit he had worn to the Revel.

All the heat rose to Ida's face, which was impressive, considering half her body felt frozen.

"What are you doing?"

"He needs to get in the pool," Lenore said, tugging open Vegard's doublet with both hands, hard enough that Ida heard fabric rip. "He'll be too heavy if we have to pull him out with these on. Help me!"

Ida flushed, but urgency won over modesty. She hurried to help Lenore, wincing as her bloodied hand smeared red all over Vegard's white clothes. It froze on contact, prompting her to work faster. She helped get him out of his doublet, tossing the fabric aside, and tugged on his undershirt as Lenore tossed his mask away and moved around Ida to pull off his boots.

The shirt was frozen to his skin. Ida muttered an apology as she yanked it away, the shirt making a sound like ice being scraped off glass. Vegard let out a strangled shout, his eyes opening, but he said nothing, and didn't protest when Lenore started working on his trousers. Ida got the shirt over his head, trying not to think too much about what she was doing as she tossed it to the side.

There was a horrible scar on Vegard's chest, just over his heart. At the center of it, the skin was puckered around a wound that had healed badly. Tendrils of raised skin radiated from it as if he had been struck by lightning. The sight gave her pause, and she might have stopped moving entirely if Lenore hadn't chosen that moment to shove Vegard into the pool.

He fell in with a splash, dousing both her and Lenore in hot water. Ida cried out in surprise, raising her hands to protect her face. Lenore sank back onto her heels, breathing heavily, her eyes fixed on Vegard. Her mask was askew, her gown in disarray, her hair soaked. Ida was sure she didn't look much better.

Vegard floated to the surface of the hot pool. Then, with a groan that sounded like relief, he opened his eyes.

They were silver entirely, iris and sclera both. That was the last thing Ida saw before an explosion of power took her breath away. It radiated from Vegard, a winter wind so bitingly cold that Ida shivered despite the amulet's protection. Beside her, Lenore let out a hiss like someone had pushed all the air out of her.

The pool that Vegard floated in, which had been hot enough to steam, froze solid in the blast. Ice stabbed through the air above Vegard's head and body, jagged icicles reaching skyward.

And then it was over.

The winter storm faded to nothingness and Vegard exhaled, his eyes closing as he rested limply above the spears of ice he had conjured. His muscles were slack, and even the pulse and flutter of his magical aura, so much a part of him that Ida had learned to tune it out in his presence, was still. If it wasn't for the rise and fall of his chest, Ida would have thought he had died.

She looked over at Lenore, who was picking herself up from the heap she had fallen into. Lenore looked a little rattled, her gaze fixed on Vegard's still form.

"Is he . . . ?" Ida began. She couldn't bring herself to say the words "all right." What she had felt, what she had seen, was the farthest thing from all right.

Lenore let out a little sigh. "He'll sleep for a little longer. Help me put him somewhere more comfortable, and then we can look around."

The ice was already melting by the time Ida and Lenore finished cleaning the area around the pool, bundling Vegard's stained clothes into a laundry basket and mopping up the puddles of water so that none of them would slip. It wasn't hard to pull Vegard—who thankfully was still wearing undergarments—out of the slush. Between the two of them, they maneuvered him up the stairs and into the austere bedchamber at the top, then tipped him into bed and bundled him in blankets. That done, they slumped to the ground, exhausted.

For a moment, there was just the two of them, sodden and drained, propped up against the wall of Vegard's bedroom, breathing. It took a while before Lenore turned to face Ida and whispered, "Vegard said the tower's base was in this room."

Ida nodded, her gaze on Vegard's sleeping form. "How did he get that scar?"

"I don't know," Lenore admitted with a sigh. "I don't think he remembers."

"Which means it had to do with that night, right?"

Lenore nodded slowly. "That's been my guess for a long time. But Ida—"

She broke off. Ida waited for Lenore to find the words.

"I've seen Vegard heal from cuts in seconds. Once, in a fit, he put his hand through a glass pane without a scratch. I've never known him hurt by anything other than his own power. So, for something to hurt him so badly it's left a mark like that . . ."

"It has to have been bad," Ida said.

"It has to have been *terrible*. I can't imagine the force it would take to leave a wound like that on him. And I don't want to."

Lenore hesitated, and seemed to curl into herself, drawing up her knees close to her chest and resting her arms on them. Ida waited, sensing in the silence that Lenore was working through something.

"Do you remember," Lenore said at last, "during the Starborn Revel, when I said you must never ask the king about these memories?"

Ida nodded. She had wondered why, but Lenore had been so certain, and if Ida couldn't trust Lenore about how her own father would behave, Ida couldn't trust anyone. She kept her eyes on Lenore, watching the emotions play across her face, a kaleidoscope of uncertainties and regrets, before Lenore finally spoke up.

"I asked him once," she admitted. "I asked him about my mother, and why I couldn't remember her."

"And?" Ida asked gently.

"It was like a change came over him," Lenore said. "Not unlike the changes you described in the library, in the castle itself. He became unhinged . . . frightening." Her fingers closed tightly around her knees, wrinkling the fabric of her dress. Ida felt strangely helpless, longing to reach for her, to ease her worries somehow. "I've never seen him like that before. I fear that . . ."

Lenore trailed off, her gaze drifting from Ida to Vegard, lying huddled on his bed. She looked miserable, uncertain, so different from the confident Lenore that Ida knew, that it gave Ida her own courage. She placed a hand over Lenore's. It was cold, but at Ida's touch, she relaxed a degree.

"Do you . . . think your father might have hurt Vegard?" Ida asked.

Lenore let out a ragged breath, and Ida knew that she had uncovered the right fear. She knew, because there were fears she was running from too, fears that she herself could not look in the eye.

Lenore was braver than Ida. She didn't look away from her fears. She slumped down against Ida's side, turned into her. And when she spoke, she spoke so softly, but Ida could hear her voice as if she had shouted.

"I've already lost my mother. My father and I are not what I would call close, but . . . he's the only family I have. I . . . I don't know who I'd have if I lost him too."

"You'd have me," Ida said, without thinking. Her words caught up with her a moment later when she felt Lenore look up, staring at her with wide eyes. "Oh—and—uh, Vegard too," Ida stammered, looking away. "You'd have both of us, really. You wouldn't be alone—"

"Ida . . ." Lenore said, drawing Ida's attention back to her.

Face burning and heart racing, Ida turned back to face Lenore.

Lenore, curled up beside her, mask askew, wet hair plastered to the side of her face, smeared eyeliner tracing dark whorls at the corners of her eyes. Lenore, rouged lips parted, so very close, an inch away. Lenore, her green eyes on Ida's, wider than Ida had ever seen them, overflowing with . . . something. Hope? Longing?

Lenore's breath fanned over her skin. Ida's eyes darted to her lips. She was so close.

It would be so *easy*.

Her breath hitched. She drew a little bit closer.

Lenore's eyes fluttered closed.

A noise from Vegard snapped her back to reality. Ida drew back sharply, her eyes widening, her heart jumping into her throat. Lenore did the same, the two of them whirling to look at Vegard.

He was still asleep, his eyes closed, his breathing slowly evening out as he settled.

Ida's face was bright red, her heart pounding so quickly she was sure Lenore could hear it. When she glanced to the side, she saw that Lenore was blushing too, her hand raised to her mouth, fingertips lightly touching her own lips. Ida swallowed. For a moment, neither of them spoke. Ida's mind raced, thinking of how she could explain herself, the excuses she could give.

Lenore cleared her throat, getting to her feet before Ida could say anything.

"Let's search the room," she said. "If whatever happened that night started here . . . perhaps there's something we can find."

Ida threw herself into the search, because it was easier than looking at Lenore.

Vegard's room was a contradiction. On the outset, it was cold, forbidding, the room of someone who hardly spent any time there and didn't care to make it pleasant. But there were traces, here and there, that suggested Vegard had once tried to live like a human being. A rug that had been thrown down to soften the room's harsh walls, a low bookcase full to bursting with books that were gathering dust, an armchair that looked almost like a display piece. A vase on a nightstand that might have once held flowers. There was a division in the room, Ida felt, a line drawn straight through the past. A Vegard before, and a Vegard after.

She paced the room, using both her eyes and her magical senses, looking for anything strange, but she saw no sign of the missing tower. No sign that this had ever been more than a home to a lonely, homesick spirit of winter.

At length, with nothing left to search, she met up with Lenore on the bottom floor. Lenore shook her head. Nothing.

"It's an ordinary room," Lenore said. In the time it had taken them to search, she had recovered her composure. She barely sounded out of breath. "No secret doors, nothing that looks like it could be hiding a tower. Nothing even uncommonly magical."

Ida nodded. She'd come to the same conclusion, but it didn't sit well with her. She glanced back at the stairs leading to the loft where Vegard slept. Her mind was working, shaping itself around the illusion. A missing tower, an altered reality. An image that Lenore and Vegard had only been able to see because *Ida* remembered it. The Dreaming Revel, tearing a window open in time, so that what was lost could be found.

She bit down on her lip in thought, letting her eyes move over the room. There was something . . . unfinished about it. The ceilings were tall enough, the walls plain enough. She could easily imagine that this wasn't Vegard's room. That this whole space was the base of a tower, with stairs leading up and up and up. Leading somewhere else.

She looked back at Lenore. It was easier to talk to Lenore if Ida kept the conversation to their shared mission. Easy not to think about what had almost transpired, to keep it to a skip in her heartbeat, just beneath her skin. "We need another window."

"What do you mean?"

"Whatever happened here changed the world, but not completely," said Ida. "It erased your memories and erased any records of a tower here, but it couldn't totally erase all its traces. You and Vegard both have lingering memories. I still remember my father and the castle as it was. That means that if something happened here, it's probably left some trace we can't see. An echo of the past. With magic like at the Dreaming Revel, maybe we find that echo and . . ."

She trailed off uncertainly. The idea had been solid in her head, but like many magical concepts, it was difficult to explain. Thankfully, Lenore caught up quickly.

"You mean we could use any lingering magical energies as a catalyst? Something to anchor one of your illusions to, and figure out what happened that night."

Ida nodded.

"And the backlash?" Lenore asked, suddenly hesitant. "If you were worried about peering into the past on your own, wouldn't this be just as bad? Worse?"

Ida breathed out. This was the crux of her plan, but to say it out loud . . .

She glanced down at the back of her hand. The wound hadn't been deep, and the bleeding had already stopped. She didn't even think she needed a bandage. Vegard's door identified people with blood, which wasn't wholly unusual. Blood was a potent source of magic. She was fairly certain she had some of Vegard's with her already, in the amulet around her neck, shielding her from his power.

With blood shared between the three of them, she could bind a candle so that it drew its magic not only from her alone, but from all of them. It might work.

But it was such a personal cost to pay.

"Ida?" Lenore asked.

They all wanted this. Ida knew that if she was in Lenore's place, she wouldn't forgive her for shying away now.

"I'd need blood," Ida said, "from you and Vegard. I can anchor the spell in such a way that we all share the consequences. Not just me."

"Done," Lenore said simply, as if Ida had asked her for a bit of sugar. "You'll have to ask Vegard when he wakes, but I don't see why he'd refuse. What else do you need?"

"I . . ." Ida blinked at her, stunned. She hadn't been expecting that to go so smoothly, but she recovered quickly. Her mind ran down a list of ingredients, everything she would need. Something to make it easier to see the truth, and something that would blunt the costs of the illusion, an additional power source that would take on some of the burden and some of the pain.

"Another memory orange, and some of that elixir from the Revel. I can figure out the rest later."

Lenore nodded. "We have to go now," she said, checking her

pocket watch. “The Revel ends in less than two hours.”

“Will Vegard be all right if we leave him?”

“He’s safer here than anywhere else. I’ll ask Gloam to look after him.”

“Then let’s go.”

PART THREE

CHAINS

Indeed, if we are to truly search for the catalyst that brought an end to the monarch's reign, we must point toward his obsession with the arcane. Toward the end of his life, King Aurel was an avid collector of powerful and unknowable things, the sort of beings that lesser and—I posit—wiser men would have left well alone. This hubris, in the end, is likely what led to his downfall.

—Herbert Ardinger, *The King of Moonlight: A Comprehensive History of Aurel IV*

Chapter 18

BOUND BY BLOOD

"The palm is truly the worst place to draw blood from," Lenore said, pointedly, to Vegard. "Not only is it extremely painful, it contains a variety of tendons, many of which may not heal properly. It's also a rather inconvenient—and visible—place to have an injury."

It had been just three nights since the Dreaming Revel, and only two since Vegard had opened his eyes—but with how close they were to finding the truth, a frenzy had built within the three of them, and Ida hadn't been surprised to open the door of her room that evening and find both Lenore and Vegard on the other side. Vegard looked paler and more drawn, but otherwise none the worse for wear, and before she knew it, the three of them were in her workshop with bowls and knives, Lenore and Vegard ready to give her whatever she needed.

Vegard stood now at one of Ida's worktops with his hand outstretched, the point of a silver dagger hovering over the skin of his palm, nearly touching his lifeline. Below him was a small bowl that Ida had set out for the purpose. He glanced at Lenore, and said calmly, "Is that so?" before slashing the dagger across his palm.

Ida sucked in a breath, but Vegard didn't even wince. Silvery blood welled up from the cut, and he let it pool in the hollow of his hand before tipping it into the bowl. With each drop of blood, Ida felt an echo of magic, an answering pulse in the amulet that hung around her neck. She wiped her palms on her trousers to shake off some of the sweat. Vegard's blood was potent, a concentrated source of power.

The last drop fell into the bowl. Vegard's eyes flashed silver as he turned away from them. When he opened his hand, displaying it to them, the cut was already gone.

Lenore rolled her eyes. "Show-off," she muttered under her breath. Her own forearm was bandaged, the wound hidden under the wrist-length sleeve of her dress.

Ida stepped forward to collect the bowl from the countertop. Even with the protection from the amulet she wore, her fingers went numb as they touched the bowl. She held her breath, carefully poured the silver liquid into a glass vial. It flowed easily, every drop, and it didn't stain the bowl the same way Lenore's blood had, as if it knew how much each magical drop was worth.

She stoppered the vial and took it—and Lenore's vial of blood—into her bedroom. It felt macabre, storing them close to where she slept, but she didn't want Sabine to find them. She put them in the top drawer of her desk, and made sure it was locked before she went back into the workshop.

Vegard was already cleaning both the bowl and the dagger. Ida shut the door behind her, exhaling. The samples were the last thing she needed. She could begin work on the candle tonight—could have it ready very soon. And then . . .

She worried at the chain around her neck with her fingertips, thinking. There was no guarantee that this would work. She had asked both Vegard and Lenore for more blood than she needed, in case she had to try again. But Ida had already done a lot of the groundwork. She'd spent hours in this room, going almost without sleep, trying to figure out how to do the impossible.

How to weave their magic together, to create the same feeling she had when she and Vegard and Lenore had worked together at the Dreaming Revel, but to stabilize it so that it could work apart from them, and to make it work with three strands of power.

And how to make an illusion not an illusion. How to make an illusion give her the truth.

What she'd realized was that her magic was far too focused on her.

With herself as the anchor for every spell, her illusions would only show her what *she* wanted to see. They were tied to her mind, to her imagination, which was great for creative pursuits, but terrible for wanting to see objective truth. As she had puzzled on this, though, she realized that anchoring her illusions to her own mind wasn't a requirement of her magic, it was something *she* had learned to do. A shortcut, to make things easier.

Maxwell Mueller hadn't needed to do that. He'd crafted the Dreaming Rooms by anchoring his illusions to the doors, to the rooms themselves. Over the last few nights, Ida had experimented with the same.

She found that she could, with a little more effort, anchor the spell on someone else. She'd tried this with Sabine, under the guise of wanting to fulfill Celeste's commission. Ida had made a simple taper candle, with barely any scent or alternate ingredients, except that she had embedded a strand of Sabine's hair in the wick. When that was burned, Sabine had—with effort—been able to create shapes and illusions, something that had delighted her. The spell became a collaborative effort, Ida's magic and Sabine's mind. It was a great leap forward for her own abilities, but in the end, the results were still fake. Only the mind directing them changed.

Ultimately, what she had to do was find a way to anchor the illusion not on a person's will or intent, but on reality.

She'd tried it next with dueling illusions. She'd burned a simple illusory candle, one that transformed her workshop into a summer garden, and set it on a worktop. Then, she'd burned a second candle, one that incorporated wood shavings from the support beams around the workshop. She tried to anchor the candle onto the room itself, the space as it existed. When the summer garden flickered and struggled to stay coherent, Ida knew she was onto something. She'd altered the recipe until the candle bound to the room managed to dispel the garden illusion entirely.

Then she returned to Vegard's rooms and collected several items from the space. Mindful of the fact that she wanted to reveal the room's true reality, and not whatever had been imposed on it, she'd deliberately gone for the parts of the room that seemed off, the parts that didn't perfectly align with this new reality. Dust from an empty vase, flakes of paint from the faded space where a portrait had been, a loose thread from Vegard's bed, water from the heated pool. She had no idea which ingredient would be best, but she intended to try them all.

That left only one ingredient.

Blood.

"How long do you think it will take?" Lenore asked, startling Ida out of her thoughts.

Ida couldn't afford to waste time. Since the library, there had been no other odd incidents, and Lenore had placed so many spells of protection in her room that it practically glowed with magic, but Ida wasn't taking any chances. Every day she waited, every day they continued to unearth this mystery, only increased the likelihood that things would get worse.

"I want to have this done in the next couple of weeks. But it will depend on how well I can manage the recipe. And I have the king's commission to think about too."

The Mythic Revel was fast approaching, and while Ida had the base recipe for her candles done, it was a lot of candles to make and not a whole lot of notice. Each candle would have to be slightly distinct, to support a different illusion. The task was irritating in the face of everything else, but she knew that her place in the castle, that her *magic*, depended on her doing it without complaint.

"Let us know if we can help you in any way," said Vegard, looking up from the sink. He stacked the bowl and knife, now clean, into the drying rack and wiped his hands off on the dishrag.

"I think this one will have to come mostly from me," Ida said. "But if you can spare the company, I'd appreciate it."

"You should get more comfortable chairs," said Lenore, shuffling a little on the wooden stools that passed for seating in the workshop. "Then we can spend the evenings in here."

"I'll . . . add it to the requisition list," Ida said, heart skipping a beat at the thought of Lenore spending her evenings here, with her. She and Lenore had not had the time alone to discuss what had nearly happened in Vegard's rooms. But even the thought of an evening together brought forth the memory of Lenore curled so close to her. Her hair brushing against her neck, the intensity in her eyes as Ida—

"Are you planning on starting tonight?" Vegard asked.

Ida blinked at him slowly, startled out of her daydream. "Uh—"

"The candle," Vegard clarified. "Our candle. Are you planning on starting on it tonight?"

"Not yet," Ida said. "There are herbs that need to soak in moonlight for a few nights—"

"I can help with that," said Lenore. When Ida turned to look at her, Lenore's gaze slid away. She added softly, "My window gets the best view of the moon."

Ida swallowed. The promise of being alone with her threatened to be her undoing, but she couldn't let her attention slip now. She needed to focus, for all their sakes.

"I'd appreciate that," Ida said, swallowing past the knot in her throat. "Thank you."

"What else?" asked Vegard.

"The—uh—the wax," said Ida. "There are a few blocks I've selected, but I'd like for them to get attuned to Vegard's aura."

"I'll put them in my rooms," said Vegard. "Hand them to me."

"And the rest?" asked Lenore.

The rest? Well, there was the wax, the ingredients, and . . .

The magic. Which could only come from her.

"The blood. And other things. That, I can do tonight."

Vegard and Lenore left Ida not long after that, which she was grateful for. As much as she liked the company, it was difficult to focus with them looking over her shoulder. She didn't want them to witness her first fumbling attempts with a magic she was worried was beyond her. A magic she would have never attempted before coming to Asteria.

Blood was a conduit for power. That much, Ida had always known. But she'd never thought to use it. When all her magic came from sweet scents and gentle herbs, she was simply an illusionist. A harmless mage, not someone to be feared.

Blood magic was something different. Something whispered about in the dark, something that drew equal parts fascination and revulsion. It was a darker side of magic, a side she'd never thought she would ever dabble in. If her mother knew, if her cousins knew what she was doing now, they would likely disapprove.

It wasn't proper. Wasn't Arreden.

It was the type of magic *other people* were always accused of.

Foreigners, like her father. Like—like her.

This felt like crossing a line. If she did this, would she be able to go back to pretty illusions and artful designs again?

She set her ingredients out on the worktop, oils and emulsions and dyes, the vial of fragments she had taken from Vegard's room, a bit of memory orange juice, the bottled dream from the Subterrane, and the two vials she had taken from her friends earlier that day. One red, one silver, both redolent with magic.

So much of her ability was tied to her perception. Her imagination.

That was one of the things her father had explained to her, in those early lessons when she sat on his lap and watched him work incense into wonders. Her magic worked because she believed it would work, because she believed that the things she incorporated into her designs had these properties, these natures.

Blood didn't have the best of associations. There was too much horror written into the concept, too much pain.

If Ida wanted to create a candle that would reveal the truth instead of create nightmares, she'd have to find a way to change the meaning.

She started with the fragments, a few pieces shaved from Vegard's wall, suspended in oil and a little bit of juice from a memory orange. They hovered like a cluster of stars at the bottom of Ida's smallest mixing bowl. To that mixture, she added dye, turning the whole concoction a very light gray. Carefully, she tipped in a drop of the elixir that she and Lenore had taken together from the Dreaming Revel. That darkened the solution to a clear silver, the color of Vegard's eyes on a good day, the color of a winter storm.

Then, carefully, she pulled out the stoppers from her vials of blood.

Among the Arreden, blood magic was a fearful practice, but there were other ways of thinking about it. In the Niressians, the mingling of blood meant something else. Those associations were buried in her memories, fragments rising to the surface of her mind like smoke from a fire. Her father had told her stories, when he was very young. Of the islands that had once been his home.

She took a dropper and measured a single drop of Vegard's blood, placing it carefully into the solution. Magic flared as it mingled with the elixir, bright swirls appearing in the heart of the mixture. Ida tasted snow on her tongue, and when she tapped the side of her dropper, it was cold to the touch. She could sense the rising of winter in Vegard's blood, the waxing of his power. She set the dropper aside and used a second one to do the same for the vial that came from Lenore.

The drop she released into the bottom of her bowl was deep red, bursting with the feeling of dark forests and secret paths and things growing in the undergrowth. Lenore's magic was waning in the same way Vegard's was waxing, but when the two of them mingled in her bowl, they rang in unity. She set aside the dropper, shaking the smell of trampled leaves and autumn herbs out of her nose, and carefully picked up the last implement on her worktop: a long, thin needle.

Blood was a promise in the Niressians. A pact.

A treaty, between those who bled together. Of friendship, of loyalty, of something almost like family.

That was the association she wanted her spell to carry. A perfect unity of the three of them. Herself, Vegard, and Lenore, all committed to finding the truth.

This would only work if Ida had as much courage as they did.

She sucked in a breath, and before she could let her fear get the better of her, she stabbed the needle into the pad of her thumb. The pain was surprisingly sharp for such a small wound. She cried out and was grateful when no one heard. Ida pulled out the needle, gasping, and carefully tipped a drop of her own blood into the bowl.

She'd never been able to sense her magic. It was a bit like asking her to look into her own eyes. Her magic was so much a part of her that she didn't know what the world would feel like without it.

But she felt this, the moment that her drop of blood struck the surface of the liquid.

The moment that Vegard and Lenore's magic rose to catch hers, wrapping themselves around her into a tight knot from which Ida couldn't see any beginning or end. She didn't feel the warmth of the summer sun on her face, didn't feel the golden aura they both swore emanated from her. But she did feel as if the world shifted into place.

As if someone had fitted a key into a lock, and all that was left was to open the door.

And then the magic flowed out of her.

Ida sagged forward, her vision darkening, and caught herself on the edge of her workbench. She gasped, blinking stars out of her eyes. The solution in the bowl had become a nexus of magic, its aura flickering and shining, something greater than the sum of its parts. And when Ida recovered enough to stand up straight, to look down at what she had done, she let out a ragged breath of relief.

Because it was beautiful.

And because it would do.

Chapter 19

THE WILL OF ASTERIA

The blood-bonded candle lay cooling on Ida's workshop desk, a creation of power, grace, and beauty. It was by far one of the most intricate candles Ida had ever made, and she could sense from the moment she pried it from its mold that this was a candle that hummed with magic, that would readily pierce the veil of reality. This was a candle that would search for the truth.

Which was why it galled Ida so much that the candle was *there*, in her workshop, and she was *here*, standing in the central lobby of Asteria's library dressed in a dark suit, high boots, a feathered cap, and a silver mask like a surreal version of one of Arred's messengers.

She tried not to let any of those thoughts show on her face. The mask she wore only concealed her eyes, crafted to accentuate rather than to hide, and the crowd had already gathered in anticipation of the Mythic Revel. They were dressed in costumes that seemed plucked straight out of the pages of the same fairy-tale books Ida had used as reference for her performance. Despite the flashiness of most of their attire and the understatement of Ida's own clothing, many of them took note of her. By now, Ida had grown used to drawing the attention of a room, particularly for Revels where her candles were meant to be a centerpiece, and she could tell from the hushed whispers that trailed her that the crowd was wondering what she would show them today.

She tried to force her mind from the candle in her workshop, to focus on the task at hand. The commission for the Mythic Revel had been ambitious, and Ida had never made an illusion with so many moving parts before. She felt torn as she walked across the library from station to station, inspecting each candle. A part of her wanted to be focused entirely on this task, was afraid that if she let her attention waver for even a second, the illusions would fail. Despite everything, she wanted so very badly for this to work, but thoughts kept creeping into her mind, uncaring of her efforts to keep them at bay. Thoughts of Vegard and Lenore and the candle, thoughts of how close they were.

You can't think about that, she reminded herself. *Not in the library.*

She hadn't forgotten the way she had been dragged through dimensions the last time she had come here, the way she had ended up in that space in between, alone and hunted. She needed to focus, no matter how much she felt like she was playing entertainer.

But the audience was building, filling the space around her with more sound and color than Ida had ever seen in the palace library, and Ida reminded herself that she wasn't playing. That at the end of the day, this was also a part of who she was. An entertainer, a performer. A luminaire.

The lights dimmed as Ida checked her final candle, returning to the first station she had set up underneath the library's astrolabe. As she settled, the artificial sunlight in the room went dark, the skylight above twinkling with stars of different colors, streaked with an entire galaxy that spanned the length of the room. With the dimming of the light, conversation quieted to a hush, and Ida felt their eyes settle on her.

She smiled, head bowed, surrounded by creatures out of myth and fairy tale, and resisted the urge to raise her head and search for the two people she knew would be in the audience—King Aurel and Lenore—as the clock struck midnight and the Revel began.

"Good evening, beloved courtiers of Asteria," Ida said, and it was always amazing how little she sounded like herself, how easily she became someone else. As if her body and mind had also fallen under one of her illusions. "Tonight is a Revel of magic and myth and adventure. The centerpiece of this Revel is a procession through the worlds of our nation's greatest tales. I will be your guide."

She bowed, placing one hand over her chest, and her wandering thoughts were quieted by the appreciative murmur that rose up from the crowd, the applause, even though she hadn't said her name. There were so many things about her situation in Asteria she would change if she could, but when she was on stage like this, Ida couldn't deny that she loved it. She took her father's firestrike out of her pocket and allowed herself to revel in the anticipation for a moment longer.

The candles for the Mythic Revel had taken some time to design, but once the idea had been formed and tested, actually making the candles was easy. She had incorporated ashes from seven chosen fairy tales into the wax, had placed a few key components in each one that would link to the world of the tale—pine needles and gingerbread seasoning for a dark forest where a witch waited, a drop of water for the tale of a river queen, a hint of smoke for the story of a mischievous little fire, brambles for the childish tale of the race between a hedgehog and a hare. Because she was working on seven candles at once, she had kept the decorations simple, a paper-and-ink theme that bound all the candles, with words from the fairy tales inscribed across each surface.

She had set up seven stations throughout the library, each with a candle that would transform the space into the world of the fairy tale, allowing them to view events as observers. The Revel had been set up around those candles, with the main event being a procession that took Revelers from station to station, letting them wander from one fairy tale into the next. Given that it would take quite some time for the Revelers to get through each tale, Ida had worked with the other staff to make sure that there was plenty to do at the Revel besides follow along with the procession. Each station was themed in a way that connected to the fairy tale, with food, drink, and other diversions, ensuring that people could drop in and out of the procession as they pleased.

Looking around at how everything had turned out, Ida was quite happy with herself. Given the impreciseness of the king's request, she thought she had done a good job of accommodating him.

Of course, King Aurel would be the final judge of that.

She promised herself that she wouldn't look for him, but she couldn't help but wonder, as she flipped open her father's firestrike, whether he was in the audience now. Whether he would experience the illusions himself, or whether he would make his final judgment based on what others had to say.

Whatever he chose to do, nothing would change. Ida held up the lit flame in one hand, turning toward her audience.

"First," she said, "I would like to tell you of the Maiden of the Stars."

She set the flame to the candlewick, and the whole world froze in place.

It was like stepping through a fall of cold water.

One moment, Ida was standing with the crowd in the library's atrium, their eyes on her and her father's firestrike in her hand. In the next, she was standing in the center of a room that looked very much like the atrium, but was not quite the same. The colors were more muted, grayed, the multicolored lights that decorated the ceiling nothing more than silver dots. The air was heavy and difficult to breathe. And the crowd that surrounded her was gone, but Ida was not alone.

A figure floated in the air before her, wreathed in cold light, a monolith, stretching from the floor to the ceiling. Their shape was recognizably human, but indistinct, as if Ida was looking at them through several layers of gauze. They were floating just a few feet above Ida's head, centered over the space where the crowd would have been. As their head tilted down toward Ida, face merely an impression of eyes, nose, mouth, and ears, Ida felt the weight of their power settle onto her and realized that this was the same being that she had fled from in her last trip to the library.

Except this time, it seemed, being in a crowd had not held them off. This time it didn't seem to matter whether or not Ida was alone.

Ida took a step back, flinching as she crashed into the table behind her, the one where her candle was set up. The impact felt odd, as if Ida were moving through water. There was pain, where her hip caught the edge of the table, and even movement as the table slid backward across the stone floor, but the candle didn't even shift off its stand, as if both candle and stand occupied a different space from the table, unaffected by gravity. Looking at the candle now, Ida realized with a start that it had been frozen in the *act* of being lit, the flame only just beginning to catch at the tip of the candle.

The figure continued to watch her. Ida turned her face up toward them and fought down a shudder, the firestrike warm in her hand. But the figure didn't move, didn't attack.

It only stared at her, as if it were . . . studying her?

Ida swallowed her fear. She didn't know what had happened, or where she was, and didn't have any idea how she would get back. She didn't know what the crowd was seeing now, if they were seeing her frozen in place, or if she had vanished, or if no time had passed at all. It was difficult to fight down the sensation of rising panic.

But the figure was only *watching* her. Waiting for something.

For her to speak? To acknowledge them at all?

". . . Hello?" Ida ventured.

They cocked their head to the side, still studying her. They did not attack. Slowly, Ida uncoiled, taking a step away from the table and toward them. Now that Ida was looking at them, face-to-face with the thing that had haunted her on her last library visit, she realized that the power she had felt was nothing more than pressure, the weight of something much larger than herself.

It wasn't malice. Whatever this thing was, it didn't *seem* to mean her harm. At least not yet.

"Who are you?" Ida asked, daring another step closer. "What do you want with me?"

The figure didn't respond. With startling clarity, Ida realized that perhaps they couldn't. But they were watching her still, so intently that it felt like a physical weight, that Ida could barely breathe beneath the force of their regard.

And then Ida felt a surge of power from the figure in front of her and she understood.

It came at her in a rush, a sensation that left her breathless. She saw stones arching toward the sky, drinking down the moon, heard music and revelry, tasted magic in her lungs. She saw air charged with power and felt the bite of winter magic and the warmth of the sun on her skin, and she knew suddenly who this was, who she was speaking to.

It seemed impossible, but then again, so much of the castle was an impossibility. Why would this be any different?

"Are you Asteria?" Ida asked.

The figure said nothing, only dipped their head in acknowledgment, face still turned expectantly toward Ida.

Ida felt a surge of excitement, a manic glee that cut through any lingering fears. She was speaking to the *castle*. She and Lenore had speculated that Asteria had a will of its own, but she hadn't expected it to be so fully formed, so concrete. If the castle was sentient, then surely it could give her answers. Surely *it* knew what had happened here.

"Then you can tell me about my father," Ida said, the words leaving her in a rush. "Please, he was a luminaire here. Before Maxwell Mueller. His name was Tomas Rosales. Surely you remember him."

The will of Asteria stared down at her as she approached, desperate. They shook their head.

Ida stopped moving. She hadn't even realized she had been walking, advancing steadily toward the figure with a hand clutching her heart. Hadn't realized it until that moment, because the figure's response was like a splash of cold water.

No.

"What do you mean, no?" Ida asked. "Why can't you tell me?"

The figure's response was to raise their arm. They moved slowly, as if they were carrying the whole weight of the castle along with them. The fingers of one hand uncoiled, until the figure was pointing directly at Ida.

Ida held her breath.

It seemed like time stopped, a space between moments, frozen and alone on the library floor. Ida, standing there with one hand pressed to her chest, in the middle of an impassioned plea. The figure, the will of Asteria, floating in the air with one hand outstretched toward her.

It was clearly meant to be a response, but Ida didn't understand. Was it an accusation? A reprimand? An answer she somehow couldn't interpret?

"What do you mean?" Ida asked, slowly lowering her hand. "What are you trying to tell me?"

The figure said nothing. They slowly lowered their hand, and Ida saw them begin to fade, the glow that surrounded them consuming them from the bottom up. Ida had the sudden fear that if she let them go, if she let this moment pass, she was never going to see them again.

"Wait!" Ida cried, rushing forward with hand outstretched. "Don't go!"

The world shattered, falling apart.

Ida's words echoed in her ears, and then she was stepping forward, one hand flung out desperately in front of her, looking into the stunned eyes of her audience. The weight over the library had lifted, time flowing normally again, her breath coming easily into her lungs. Over the pounding of her own heart, Ida realized that people were staring at her. That she was in the middle of her performance.

She felt the heat rise to her face, fought the urge to stammer an apology. How much had they seen? The illusion was already beginning to take hold, the candle behind her conjuring a view of a lakeside in the middle of the night, the sky above and the surface of the water sparkling with stars, and Ida fought down the urge to scream, to call for the castle's will to bring her back into that space and keep her there until she had *answers*.

The illusion was beginning.

If she maintained her composure, the crowd would think it was all part of the act. All part of the show. She swallowed down her rising panic, turning to face the Revelers as she straightened up, clearing her throat.

This time, though, she did let her eyes sweep the crowd, looking for someone in the audience.

She found Lenore.

Lenore was watching her, and from the expression of concern on her face, Ida's lapse hadn't gone unnoticed. The sight of her there grounded Ida. It reminded her of the candle in her workshop, the one she had created with the three of them. The candle meant to uncover secrets.

If the castle wouldn't give her any answers, that was fine.

Ida would simply find them herself.

Chapter 20

MOMENT OF TRUTH

The candle was a simple taper, its silver sheen the only thing that separated it from the candles that could be bought in packs of ten or twenty at any corner store in Trissaire. Standing on a scuffed brass candleholder on Vegard's nightstand, which had been relocated to the center of his entrance hall, it didn't look like the sort of thing that had taken Ida weeks to prepare. It didn't look worth her sleepless nights, the bags under her eyes, the way her left hand still trembled from the magic she had poured into her endless attempts.

That was, at least, if you couldn't sense magic.

The air around it shimmered, laced with power. An invisible lattice hung over the candle's surface, hers and Vegard's and Lenore's magic woven together like a net, its threads so tightly wound that it was difficult to tell which strand belonged to whom. Underneath the framework, the candle was bursting with power—the herbs that Lenore had grown for Ida boosting and supporting the already potent mixture of dreaming elixir, silver, and blood.

Ida knew that it was possible to create a candle that would be dangerous for her, knew that she could burn herself out if she wasn't careful with her own power. But she had never come close to risking it until now. This candle felt like a restless bull, like the second it was free of its fetters it would go into an unstoppable charge, tearing through anyone and everything in its path. It was beautiful, and powerful, and deadly, the first thing Ida had ever made that felt like a weapon.

Even Lenore and Vegard seemed impressed. She could tell by their silence, the two of them standing on either side of her, surveying her work.

At length, Lenore said, "This is nicely done."

Ida exhaled, too numb to feel anything at the praise. She had spent the past few nights perfecting this technique, to the exclusion of everything else. Either this candle was going to be enough to show them the past, or nothing would. There was no middle ground here.

She reached into her pocket, drawing out her father's firestrike. Her fingers ran over its familiar weight, the coolness of the metal.

"Should we get started?" she asked the other two.

They nodded. They were uncharacteristically silent as they approached the end table, each of them standing equidistant from each other, the three points of a triangle. There had been surprisingly little conversation that evening. It was as if each of them were focused on what they had lost for so long, and what the end of this mystery would mean.

"How do we do this?" Lenore asked, when they were standing in place.

"It would probably be best to hold hands . . ." Vegard said. He trailed off uncertainly, glancing at Ida.

It was flattering that Vegard deferred to her when it came to this. It was his room, his memory, and he had enough magic in a strand of his hair to knock Ida out for a week without the amulet he had given her to guard against just that.

But this was still her project. *Her* magic.

"The candle's built on a connection between the three of us," she said. "Once it's lit, it will release a lot of energy. We'll need to maintain that connection, to guide it and use it to break through whatever's getting in the way of our memories. But I'll need a hand free for a moment, to light the candle."

Lenore nodded, extending a hand toward Vegard. He took it. Ida held her left hand out to Lenore, and froze as she felt Lenore entwine her fingers with hers, holding tightly. She glanced over at Lenore, but Lenore's gaze was fixed on the candle, her expression like stone. Only the slight tremble in her hand as she held tightly to Ida's, and the roil of her aura, told Ida how nervous she really was. Ida squeezed back, reassuringly, and felt Lenore start to relax. She used her right hand to flick the cover off the firestrike. Her thumb moved over the striker, two quick motions until it caught.

Ida needed to be quick. She had no idea what would happen once this began.

She set the flame to the wick and quickly dropped the firestrike onto the end table, grabbing Vegard's free hand.

Her fingers had barely brushed against his skin, the bite of winter around her, before the force of all that magic hit her like a battering ram.

It knocked her off her feet. Figuratively speaking.

In her head, Ida knew that she was standing in Vegard's room, knew that she was holding hands with both Vegard and Lenore, the three of them like statues arrayed around a quietly burning silver candle. But her mind had been flung out of her body, tossed headlong someplace else entirely.

The violence of it shocked her. Her illusions were normally gentle things, overlaying reality, leaving the audience feeling as though the world had changed, but not unmooring them from their bodies.

This felt like being torn. Like being ripped from her mortal coil and set adrift. She would have panicked, if it wasn't for the fact that Lenore and Vegard were with her, if it wasn't for the fact that she could still feel their hands in hers. As it was, she gripped their hands tightly and clenched her jaw until it was over.

When the world finally stopped spinning, it felt like a crash landing.

One moment, Ida's mind was in free fall, in the next, she was standing in a chamber that looked very much like this one. Vegard's room, but different. Larger, somehow. Warmer. True to life in a way that the real room, in the real castle, wasn't. The season was slightly different, and it was daytime, sun shining through the large windows that occupied one wall. The sun turned the white stone of the walls from funereal to refreshingly cool, and the sight of it, warm and buttery and golden, was so foreign to Ida that for a moment all she could do was bask in it like a cat, face turned toward the light.

The moment passed, and Ida looked around for the others.

Lenore and Vegard were gone. Her hands were closed around empty air. She couldn't even sense them. If she strained herself, searching for them, she *thought* she could feel the hint of their hands in hers, a brief sensation against her skin. But it felt like straining to wake from a nightmare, a smothering, panicky sort of paralysis. Ida shied away from the disconcerting feeling, letting herself slip deeper into the dream.

She chided herself as she tried to slow her racing heart. This was exactly what she had hoped for, the effect she'd tried to achieve. A dream rooted in reality, an illusion that showed her what had actually come to pass. If she got scared and backed out now, this whole endeavor would be pointless.

She just had to trust that Lenore and Vegard were with her somewhere. Perhaps they were viewing the same thing she was, or perhaps they were in separate dreams. Either way, it was her job to learn as much as she could now, so that she could tell them about it later.

She swallowed against her nerves and started to explore her surroundings.

It was the same room, but newer somehow, the air filled with the scents of sawn wood and fresh paint. The room was less furnished than Vegard's rooms were in the present day, but the vase that sat on the end table was full of flowers, wild, alpine blooms that looked like they had been freshly picked from the world outside. The pool of hot water that occupied pride of place at the foot of the stairs in the real world was absent in this dream. Instead, someone had gamely placed a cushioned bench on the tiled floor, its arrangement looking like the beginnings of a small sitting area. There were crates of belongings stacked against one wall, a kind of clutter and sentimentality she had never seen in Vegard.

And there was a door on the far side of the room, set into the stone wall, that had never been there before.

Ida stepped toward it, hand outstretched for the doorknob. Just as she was wondering if she could touch things in this dream, or if it would be like during the Dreaming Revel where her hand had passed right through the door, it swung open.

Ida jumped back, avoiding the door by a hair. She looked around, desperate for a place to hide, but it was too late. There were people walking through the door.

"—perfect," a boy's voice was saying. "From here, I'll be able to anchor Asteria's spells, and it has the best view of the glacier. Of course I'm happy with it."

The boy was Vegard, but Vegard as she'd never heard him. If she hadn't known how age washed over Vegard like rain, if she hadn't known that this couldn't have been that many years ago, she would have sworn that this Vegard was younger. He was the same height as the Vegard she knew, his black hair the same length, his eyes the same shade of silvery gray. But there was a warmth to his pale skin that Ida had never seen, a gleam in his eyes. He was smiling, brightly, openly, and he had tucked his hair back behind one ear. He looked like at any point he might burst into laughter, when the Vegard Ida knew hoarded his smiles like they were gold.

Any other time, Ida would have wanted to study him. To look at this Vegard, glowing and golden, and try to understand how he had shattered into the Vegard she knew. Any other time, this mystery would be all that consumed her. But not this time, because the man who was coming down the stairs behind Vegard, the man who said quite reasonably, "Well, it's very far away from everything in the castle. You may feel isolated out here. Don't you want your rooms a little closer?" was someone whose presence made her heart leap into her throat, made breathing feel impossible, made her eyes prickle with happiness and grief and longing.

The man walking down the stairs behind Vegard, his skin a dark shade of brown, his brown eyes an echo of her own, wearing the dark liveried jacket and trousers of a court artisan, was her father.

Tomas Rosales, Court Luminaire.

They couldn't see her.

Ida was grateful. If they could, they would have seen her gaping, blocking the doorway with her mouth open like a fish, unsure whether to scream or cry. Instead, they continued talking, walking right *through* her as if she wasn't there. A part of Ida, detached and analyzing the situation with a mage's eyes, realized that of course she would be immaterial to them.

She was only an observer, watching events that had already happened.

And this was a memory.

"—prefer to be as close to the anchor as possible," Vegard said, and Ida realized that she'd missed part of their conversation, that she'd been so stunned at seeing her father again that she had let herself forget why she was here. She spun around to watch them as they paced over to the window, resolving to pay closer attention.

"It's still quite delicate, and I want to make sure I'm on hand if it needs an emergency replenishment."

"I don't think you need to worry there," her father said. They'd come to a stop in front of the window, looking out at the mountains arrayed before them. "It's quite well-constructed. From the tower, it should cover the entire castle. You'd sense any problems the moment they arise."

This was a side of her father she had never seen before. He was calm and professional, his tone reasonable, words thoughtful and analytical. At home, she mostly remembered her father being tired and gentle, careful when it came to teaching her how to use the magic he'd given her. Here, he was in his element. She wished fervently that she had been able to see more of *this* version of her father. She had so many questions to ask him.

"Maybe so," Vegard said. "Still, better safe than sorry."

What were they talking about? Something in the tower?

She looked back over her shoulder at the door hanging open behind her. From this angle, she could see that it led to a stairwell. The missing tower was likely at the top, and Vegard had asked for his rooms to be placed at the foot of the tower, so that he could monitor something.

An anchor. That was what Vegard had been talking about when he first descended the steps.

When she built her candles, she anchored magic to them. Had Vegard done the same thing in the tower? Was there a spell up there, and if so, what was it supposed to *do*?

She tore her eyes away from the door as Vegard asked another question.

"What about your core?" he asked. "Did you find a safe place for it?"

Her father smiled, mischief in his expression as he looked out the window. "Oh. I've found the perfect place. You won't believe . . ."

The memory changed.

Ida fought to grab hold of her father's words, the beloved image of his face, but it melted away like sugar in water, the image vanishing in a blur of color as the scene shifted again. She cried out in frustration, her voice echoing against the stone walls of the chamber, but she had no power to bring the memory back. The spell had been anchored on Vegard's room, on the things that had happened here, and unlike her illusions, unlike the dreams from the Dreaming Revel, she was not in control.

She could only watch the story unfold.

When the scene resolved around her, it was nighttime, a more familiar view of Asteria. Time had clearly passed. Vegard had unpacked the boxes, and a familiar bookshelf now stood next to the sitting area that occupied the space where the pool would be. He was seated on the couch, the full length of his body sprawled across it, his back on the armrest. And he was reading. The Vegard Ida knew occupied spaces like he was walking on eggshells, like at any point the world might collapse out from under him. Seeing him like this, utterly at ease, relaxing on a couch like any boy their age would, was a shock to Ida's senses.

"What happened to you?" she asked him.

Vegard didn't answer. He lazily flipped a page, a faint smile on his face.

Nothing else happened. Ida hesitated, then took a step forward to perch on a nearby armchair. She didn't fall through it, so she was clearly allowed some ability to interact with the furniture. She just couldn't speak to anyone, and she couldn't do anything to interrupt the flow of the memory.

She settled into the armchair and watched, hoping that the room hadn't taken her out of a vital conversation to show her Vegard reading a book. The moment to catch her breath was useful, though, and Ida found herself almost falling asleep before the door to Vegard's room swung open.

Both she and Vegard sat up—Ida suddenly, Vegard slower. The languid expression on his face vanished when he saw who it was.

Tomas Rosales was coming into the room like a hurricane. His hair was disheveled, and there were bags under his eyes that hadn't been there in the last memory. He looked like he had been working all night, but the expression on his face was pure fury. Ida had never seen her father this angry, and likely neither had Vegard, because he immediately sat up straight and set his book aside.

"Tomas—" he began, but her father interrupted him.

"It's happened," Tomas said, casting the words out like a snarl. "He's bringing *her* here."

Chapter 21

BEFORE THE FALL

Her.

The dream froze for a single moment, slowing to a glacial pace around Ida. Her mind was racing, rocketing from one memory to another. She remembered Vegard's version of events, shared with her in a quiet theater a lifetime ago. Remembered Vegard saying that everything began to change when a girl had been brought to the court.

Lenore.

Tomas stormed over to the armchair, and Ida realized he intended to sit in it. She sprang up quickly, practically leaping out of the chair to get out of the way before her father could collapse right through her, and came to a stop a few feet away from them, eyes wide and heart racing. Her father sat down heavily, resting his head in his hands, elbows on his knees. He dragged his fingertips over his face, a gesture she had only seen him make in the depths of exhaustion. Or frustration.

Vegard studied him for a moment before speaking, the lost expression on his face achingly familiar to Ida. He hesitated for only a moment before he said, "Surely . . . that's not a bad thing.

You yourself have spoken about wanting to bring your daughter to Asteria."

"That's *different*," Tomas snarled. "And anyway, I wouldn't bring Ida here if I couldn't get her mother to agree. That wouldn't be right."

"Lenore's mother doesn't agree?"

"Lenore's mother is *furious*. And I've told His Majesty a thousand times—beings of power aren't to be taken lightly."

Vegard looked truly worried now. His brow furrowed in concern. "Surely the Witch of Callania could *stop* His Majesty from bringing the child here. She's powerful enough, and Aurel isn't her king."

Tomas said nothing, his lips pressed together in a fine line. He sat back in his chair, his gaze fixed on the middle distance. Ida wondered if Lenore was watching the same scene she was, listening to the same story unfold. If Lenore now knew that her mother had never wanted to let her go.

At length, he said, "He has a whole court of magical beings to draw from, many of whom you and I found for him. If he really wanted to bring Lenore here, I'm not sure the witch could stop him."

"He would steal his child from her mother?" Vegard looked disbelieving, but her father's expression was steel and storm. It was the hard look of someone who realized that the person they had devoted so much of their time to had changed, had become someone unknowable. Perhaps even someone monstrous. It was the look of a person quietly calculating how much they had contributed to this fall, how much blame lay with them.

"I truly fear that he would," Tomas finally said. "He's angry enough to do it. And the King of Callania would let him. He doesn't have much love for the witch."

"The witch would retaliate, though," Vegard said. His eyes were wide, imploring. "The king must know that. Doesn't he?"

"I think . . ." Tomas said, carefully weighing the words out as though each one might be treason, ". . . I think he believes himself beyond that."

Ida stood at the top of the tower in the next vision given to her by the dream. The room at the top was small and circular, and it hosted very few items of furniture. Very little, in fact, besides a pedestal on which rested a shard of ice seemingly suspended in the air over the stone. Ida was sure that if this were the real world, if she were truly standing in this lost chamber, the room would be drowning in magic. As it was, she didn't feel anything but the ghost of a prickle on her skin, a sensation like air blowing over the back of her neck.

The room was fascinating, but she couldn't expend too much focus on it, because both she and a past Vegard were absorbed in what was happening outside the window.

The tower had only two windows, both of them high archer's slits carved into the stone. One faced the mountains and was almost certainly the source of the light Lenore had seen from her window on the night of the incident. The other faced the entrance of the castle, the courtyard that greeted visitors.

There was a great procession in the courtyard. A carriage decorated in the royal insignia had pulled up the road and was being attended to by a flock of servants in black and guards in gleaming uniforms. Only one person in Asteria merited so much fuss, so Ida was sure that the king was in the carriage. But when the door opened, it wasn't Aurel IV that stepped out, but a girl, young, with messy auburn hair tied back, a child Ida knew on sight.

Lenore.

She wore a black dress like she was in mourning. When someone in the courtyard reached up to help her down from the carriage, Lenore pushed their hands away and stumbled out by herself. She stood stiffly at the edge of the courtyard, and though she was much younger in this vision, she was so obviously hurting that Ida's heart broke, watching her. She hoped that present-day Lenore, *her* Lenore, wasn't also watching this scene.

But those thoughts died away, because Aurel stepped out of the carriage next.

From beside her, the Vegard of the past hissed in surprise. Ida couldn't blame him. The King Aurel that stepped out of the carriage, gripping the door for leverage and all but stumbling into the arms of the startled footmen that hurried to receive him, was *not* the Aurel she knew. He was—somehow—older. From this distance, it was difficult to see his expression, but he swayed like a drunk as the footmen tried to keep him upright, his back bowed as if by a great weight. He looked sick, as if he'd been affected by the long drive up the mountain. But from the way Vegard watched him, practically pressed against the stone, this wasn't something as prosaic as motion sickness.

Something was *wrong* with the king. And as Ida's eyes landed on the small girl on the other side of the courtyard, currently surrounded by helpful maids in black-and-white uniforms, she had a feeling she knew why, if not how.

King Aurel was cursed.

The world spun away with a dizzying lurch, and this time, when it resurfaced, it took Ida a moment to come back to herself, as if she had left pieces of herself in the last memory. It took her a breath to realize where she was, one more to take hold of the edge of a table above her and pull herself up off the ground, the pounding echoes in the back of her mind slowly asserting themselves into actual conversation. She gasped as the room snapped into focus, shooting to her feet, and was grateful that she couldn't be seen in this vision. That the argument unfolding between three players—Tomas, Vegard, and King Aurel himself—continued without her.

She was standing in Vegard's rooms, next to a heavy wooden table that had been set up beside the room's outward-facing windows. Food had been set out on the table's surface, an assortment of small cakes, pastries, and cups of coffee long since grown cold, but it looked like only Vegard had actually had anything to eat or drink. The plate in front of him was full of crumbs, the remnants of his coffee cooling dregs. The other parties at the table, Aurel and Tomas, hadn't eaten anything at all.

They seemed to be doing most of the arguing. And Vegard, unfortunately for him, seemed to be in the same position Ida occupied when her grandmother and mother chose a family meal as the venue for one of their arguments. He glanced between the two of them and reached for another pastry, as if by continuing to eat he could make them forget that he was even here.

Neither of the others were looking at him. Ida, standing between Vegard and her father, was surprised by two things—the rage in her father's voice, and the change that had come over King Aurel.

"There is *nothing* that can be done!" her father insisted. "Not in my power, not in Vegard's! You must return the girl."

Aurel sniffed, as if her father's impassioned pleas were something that could simply be brushed away, like a particularly annoying fly. Vegard looked pained at having been mentioned at all—if he could disappear into the upholstery of his high-backed chair, he would have. Aurel raised his head, and Vegard flinched, but Aurel's eyes were only for Tomas.

Aurel looked thinner than Ida had ever remembered seeing him, as if all the vitality in his bones had been sucked away. His hands, as he folded them together in front of him, were shaking. His breath rattled in his chest in a way that suggested illness. And although Ida remembered never being particularly impressed by King Aurel, in this vision he looked like he had one foot in the grave. Yet his eyes, when he raised them to study her father, were completely clear.

"You cannot seriously be suggesting I return my daughter to the woods to live in a *hovel.* What would my people say?"

"Your people hardly know a thing about her," said Tomas. "You don't present her at parties, you haven't brought her to Trissaire, you haven't named her as an heir—"

"She isn't *ready* for that sort of attention."

"She isn't *happy* here! She wants to go home!"

"She doesn't know any better!" Aurel roared, and the sound of his voice, bouncing off the high stone walls, made her father shrink back for a moment. Aurel's eyes blazed. "You overstep yourself, Tomas. Simply because *you* don't have the courage to bring your daughter to Asteria, doesn't mean—"

"This isn't about my daughter," Tomas said very softly, his voice a warning. The low tone of his voice was enough to cut through Aurel's speech. It wasn't enough to dull his anger, nor the way he glared at Tomas. "This is about yours, sire, and about you. Forgive me if I am speaking out of turn, but as your *luminaire*, as your adviser of magic, I am telling you that if you do not give the girl back, you will die."

Aurel shook with rage, and Ida held her breath, afraid that the king would throw something at her father, or worse, order him thrown in the dungeons. But then, as if by great force of will, he mastered himself, his jaw clenched tightly as he settled back into his seat. He said nothing for a few long moments, looking between Tomas, who was watching him with a pleading look on his face, to Vegard, who was trying very hard not to catch his eye. At length, Aurel sighed, and when he spoke again, his voice was calmer.

"Tell me again, Tomas, about the nature of this curse."

Tomas breathed out a sigh of relief. He tapped his finger on the table, and though Ida couldn't see what he used to focus his magic, no hint of a censer or an incense stick or any of the small things that he had used at home, the air above the table shimmered. It formed an image of a man wreathed in smoke, a featureless representation of a human being. At the slightest gesture from Tomas, a glow began to shine from within the haze, just over where the man's heart would be, as if the smoke housed a glowing coal. The glow was spreading, taking over the indistinct form of the man's body. As Ida watched, it seemed to burn him up from the inside, until the glow was too bright to look at, until there was nothing left of the smoke that made up the man.

"This is the issue, sire," Tomas said, the sequence reversing itself until the smoke man returned, his heart a burning ember. "The curse is a type of parasite, tied to your heart. It feeds off life essence. As it feeds, it grows, and you diminish. It's designed to act slowly, likely to give you time to consider your options. But make no mistake, it will still kill you in the end."

"And you cannot remove it?"

"I can only affect the intangible," Tomas said. "I can make you *feel* as if you are not cursed, I can make you forget that the curse exists. But that would only be an illusion. I cannot remove the curse, which means I can't save your life."

"I see," said Aurel gravely. "And you, Vegard?"

He turned his gaze onto Vegard, who tensed, sitting up in his seat. Ida saw the uncertainty play out across his face, his emotions so much more transparent in this memory than they had ever been in her time. She could see how little Vegard wanted to answer this question, how much Vegard longed to not be a part of this conversation. At length, Vegard sighed and put his half-eaten pastry back down onto his plate.

"I can feel the curse at work in you. I can . . . see it, actually, when I look at you." His eyes flashed silver, just for a moment. "But I fear that separating it from you would only kill you."

"Why is that?"

"It's tied too closely to your life. It's entwined with you. If I were to use a physical analogy, if I tried to cut it away from you, I would likely end up cutting into you. I couldn't remove it without hurting you as well."

"So there's nothing you can do?"

"I . . ." Vegard hesitated, glancing down at his plate. His fingers flicked crumbs off the table, a distracted gesture. "I . . . wouldn't say that."

Tomas was watching Vegard closely now, his mouth pulled tight in disapproval. It was a stark contrast, Ida thought, to the look in Aurel's eyes, the naked greed there as his attention focused entirely on Vegard.

"What can you do?" King Aurel asked.

Vegard sucked in a breath. He lifted his head. "The main issue with the curse is that it siphons off your life energy. And as a human, you only have so much life to lose. If we could supplement your natural energies somehow, we could . . . give the curse more to feed on. It would prolong your life, but it wouldn't exactly cure you, and if we start on this course, we won't be able to stop. The curse will grow stronger. Once we stop, its power will overwhelm you. It's simply not a sustainable solution."

"But it would buy me time?"

"Yes . . ." Vegard said slowly. "Yes, it would. But you would not feel like yourself."

"That's hardly an issue," Aurel said dismissively. "Tomas already said he could take care of the mental and emotional aspects of the issue. All I need is time. Lenore has the same magic as her mother. I only need to wait until she is grown, until she comes into her power . . ."

"There's no guarantee she will ever be capable of lifting the curse," Tomas said. "Magic doesn't work that way. The inheritance of magic doesn't always follow straight and simple lines—"

"She *will*," Aurel said. "She is the daughter of a king. I only need a decade, perhaps less." He looked back at Vegard. "How do we begin?"

"Well . . ." Vegard looked uncomfortable. "You need a donor. Someone with enough life energy to spare, someone with enough magic to feed the curse and keep it at bay."

Aurel and Tomas were both looking at him now. The former with slowly dawning comprehension, the latter with horror.

Vegard sighed. "I suppose . . . it may as well be me."

Chapter 22

SHATTERING

Silver droplets ran down the inside of Vegard's forearm, gathering into liquid pools at the bottom of the bowl Ida's father was holding. Tomas Rosales's eyes were narrowed in anger, lips pursed as he waited for the bowl to fill. Vegard watched with a vacant expression as blood dripped from a cut on the outside of his arm.

When the bowl was nearly full, Tomas said, "That's enough," and handed Vegard a small cloth. Vegard took it, pressing the cloth to the wound as Tomas whisked the bowl away with businesslike efficiency. He held it with the tips of his fingers, set it aside gingerly, and looked back at Vegard.

"Doesn't that hurt you?" he asked.

Vegard frowned, dabbing at a few stray droplets that glittered on his skin. The wound had already closed.

"Not really. I heal quickly."

"It's not just about *healing*." Ida was struck by the vehemence in her father's tone, the way his eyes blazed. It was an expression she recognized, because she wore it on her own face when she was angry. "He's draining you of your power. I cannot believe you agreed to this."

"It's not so dramatic as all that, Tomas," said Vegard. "Blood doesn't mean to me what it does to you. It's . . . a bit like giving the king a few strands of hair. It will grow back."

He turned away, his gaze already fixed on something in the distance. Ida saw that he was trying to seem unbothered, nonchalant, but her disbelief was mirrored on her father's face. She could hear the exhaustion in his tone. The strain in his voice, the echo of the Vegard she knew. She bit her lip, looking over at her father, who seemed to be struggling to compose himself, to find the right words.

At length, Tomas said, "You're not as invincible as you think you are, Vegard."

"I don't see what the problem is," Vegard said. "I have plenty of power to spare."

"Do you?" her father asked. "I can *feel* your aura, Vegard. You're growing weaker by the day."

Vegard removed the cloth from his arm, displaying unbroken skin. "I'm fine, Tomas. I'll recover."

"Why does this matter so much to you?" Tomas asked. He spun away from Vegard stiffly, pouring the blood into a series of stoppered glass vials laid out on the table beside him. Ida stood over Vegard's shoulder, watching as realization dawned that Tomas wasn't angry at *him*. "This isn't your realm. You could *go home*."

"Without my blood, the king will die," Vegard said, and he looked so disturbed by that, so frightened, that it only occurred to Ida at that moment that Vegard had not seen a lot of death. That he might have lived for centuries and yet lived in a world unchanging, that *this* Vegard still thought of humans as something fragile, something to be protected. "Doesn't that matter to you?"

"It is the nature of humans to die," said Tomas. "It's *not* yours.

And if you keep this up, Vegard, my concern is that you will die. Or at least, you'll lose something vital that you'll never recover."

"Tomas . . ." Vegard said, lowering the stained cloth back to the tabletop. "This isn't enough to hurt—"

Ida would never know what Vegard had been about to say, because it caught in his throat, his sentence ending in a choked-off gasp. The cloth tumbled from his fingers as his eyes flashed silver, as he dropped to a knee, clutching his forearm. He started breathing heavily, chest heaving. Ida was only half there, hidden away from the violence of Vegard's aura, but she had stood close enough to it before to know what it had to feel like.

Like a storm, like ice shattering beneath your feet, like frigid water rising up to swallow you whole.

Tomas turned toward him, alarmed, and stopped as a wave of frost and cold pulsed outward from Vegard, forming patterns of ice on the ground at his feet. The ice washed harmlessly over Ida, but Tomas shrank back, letting out a bitter curse in a language she didn't recognize. When he shook his arm out, Ida saw ice on the surface of his sleeve, on his skin.

"Tomas!" Vegard said in alarm. The moment had passed, and he stepped forward, taking hold of Tomas's arm gently between the elbow and wrist. As Ida watched, the ice retreated, leaving skin and cloth untouched. Vegard turned Tomas's arm over, inspecting it closely. He let out a shaky breath.

"I'm sorry."

Tomas's skin was an ashen shade of brown, and he leaned against the table, catching his breath. Ida watched him, seized with a sudden fear that this was it, that this was when she discovered exactly what happened to her father, that Vegard had been the unwitting architect of his demise. But then Tomas took in a breath, running his hand over his face. He pulled his arm out of Vegard's grasp.

"I'm going to speak with him," Tomas said, and the calm in his voice made Ida shudder. It was a deceptive calmness, hiding the rage underneath.

"You can't—"

"I can. This can't go on." Tomas finished pouring the last of the blood into the vials and, as if he could no longer stand to look at what he had done, began quickly putting his tools away. "I can't *let this* go on any longer."

"He's your king—"

"Not my king." Tomas drew in a breath, as if gathering himself, and said something soft that Ida couldn't quite make out. Something in the same language he had spoken earlier, when he'd cursed, except laced with so much more meaning. She thought he was speaking Niresso, and her heart ached at the sound, because her father's voice had never sounded natural in Arreden, but the words came to him effortlessly now. When he switched back to Arreden, though, Ida could easily understand the defeat in his tone.

"I should have listened to my wife. Stay in your room, Vegard. This will be over soon."

He strode out of the room, marching toward the door like someone on a mission. Ida saw Vegard hesitate, saw him raise his hand as if to call Tomas back and then, as doubt flickered across his face like a cloud racing across the summer sky, saw him lower his hand back to his side.

The argument was fast, explosive, and came without warning.

One moment Ida was standing next to Vegard in the room,

watching her father walk away, and the next she was caught in the middle of the storm, raised voices coming at her from either side. Her father and King Aurel again, standing on either side of Vegard's sitting room, while Vegard himself sat on the couch between them, his eyes flicking from one to the other. There was a listlessness in his expression that hadn't been there before, an apathy that was painfully familiar to Ida. But his eyes were still sharp as he listened to them argue his fate.

Listening was all he could do. It didn't seem like either of them would give him any room to join the conversation.

"—you have *no right*! *No right* to tell me what I can and cannot do! Vegard is older than you or I—"

"Vegard is a *child*! I don't care how old he is, in the reckoning of his own people, he is a *child*, and you're bleeding him to death because you can't accept that you stole *your* child from her mother!"

"Lenore is *mine*! And Vegard knows his place—"

"Vegard and I are not your subjects! We are your allies—we are *not* citizens of Arred—"

"I am still a king, and you are still my servant, or have you forgotten your place so readily—"

"You once called me your friend. Was that worth nothing to you?"

"You *are* nothing, Tomas. Just a Niresso hedge witch! You are *nothing* without me!"

Tomas recoiled from the words as if slapped, the violence of them stealing the air out of the room. Ida sucked in a breath, sharp and painful, at the look in her father's eyes, at the emotions that warred across his face. Even Aurel seemed surprised at the words that had come out of his mouth, though his expression settled quickly into resolve. He stopped talking, staring at Tomas, as if daring him to say anything about it.

Shock, anger, betrayal.

There was a moment when Ida thought, genuinely thought, that her father would turn around and leave. But he held his ground, his eyes flicking away from Aurel to Vegard between them. He drew in a breath. "You are going to *break Vegard.* And I'm not going to stand by and watch you do it."

Aurel's response was dangerously soft. "Am I to take that as your resignation, Tomas?"

Tomas's eyes flashed, but before he could open his mouth to speak, Aurel went on.

"Think *very carefully* about the next words you speak in my presence. And pack your bags. I want you out of my castle by midnight. Count yourself lucky that I am sending you home to be with your family, instead of back to your *islands*. Get out of my sight."

Tomas gritted his teeth. His hands were clenched into fists, and for one terrible moment, Ida thought he would reach out and strike Aurel. But he didn't. Instead, his eyes flicked toward Vegard, one more time. Aurel scowled in distaste.

"Go!" he shouted. "I gave you an order. You may not be my subject, but if you will not serve, you will *leave*. Or you will be removed. *Now.*"

Tomas sucked in a breath and then, stiffly, as if all his limbs were made of metal, he started for the door. Aurel watched him go, saying nothing until the heavy doors that led to Vegard's chambers had opened and shut behind him.

Then Aurel turned toward Vegard.

The expression on his face made Vegard recoil. It was anger, and fury and greed, and Ida, who was only an observer to this scene, who could not affect it or be affected by it in any way, still found herself shaking at the look in Aurel's eyes. As if Vegard were not alive, as if he were simply another mark of Aurel's dominion, a bauble no more useful than a scepter or a crown.

At length, he said, "Vegard, attend me in the upper room tonight. Tell no one. I command you by your name."

Something happened, a shift in the air, like a thread between Vegard and Aurel had been pulled tight. Vegard gasped, doubling over, his hands clasped tight around his arms. Flashes of white light danced across his skin, as if the magic inside of him were struggling to break free. His face was contorted in pain.

Ice spread across the couch he was sitting on, his arms, his face, the floor. It inched across the stones until it touched, barely, the soles of King Aurel's boots. And then it stopped, as if unable to move any closer.

Vegard struggled to raise his head, looking at King Aurel from underneath a fall of black hair. His eyes were silver. And King Aurel's, as he looked back at Vegard in that moment, were the same.

Vegard sagged, defeated. And the king didn't spare him another glance as he turned and walked away.

This was a scene of sacrifice.

Ida screamed when the world fell into place around her. It ripped from her throat, sharp and piercing, but no one else could hear her. No one could help, because this was only a memory.

A memory of Vegard in the upper room, the missing room.

A memory of him lying shirtless on the stone pedestal, his eyes filled with fear. A memory of the king standing over him, a silver knife in his hands. Of Aurel's wild eyes and Vegard's mouth straining to make a sound. Of every muscle in Vegard's body going taut as he saw his death reflected in a silver blade.

The king tipped the knife, angling its point toward Vegard's heart. Ida clenched her fists, nails pressing into her palms, and told herself that this wasn't happening, that this wasn't real. That this was only a *memory*—

"Stop!"

The voice bounced off stone walls, echoing up the stairwell. The blade halted in its descent, Aurel's eyes flashing with rage as he spun toward the stairs. Ida heard footsteps, two at a time, as frantic as the beat of her heart. And then her father was at the top of the stairs, gasping for breath, one hand clutching the railing tightly as his eyes fell on Aurel with disbelief.

"Your Majesty," he said, still catching his breath, "what are you doing?"

"I thought I told you to get out of my castle."

Tomas's eyes drifted past Aurel to Vegard, lying on the stone behind him. He drew himself up to his full height, breathing deeply as if he were drawing power from the air. And then he took a step away from the stairs.

A step toward the king.

"Your Majesty, be reasonable." Tomas held his hands out in front of him, a placating gesture, but his eyes drifted between Vegard, the knife, and the king. "There's no need to go to such extremes."

"This is no longer your concern, Tomas."

"I can't let you kill him."

"He's *mine*! Everything in this castle is mine to do with as I wish! Everything except—"

The king stamped his foot, his eyes flashing Vegard's bright silver. Silver light flooded his veins, tracing grotesque outlines across his skin. It erupted across the floor in violent, coruscating patterns, a wave of power that made Ida flinch.

It didn't touch Tomas.

The light broke against him like a wave on the shore. It splashed over him and left him unharmed, gleaming.

Tomas's eyes were dark as moonless nights, his gaze fixed solemnly—sadly—on the King of Arred. "Everything except me. You don't have my blood. You can't bind me by my name. And you don't have my fealty. You had my loyalty. Once. I pledged it to a good man. A good friend and a good king. Please, sire. Put down the knife. Be worthy of that trust again."

It was precisely the wrong thing to say.

"You *dare*—" Aurel was practically shaking with rage. "You *dare* to tell me that I am not *worthy*?"

"Your Majesty—"

"You will be the last Court Luminaire who does not give me their *fealty*!" Aurel roared. He spun around, plunging the knife into Vegard's heart.

"No!" Tomas screamed, running forward.

Vegard's entire body seized, back arching, mouth opening in a silent scream. White light gathered at the dagger's hilt, crackling like electricity where blade met skin. It grew so bright it was painful to look at, the core of Vegard's power, the entirety of him starting to flow up the dagger and into Aurel's waiting hand. Aurel leaned over

Vegard, looking down at him with avarice in his eyes, ready to take it all into himself.

Until her father practically shouldered him aside, covering Aurel's hands with his own.

The second his hands touched the knife, Tomas screamed. Ida saw Vegard's light lash out at him, stinging his hands, crackling over his skin. But he didn't let go. Instead, he struggled, fighting with Aurel as the king tried to regain control of the knife, the two of them shoving and pushing against each other.

Ida realized what her father was going to do the second before he did it.

He elbowed King Aurel in the head. The king's head snapped back, blood flying from his nose. He stared at Tomas in disbelief as he staggered back a pace.

And in that moment of distraction, Tomas pulled the blade from Vegard's chest.

Vegard bucked and gasped, the ragged wound in his heart already beginning to seal itself. But the damage had been done. Power had been taken from him. It hung in the air above Tomas, an angry white orb spinning at breakneck speed, flashes of light emanating from it like the center of a storm. Tomas gasped for breath, staring at it helplessly.

And Aurel recovered his senses for long enough to tangle his fingers in Tomas's hair, shoving him face-first into the orb.

Vegard's eyes snapped open. He sat up.

"Tomas!" he screamed, and Ida screamed too, for everything it was worth.

All that power surged into her father, his limbs jerking under the strain. He tried to push back, but Aurel held him there. He grinned in triumph, blood pouring from his nose, dripping red and silver on the stone floor as he declared, "I free myself from this curse! I deny this curse was ever placed on me. I deny this curse and everything that would take Asteria from me!"

White light erupted from Tomas's back, stained with gold. It spread, filling the entire room.

And then everything shattered, breaking apart until Ida was the only person in the world still screaming.

Chapter 23

CRASH

When Ida came to, she was lying on cold stone, her face wet with tears and her throat hoarse. She rolled over onto her side, her breath coming in hitching gasps as she tried to reorient herself.

Sunlight came in at a low angle from high windows, illuminating a familiar set of stone floors. To her left, steam rose from the surface of a warm pool, dampening the air. Above her head, a wooden table lay on its side, her carefully crafted candle on the floor next to it. And from somewhere behind her, Ida heard a groan as one of the other two started to wake up.

It was that sound that reminded her where she was, what she was doing. She was in Vegard's rooms. She and the others had come up with a plan to discover the truth about the evening missing from Vegard's and Lenore's memories. And they'd found—she'd found—

She sucked in a gasp of air, pressing her hand over her face. The memories threatened to overwhelm her. When she closed her eyes, all she could see was Vegard on a stone table, King Aurel's hand in her father's hair, the white light that took apart the world. Vegard, betrayal in his eyes as he watched the king advance, Vegard with a silver dagger in his chest, Vegard—

Vegard!

Ida pushed herself up into a sitting position, pulling her hand away from her face. She searched frantically, eyes sweeping over the mess on the floor of the room. Lenore lay groaning on her side, her face obscured by a curtain of reddish-brown hair. And directly across from her—

Vegard was curled in on himself, one hand fisted in his dark hair. His shoulders shook like he was crying.

Ida pushed herself up to her feet, running over to him. She dropped down to a crouch at his side.

"Vegard—"

Her voice sounded rough to her own ears. She hesitated, then reached out and touched his arm. His skin was cold as ice, but the cold had no bite. When he tipped his head up to look at her, opening his eyes, they weren't the bright silver they became when his magic grew too much to bear. They were only a flat gray, like a cloudy sky, red-rimmed and pained. His other hand clutched the fabric over his heart. He was shaking.

"Ida . . ." he said. "Ida, I—"

Ida sat down and gathered him into her arms.

He shuddered, shaking against her, and then the tears came, bursts of frigid cold against her shoulder.

Ida cried too, all the pain she had been holding back breaking free, until it was just the two of them, holding each other, crying.

At some point, Ida wasn't sure when, Lenore joined them. She was much more composed than they were, composed enough to coax them both to their feet, one at a time. She helped Vegard over to the couch that was the only remnant of what had once been his sitting room, and then came back for Ida, wrapping an arm around her as she helped her to stand. Lenore paused, turning Ida gently to face her, and Ida rested her head on Lenore's shoulder, too drained to do more than sink into her warmth and take comfort in her strength. In the warmth and the feel of the deep and living earth, of Lenore's magic, growing tightly all around her. For a moment, they simply stood together, wrapped up in the small world they had created in each other.

Then Lenore gently led Ida over to the couch as well, sitting her at the other end of it. She left them there, had a whispered conversation with Gloam at the entrance to Vegard's chambers, and returned a few moments later with a tray of hot tea and pastries. The cups she poured went ignored, cooling on the table between them as Ida turned what was left of her candle over in her hands.

The candle had split down the middle as if it had been struck by lightning, wax charred and blackened around the wick. It crumbled at Ida's touch, leaving sooty residue on her fingertips. Although parts of the wick were still intact, Ida knew that this candle would never light again.

Lenore let the silence drag on for an appropriate amount of time before she spoke.

"So . . ." she said.

"So," Ida repeated, setting the candle down. The base was solid enough. It remained standing, pieces of it splayed grotesquely in all directions, its interior exposed to the open air.

For a moment, Lenore looked at a loss for what to do. She looked down at her hands, drew in a breath to steady herself, and looked back up at Ida and Vegard.

"Did we all see the same vision?"

"That depends," said Vegard dryly, looking up from where he was curled up at the edge of the couch. "Was it a vision where His Majesty tried to tear out my heart?"

Lenore flinched. Ida roused herself out from under her shroud of self-pity for long enough to remember that whatever else Aurel had done, he was still Lenore's father. She looked at Lenore and tried to come up with something delicate to say, but the memory of her own father stopped her. That moment—

She couldn't think of it as his last moment. He was still alive. He had to be.

"I saw that too," she said, keeping her voice as soft as she could make it. "He was desperate to break a curse placed on him by your mother."

Lenore exhaled. Her hands were tangled in the fabric of her skirts, holding on so tight they were almost shaking.

"All right," she said. "Same vision then."

"We likely saw three reflections of the same event," Vegard said. "There may have been slight differences in our visions. Breaking down what we saw and seeing where our visions diverge would be an interesting exercise. But ultimately . . . ultimately, I think we all saw the most important parts."

Ida nodded. The story was clear enough.

Lenore was brought to the castle against her mother's will. Her mother cast a curse on King Aurel in retaliation. Rather than return Lenore to her mother, the king decided to seek alternate means of breaking the curse. He first used Vegard's blood to strengthen himself, and then attempted to sacrifice Vegard to break the curse entirely. And since then, the luminaires had all sworn fealty to the king, and something had happened to make the oath stick. To make the luminaires part of the Collection.

There were only a few more holes in the story.

As much as Ida's mind recoiled from it, they were going to have to talk about that room.

"What happened at the very end?" Ida asked. Her voice sounded flat to her ears, a dull monotone. "Why did everyone lose their memories?"

"It has to do with what my father did, doesn't it?" Lenore's voice was much the same as Ida's, a dry, academic tone, as if they were talking about something they had found in books. "What he said. He denied the curse. And in doing so, he denied everything that came from the curse, including the very spell he was performing. Including my . . ."

Her breath caught. Lenore stopped speaking, looking back down at her cup of tea.

"It went too far." Vegard's hand rose to his chest, his thumb tracing the hidden lines of his scar. "The king is, at best, a novice mage. He used far too much power to fuel the spell. Far too much of *my* power. The magic likely spread beyond the boundaries he'd envisioned."

"So he erased the curse." Ida counted the effects off on her fingers. "He also erased any memory of the curse having happened. That's why Vegard can't remember where he got that scar, why no one can remember what happened that night, and why Lenore can't truly remember her mother. But what happened to . . ." There was a question she wanted to ask, a question buried in her throat. It was a question whose answer she wasn't ready for. "What happened to the tower? It existed before the curse. So it shouldn't have vanished, right?"

"It's . . . probably collateral damage." Lenore picked awkwardly at her skirt, not meeting Ida's eye. "The spell was clearly out of control by the end. It destroyed the tower and then—in a rush to fulfill its conditions, erased the tower from memory to make it so that the curse had never happened in the first place, and the spell had never been cast in the first place. Like a child making a mess, and covering it up with an even larger one."

"It created a reality where the tower never existed in the first place," said Vegard, "and because minds abhor a vacuum, everyone came up with their own explanation for what was lost."

"Where did the tower *go*?" Ida thought back to those last terrible moments, thought of the light that spread into every corner of the room, A pure, destructive light that erased everything it touched. But she hadn't seen the light tear into the stones, hadn't seen it destroy the pedestal, the steps, the railings. There were no explosions, no shattering. Nothing had been physically destroyed. "It can't have been destroyed. Vegard and the king are still alive, and they were right in the middle of it."

No one answered for a long moment. Ida sat there, squirming in her seat, enduring the looks her friends shot her. She knew, and they knew, that she wasn't truly asking about the *tower*.

At length, Lenore said. "This is just a theory, but . . ."

Ida sat up sharply. "But what?"

Lenore looked a little uncomfortable. She cleared her throat, smoothing out her skirt before she went on. "But . . . I think that . . . rather than being destroyed in the physical sense, the spell simply, well . . . it simply . . ."

She straightened up, holding her right hand out in front of her, palm facing the floor. Slowly, she rested her left palm on the back of her right hand.

"It overlaid another reality onto this one. One where my father had never been cursed, one where he never needed Vegard's blood in the first place. One where the tower had never been built. There are some gaps, of course. The old reality still exists in our minds, in some of our memories. That probably explains the strange events that have happened to you, Ida. That first time you were lost in a castle, you said it looked like a ruin. You likely were seeing the castle in its former reality."

"And the hounds?" Ida asked, remembering the way they had formed out of the shadows, the way they chased her like they were going to devour her.

"Maybe it has something to do with *that* reality," Lenore said. "If the hounds existed in that version of Asteria. Some sort of . . . security spell?"

"Or it has to do with the king's wish," said Vegard. "If this reality *is* overlaid on top of another one, it's probably fighting to keep its integrity. It would see someone like Ida, who still *has* memories of the past, as something to be destroyed."

"And it doesn't affect Lenore, because . . . ?"

"That's what I'm trying to understand," said Vegard. "It could be because the original curse was cast by Lenore's mother, and the spell was altered by her father. Neither of those people would want to harm her, so *this* version of reality won't put her in danger. But it's hard to say."

Ida couldn't hold back any longer. "What about *my* father? The tower was never built in this reality, all right, I accept that. But my father was *here*. I remember him. My mother remembers him. *I'm* here!"

She pressed her hand to her chest, startled to feel how fast her heart was beating, how her breath came into her lungs, quick and furious.

They couldn't look at her. Not Lenore, whose eyes were fixed back on her lap, and not Vegard, who said, "Well of course, the spell couldn't erase *you*. You were already born. The spell had to make certain allowances for you to exist. You needed to have a father in this reality."

It felt like there was a buzzing in her head, like her mind had been taken up by a swarm of bees. She could feel the prickles as they leaped and danced across her skin.

"What are you saying?" She'd have to turn her head to look at Vegard, and that was more than she could manage. She looked directly at Lenore, whose gaze had finally risen to her own.

Lenore reached over, slowly taking Ida's hand. Her touch would have normally been comforting, but Ida felt her stomach twist with dread at the look in her eyes. She didn't want to hear Lenore's words, didn't want to understand why Lenore felt she needed to look at Ida like that.

"I think we have to assume," Lenore finally said, "that your father is . . . well, we should assume that he's dead."

Her world came apart at the seams.

Everything inside her was screaming, crashing, falling, but she couldn't make a sound. And over the chaos, over the rush of blood in her ears and the shrieking in her heart and whatever small, clawed beast was tearing up her insides, they *just—kept—talking*.

"That unfortunately makes sense," said Vegard. "Aurel killed your father because of the curse. If the curse had never existed, he wouldn't have done that. But no magic can bring someone back to life, so the spell simply pretended he never existed—"

"My father's not dead."

The words came out of her in a whisper. Vegard broke off, staring at her.

"Ida . . ." Lenore began.

"My father's not dead!" Ida snatched her hand back from Lenore, getting to her feet. The table banged her shins as she stood, a sharp flash of pain, and it rattled her cup, spilling hot tea across the wooden surface. Her candle fell over, rolling into the plate of pastries.

Ida couldn't care less. She wanted everything to spill, everything to *break*. "He's *not*!"

"Ida, listen—" Vegard's hand closed around her wrist. Ida was used to Vegard's touch burning, but she didn't feel the bite this time. She yanked her hand out of his grasp and Vegard flinched, pulling away from her as if he'd been burned instead.

"Don't touch me!"

Her skin was buzzing, energy bubbling just beneath the surface. She had never wished until then that her magic was the type that could be brought into the physical world, that could affect corporeal reality. She wanted to let her magic pour out of her, let it crash into the walls and smash open the windows and bring Asteria down.

Ida forced a breath deep into her lungs, tried to fight through the waves of panic and anger. It was like trying to claw her way out from under a stack of thick blankets. They were pressing down on her, smothering her. She grasped at any shred of rational thought she could find. "He's—he's just lost. Like the tower. Something went wrong with the spell, and he never made it over to this reality."

Lenore's face fell, and Ida *knew* that she didn't believe it. Ida hated her for it then. The feeling was like a punch to the gut, knocking all the wind out of her.

"Ida, given what we saw, it's highly unlikely that he—that anyone could have survived."

"Vegard did." Ida's voice was coming out in quick breaths, desperate and pleading. "Your father did. There has to be a way."

They were both staring at her now, with eyes so full of pity, so full of regret. She didn't *want* their pity. She didn't want their regret.

She wanted them to say they believed her. That they would *help* her.

It was what she would have done for either of them.

But they didn't. They watched her with those pitying eyes, and they didn't move, didn't say another word, even when her vision blurred with tears.

When Lenore reached out to touch her arm, Ida pushed her hand away.

"I have to go," she said, her voice thick in her ears. "I have work to do."

She didn't wait to hear what either of them had to say, didn't give them the chance to try to stop her. She walked over to the door, pushing her way out into the corridors, and gasped in a breath of cool air. Then she started to walk, striding through the halls with single-minded determination.

The castle felt like it was closing in on her. The noise from the Revel—already well underway—filled the corridors. It made Ida sick. The sound of laughter, the sound of music—what were they laughing for? What were they dancing for?

She saw very few people on her walk, and didn't acknowledge those she did see. She didn't stop until she reached her room, until she pushed open the plain, narrow door that led to her bedchamber and found Sabine inside, making her bed.

"Oh, Mistress Ida," Sabine said, her back turned toward Ida as she worked. "You have another commission from the king."

"Yes, thank you, Sabine." The words came out of Ida's mouth without her having to think of them. The envelope on her desk taunted her. Heavy paper, sealed with the king's crest. The highest honor an Arreden artisan could ever receive—to be appointed to serve the king. It had made Ida proud once. "I'll get started on it right away."

Sabine nodded, humming to herself as Ida picked up the envelope and moved around her to pass through the door to her workshop. She didn't know how she managed it. To keep a straight face, to keep the pain out of her voice until the workshop door was closed behind her, until Ida was finally, finally alone.

She crumpled up the royal letter in her hand, tossing it against the workshop wall with as much force as she could manage.

And then she dropped down to the ground, buried her face in her knees, and let herself cry.

Chapter 24

A DOSE OF POISON

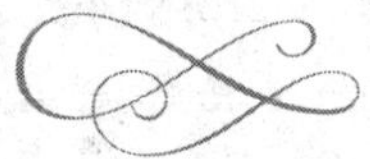

"Hmm . . ."

Ida fought not to fidget as Celeste frowned at the candle resting on the countertop, her eyes moving from it to Ida and back again. She had worked hard over the past two days to finish this candle, to rid herself of her obligation to Celeste once and for all so she could focus on finding her father, on finding out the truth, and be done with this cursed place. She'd walked into Celeste's rooms thinking this would be it, but instead of thanking her, Celeste didn't seem pleased.

Ida fought down a sense of irritation, wishing Celeste would just get on with it. She was so tired. Her limbs felt like they were weighed down with lead. Over the past few days since her return from Vegard's rooms, she'd hardly slept.

She let Celeste study the candle, her eyes moving toward a splash of scarlet paint on Celeste's countertop. She wondered how long that had been there.

"It's . . . good," Celeste said finally. "But I don't believe this is your best work, Ida."

Ida's head snapped up, her gaze fixing on Celeste. "What do you mean? It's a candle crafted specifically for you. It works just like I intended. What else do you *want*?"

She heard the petulant edge creeping into her tone and clenched her hands into fists, fighting down a wave of shame. She had worked *hard* on that candle. She'd used every technique she had learned during her ill-fated adventure with Vegard and Lenore. She'd created a candle that let Celeste project her own illusions, giving her imagination *life*. How could it not be enough?

Celeste seemed unfazed by Ida's outburst. She cupped her chin in her hand, looking at the candle. "It's true that it does what you intend," she said, after a long pause. "And it's true that I'll be able to find some use for it. But I don't need a candle that shows me *my* imagination, Ida. I wanted a candle that shows me *yours*. Your artistic soul. Something that took *risks*, that you've never done before."

Ida wanted to scream. Take *risks*? Hadn't she taken enough risks already? Her *risks* had cost her everything: her freedom, her family, and the friendship of the only two people in Asteria who understood her. Wasn't that *enough*?

"I *can't*," Ida said. "This is my best work, Celeste. Take it or leave it."

"I'm happy to accept *this* candle, of course," said Celeste. "I'm sure it will help me visualize my next piece. But I'll pay you for it, one artist to another. Name your price."

Ida forced down her frustration, her embarrassment. She didn't want to name her price, didn't want to be paid. She wanted to be *done*. To not have her promise to Celeste weighing down on her when she was trying to find out the truth about what happened to her father.

"I can't take your money—"

"Of course you can," said Celeste, already reaching across the worktable for her coin purse. She pulled a heavy gold coin out of the purse, setting it on the countertop. It was more money than Ida had seen at once, but her eyes were fixed on the face staring up from the table at her. King Aurel in profile.

She couldn't get him out of her head. King Aurel, his hand in her father's hair, forcing his face into the light.

"Ida?" Celeste asked. "Are you all right? You look like you've seen a ghost."

Ida blinked, snatching the coin up from the table with entirely too much force. "I'm fine," she said, tucking it into her pocket where it could no longer look at her, where it could no longer make her *remember*. "Nothing to worry about. I'll make you a new candle."

When, she didn't know. She had another royal commission—a task she'd rescued from the crumpled ball she'd made of it. The last thing she wanted to do was work on another candle for *him*, another commission where she had to channel magic through her fingertips and make pretty scenes and pretend that she didn't *know* the truth.

This King Aurel didn't even remember what he had done. That didn't make him any less complicit, but what was Ida going to do in the face of a monarch?

If she thought about this too much, she was going to start crying again, and she couldn't afford tears. She swallowed hard against the knot in her throat, looking back at Celeste. "I'll think of something else. Something . . . riskier."

"I'm looking forward to it," Celeste said. She looked concerned. "Try not to be too worried, Ida. Creative blocks happen to everyone. I have every confidence that you'll find your way out of this eventually."

Ida wasn't quite so hopeful. Celeste might think this was a creative block, but Ida knew that it was something different. It was the nightmares that kept her up at night, the exhaustion dogging her every step as she tried to get through her day. Her magic, which now felt like a chore, like a tool in her arsenal to find what really mattered.

To find her father.

That was *all* she cared about. She didn't care about this commission, not truly. She wanted it *out of her way*. But now that Celeste wasn't happy with it, now that Celeste was demanding more from her, she just wanted to scream. She had *no idea* what to do, to find her father, *or* to please Celeste. She had already stretched her magic to its limits, shattering the boundaries she had once placed on her art. And now Celeste was asking for more risks. What other risks could she *take*?

The answer came to her slowly, an idea breaking through the mire her thoughts were trapped in. She sat up straight, her eyes widening. Up until this point, she had pushed boundaries with the mechanics of her magic, true, but had barely scratched the surface of taking risks with her ingredients. The blood of other mages and the dreaming elixir were *unconventional* ingredients, to be sure, but they were applied with a logic that any mage could easily follow. Someone else had enchanted the dreaming elixir—Ida had only taken advantage of their hard work. And blood was well known to be a potent source of magic.

What she had in mind would raise some eyebrows. It was definitely more reckless than anything Ida had ever tried. A risk in every meaning of the word.

But would it work?

Celeste smiled at her expression. "See?" she asked. "You have an idea already, don't you? I can tell."

"I have to go," Ida said, scrambling off of her seat. "There's something I want to try. Thank you, Celeste."

And this time, she meant it.

Celeste seemed rather self-satisfied as Ida rushed out of her workshop, back to her own world, but her commission was the farthest thing from Ida's mind. Ida thought only of her plans, the idea just starting to take shape in her mind: a recipe for a candle that would show her, once and for all, what had *really* happened that night in the tower.

"Mistress Ida, are you quite sure about this?"

It was odd for Steward Dallenbach to come see her, odder still for him to come to her door with her last requisition slip in his hand, brow creased in worry. Her agreement with the king meant that she could request whatever she wanted, and she'd asked for quite a few strange things over the course of her tenure here. No one had ever questioned her.

Ida knew, from the way the steward watched her now, that she had finally found the limit of His Majesty's largesse.

"I need it for a research project," Ida said. "I have an idea for how to improve my technique."

"But nightflower is—" Dallenbach's eyes moved from her to the scrap of paper in his hand and back again.

"A poison, I know," Ida said. "I'm not planning to eat it."

Steward Dallenbach didn't look convinced. That didn't surprise her. He was still in charge of managing a royal court, and kings didn't generally feel comfortable with deadly poisons on the premises.

"I'm trying to play with the effects of sleep," Ida said. "I was inspired by the Dreaming Revel. Nightflower is an extremely powerful sedative." That was true enough.

"Then surely you can use any other sedative."

"I've tried others," Ida said. "They aren't potent enough. Once they're mixed in with the rest of the ingredients, they lose their charm." She sighed. "Look, I know how unorthodox this is. I promise to be *very* careful. I only need one bloom, and I promise not to let it out of my sight."

Dallenbach hesitated. For a moment, Ida worried that he would refuse, that he would look at her and see what Celeste had so clearly seen the other day, that Ida was at the end of her rope.

But for good or ill, he didn't know her as well as Celeste did.

He glanced once more at the sheet of paper in his hand, nodded solemnly, and said, "Very well, I'll hold you to that."

The nightflower appeared in her workshop the next day, a single white blossom in a sealed glass vial. It came with a note detailing the properties of the flower, a reminder—in Steward Dallenbach's harsh handwriting—that every part of the blossom was extremely toxic, that even the pollen could kill her. It also came with Sabine's strong disapproval. The maid fixed her with an iron glare as Ida stared at the flower.

"I'm a court artisan, Sabine," Ida said. "I'm allowed to experiment."

"And if your experiments strike you dead or worse, what then?"

"I'll be careful."

"I'm sure you will," said Sabine. "But you've said it yourself—you don't always know what your magic will do."

Ida tried to give Sabine some grace. She tried to remind herself that Sabine was just doing what she thought was best for her, that Sabine was trying to look out for her in her own way.

But all she felt was irritation at Sabine nagging her, at yet another person telling her she didn't know enough.

"I know what I'm doing," she said, turning away. Sabine said nothing as Ida started opening cabinets and taking down tools, making a neat pile of bowls, vials, and instruments in preparation. Ida could still feel her standing there, watching her judgmentally, but Sabine didn't respond. The silence stretched on for long enough that Ida began to think Sabine had given up, that Ida had won.

But then Sabine spoke up on her way out the door, and what she said made Ida want to scream.

"I can't believe I'm saying this, mistress. But I miss your friends."

Vegard and Lenore were the last people Ida wanted to see.

She hadn't quite decided what she would do if she ran into them, somewhere in Asteria. On one level, she missed them terribly. She found herself sitting at her writing desk in the middle of the night, composing the beginnings of several letters. But she crossed out each one before she could write more than a few lines, crumpling the paper and tossing it below her desk until it seemed like the floor of her bedroom had accumulated a snowfall, a thousand frustrations scattered where they could never hurt her.

She missed their company, their closeness. She wanted to speak to them again.

But when she did, she didn't know what she would do.

She ran into Lenore only once, at a Revel. She had just finished going through the motions of an illusion, conjuring up a woodland scene. She could tell that her heart wasn't in it, that she was distracted, but thankfully, her magic wasn't the centerpiece of the night's festivities. She was only meant to add ambiance, to bring a summer's day to a winter night so that the king's other performers could dazzle the attendees with their arts.

It was as she was turning to leave that she heard someone call her name. She froze, because she recognized that voice, and the sound of it made her heart seize up, made her feel as if the room had lost all its air.

"Ida, please? I just want to talk."

Lenore's voice was so soft, so sweet, so uncommonly uncertain. The expression on her face was tentative, hesitant. She looked like she was hurting, and that made Ida feel like something was clawing her up from the inside.

She wanted to talk to Lenore. She couldn't.

Ida walked briskly toward the exit, swallowing hard against the lump in her throat. She pretended she hadn't heard, hadn't seen the way Lenore looked at her, but both she and Lenore knew it was a lie. Lenore continued to call for her, and Ida practically ran away.

Neither of them tried to contact her after that.

Now, as Ida stood alone in her workshop, holding death in her hand, she found herself thinking back to that moment, to her reaction. To her conversation with Celeste, and the resolve she had found.

She had to do this first. To understand what had really happened to her father.

To find out if he was alive, or . . .

She couldn't even think of the alternative. But she had to know. Only then would she be able to face Lenore.

Before Ida could incorporate the nightflower into a candle, she had to reduce it down into something soluble, something she could infuse into wax. Given the plant's toxic properties, she also had to do this without killing herself. If Ida had been at home, in her mother's workshop with the small handful of tools that she'd been allowed to use, she never would have attempted it. But she was the Court Luminaire, with all the resources of Arred at her disposal, and her time as luminaire had taught her how to handle dangerous substances. She made a few inquiries and received permission from the royal physician to use his laboratory.

The physician had a workbench that was uniquely suited to her purpose, because it had been engineered so that air flowed away from her, rather than toward her. A sheet of glass separated her from the main body of the bench, with just enough open space at the bottom for her to reach her hands through. This, according to the physician, would protect her from any untoward vapors, but Ida was extra careful. She wrapped cloth tightly around her nose and mouth to keep her from inhaling any pollen, and when the physician found out what she wanted to do, he lent her gloves, a heavy coat with a vaguely chemical smell, and a pair of heavy goggles for her eyes.

When she was finished, she felt a little like a doll wrapped in cotton, but no part of her skin was exposed to the air, and she felt protected enough to carefully slide the nightflower behind the glass and uncap the vial. It rested at the bottom of a bowl, a seemingly innocent white bloom beginning to wilt around the edges.

Normally, she would grind her herbs to better release their oils and scents, but that felt like tempting fate with this blossom. So instead, she used tweezers to carefully pry two petals and one pistil from the flower, laying them in the bottom of her bowl, and placed the rest of the flower back into the vial.

She was left with two petals and a dash of pollen. If the stories about nightflower were to be believed, that would be enough for a handful of murders. On top of those, she poured a little of the oil she used to capture scent and put the bowl over a fire. She spent the whole evening waiting, sweating, in the doctor's laboratory, not wanting to take her eyes off the solution for a second, and after several hours, strained out what was left of the petals and collected the oil.

She was just cleaning up when the doctor appeared over her shoulder, squinting at her work from behind his thick, round glasses.

"You know," he said, "it's quite remarkable what you're doing. I've always been of the belief that it's the dose that makes the poison. Some of what we've considered toxic substances are medicinal, when applied at the right concentrations and under the watch of a trained physician."

Ida was tired, sweaty, and wanted nothing more than to finish for the day and get started on her candle tomorrow, but the doctor had been kind enough to let her hang around his office for hours, so she offered him a smile. "I'm hoping I can dilute it down so that it has a sedative effect. Something strong enough to immediately transport someone into a dream."

"I wasn't aware you needed such things," the doctor said. "From what I've seen, your illusions work well enough awake."

"Yes, but they aren't as immersive that way. People still know they're viewing an illusion. They don't think that what they're seeing is reality."

"And is that what you want to do, then?" the doctor asked. "Make someone believe that something that isn't real, is?"

He frowned at Ida. Was that suspicion in his eyes? Ida tried not to fidget.

"I'm trying to capture the feeling of being in a dream. Where you think that anything can happen." She saw that the doctor was still unconvinced, and so told the story she had been telling since Steward Dallenbach first showed up at her rooms, demanding to know what she wanted to do with poison. "I've been inspired by the Dreaming Revel. There are so many things my illusions can't do. I can't make someone fly, for instance. I can only make them feel like they're flying."

"And what dreams would you show someone? Only good dreams, I hope."

Ida tried not to think about her father, tried not to think about that terrible scene at the top of the missing tower where everything had gone so horribly wrong.

"Of course, Lord Doctor. Only good dreams."

By the time she made it back to her workshop, dawn was filtering in through the windowpanes and Ida was exhausted. She stayed awake long enough to strip out of her clothes and leave them in a burlap sack for Sabine to take to the specialized cleaners the doctor had suggested, and to stand shivering in the servants' bath and pour a few buckets of water over her head to make sure that no pollen remained anywhere on her. Then, dressed in her oldest and most comfortable nightgown, she trudged back to her room and went straight to sleep.

The next night, she went to work.

She melted wax on her hearth and added to it the same potent mixture of blood, elixir, and silver that had taken them past the veil of secrecy surrounding the castle and into the truth. Then, she added two more ingredients—iron shavings, carefully scraped from the bottom corner of her father's firestrike, and a single drop of nightflower oil. The combination turned the wax a shade of violet, like the deep velvet of a moonless night.

If this didn't show her where her father was, nothing would.

The candle required a night to set. Ida always left her spells to cure before she tested them, but it had been a while since any of her magic had left her as impatient as this. When she finished dipping the tapers, she'd left them on the rack to dry, their slender forms still hanging by their wicks from the rods she used for them. It was so tempting to take one and burn it immediately, to see what she had done.

But that wouldn't do. Ida had only a handful of chances at this.

If the magic went wrong, there was no guarantee she would be able to try again.

The next day, she rose, bathed in the Knights' Bath and ate breakfast without speaking to anyone, then went back to her workshop, locked the door behind her, and took down one of the candles.

She studied it, feeling the interplay of Vegard's and Lenore's magic against her own. The memory of what they had created together was at the forefront of her mind, and if Lenore and Vegard were here, she was sure they would be angry at her for using their gifts the way she had. She was tempted to call them, to summon Gloam and tell them to bring her friends here immediately. She would tell Vegard and Lenore how sorry she was for the way she had treated them, would explain that she had been under a lot of stress. She would remind them how much she missed her father, and how much the vision they witnessed had distressed her. And she would ask them to help her with this, just one more time. To help her see if . . .

But that was where her mind ground to a halt. That *if.*

If what? Because if she called Vegard and Lenore here, if she invited them to her workshop and tried to make peace with them, it would be tantamount to admitting that what they had said to her was possible.

That her father really was—

Ida flicked open her father's firestrike, touching a tongue of fire to the candle's wick.

It happened so suddenly, from one indrawn breath to another. Ida stared at the lit flame, at the fire in her hand. She hadn't really intended—she hadn't been thinking at all. But before she could even stop to think about what she had done, the magic hit her like a wave. It crashed over her, dragging her under, and Ida had one last thought, a sudden note of panic that she had *locked herself in her office alone*, before the world blacked out.

Chapter 25

THE OTHER SIDE OF THE LIE

Ida felt like she was falling through time and space, like she was dreaming again, except this time, Vegard and Lenore weren't there to catch her. She tumbled end over end through a dizzying void and tried to grab at the illusion, tried to pull it from something formless into something with shape and meaning, but it was like trying to grab smoke. Her body felt heavy, weighed down as surely as if she were buried deep under the earth.

The nightflower. The single drop she'd infused the candles with. It dulled her senses, so that she couldn't take control of the dreaming. She realized with a growing horror that she was going to drown. She believed it so strongly that it felt like her lungs were burning, crying out for air.

And then she surfaced, but the place she found herself standing in didn't look like it belonged to any world.

She stood in a narrow strip of darkness between the wreckage of two large mirrors. Through the shards of the mirror on her right, she saw Asteria as it was, saw the court of the Night King awash in glory, magic, and power. And through the panes of the mirror on her left, she could see . . . something else. Dusty halls draped in black, empty except for the occasional scurrying rat. Sunlight gleaming through high windows. A young woman Ida didn't recognize dressed in an expensive black gown, a crown on her head and a scepter in her hands. A casket being led through the streets of Trissaire, draped in flowers and banners, flanked by horses and soldiers, draped in the royal banner of Arred.

Fragments of both mirrors sparkled on the ground at her feet, so intertwined that it was hard for Ida to move for fear of catching her foot on one of them. As she watched the mirrors, she understood that she was looking at two different realities. The world on the left was the world that they would have been living in, had King Aurel not done what he had done. It was a world where the king had succumbed to his curse and his pride, a world where Aurel died and the crown princess succeeded him as Queen of Arred. A world where the Night King's Court and all of its wonders had never come to fruition, where Asteria remained unfinished in the mountains. It was the world Ida had found herself in, the night of her first performance as Court Luminaire.

The second world, the one on her right, was the world she lived in now.

Vegard and Lenore had been right about one thing—Aurel's spell had propelled them into a different reality. But what were they supposed to do from here?

She hesitated and then reached out, resting her fingers lightly on the surface of the glass to her left. It felt cool under her fingertips, like ordinary glass. But as her fingers came to rest on the pane, the glass that surrounded her glowed briefly, its surface clouding over and shining with golden light.

When the light settled, Ida saw herself.

Not as she was now, but as Court Luminaire. In her workshop, in the palace halls and ballrooms, in the chandler's studio that belonged to her mother. She saw herself as she remembered, a child in Trissaire, running across the carpet of their apartment, saw herself with her father. She saw herself following her mother onto a Trissaire train for the last time, saw the way she cried as the train left Trissaire for the countryside. She saw herself studying magic, looking through dusty notes and trying to reconstruct everything her father had left her, his only legacy a few notebooks and a handful of fractured memories.

And on her left . . .

On her left, another reality.

She saw herself as she was now, but she wasn't in Asteria. Neither was she in the mountains, elbowing for space with her cousins and trying to ignore her grandmother's pointed barbs. She was sitting at the window of their old apartment in Trissaire, sipping coffee from a chipped cup at a round wooden table she didn't recognize. She was dressed fashionably, like a girl from the city, in a long skirt of a deep red color and a white ruffled blouse, her wavy dark hair pinned out of her face. She was reading a book and she looked . . .

Ida couldn't describe how she looked.

Her eyes were solemn, less bright, not as animated as her eyes on the right. But there was a lightness to her that Ida didn't understand, as if the world didn't sit quite so heavily on her shoulders. As she flipped a page, she smiled.

This must have been an Ida whose father was still with her, but even as the thought occurred to her, the images on the left changed. They showed a young Ida dressed in black, crying with her mother beside a grave. They showed a casket and mourners standing in the rain. They showed Ida's mother slumped over the old table in the Trissaire apartment, her head in her hands, a crumpled telegram beside her. They showed a portrait in the living room of Tomas Rosales standing proud, dressed as a Court Luminaire.

Ida jerked away from the images, crashing into the mirror behind her. Glass cut her, piercing through cloth and skin, but Ida barely noticed as she shoved fragments aside in her haste to get away. That couldn't be real. She would never believe it. There could *never be* a world where her father had died and Ida would be sitting at the kitchen table reading a book and smiling. Those things could *never be*, not in any reality.

She stumbled and fell, tumbling backward through shards. As she fell, the glass vanished, winking out of existence and leaving her in the dark again. She landed on something hard and sat there for a moment, her head spinning, the cuts on her arms and legs stinging. Blood stained the fabric of her clothes, a warmth she could feel but not see.

She sat there, shivering, her legs pulled up close to her chest. It took Ida a while to master herself, to remember that what she was seeing and feeling was an illusion, no matter how real it felt. She willed the cuts on her body to fade, willed herself to remember that this was only a dream, that she was master of her own illusions. But nothing happened. The space remained dark, and Ida continued to bleed.

The depth of her arrogance was just beginning to dawn on her. Her body was alone, in a workshop with a locked door, and her mind was trapped in a dream she couldn't control. Her heart started pounding, breaths coming shallowly in her chest. If she couldn't get out of here—if she stayed sleeping forever—

It would be what she deserved. She pressed her forehead to her knees, feeling as if the darkness around her had weight, resting on her shoulders, pushing her into the ground. She felt tears prick at her eyes and sniffed, wiping them away with her hands. The last thing she needed to do was panic.

She remembered her father, his hands over hers, teaching her how to create her first illusions out of scent and smoke, guiding her through her first wavering dreams, the way he'd held her to him when those dreams had become nightmares.

"You are the master of the dream, Ida," her father had said, holding her close as she trembled and shook and cried. *"The dream belongs to you. If you let yourself be scared of the dream, it will become a nightmare. But if you remember that you're in control, that nothing can take that control from you, you can do wonders. Remember that."*

Wonders.

Ida clenched her hands into tight fists, forcing herself to her feet. That was it, wasn't it? At the end of the day, it was still her dream, and if she let herself be afraid, it would only show her things that made her afraid. Things like her father dying in another world. Like the person she had become without him.

She choked down the bile that threatened to rise into her throat, facing the darkness.

"Show me my father."

Her voice echoed in the space, and something shattered, bursting to life around her. The mirror shards came back, but this time they filled every open space, so that Ida was standing in the center of a world of crystal and light, reflections shimmering in every direction. And in each mirror, she saw her father. A hundred versions of him, a thousand. Her father as Court Luminaire, her father at home with her and her mother, her father sitting in Vegard's room with that haggard expression, eyes fixed on the distance as he talked about Lenore and what the king would do. There were visions she had never seen before, images she would never have been able to see. Her father at King Aurel's side, her father entertaining the king's guests with magic, her father walking a mountain trail in the daylight, the unfinished construction site of Asteria behind him as he took deep breaths of cool air. There were even images of her father on the deck of a ship, the ocean's endless blue spread out before him, images of her father not much older than she was now, in an unfamiliar house with unfamiliar people who looked just like him. Images of her father in a marketplace, on a street, kneeling before an older woman with graying hair that Ida realized with an aching sense of familiarity was her grandmother, and pressing the back of her hand to his forehead while she cried.

But every vision of her father was old. Every vision of her father showed him in the past, before that terrible moment in the tower, before he seemingly vanished from existence. Fear coiled tight around Ida's chest, a snake wrapped around her heart. She could still hear Vegard's and Lenore's words—those terrible, terrible words.

Your father might be . . .

"Show me my father *now*," Ida demanded.

The visions vanished at once, leaving Ida in that darkness again, that void.

Ida wanted to scream.

She choked it back down. In this place, in this dream, the last thing she wanted to do was give it a reason to change, to show her something that might not be true.

Ida reached out, feeling the space beside her. She was surrounded by solid objects, cool to the touch, like glass beneath her palms. She breathed out, laying her hand flat against the surface. The mirrors hadn't vanished. They'd simply gone dark. Maybe her father was in a place much like the one she stood in now, a place without any light. Maybe the mirrors couldn't show him to her, because he was lost between dimensions.

Maybe Ida simply wasn't asking the right questions.

"Show me where my father went," she said, "after his confrontation with King Aurel."

The world exploded back into light. Every mirror showed the same image now, a blinding light that made Ida feel sick to look at. It wasn't a stationary light. It wasn't simply bright. There were patches of gray and silver in the light that shifted in a sinuous, undulating pattern, as if everything around her was spinning and moving. She swallowed against a wave of nausea and squeezed her eyes shut, but it was as if the light was a living thing, as if it could seep beneath her eyelids. She choked back bile and forced herself to open her eyes, to look into the light.

It was like looking into infinity. The more Ida stared into the light, the more she felt like the air was being sucked out of her throat, like she couldn't breathe. It was beautiful and terrible and it stole everything from her. She stood in the light until she couldn't bear it anymore and said, voice hoarse and close to breaking: "Stop."

The world came to a sudden halt, all the lights winking out at once and leaving Ida in the sweet dark once more.

She gasped for breath, resting one hand on the closest mirror as she doubled over. The space was completely black, so dark Ida couldn't see her hand in front of her face, but the light still flashed before her eyes. It was horrifying and all-consuming and somehow she just knew, *knew* that if she had been doing more than simply observing, if she had been in the currents of those lights, being swept away by them to parts unknown, she would never find her way out again.

It was a violent light, a killing light.

No.

She bit her lip, fighting back a growing despair. No. That couldn't have been the right place, the place her father had gone. Or maybe it wasn't as bad as she had imagined it. Maybe her father, with his greater knowledge of magic, with his skill, would have survived where she could not imagine surviving.

Maybe, maybe, maybe—

"Again," Ida said, voice hoarse.

The light started again, and this time it felt like it was flaying her apart, ripping at her from the inside. She closed her eyes against the intensity, peered at the light through the gap between her eyelids, twisted herself this way and that as she tried to find some shelter, some place where the light was weakest, where a human being with enough power could find their way through. She could find nothing. The light was relentless. Endless.

"Show me how this would have looked to my father."

The light didn't change. It didn't even diminish in brilliance. Ida steeled herself, opening her eyes and giving the room a quick look, but there was nothing. No shelter, no easing of the onslaught, no escape. No turning back. And her father wouldn't have had as much time as she did now. He wouldn't have had the luxury of distance, of being able to stop and consider his next move. He would have had moments, mere moments to save himself.

Her heart was hammering so quickly behind her ribs that it

felt like something else, something that wasn't part of her. Like it belonged to someone else. Hot tears pricked her eyes and she wanted to throw up, but no, no, no, this couldn't be right, this couldn't be where it ended—

"Show me where this *ends*!" she screamed. "Show me what's on the other side!"

The mirrors exploded outward, shards of glass bursting one after another with a noise like cannon fire. Large shards flew inward, piercing skin, impaling her, and Ida had half a second to comprehend what she had done, what she had asked, what was *happening* to her before she was falling to her knees, eyes wide, the feeling lost in her fingers—

"—*Ida*—Mistress Ida—"

Ida groaned, trying to open her eyes, but her vision wouldn't focus. The world was a wash of colors and haze, and none of it made any sense. It felt like she was burning. Her skin ached where her clothes touched it, and she wanted to scream, but all she could manage was a whimper.

There were people around her, voices. She tried to focus on what they were saying, but it was like each voice slithered out of her grasp before she could take hold of it. Words passed through her mind, but they lost all their meaning. A cool hand touched her cheek, and the contrast to her heated skin was a pleasant pain.

". . . burning up . . ." one of the voices said.

". . . doctor . . ." said another.

"No time," said a third, and Ida saw a blurry figure lean forward, pressing a thumb to her forehead. Cold radiated through her, making her gasp and arch her back, quenching the flames and pulling the world into sharp focus. Ida had half a moment to register the inexplicability of Vegard crouched over her, framed in the absolute ruin of her door, his eyes shining, before Lenore pulled his hand away and instead of burning, Ida was shivering, a great full-body chill that racked her frame and made her curl up into herself, desperate for warmth.

"See what you did?" Lenore's voice asked, but then the hand was back on her forehead, and this time the touch was uncomfortable. She flinched away from it, crying out, but the person touching her wouldn't be deterred.

"No, her temperature's better," the voice said. Female, older, with a touch of impatience. *Sabine.* "Help me carry her to bed."

Hands came to either side of her, lifting her up. Ida wanted to protest, to say that she would be fine in a moment, that she didn't need or want them to fuss over her, but she couldn't move, and her protests came out as incomprehensible murmurs as they carried her into the next room and let her tumble down onto her bed.

When her body hit the mattress, Ida forgot about her protests and blacked out, falling into a mercifully dreamless sleep.

Chapter 26

FEVER DREAM

Ida was coming apart at the seams.

She felt as if she were drowning, caught in a violent current. The water would push her under, holding her beneath the depths, and she would claw her way to the surface, gasping for air. But the water never stopped running, never stopped moving, and no matter how hard Ida fought to stay up, to *breathe*, the water pulled her down again.

When she surfaced, she would be lying in her bed, blankets rumpled around her limbs, sweat soaking through her clothes. Sometimes, it would be dark. Sometimes, the thick shades drawn over her windows would be open to let in the morning light. Sometimes she would be alone. Sometimes Sabine would be with her. One time, she swore she heard Lenore and Gloam, speaking over her, before the dark closed over her head again.

And then there were the dreams.

They haunted her, dreams of funerals and tears, of ruins and graves. Each time she surfaced, she always tried to hold on to reality, but it seemed determined to escape her. No matter how hard Ida fought, how much she tried to remain on the surface, she drowned anyway.

When she finally found herself tossed onto the shore, gasping for breath and fully aware, it was nighttime. She was alone in her bedroom, lying in the middle of sweat-soaked sheets. Her limbs felt heavy, weighted. She raised one hand a few inches off the covers before letting it flop dejectedly back down beside her.

When consciousness no longer tried to flee from her, Ida took stock of herself. She had the weak, hollowed-out feeling of someone who had been sick for a long time. Her throat was dry, her lips chapped. She no longer felt feverish, but it was as if she had been reduced down to skin and bones. And although she had been sleeping for gods only knew how long, she was exhausted.

The door to her room swung open. Ida turned to watch as Sabine came in, balancing a basin of water against her hip. Her eyes met Ida's, and she didn't look particularly worried, or surprised to see her up. They hardened, and Ida would have flinched if she had the energy.

"Well," Sabine said. "You're awake. Do you remember who you are?"

Ida tried to say *yes* but her mouth was so dry that no sound came out. She tried again and managed to croak out the word.

"No permanent damage, then." Sabine walked over to Ida's bedside, setting the basin down and putting her hand on Ida's forehead. Her touch was warm, but the warmth no longer felt like pain. "And your fever's gone as well. That's good. I suppose you've learned your lesson?"

"What happened?"

Sabine's lips pressed tightly together in disapproval, and Ida was afraid Sabine would start with a lecture. But apparently seeing that Ida was in no state to bear one, Sabine held back for now.

"Lady Lenore found you," Sabine said. "She's connected to those . . . spirits, the ones His Majesty uses to show guests around the castle. Somehow, she realized you needed help. She and—and Vegard"—here, Sabine hesitated on the name—"came to fetch me. As soon as we noticed your workshop door was locked, we knew something had gone wrong. But we didn't have the key. We caused some damage. I'm sorry about that."

Sabine didn't sound sorry. Ida's eyes moved from her to her workshop door, now a blank space covered by a canvas tarp.

"Vegard did something to open the door," Sabine said. "He broke it open, with his magic. And we found you lying on the floor." Sabine paused, and Ida wondered what it had looked like, what pathetic figure she had cut, lying on the ground, writhing.

"You . . . weren't yourself. You were burning with fever, delirious . . . we all thought you had poisoned yourself. And your candle . . ." She gestured with both hands, grasping in the air, trying to act out something that Ida only registered as frightening.

"Can you show me?"

Sabine picked her way around the canvas tarp and stepped into the workshop, coming out with a wooden box held in both hands. She touched it very lightly, as though it contained a venomous serpent. There was something magical inside the box, an aura so confused and tangled that it was difficult to parse. It made her start to feel nauseous again. She swallowed hard and carefully lifted the lid with both hands.

Her nightflower candle, the one she had spent days crafting, was a charred and melted heap in the center of the box. Wax had pooled in rivulets around the candle's body and base, then hardened again so that the entire piece looked shapeless. The wick was a ruin, blackened and scarred, the wax around the candle pitted with gray ash. A faint floral scent was rising from the box, making Ida's eyelids feel heavy again. She shut it in alarm, pushing the box away from herself.

"Put it back in the workshop and don't touch it," she told Sabine. "Ask the doctor how best to dispose of it. I'm not sure it's safe to be around."

Sabine nodded tersely but hurried to do as she was told. As she went, Ida burrowed deeper into her blankets and tried to breathe under the weight of her failure. An illegal substance obtained at great personal and professional cost, a risk to her life and the lives of anyone who might have come into that room after her, and for what?

She still hadn't found her father. She hadn't found anything useful at all.

She waited for Sabine to return, trying to make sense of what she had seen. That space between dimensions, the thing that happened after. When she thought about it, she could still feel shards of glass piercing her body, still felt like she should be covered in blood, dying on the ground.

Dying.

Ida squeezed her eyes shut at the thought, clutching her blankets tight in her fists. She could still hear Lenore's voice ringing in her mind.

Your father might be . . .

There had to be something else. There *had* to be. Some other truth, some other answer. Something Ida hadn't yet been able to find.

Her father couldn't be *dead.* Maybe—maybe he was dead in *this world*, the world the king's spell had taken them to. Maybe he was alive somewhere else, in some other reality.

Maybe, maybe, maybe.

The sound of water running in the next room made her open her eyes. When she came back, Sabine was drying her hands on her skirts. The skin was pink, like she had scrubbed them many times.

"Steward Dallenbach isn't happy with you, you know," Sabine said.

Ida found it difficult to care exactly what Steward Dallenbach thought of her at that moment. She found it difficult to care about anything.

"So?"

"You might be a little more concerned. He's planning to write a report to the king."

Ida ran her finger over the top of her sheets and tried to divine exactly how she felt about that. If Steward Dallenbach's complaints reached the king and he decided to throw her out of Asteria, she would leave, but without her magic. Even as exhausted as she was, the thought of going home without her magic filled her with a creeping, all-consuming dread. Her magic had been with her her whole life. It was more than a tool for her. It made her feel *alive.* A world without magic was like imagining a world without color.

And on the practical side of things, without magic, what would she do? How would she survive?

With magic, at least Ida was special. *Unique.* Without magic, she was just a half-Niresso, not-quite-Arreden nobody from a small town in the hills.

It made her want to toss all the sheets off the bed and scream. She forced herself to think calmly, to think past the fear and rage. There had to be a way out of this.

"How long was I sick?" she asked Sabine.

"Four days," Sabine said, which explained the weakness in her limbs, the emptiness in her stomach. Four days was bad, but she hadn't missed a deadline. She could still finish her work in time for the king's next celebration. Professionally, her position as a luminaire was safe.

If Steward Dallenbach wasn't about to blow her career out of the water.

"Isn't there any way to stop the steward?"

"I'm afraid not," said Sabine. "He thinks you've been reckless. Dangerously so." The way Sabine said it made it clear that she agreed with that assessment. "He thinks that His Majesty ought to know, especially since you're still in your probationary period."

"What do you think will happen to me when Steward Dallenbach informs the king?"

Sabine frowned at her, but said, "I suppose His Majesty will invite you to an audience. You'll have a chance to explain yourself."

An audience with the king was out of the question. The way she was now, Ida had no idea what she might do, the things she might say. And this version of King Aurel had *no* idea what had happened to her father. She would only end up sounding unhinged.

Ida chewed her lip, considering her options. She needed more time. Maybe there was something she hadn't considered, a problem with the spell, something she could fix. She couldn't leave Asteria yet, and she couldn't have the king's eyes on her.

"What can I do?" she asked Sabine.

Sabine fixed Ida with a long stare, resting her hands on her hips. "Are you seriously asking me?"

Ida winced, remembering how she had brushed off Sabine's

concerns about the nightflower. “Yes. I’m sorry about the way I acted before, Sabine. I need your help.”

Sabine kept her eyes on Ida for a moment longer. Ida squirmed, wondering if she had finally crossed the line, but Sabine relented. Her expression softened, her hands falling to her sides.

“You should get ahead of Steward Dallenbach’s story,” she said. “Write a letter to the king.”

Ida blinked. “I can do that? Just reach out and write the king?”

“You know someone who can.”

Ida’s heart sank like a stone.

Lenore.

It was easy to forget that Lenore was the king’s daughter. That she could appeal to her father on Ida’s behalf. But that would require speaking to her. And the last time they’d spoken, Ida had . . .

Ida plucked at a stray thread on her sheets, miserable.

“Lenore and I . . . aren’t speaking right now.”

“Really?” Sabine asked. “Is that why she’s so concerned about you? Why she’s been here constantly to check on you? She would help you if you asked her. You know she would.”

Ida knew, but the thought of having to go to Lenore’s rooms, head hung low, asking Lenore to speak to her father for her, made her feel utterly miserable. She knew that Lenore didn’t like speaking to her father, knew that Lenore had to be going through her own reckoning with everything she had learned about the curse and her mother, knew that she still owed Lenore an apology and an explanation for why she had pulled away.

She wanted to see Lenore more than anything. And she wasn’t brave enough.

"I can't let her see me like this. The last time we spoke, I ran away. I need to figure this out myself before I can . . ."

Before Ida could face her. It sounded childish in her mind, and she trailed off, unable to give voice to the thought. She could practically *feel* Sabine's frustration with her, braced herself for Sabine to tell her to get over herself, to stop being so proud.

Sabine only sighed and said, "Well, then I suppose you'll have to write His Majesty directly. As a royal artisan, you should be able to make an appeal, only there's no guarantee he'll actually read your letter. And there's no guarantee he'll reply promptly, or even read it before Steward Dallenbach can get to him."

A letter. Ida perked up.

Formal letters needed to be sealed. And what was a seal if not wax? And wax, she could work with.

It was a risky idea. If she were caught . . .

But she wasn't *really* doing anything wrong. Only making sure the king paid attention to her letter.

"I'll write him," Ida decided. She pulled the blankets off herself, starting to push herself up. "Help me, Sabine."

Sabine helped Ida into her desk chair and left with the laundry and a promise of food and coffee. While she was gone, Ida sat alone with a pen, a few sheets of paper, and a thousand thoughts chasing each other around in her mind.

The contents of the letter would be easy enough. Ida began with a brief explanation of the situation she was in. She made sure to point out that the nightflower had been obtained for legitimate reasons, that the royal physician could vouch for her, and that even though she had been as careful as possible (a small lie here would make no difference), accidents had occurred. The accident had only affected her, and so Steward Dallenbach's behavior was, in Ida's opinion, an overreaction. She asked the king to consider what he expected from his artisans, the way he always encouraged them to push the boundaries of what was reasonable, and then as a last touch, she promised to use the nightflower to produce something spectacular at her next performance. Then she signed the letter with her name.

Once she was done, Ida glanced behind her to make sure the door was closed. Then, she reached into her desk drawer for the stock of candles she kept for her own use. She selected a small orange taper. This one had been made with a very simple effect, to draw attention. She'd only used it a few times, burning it to divert her grandmother's or her cousins' attention to other things so Ida could slip by unnoticed.

Ida flicked open her father's firestrike, lighting the candle again. She held it over the envelope, letting wax drip onto the fold. Then, she blew out the candle and hid it in her desk drawer, pushing her seal of office into the wax.

Candle wax was of a different consistency to sealing wax, but Ida only needed the seal to hold for a short while. If all went well, His Majesty would read the letter today.

She stared down at the letter, at the emblem of the Court Luminaire embossed onto the wax seal. Ida only needed this position a little while longer. One way or another, she was coming close to the truth.

The first night after sending her letter, Ida stayed in her workshop. She waited with bated breath, but no response came from the king. On the second day, although Sabine had told Ida that Steward

Dallenbach had gone to see His Majesty, no response came. Ida held her breath. On the third day, Ida received a short letter, in the king's hand.

It said only: *I am looking forward to seeing what you create.*

Chapter 27

BLURRED LINES

The world dissolved at the touch of flame to wick, the candle swallowing all the room's light. Ida waited, fearful, but there was none of the awful tug she had felt when lighting her first nightflower candle, that shift that made her feel like she was being pulled through the eye of a needle from one world into another. Instead, a floral scent rose into the air, the gentle hint of jasmine. She'd diluted her nightflower even more, until only the faintest traces remained and it did nothing but whisk her audience into a gentle sleep.

She could feel her audience starting to grow restive in the darkness, uncertain. From personal experience, she knew it was an uncomfortable journey through the void.

Ida would be their guide.

Light bloomed in the heart of the darkness. It was a fragile, golden thing, lacing its way between her cupped hands. The light expanded, flooding the room, filling the space from edge to edge. And where the light touched, it created a world.

A garden on a hilltop, high hedges and marble statues and overflowing flower bushes, insects humming as they drifted through blades of grass and alighted from leaf to leaf. The air was filled with the sound of birdsong. At first glance, it might have seemed almost ordinary, if not for the pink hue to the sky. But closer inspections would reveal something different: The insects were clockwork, beetles and ladybugs made of elaborately constructed gears that somehow managed to convey the feeling of life. The birds were small dragons, flitting and cavorting from branch to branch, chirping and cooing and breathing out puffs of fire. The flowers, if anyone chanced to try one, were spun sugar, each one with a different flavor. And the fountain, decorated with a statue of a young knight raising his cup, poured sparkling wine instead of water.

It was a complete illusion, a full immersion of the body into the dream. Ida breathed out and watched with satisfaction as her audience fumbled around in the spaces they were standing in, groping for the edges of dinner tables, chairs and couches, furniture that was no longer there.

She felt a flash of pride. The illusion was a culmination of everything she had learned—how to anchor a spell to a room instead of herself, how to use the dreaming elixir, how to dilute nightflower. Ida could only imagine what Lenore and Vegard would say about it if she had the courage to discuss it with them.

The thought was enough to dampen her mood. She swallowed it back, pushing it away from herself as if she were swatting at a troublesome insect, and faced her audience. With her voice magically enhanced by her surroundings, it was easy to get their attention and announce that they could move freely in this space, that their real bodies were still sitting at the tables in one of Asteria's many banquet halls and would remain there for the hour it would take this candle to burn out to nothing. They were free to go anywhere, try anything, except that they would be unable to push past the ivy-covered wrought-iron fence that bordered the space, because the world behind the fence was only a painting. And that nothing in this space truly existed, so they would not be able to take anything with them when the hour ended. The crowd dispersed eagerly, cavorting through the gardens, and Ida sighed in relief.

After the king's answer, Ida had gone exactly by the book. She'd diluted the nightflower oil even further and tested the illusion until she had full control over the world she built, until she could come back without feeling feverish or nauseous. When the recipe had been perfected, Sabine had volunteered to be Ida's first guest.

It was more than anyone would have expected of her, and Ida resolved to make it count. After this, she would take no more risks. She would go slowly, carefully, and find the truth once and for all.

"You've done well," said a voice at her shoulder, and Ida froze, feeling a chill ripple down her spine. It was a voice she had heard many times since coming to Asteria, but had only addressed her twice before.

Her most recent memory of that voice was full of pride and rage.

A silver blade, a void of white. Her father's head in his hands.

She swallowed, torn between dropping to one knee or running as far away as she could. Her mouth had gone completely dry, and her heartbeat was pounding in her ears, a drum so loud it astonished Ida that no one else could hear it. She was glad suddenly that she had anchored the illusion to something else, that the garden was not now warping into a nightmare from the state of Ida's mind and heart.

Ida managed to bring herself under control. Managed to turn, stiffly, and address her king.

"Your Majesty," she murmured, dropping into a quick bow

so that the king couldn't see the conflict and uncertainty in her eyes, the anger she felt at his presence. "Is there something I can do for you?"

King Aurel's eyes drifted mildly across the entire scene, taking in Ida's masterwork the way he might have taken in a vaguely amusing painting. "I must confess that after reading your letter and entertaining my steward's grievances, I've been finding myself curious about your work. I was hoping you could assist me with something."

That damned attention-drawing candle. She'd hoped that a single dab of wax wouldn't have made a lasting impression, but she supposed it was more potent than she'd thought.

"I am your loyal servant."

The words were rote. Like Ida was addressing a concept, rather than a person. It was so much easier to talk to King Aurel IV than it was to talk to the man who had betrayed her father and both of her best friends.

She kept her eyes to the ground, hoping the answer was enough.

King Aurel, thankfully, was used to people addressing him with deference and not much else.

"Lately," he elaborated, "I find myself troubled by dreams."

Ida looked up sharply, then quickly looked back down at the ground again. "Dreams, Your Majesty?"

"Yes," King Aurel said. "The contents of the dreams are . . ." He frowned, looking slightly perplexed. ". . . well, I confess, difficult to remember. But they are upsetting enough to cost me my sleep, which is why it intrigued me when I heard from two separate sources"—the doctor, Ida supposed, and Steward Dallenbach—"that you've been dabbling with nightflower. I want you to create for me a candle that will ensure a deep, restful sleep, while keeping away those dreams. Can you do that for me?"

Ida's heart was racing. What were dreams, after all, but a window into the mind, a window into memory? King Aurel had been *there* that night. If any trace of it remained in his mind, if there was anything he remembered, she might be able to uncover the real truth. She could push past his dreams and into his memory, have free access to his thoughts while he slept. She could find out what happened to her father, not just as an outside observer, but from someone who had actually been there.

She could find out if her father was still alive, and if so, how to get him back.

Warning bells were ringing in her mind, urging caution. This might be Ida's chance to get close to the king, to observe his dreams. But to attempt such a thing, much less to pry anywhere else, would be a risk. Using magic on the king without permission might even be considered a threat. She hadn't forgotten her mother's warnings. In places of power, bad things happened to girls like her.

She had just told herself she would take no more risks, that she would go *slowly*. Carefully. But this was a *chance*. Maybe her only chance. It dangled in front of her, golden and inviting, and Ida couldn't help but leap.

"I . . . would be happy to help Your Majesty achieve a more restful sleep," she said. "But it will be difficult to do without knowing the content of your dreams. If I knew what they were about, I could more easily design a candle to keep those dreams at bay."

King Aurel's eyes narrowed at her. His expression was surprisingly shrewd, and Ida wondered if she had miscalculated, if her motives were so clearly written on her face. But the king only said, "What do you suggest?"

"Let me keep watch over you for a few days." Ida spoke the words quickly, afraid that if she slowed down, she would lose her nerve. "While you sleep. Let me explore your dreams. If I can find any common thread between the ones that disturb you, I can create a candle especially for you."

The king was watching her, and Ida fought to keep herself still, to not wring her hands, tug at the fabric of her clothes, to do anything that suggested she was more than a loyal luminaire.

The king was staring at her.

He had to know what she was planning. She was going to get thrown out of Asteria, or worse.

He knew—

"Very well," King Aurel said. The words felt like a blade, cutting the threads of tension that held Ida upright. It was so hard to maintain her posture, to not breathe out, to not let the astonishment and sheer *relief* show on her face. She almost didn't hear King Aurel's next question. "How many nights will you need?"

"How—how often do you have these dreams, Your Majesty?"

"Every few days or so," the king said. He paused in thought. "Perhaps twice a week."

"Then let's start with three consecutive days." Three days in a row. She could go three days sleeping only at night. It was hard to remember at times that that had once been her life: sleeping at night, awake and working during the day. "That should cover it. If it doesn't, we can always take a little more time. I only need to witness the dream once."

"Three days, then," King Aurel said, nodding. "You will write to me when you've finished your preparations?"

Questions, from the king, were anyone else's orders. "Yes, Your

Majesty," Ida said, bowing. "Of course."

He didn't dismiss her, not exactly. But he walked past her, hands clasped behind his back, and Ida understood the conversation was over, that she was no longer worthy of King Aurel's attention. She waited, keeping her head bowed, until the king's silhouette passed her by, until she was standing in his shadow.

She was just about to straighten up when King Aurel raised his head and looked back at her.

"Miss Rosales."

He said her name strangely, like it tasted odd in his mouth. Ida looked up to see him frowning, somewhat confused, as if he had been wandering in an unfamiliar place and stumbled upon a room he had once lived in.

Ida felt something snag at her, pounding in her chest. Not excitement, not exactly. Not even hope. But a relative of theirs, possibly. A dose of adrenaline that made the whole world sharpen at the edges, so that Ida wasn't sure if she was afraid or energized or angry.

Her answer was automatic.

"Yes, Your Majesty?"

The sound of her voice shook King Aurel out of his trance. Whatever familiarity her name had to him, she was a stranger. His gaze landed on her, and Ida was struck once again by the weightlessness of it, the utter lack of gravity in his bearing. His posture was intimidating, his voice calculated to spark admiration or fear, but he was a king and those things could be trained.

His aura was nothing. It brushed up against hers, a whisper of a touch, barely anything at all.

He might have been King of Arred, but he knew nothing about magic.

Nothing except that he wanted it.

"You've been with us a season, and we haven't had a moment to discuss the matter of your probation. In general, I've been pleased with your work. While some might have doubts about your youth"—the words "Steward Dallenbach" went without saying—"I've always believed in cultivating talent where it can be found. Should you succeed in ridding me of these dreams, I'm prepared to end your probationary year early and name you Court Luminaire in full, with all the rights and privileges therein."

He said it like an honor, like a gift, and Ida might have once taken it as that if she hadn't remembered the rage in his eyes as he stood over Vegard and stared at her father, the venom in his voice as he promised that all other luminaires would swear fealty. The memory of the ring she'd kissed was a brush of cold against her lip, the taste of dull metal in her mouth. She imagined being bound by her oath for a lifetime.

She dropped her head to keep her feelings from showing on her face.

"I'm honored, Your Majesty."

King Aurel didn't respond to this. What response was there?

Of course she would be honored to receive the recognition of her king.

He started to walk again, making his way across the grounds of her garden. The garden Ida had crafted out of nothing, every blade of grass and every drop of water and every buzzing, improbable clockwork insect her own creation. He walked like he owned it all, her and her magic both, but the magic—the magic was in Ida, and it wasn't in him.

And he might be her monarch, but Ida swore silently to herself in that moment that he would never own that.

She kept her eyes on the king's back as he walked away, and because he was only mortal after all, and not a mage, he didn't notice the naked anger in her gaze, the shift in her aura as all her magic bent, curving like blades toward him.

PART FOUR
FALL

I have often heard from many critics of my portrayal of the late monarch that I simply do not understand what our nation lost when it lost Asteria. And perhaps that is true. I confess that I never visited the court of the Night King, that for all of King Aurel IV's largesse in allowing what—at times—seemed half the realm to take up residence in his castle, he did have a particular hatred for the modern journalist, and the historian even more so. However, though I acknowledge that it is a shame to have lost the court and all its peculiarities and wonders, I must ask—where did the magic go? Does it not still exist in the world? Was not King Aurel IV merely curator of magic, and not creator? If magic interests you, dear reader, I encourage you to search for it where it may be found. Perhaps you will find things stranger and more wondrous still than anything housed within the walls of that castle.

—Herbert Ardinger, *The King of Moonlight: A Comprehensive History of Aurel IV*

Chapter 28

WHAT MAKES A KING

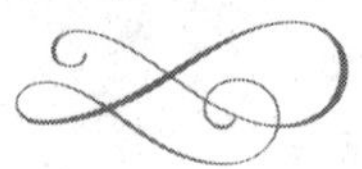

There were moments in life that felt like paths were diverging, like one single breath could change everything. When Ida's mother had returned from the post office that one summer evening, hard-eyed, and told Ida to pack all her things. When Ida had looked down at the dinner table and seen just a glimpse of the broadsheet, a glimpse that happened to show her the advertisement for a new Court Luminaire. When she had decided to pack her bags and steal away in the dead of night to go to Asteria and find out for herself what had happened to her father. Meeting Vegard. Meeting Lenore. The candle they'd made out of blood and dreams.

There had been a lot of those moments recently. Changes coming closer and closer together like waves crashing against the shore, so frequent that they had become the only constant in Ida's life. She had gotten used to it, to the reordering of everything she'd known and believed, sometimes gentle, sometimes violent. But that didn't mean she wasn't aware of how much she had lost, or how much she had left to gain.

Standing in the royal bedchamber that day, beside the heavy curtains that blocked out even a hint of the golden sun, Ida felt like this was another change: something momentous entirely in her hands. Because if she did all the right things, she might walk away from this with real answers, with a way to get her father back and set things right. And if things went wrong, she could lose everything.

King Aurel's bedtime routine was a surprisingly involved affair. Servants bustled around him as he lay down, plumping his pillows, sliding warming pans beneath his sheets, setting out a pitcher of water and a glass in case the king woke thirsty during the day. The king's servants moved like clockwork, sweeping past Ida as if she wasn't even there. She stood with her back to the curtains, facing the king on his bed, and waited for the activity to die down.

So much fuss for one old man, Ida thought. They all had maids, all of them who worked in Asteria in any official capacity, but Ida couldn't imagine Sabine fussing over her bed like that before she slept, as if Ida were an infant who needed to be tucked in.

If Lenore were a princess in truth, and not just a king's daughter, would this be her life? Cosseted and fussed over from the moment she opened her eyes to the moment she closed them again?

Was this why King Aurel was so fascinated by magic? Because it was the one thing that escaped him, no matter how hard he tried to grasp it? Because it was the one thing that remained out of his control, in a world that laid everything at his feet?

She was having uncharitable thoughts. The sound of the king's heavy bedchamber door closing snapped her out of them. She straightened up as Aurel, lying in bed among his many pillows, turned toward her and said imperiously, "You may begin."

Ida cleared her throat and pulled her father's firestrike out of her pocket. She flicked it open and paused with her thumb on the wheel. "This first candle is one for ordinary sleep," she said, gesturing at the black candle nearest her. "It contains no nightflower, and so there's no risk to Your Majesty from its use. However, it isn't as potent as the nightflower candles. When I light it, you'll feel drowsy, but not so much that you won't be able to fight it if you need to. It's only meant to relax you, to make it easier for you to fall asleep despite my presence."

King Aurel nodded. "And the other one?"

The other candle was silver, anchored to the room. She'd had to ask the royal maids to give her a few shavings of stone, a thread from the king's carpet, a single feather from his bed. They, under instructions to give Ida whatever she needed, had complied.

"This is the one that does all the work," Ida said. "It's the candle that will let me into your mind, to observe your dreams." This was the part that made Ida the most nervous. A lie of omission to a monarch could be damning, and she had made this candle to do so much more than that. "It's designed to give me a window into your subconscious mind. I won't be able to access your thoughts, only what you're already willing to show me."

"And what you see," King Aurel said, "you will report directly to me?"

"Your secrets are safe with me."

The words tasted like poison on her tongue.

On the first night, the king did not dream. Ida spent a handful of hours floating over the murmuring currents of King Aurel's consciousness, waiting for the fragments of thought, emotion, and words to coalesce into something solid, but they never did. King Aurel woke telling Ida that the sleep had been quite restful, and Ida told him they would try again the next day.

On the second day, she thought she saw a spark fluttering across the surface of the king's mind, a racing thought that almost came together into something useful. But the dream it formed was a simple thing, a comforting haze of color and images and motions that likely made sense to King Aurel but meant nothing to Ida. The king woke that night telling her that he had dreamed, but because it was pleasant, it wasn't the dream that he'd asked Ida to help him with. Ida could have told him that, but simply accepted it with a nod and said that perhaps the right dream would come tomorrow.

On the third day, it happened.

Ida was hovering above the king's consciousness, bored now of watching silvery thoughts spark and race across a ghostly river made of threads of spider silk, gossamer waves shining as they twisted around each other and cut through empty, void-like banks. Then a thought darted across the threads, a quick burst down the river from end to end until the whole structure was shining, and Ida plunged headlong into the dream.

It wasn't a coherent story, but rather a collection of vignettes. A little girl Ida didn't recognize, with King Aurel's nose and King Aurel's eyes, staring at him from across the room. A tall, imposing woman, wearing fine clothes and a gilded crown, who Ida had only ever seen in portraits of the royal family. Another woman, with Lenore's auburn hair and Lenore's piercing stare, watching the king from across a wooden table covered in herbs, her expression dripping with something that might have been scorn or might have been pity. An old man, sick and dying, lying in bed with a crown on his head and staring at the king with a hateful expression. A storyline never resolved, but as the images raced one after another, Ida understood what was plaguing the king.

It was guilt. The crown princess, the late queen, Lenore's mother, the previous king.

All of them staring at Aurel in the bright light of day, with accusatory eyes as if they knew he wasn't fooling anyone, as if they were aware of everything he had done.

When the king awoke early, looking troubled, Ida told him that she thought she had an idea, but that the vision hadn't been so clear. She asked for one more night, to better explore her suspicions, and to make sure she was correct. She explained to him that she had seen visions of the queen, of the princess, and of the king's father, but she omitted any mention of Lenore's mother, and said the meaning wasn't yet clear.

That was her next lie. When she retreated back to her rooms that evening, Ida stayed awake long enough to lace wax with lavender and bittersweet, one a symbol of distrust, the other a cry for truth. She poured the wax into a small mold, creating a simple votive candle, and let it set while she tried to get some sleep. The next day, she told the king that the smaller candle would heighten her powers of perception, allowing her to discover the root of the issue.

King Aurel didn't question her.

He lay back, with all the confidence of someone who believed they owned the world, and let Ida usher him into sleep.

Ida waited until King Aurel was sound asleep, until his eyelids began to twitch in dream. And then, moving as quickly as she could, she lit first the silver candle and then the newest votive. Twined scents rose up into the air, and Ida followed them into the void.

King Aurel wasn't dreaming just yet, the currents of his mind quiescent, peaceful. But now that Ida knew what he dreamed of, it wasn't hard to tug at those currents. She thought of guilt, the sinking feeling in her chest, the cold, clammy sensation that ran across her skin, the way it ate at her from the inside knowing that she had done wrong, that she needed to set things right.

Guilt came easily to her. It was so close to the surface, both because of the risk she was taking here and because of what she hadn't yet done. The words spoken between her and Vegard and Lenore, the apology she had yet to make, the things she couldn't say. The complicated mass of emotion that threatened to rise to the surface every time Ida thought about her father or her mother.

Her feelings echoed in the black space, and, buoyed by the power she'd imbued into her second candle, they scattered across the threads of the king's dreams, calling up similar memories in him. Ida found herself once more standing in the bright light of day, in a garden, staring at a child whose eyes were too sharp for her age, a child who was already looking at her like Ida had failed her.

No, not Ida.

The king. Ida was seeing out of King Aurel's eyes, looking out at the world as he had seen it then. And this girl was the crown princess, Aurel's trueborn daughter. His oldest child, the woman who would someday become Queen of Arred.

There was an accusation in her eyes, a knowingness that made King Aurel recoil. Ida pressed at that image, urging it to fall open, to show her what lay beneath.

She didn't even have to think too strongly about where to press, about how to make the world fall open before her. It was like the king wanted her to see, wanted her to ask.

It was true what they said about the guilty. They were always looking for a confessional.

There was a rush of air, and then the scene unfroze. The girl stepped forward, her eyes on him, and spoke.

"You're *never* here," she said, sounding more like a wraith in her inflection and tone than a child. "You were in your library when Mother fell ill and you were playing with your magic when she worsened and you were traveling when she died. None of this meant anything to you. None of us meant anything to you. You left me, you left me, you *left me*—"

The child's screaming cut off as Ida recoiled from it. Before she could fully get her bearings, the scene changed. She saw the previous king, lying in bed. Although he looked emaciated, in the dream, he was sitting up straight, his eyes fixed on King Aurel. He pointed one withered finger at him.

"—be the ruin of us," he was saying. "You'll be the death of this kingdom. This obsession of yours with the *unnatural*, with these freaks—"

The queen was gentler, but no less cutting as she stared at Aurel, looking down at him as if from a height, as purposeful as it was disdainful. "A king must do what is best for his kingdom, and a queen must support him. My mother told me this, when I came to marry a king. So why am I alone? Why do I sit in councils alone, hear grievances alone? Why do I rule this country alone, while its king hides in the wilds? Where is the King of Arred?"

The last vision was the woman who looked so much like Lenore. Ida found herself staring at her as she appeared in front of the king, sitting calmly across from him at the table. She wanted to memorize her features, to bring her to life later for Lenore, who could hardly remember her mother.

She wasn't raging at King Aurel about Lenore, which Ida would have expected. Instead, she had fixed the king with a calm, cool gaze. When she spoke, she didn't speak with the voice of a nightmare, but with a voice that seemed drawn directly from memory.

"You say you are great because you are the King of Arred. But what does Arred mean to me but a land on the other side of the mountains? You haven't yet shown me where your greatness lies. You haven't shown me what makes you a king."

In the darkness, in the space behind Aurel's mind, Ida lifted a hand. The memory froze, slowing to a stop, King Aurel's gaze fixed on Lenore's mother's face.

This moment, face-to-face with someone else who had been lost to memory, was as good enough a place to start as any.

Ida held her breath and began to do something forbidden.

The dream turned liquid, the scene around her dripping as if it was melting, colors running liquid at her feet as she pushed deeper into the king's mind, deeper into his memories.

Deeper into the things that he himself had forgotten.

Chapter 29

IN LIVING MEMORY

At first, Ida thought it wasn't going to work. That even here, the truth of her father's fate would escape her.

Then the shifting watercolor world around her flowed into a solid shape, and Ida found herself standing somewhere else, somewhere different.

It took her a while to recognize it as Asteria.

The castle didn't have any of the grandeur she had come to know. The smell of freshly cut wood hung in the air, and the hall they were standing in was yet unfinished—to Ida's left, hulking structures of scaffolds reached to the ceiling. There were gaping holes in the floor where stones hadn't been laid down, and whole sections were supported only by exposed beams to keep the castle from falling down on top of itself.

It felt like she was standing in the belly of a beast that had been torn open, its bones exposed to the sky.

Her father was in front of her, facing the dream's version of King Aurel.

He looked younger, as young as he had been in the earliest of

Ida's recovered memories. He had a piece of paper spread open in his hands and was reading it by the light of a single candle because it was night here, a proper night where the shadows crept in at the edges. The candlelight played on her father's skin, darker than hers, too dark to pass as Arreden. It played against his dark eyes, against the dark brown of his hair.

The father she had seen in Vegard's memories hadn't been smiling, and Ida realized then how much she missed that smile. How much her heart ached to see him happy and alive.

But her father wasn't smiling at her, of course. He had no idea she was there.

He was smiling at Aurel.

"This is incredible," he said, gesturing at the sheet of paper in front of him. "What you've planned here, Your Majesty, it will be the envy of everyone on the continent."

"And the modifications?" Aurel's voice startled her, because it seemed to come from where Ida was standing. It was also more uncertain than any other time she had ever heard the king speak. "You don't think they're too . . . extreme?"

"Not at all." Tomas frowned, squinting at the paper, which Ida now saw held plans. Sketches of the castle, of the Asteria it would become. He frowned, some of his enthusiasm tempered as he studied them a second time. "They're certainly ambitious . . ."

"Speak freely, Tomas," King Aurel commanded. "You're my magical adviser. Can it be done or not?"

Her father looked a little startled. He blinked up at the king as if he had briefly forgotten Aurel was even there, so engrossed was he in his thoughts. It was an expression achingly recognizable to Ida, because she got like that sometimes, when she was deep at work on one of her candles. But at the king's command, her father studied the plans again.

"It can be done, in theory," he said. "But something this large . . . I won't be able to sustain it. I don't think any human mage can."

"And what about nonhuman mages?"

The question was like dropping a coin in a well. There was no sound at all, nothing but the lurch of the sudden drop, until the echo of the splash. Her father turned toward the king.

"What do you mean?"

"I've found a spirit willing to help us," Aurel said, and he sounded so pleased with himself, so proud. As if he had been sitting on this news all day and was just waiting for the moment that he could tell Tomas this, could watch Tomas's expression go from confused, to guarded, to delighted. The smile was just starting to catch at the corner of her father's mouth again when he said, "You didn't."

"I did."

"But you've told me that the local spirits are unfriendly to human kings."

"I am still a king, am I not?" Aurel asked. "I went north."

"North," Tomas repeated.

"North." She could practically *hear* Aurel's self-satisfied smile. "My tour last year, to the northern kingdoms. When I finished, I crossed their boundaries and went farther north still, to the place where the ice never melts, where the entire country lives in a yearlong day. I went to the Kingdom of Winter."

Tomas was hanging on the king's every word. And Ida wanted to yell at him, to say that that was wrong and the king was a fraud, but she couldn't, because she knew, because Vegard had told her that this part was real.

It was real and it would end badly for all of them, but it was *real.*

"And?" Tomas asked. He looked like he was bursting to ask for details, to know who the king met and where and how, and what the country was like, but he contained himself to a single question. "What happened next?"

"I spoke to the winter spirits about the Asteria project," King Aurel said. "Their elders were predictably disinterested. But I did manage to convince one to come and observe the project. A young spirit, considered a child among his people."

"A child?" Tomas asked. He looked a little concerned, and Ida wondered how old she was in this scenario. A toddler? Was he picturing her when he thought of Vegard?

If Vegard had ever been a toddler, it had been centuries ago. For some reason, the thought made Ida feel incredibly lonely.

"Don't give me that look, Tomas," Aurel said. "I say 'child,' but the boy seemed more like a young man. Certainly old enough to make his choices. Like all young men, he thinks his homeland is the most boring place in the universe. Spending some time down here would be a holiday for him."

"Oh . . ." Tomas relaxed by degrees. Ida remembered Vegard lying on a stone slab, remembered a silver knife, and thought this was perhaps premature. But Tomas would have no way of knowing what was to happen. He brightened—Ida could see the curiosity in his eyes, the sudden knowledge that all was perhaps not as lost as it seemed. "And he's willing to help?"

"He expressed great interest in the project. He hasn't seen much of humans and seems interested, although why any being with that much power would be interested in *us* is a mystery for the ages. He'll help however he can."

"In that case," said Tomas, looking back down at the plans, "we may have something here. I'll have to meet him, find out how well we can work together, if he has enough raw power to fuel the enchantments . . . but a true spirit of winter . . ." Her father had begun to pace, muttering to himself as he looked at the plans, his voice echoing in the expanse of the unfinished hall. Looking at him, Ida felt a sharp stab of pride mingled with grief. Her father hadn't just been another luminaire, an entertainer. He had *built* Asteria.

How had she not seen it? The layout of the castle, the rhythm and schedule of its Revels, the way the castle itself existed like a thing out of dream? How had she never noticed her father's hand at work when she had spent all her time reading his journals, so many years trying to recapture the magic he could invoke with a thought?

There were two answers, and both could be true.

The first was that she had been a child, and despite her best efforts, she simply didn't *know* her father well enough to recognize his work on sight.

And the second, that Asteria had *changed*. Had been changed. That whatever gleaming vision her father saw in the plans before him had been altered beyond repair, transformed into something unrecognizable.

Grief was so heavy she could taste it. It coated the air, her lungs, the inside of her throat. She felt like she'd been running from it for so long that she was starting to tire. That grief was a monster bearing down on her, and its breath was on the back of her neck, and its fangs were inches from her skin.

She could remember, as clearly as if it happened yesterday, Lenore's careful words.

. . . we should assume that he's dead.

Ida sucked in a rattling breath and took hold of the king's mind. She forced it to push forward, past this memory, this image of her father in his prime, buried layers deep in a dream of guilt. She didn't want to see any more but she had to, she had to *know—*

Show me what you did to him.

The dream struggled.

It shuddered in her grasp, as if King Aurel himself didn't want to see this, didn't want to know. As if she wasn't the only one running from a demon.

But the king had never had any magic.

He might have been one of the most powerful men on the continent, but in this space, *she* was stronger than him.

The memory shuddered, the image of her father frozen on a smile. It all came apart, and when it pulled back together again, Ida was *there*. In that terrible place, above Vegard's rooms. In the tower that never was, on that stone pedestal where Vegard bled and her father fought a king.

Seeing it from Aurel's perspective was brutal, and visceral, and sickening. She could smell blood in the air, its quality different somehow from human blood and yet still so real, so *vital*. She could see her father thrashing in Aurel's hand as he put him between himself and the light, the king shielding himself with her father's body. She could *feel* every desperate animal twitch of his limbs as the universe fell apart and then—

—and then. In that moment before it ended.

A silence.

A stillness.

Her father's body going slack.

And Ida knew.

The world shattered around her, the dream falling apart, but it didn't matter. Ida didn't even try to hold on to it, because none of it mattered anymore. She was stumbling back, her heart pounding in her throat, her knees threatening to buckle underneath her, and she wasn't screaming but the scream was inside her head, a long, echoing cry that rattled against the bone of her skull, that made her feel like she was shattering.

She didn't even notice. It took her so long to notice that she was standing in the king's bedroom, one hand braced against the table behind her, the table with the candles that she had knocked down without seeing, the wax that was spreading its way across the tabletop. That her hands were shaking and that in the dim light King Aurel had risen from bed, and he was staring, angry and hollow-eyed, at *her*.

Chapter 30

RECKONING

In that terrible handful of breaths between the king opening his eyes and his first words to her, Ida prayed that he had no idea what she had done. That he had not seen or felt anything, or that he would think it was only a bad dream. But then his eyes narrowed sharply, and she realized she had gone as far as she could for a girl like her.

"Your Majesty—" Ida began.

"Silence!" King Aurel's words were sharp, cutting. Commanding enough that Ida's mouth shut of its own accord, so quickly that her teeth clacked together. For all that King Aurel lacked, he was still a king, and he knew how to command the attention of a room.

The king watched her. He didn't even bother getting out of bed. He simply let her stand there, quietly, her knees trembling and waves of cold washing over her as she awaited her fate. Ida glanced at his eyes, and saw only rage in them. And a new thought came up unbidden, one she could no longer deny, bubbling to the surface of her mind like a breath exhaled underwater.

You killed my father.

She hated him. Yet in the wake of such terrible truth, all she felt was exhaustion, weighing down on her, dragging her to the ground.

"What did you do?" King Aurel asked. He said each word slowly, carefully, as if each word were its own sentence. She flinched, and despised herself for it. That her first instinct was to cower, and lie, and hope that everything would pass her by.

Because girls like her died when they crossed kings.

"N-nothing, Your Majesty."

"Don't lie to me," King Aurel said. "I felt an enchantment on me, felt you—worming your way into my mind. What. Did. You. Do?"

Ida pressed her lips tightly together. Thought of an answer, discarded it. The truth was locked up in her throat. What came out—what came out so easily—was another lie.

"I was—searching for the source of your nightmare—"

"You *lie*." King Aurel's face was twisted in rage. "You showed me a vision—what was that vision? What was that *place*? My head—it feels like it's tearing itself apart—"

Ida looked up sharply, alarm running through her. She knew the pain King Aurel was feeling. It was the same pain that she felt, the same pain Lenore and Vegard felt, when they came too close to remembering the past. To thinking of that other reality that wasn't supposed to have existed. She knew it felt like daggers digging into her skull, like her entire being was coming apart at the seams.

And she knew, suddenly, how that would feel to a king.

One who had let her into his chamber, to watch him while he slept. One who had made himself vulnerable in front of her.

"You *tried to kill me*," King Aurel said.

"No, Your Majesty, I would never—! My magic can't—!"

"Liar!" King Aurel roared. "You were in my head. I *felt* your hate. You took your magic and tried to kill me!"

"No—" Ida gasped. Her face was wet. There were tears, she

realized, running down her face, and she must have looked so pathetic, so guilty, and she hated herself so much for it then, but the world was still yawning open beneath her, an emptiness Ida couldn't fight. And the king, the king went on as if he hadn't heard her, his rage stealing his reason and turning him into something else entirely.

"Everything I've done for you—I've given you everything, elevated you far beyond your station—how dare you—how *dare* you—" He broke off, clutching his head. Ida opened her mouth, but no words came out. All her thoughts were crowding for space in her mind, all her regrets and all her fears, narrowing down to the realization that she shouldn't have done this, that she should have listened to her mother.

To Vegard. To Lenore. To *anyone*.

King Aurel groaned, fighting through the pain in his head. When he raised his eyes toward her, there was no mercy in them.

He opened his mouth and called for the guards.

When they left Ida in a cell in the dungeons, they left her with not even a single candle.

The only light came from a torch on the other side of the bars, a flickering, uneven glow that cast long shadows on the inside of Ida's cell. Night had fallen a while ago, and although Ida had spent the past few months in the court of the Night King, the darkness had rarely felt so personal, so deep.

The cells below the castle of Asteria were rarely used. Ida hadn't even considered they might be here. There were no other prisoners besides her, no other guards except the one who had been assigned to guard her—human, mundane, and incredibly resentful of his duty. Ida supposed she was preventing him from attending a Revel.

It was damp in the cells, and cold. The guard had given her a blanket—she supposed she looked pathetic and nonthreatening enough to warrant some kindness—but she couldn't bring herself to do much more than huddle under it, her back braced against the cold stone wall of the dungeon and her knees pulled up close to her chest. One of her hands held her father's firestrike, her thumb running over the engraved letters on its front, again and again and again.

She wondered if the king had told anyone what had happened to her. If Sabine, or Lenore, or Vegard knew where she was. If they had even noticed she was missing.

It was almost funny. The whole time she had been here, she'd assumed that the worst thing that could happen was being sent away; that if everything went wrong, she would be forced to leave Asteria, to go home without her magic, to live her life as an ordinary human.

It had never occurred to her that she might be *arrested.*

That King Aurel would, in his waking state, so gravely misunderstand who she was and what she had been trying to do.

"I didn't try to kill the king," she said. The words echoed in the cell around her, flat and hollow.

"I need you to be quiet, miss," the guard said, in the same matter-of-fact tone he'd used all the other times Ida had tried to speak. She thought he was young, maybe only a few years older than she was, but it was impossible to tell in the dark.

He seemed miserable to be here. Ida supposed that made two of them.

"But I didn't," she said, letting the edge of her words trail off into the darkness.

The guard didn't respond, which was just as well. Ida didn't want to think about it, didn't want to explain that there was nothing she could have done from within Aurel's mind to kill him. Didn't want to think about the circumstances that had led up to this moment, the things she had witnessed in the dark of the king's mind, the fact that he had likely woken up thinking of murder because Ida had forced him to revisit his murderous past.

Murder.

A hitching sob escaped her, and she tried to choke it back, to keep it from echoing.

The monster she had been running from for so long had finally caught up with her. Its claws were finally digging into her back, its teeth sinking into her shoulder. In the dark, in the quiet, in the aftermath of betrayal and shame, the truth wouldn't shut up. It kept ringing in Ida's head, over and over again, and she was falling into its abyss.

Her father was dead. He had been dead for a long time.

King Aurel had killed him.

And the king did not remember.

"He killed my father, you know," Ida said. She said the words just to try saying them out loud, and was surprised when she said them without breaking, without her voice doing much more than quiver.

The guard sighed. Ida wondered if he believed her, even a little. If he took one look at her not-quite-Arreden features, her hair that was a bit too wild and her skin that was a bit too dark, and thought there was no way she could have been telling the truth, or if he thought that even if she was it didn't matter, because neither she nor her father were worth as much as a king.

He said, "You won't make things better for yourself by talking."

He wasn't unkind.

This would have been easier, Ida thought, if he was.

Grief was thick on her tongue, a cloying taste in her throat like she had eaten something rotten. Like she was rotting, from the inside out, falling apart.

Her father was dead. He would never come home.

Ida had come to Asteria for nothing. Absolutely nothing.

She started to cry. Her sobs echoed in the cell's open air, and she heard the guard's nervous shifting start again. A part of Ida was mortified that she was crying like this where someone could see her, that she was showing everyone how weak she really was. How small, how young, how useless.

But that part of her was locked deep inside her heart.

The rest of her didn't care.

She slept after her tears had been wrung out of her, after it felt like she had no more feeling left to give.

When she woke, curled up on the cot underneath her blanket, shivering and feeling as if something vital had been hollowed out of her, she was alone. The cell was still dark. She had no idea what time it was.

"Gloam," she whispered, into the darkness.

There was no answer. Ida waited for a few heartbeats, for a long stretch of undefined time. Gloam had never taken longer than that to come after she had called their name. If they hadn't responded, Ida was forced to concede that either Gloam couldn't hear her or didn't care. The former seemed more likely, but the latter thought hung like a weight in Ida's mind, one that she couldn't banish.

Why would Gloam care about her? Why would anyone?

After the way she had behaved, after what she had said to Vegard and Lenore, after the two of them had rescued her and she'd said nothing, absolutely nothing to them.

She hadn't even thanked them.

Why would they come?

Wrapped up in misery, Ida tugged her blanket tight around her and went back to sleep.

The next time she woke, it was to the sound of the bars rattling, the door to her cell swinging open.

Ida sat up sharply, a thousand thoughts spinning in her mind. She was being brought to trial. She was being freed. Someone was coming to inflict any number of cruelties on her on behalf of the king. Her mind was spinning with thoughts she couldn't escape, but—

—but no. It was only her guard. The kind young man. He looked just as startled as she was, holding a metal tray in one hand.

"Food," he said simply, setting it down on the floor between them. He still looked uncomfortable to be here, but he spoke as if to a scared animal and rose from his crouch with his hands up. "You should eat something."

"How long will I be here?" Ida asked.

He shook his head and said nothing more after that, retreating beyond the boundaries of her cell. The door scraped against stone as he closed it, the lock clicking into place with a loud clang. It seemed to take everything with it. Ida's hope of freedom, all the light in her room.

Her stomach was rumbling. Even after everything that had happened to her, everything that was still happening, she needed to eat.

She got up and walked toward the tray.

Her cell didn't have a table. She took the tray back to her cot and balanced it between her knees and her body. She'd been expecting gruel, something unpleasant, but when she lifted the cover, she saw that dinner was a thick stew, still warm, with chunks of meat and potatoes, and a roll of bread. The bread was somewhat stale—day-old—but the food was substantial.

They even feed prisoners well, in the court of the Night King.

She choked back the mad laugh that threatened to escape her, the thing that was halfway to a sob. And, because she needed to keep her strength up, she ate.

When she was done, she set the empty tray back by the door and went to her cot. She curled up against the wall, sitting on her hands to warm them.

How long had it been? She'd had one meal, and she'd been asleep.

But perhaps the real question was how long would it *be*?

Until someone came for her. Or until King Aurel decided to enact his own justice.

Ida wanted to laugh at herself. Even now, even imprisoned in the ruins of all her hopes and dreams, there was a part of her mind that was still thinking about those things. A part of her mind that still believed in escape, in a *future*.

The rest of her thought it was ridiculous. She had no options left. None.

If she were Vegard, she could blast open this cell door. If she were Lenore, she could grow vines to pull the door open, or call down any number of allied spirits to whisk her away.

But she was just Ida.

Just an illusionist, just a crafter of pretty dreams. Her magic couldn't affect the physical world.

She didn't have a candle. She didn't have her tools. She didn't have anything.

She wanted . . .

She wanted her mother. The ache was fierce, suddenly, closing her throat and making her head drop to her knees. She wanted to tell her mother what she'd found, the reality of what had happened to them. She wanted to look her mother in the eye and say the words: *He never abandoned us. He never meant to leave you.*

Because that was true, wasn't it?

Her father was dead, but at least—at least—

—at least her mother would know that he loved her. That he'd loved both of them. And maybe the ache she'd been carrying in *her* heart all these years would heal.

But that wouldn't happen now. If Ida stayed down here forever, her mother would think she'd been abandoned by both husband and child. And Ida's heart broke all over again, a thousand pieces fleeing from her center like dust from a collapsing star.

But this time was different. This time, the pieces of her didn't fly into the void, didn't vanish. They remained, swirling around a thought at the very heart of her, the gravity of this one thought strong enough to bring the pieces of herself back together, to construct something entirely new from the wreckage.

If her mother didn't know what had happened, Ida needed to tell her.

And not just her mother. Her father's family—he surely had to have family in the Niressians. They had to be alive, had to be wondering what had happened to their son. Maybe—maybe they even knew about her.

They deserved to know. All of them did. So that they could all escape that dark place Ida had been languishing in for years, waiting for her father to return, never knowing one way or another.

Which meant that Ida couldn't stay here. She needed to escape, needed to find her way back to the surface so that she could go home and tell her mother the truth.

The thought steadied her through one breath. And then a second.

She could do one more thing before she rested, before she let the grief catch up to her and consume her.

She could *find a way out.*

Ida lay on her side on the cot, pretending to be asleep. It was easier. It gave her a good reason not to talk to her guard, not to acknowledge him at all.

In the darkness, she tried to plan. She didn't know how much longer she had to wait until she faced the king's justice, and there was no way to get a message to the surface. Her guard wouldn't help her—he'd already shown himself unwilling to speak to her. She had no way of getting help from her allies, and no way of getting any tools she might have in her workshop. If she was going to escape, she was limited to whatever she had on hand.

What did she have on hand?

Not much.

Stripped-down furniture, the clothes she was wearing, and a reeking chamber pot whose contents Ida didn't even want to consider. Stone walls and the bars of a cell she would never be able to break through. A guard that seemed sympathetic to her, but not so sympathetic that she could turn him to her cause. It was a very limited arsenal.

If only she had a candle.

Some way of channeling her magic.

Some—

Her eyes snapped open fully. Her hand searched in the pocket of her jacket, fingers closing around the cool metal of her father's firestrike. She had her father's firestrike.

It didn't do her much good on its own. The flame it made might be enough to light her way, but the cell was too damp for anything in it to burn. Most of the furniture was made of metal, and even if she succeeded in setting fire to her sheets, it would likely only cause them to smolder pathetically before the guards caught her, put it out, and took her firestrike away.

But even thinking that, Ida could feel her heart starting to race, excitement and anticipation prickling in her blood, like her subconscious was close to an answer her conscious mind couldn't grasp. The metal was cool beneath her touch, the engraved letters a soothing texture on the pads of her fingers.

All luminaires had a medium. She used scent to carry the idea of her magic, to shape and craft the illusion. Scent to her was like paint to an artist—but scent wasn't truly her medium. It wasn't the source of her power.

She needed the scents. Her magic didn't.

What her magic truly needed from her was . . .

Ida's fingers closed tightly around the firestrike, her eyes snapping open in the darkness of her cell.

What her magic truly needed from her was *fire*.

Chapter 31

HEARTS ABLAZE

The blaze came up in a second, a wave of smoldering, scorching heat that pressed against Ida's skin and threatened to overwhelm her. It started from her cot, from the blanket the guard had been kind enough to give her, but it raced across everything it could find, an inferno that wanted only to consume whatever it could touch.

Ida ran forward, flinging herself against the bars, the metal already heating from the flames. She banged against them with her fist, as loudly as she could, and screamed through her hoarse throat.

"Fire! Fire, help! Help me, *please*! *Fire!*"

The sound of running footsteps answered her, heavy footfalls from somewhere off to her right. Her guard came around the corner at a sprint, his eyes wide, face red from exertion as he took in the scene in front of him. He assessed the situation quickly. In the time he'd been gone, the flames had spread wildly. Black smoke filled the corridor.

Ida coughed and retched, sagging against the bars as the smoke tickled her lungs. She gasped for air.

"Help me!" she shouted again.

The guard sprang into action. He grabbed the keys from his

belt, quickly unlocking Ida's door. It fell open, and Ida fell almost into his arms, her hands on his chest as smoke chased her out into the corridor. The guard pushed her behind him, putting himself between her and the flames.

"Stay back!" he said, looking around for something he could use to douse the fire, a bucket, a source of water, anything.

Ida snatched the baton from his belt and hit him over the head.

He was taller than her and trained. He spun to meet the strike, his eyes wide in disbelief, but she had the element of surprise. She saw the moment his eyes widened in betrayal and comprehension, felt the shock of impact travel up her arm as she struck him, saw him fall backward, back into the room filled with flames. He dropped the keys.

The blow had been harder than she expected—her fingers felt numb—but she quickly tossed the baton aside and surged forward to pull the cell door closed. She scooped the keys up from the floor before he could reach them and stumbled back against the wall on the other side of the corridor to catch her breath. Her heart was pounding, sweat soaking her clothes. In the cell, the guard leaped up with a garbled shout and ran to the cell door, the flames at his back. He rattled the bars, but the lock held.

His eyes were wide with desperation and fear, until the moment Ida let her father's firestrike slip from her nerveless fingers, and it clattered onto the stone ground.

The flames winked out, her hold on the illusion vanishing with them. There was nothing in the cell, no fire, no heat, no smoke. Nothing but the rumpled sheets from Ida's short imprisonment and the damp and the cold.

The guard's eyes widened in dawning comprehension.

"You—" he gasped, but Ida didn't have the wherewithal to respond. Her father's firestrike was a charred, twisted version of itself, the little striking wheel and the spout that produced the flame curled into each other as if they'd been made of clay. The fingers of her left hand were burned, the skin bright red and shining. She didn't feel pain, not yet, but her hand was shaking.

It had taken more out of her than she expected.

In the end, there had only been one illusion the little firestrike could produce, only one thought that could be coaxed out of the smell of metal and fuel and the remnants of burning.

The firestrike only had thoughts of fire. And when Ida brought those to life, the little firestrike, a poor vessel for magic, finally gave out.

She wanted to take it with her, this last broken memory of her father. But when she bent down to pick it up, the metal was still hot to the touch and she hissed, pulling the fingers of her unburnt hand back. She looked up at the guard, who was still watching her with confusion, and betrayal, and a little bit of fear.

"I'm sorry," she said, and turned to run the way he had come.

"You won't be able to get out that way!" the guard shouted after her, his voice echoing in the corridor, but Ida didn't bother listening. She ran, rounding the corner and racing up the set of stone steps she found there. She didn't know how long she had until word of her escape spread, or until exhaustion took her, but she wasn't going to waste her time arguing.

She ran, and nearly threw herself against the closed door at the top of the steps.

When she touched it, she was glad that her hand had closed around the handle, because the door attempted to throw her back.

It was a simple wooden door with bars guarding a small window at the top, but the force of repulsion that came from it struck her in the chest like a battering ram. She held tight to the handle, and that was the only reason it threw her just a few steps back, and not down the stairs entirely. The impact was strong enough to knock the wind out of her, a sharp pain radiating up her arm as her joints protested the motion.

Ida let go of the door, stumbling back onto the landing at the top of the steps. She stared in disbelief.

No wonder they had only bothered with one guard. It wasn't because there were so few prisoners in Asteria, or because King Aurel underestimated her.

It was because Asteria's dungeons, like the rest of it, were also magical.

The door was either enchanted to only allow specific people to pass, or to stop prisoners from escaping completely. If it was the former, there might be a key, something on the guard's uniform or something he was carrying. But, Ida thought, with a sinking feeling, that wasn't likely. She *had* the keys in her hand, a ring of keys all tied to the cells that lined the dungeon walls, and any lock tied to an object wouldn't be secure enough for the King of Arred.

More likely than not, it was tied to *her*. To keep her in.

Ida choked a sob, tangling the fingers of her free hand into her hair.

It was the cruelest irony, to be able to *feel* the magic, to be able to read its currents and track its flow, but to not be able to do *anything* to affect it. If she had a candle, if she had her tools, if she had *time*, she could have crafted a spell that would make the door believe she was someone else, could have coaxed it to open for her.

But she had none of that.

She had a handful of moments before someone found her wandering where she shouldn't be and put her back in her cell. Minutes, maybe, because if whoever had built this dungeon was as clever as Ida thought they were, the spell would likely also set off alarms.

Did you come up with this too, Father? Ida wanted to scream. *Was this part of the spells you made for him?*

It didn't matter.

It didn't *matter.*

Ida wasn't getting through that door. She'd gotten out of her cell, and that had left her with burned hands, a firestrike that no longer worked, and the last memory of her father lying cooling on a dungeon floor in the castle he had built.

And then something slammed into the door, strong enough to rattle it on its hinges. Ida's eyes widened and she stepped hurriedly back. Her breath caught in her throat, fearful, before she realized that this wouldn't be the guards.

The guards wouldn't *need* to throw themselves against the door. The door would open for them.

Which meant this—

—this was something else.

The force slammed into the door again, and this time, the wood splintered. Ida felt something seeping through the web of magic woven over the door.

A gust of cold air, biting, like the first winds of winter. The taste of frost on her tongue.

The next blast blew the door apart.

It obliterated the door, fragments of wood exploding outward from its center. A wave of frigid air swept into the dungeon, making

Ida gasp with sudden, sharp relief. Ice grew and spread along the walls of the corridor, along the roof, bathing the room in sharp, crystalline edges. And in the space on the other side of the door, wreathed in the mist that had sprung up from the cold wind, stood two familiar figures.

Ida had barely a moment to register the sight of Vegard standing there, hand outstretched toward the door with frost drawing scalelike patterns on his skin, before Lenore rushed into the room, sweeping Ida up in an embrace that nearly knocked her off her feet. She stumbled backward, startled, and caught Lenore by the waist to keep them both from falling over.

"Lenore—" Ida began.

"Thank the gods you're okay," Lenore breathed against her neck, squeezing her tightly. Ida had only a moment to relish in the warmth of Lenore against her before she had been released, and it left her reeling, strangely bereft. Vegard stepped into the room, and Ida blinked, staring at the two of them.

Vegard was wearing white, like he had for as long as Ida had known him, but instead of the finely tailored clothes Asteria supplied him with, he wore armor: a breastplate made up of what looked like interlocking scales, each one gleaming. His eyes were fully silver, shining against the dark. For a moment, he looked like what he was, something other than human. But then he met Ida's eyes, and his gaze slid away, the old awkwardness creeping into his expression.

Beside him, Lenore wore trousers and boots, a dark-colored riding jacket hugging tightly to her arms, auburn hair pulled back in a messy braid. She looked like she was dressed for a long journey. Magic hummed around her, frenetic, a drumbeat of power that to Ida felt like falling rain.

A sob caught in Ida's throat. The last time she had seen her friends, she'd been screaming at them.

Since then, they had saved her twice, and she still didn't know what to say.

She swallowed past the lump in her throat, the jagged shard that cut into her all the way down, and opened her mouth to apologize, to say everything that had been building up inside her since the start.

"We have to go," Vegard said. "They're going to come for you. We need to find somewhere safe."

Ida's words died in her throat. Of course.

Of course this wasn't over yet. Of course there was a reason why Vegard and Lenore had come as if dressed for battle.

This was going to have *consequences*.

This wasn't how she had wanted to meet either of them again. She wanted to have enough time to tell them everything that was on her mind.

But that wouldn't happen. So she nodded, and even though she felt like she was close to exploding, she said, "Okay. Let's go."

They moved quickly through the halls of Asteria, running along dusty passages and through narrow, unused corridors. They said little as they ran, but it was hardly the time for conversation. Ida wanted to know what had happened since her imprisonment, what was happening now, but from the tense look on Vegard's and Lenore's faces every time they neared a thoroughfare, or ducked into storage rooms to avoid passing servants, she guessed now was not the time.

The route they took was a roundabout one, and it took Ida a

moment to realize where they were going, but eventually she recognized the stairs leading down to the Subterrane ahead of them. Before they reached the entrance, however, Lenore pulled Ida back, the two of them ducking into an empty hallway. She held Ida's hands in both of hers, her expression serious. Ida looked back over her shoulder to see Vegard waiting at the corner, standing guard and studiously not looking at either of them.

"Lenore?" Ida asked.

"This is where I leave you," Lenore said. She spoke quickly, as if time was precious, as if she could feel it slipping away from them. "Vegard will explain everything. Go with him."

"I don't understand," Ida said. "What do you mean leave me? Where are you going?"

Lenore looked pained. She looked over her shoulder, as if they were in danger even now.

"I wish we had more time," Lenore said, shaking her head. "But we don't. I promise you, Vegard will tell you everything. Just—" She hesitated, looked into Ida's eyes. In her face, Ida saw a thousand unsaid things. Her mind went back to the night of the Starborn Revel. To Lenore, seated across from her on that ridiculously small couch, daring Ida to wager a secret.

Ida knew now that she would have told Lenore all her secrets if she could have, and she thought perhaps Lenore would have done the same, but Lenore simply whispered, "Just be careful. And be well. Gods willing, we'll see each other soon."

She squeezed Ida's hands once and let her go.

Ida wanted to stop her, to grab her and never let go. To say how sorry she was for the way she had treated Lenore, how much it made her heart ache that Lenore had come to her rescue anyway.

But Lenore's expression was so determined that Ida knew—wherever Lenore was going, whatever she was planning to do, it was something she needed. Something that she had been working herself up to accomplish for a long time.

So Ida reached out instead, pulling Lenore into her arms one last time. Lenore tensed, before melting into Ida's embrace. The moment lasted for one heartbeat. Another.

And then Ida let go and Lenore turned away, hurrying quickly down the hall.

It was only when Ida and Vegard were in the Subterrane, in that maze of unused rooms that had once housed the Dreaming Revel, that Ida felt herself uncoil. They slipped into one of the rooms, now cold and empty without their various decorations, and when Vegard froze the lock shut, she felt all the energy of escape hit her at once. She breathed out, leaning back against the wall.

"We're safe for now, but not forever," Vegard said. "They'll find us eventually."

"What's happening?" Ida asked. "How did you find me? What's going on?"

Vegard looked back over his shoulder at her, and Ida was struck again by the lost look in his eye, the sense that he no longer knew how to talk to her. As if he was worried that whatever he said would send her fleeing from the room. She felt a burning sense of shame at the way she had treated him.

"Lenore found out what had happened to you," he said. "She told me, and then she told your maid. Sabine. We made a plan to get you out. I'm sorry we were delayed."

"I'm sorry too," Ida blurted out, and just like that the shards were out of her throat, the weight lifted off her heart as if she had thrown it to shatter on the ground between them. "Vegard—the things I said, the way I stopped talking to you, the way I didn't even reach out after you *found* me, I'm so, so sorry."

"Ida . . ." For a second, Vegard looked like he didn't know what to say. And then he took in a breath, and tentatively extended a hand to her. "I forgive you. Of course . . . I've always forgiven you."

She didn't deserve this.

She didn't deserve *forgiveness*.

But Vegard was looking at her, his hand extended, and he had come to save her, despite everything she had said, despite everything she had done. And it was such a *relief* to see him, to be there, to have spoken her words and received pardon.

She raced forward, ignoring Vegard's outstretched hand as she wrapped her arms around him. Cold bloomed against her skin, a winter's night sapping her of her heat as the metal edges of his armor's scales pressed into her through her clothes, but she held tight and wouldn't let go.

And after a moment, Vegard lowered his arms, settling them around her.

Chapter 32
TEN THOUSAND THREADS

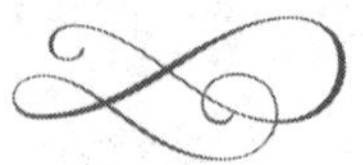

"Three *days*?" Ida asked, staring at Vegard.

In the stripped-down rooms of the Subterrane, there was nowhere truly comfortable to sit, but they had taken up places by the wall farthest away from the door, Ida against the wall, Vegard sitting between her and the entrance in case anyone came in.

Vegard nodded. "At least. You've been imprisoned for three days."

"That's not possible," Ida said. She started searching through her memory, feeling dizzy. How many times had they fed her? Once? She wasn't *nearly* hungry enough to have had only one meal in three days.

Of course, now that she thought about it, she could feel her mouth going dry, her head spinning.

She'd thought that Asteria's dungeons had been surprisingly magicless. But maybe that was a trick, meant to disorient prisoners. Maybe the truth was that the dungeon was under powerful spells too, magic meant to ensure that nobody could communicate with the outside, that nobody could escape.

Vegard confirmed her guess when he said, "We think time works differently in the dungeon, which is why we couldn't contact you while you were down there. Gloam thought they felt you call them, but . . ."

Ida shook her head. Three days. It felt like there were spiderwebs clinging to her skin. She sipped water from the flask Vegard had passed her, working through it. Her left hand lay at her side, wrapped in a cloth that he had enchanted to keep cold.

When she no longer looked like the world was falling out beneath her, Vegard nodded and continued. "We've been meeting in secret during those days, Lenore, Sabine, and I. We used my chambers, and met during the day, while the rest of the court slept. Things got a little . . . out of hand."

A little out of hand.

Ida hadn't missed the fact that they were in hiding. She hadn't forgotten that Aurel was still King of Arred, that defying him was treason, and that they couldn't stay here.

"How does Sabine fit into this?" she asked.

"Sabine is in Feld," Vegard said. "Before the castle woke yesterday, she took some of your things and handed in her resignation. She plans to wait in Feld in case you can leave by train."

Sabine. Feld.

Ida's eyes prickled at the thought of her maid giving up her livelihood for her. Sitting in Feld with all Ida's things, all her work, everything she had built in Asteria. She couldn't even begin to thank Sabine for everything she had done, and it was all worthless in the end, because Ida was still part of the Collection. Because Ida still couldn't leave.

"*How* are we going to leave Asteria?"

"By finding the source of the binding spell, and breaking it," said Vegard.

It was dawning on Ida that this plan had fallen into place without her, that no matter what she had said and done, her friends had still tried to save her. Were still trying to save her. That they hadn't given up on themselves, even if she had. Sabine, Vegard, and Lenore.

"Where did Lenore go?" Ida asked. "She promised you would tell me."

"Lenore's gone to confront the king. Ostensibly about you. It isn't the first argument they've had over the past few days. But it's a distraction. Once word gets out about the escape, she'll keep him from leaving his room."

Vegard's answer chilled her to her core. A part of her had expected it, after seeing the look in Lenore's eyes. But in that moment, Ida was suddenly, terribly afraid for her.

Ida had only seen Lenore truly use her magic once, to save Ida from the hounds in the disastrous aftermath of that first Revel. She knew that it was magic of the earth. That much was obvious. Slow-moving, complicated, but unlike Ida's, able to affect the physical world. She knew that Lenore preferred to use her connection to spirits like Gloam, found it easier to lend them a bit of her power than to use magic herself. She knew that Lenore was like her, in that she had never been properly trained. In that she'd been taken from a parent far too soon.

Lenore *could* stop King Aurel from leaving his room if she really wanted to. But that wasn't a permanent solution. The King of Arred couldn't be locked up forever—sooner or later, the tables would turn on her.

And he was still her father. There was no way Lenore got through this confrontation with her relationship with him intact.

Vegard and Lenore were too smart not to know that.

Sabine was waiting in Feld. Vegard had come to her dressed for battle.

There was a cold edge in Ida's mind, a feeling like ice in her veins as she started to grasp the enormity of the thing. If they broke this spell, it wasn't only Ida who would be able to leave the castle. Vegard and Lenore could leave. The *Collection* could leave.

Vegard smiled at her, his eyes sharp, his smile all ice and jagged edges.

"You're not the only one who's been doing some thinking over the last few weeks."

Ida felt terrible. She'd been so focused on herself, so terribly lost in her own hurts, and her own pains, and her own grief. She hadn't thought about what it *meant*—for Lenore to see so clearly how she had been stolen away, for Vegard to see how the king had tried to wrest his magic from him. She was ashamed to realize she hadn't thought about what *they* would do about it. It had been selfish, so selfish of her to assume that she was the only one who felt called to action, to move and plan and make a change.

"How are we going to break the enchantment?" she asked.

"That's where we need you, Ida."

Ida didn't know the first thing about the magic that kept the Collection imprisoned in Asteria. But Vegard seemed to think she could help, and she knew with cold certainty that she would not be leaving her friends alone again.

"Tell me what I can do."

"This isn't the first time Lenore and I have talked about leaving," Vegard admitted, seated on the floor in front of Ida. "We've considered it in the past, but we were unable to determine how King Aurel was keeping us bound. Lenore and I mistakenly believed the magic was cast by the king himself. The memories we uncovered show that that was a lie."

Ida nodded slowly, guilt cutting at her from the inside. Vegard's words only reminded her of how Lenore must have felt, seeing the truth of what her father had done.

Ida should have been there for her. Instead, she'd run away.

"I'm surprised she's helping me," Ida said, looking down at her hands. "After everything."

Vegard looked at her with surprise. "Why wouldn't she help you?"

"I left her . . ." Ida said, miserable. "She needed me. She needed help, and I—"

Vegard shook his head. "You *did* help her, Ida. I've known Lenore for . . . a long time, and I've never seen her like this. After meeting you . . . something's changed in her. For the first time, she's dreaming of a future beyond these walls. A future with you."

Ida stared at Vegard, but he didn't seem to realize the import of what he had said. Vegard looked at her matter-of-factly, as if he had only spoken the truth as he saw it. She swallowed past the knot in her throat. She didn't know if Vegard had misunderstood the situation or not, but Lenore *was* fighting, whether for Ida or for herself or for both of them, Ida didn't know. Wouldn't know until she asked her in person.

In the meantime, Ida would *stop* letting her down.

"All right," Ida said, taking a deep breath. She straightened up. "What do we know? That the king has no magic of his own?"

"That . . . isn't entirely true," Vegard said. "While it is true that King Aurel has no magic of his own *at present*, it doesn't mean he has never had any magic. He briefly possessed some amount of power, the night Asteria was moved from one timeline to another."

It was hard to think about that night without remembering her father, struggling in his last moments as the king betrayed him. Ida swallowed hard to steady herself and focused on the facts, on the memory of the king's eyes shining silver as he brought all his stolen power to bear. Vegard's magic, unleashed in an instant, strong enough to break the boundaries of space and time.

"You think it happened then?" Ida asked. "That it was part of the king's conditions, when he altered the castle?"

Vegard nodded. "King Aurel's actions then were those of a man wanting to hold on to everything he had gained. Lenore and I think that some of the castle's more peculiar rules come from his choices on that night, his desires. It makes more sense than the idea that the rules for the Collection were written in place from the beginning. Neither of us can remember much of the early days, but I do know that I was responsible for many of Asteria's spells, and I don't think there is a version of myself, no matter how young, naïve, or curious, that would have willingly written my own captivity. I don't think your father would have done that either, from what little I remember of him."

Ida remembered the bright-eyed man who had paced the unfinished halls of Asteria, looking at the plans of the castle and dreaming of what it could be. She thought of her father and remembered his patience as he taught her magic, the way he had marveled at the beauty of even her smallest creations. She remembered the way her father had died to protect Vegard, to save his life.

She couldn't imagine him writing spells of subjugation and control either.

"No. I don't think he would."

"Then we have to assume that King Aurel, whether knowingly or unknowingly, trapped us in Asteria when the castle moved, when we all lost our memories," Vegard said. "As far as we can gather, it resulted from a fundamental altering of the spells that anchored Asteria in the first place. Your father designed those spells, but my magic fueled them, and since King Aurel had access to my power, he was able to bend those spells to his will. Since the king has no magic and wouldn't be able to free us even if he wanted to, trying to convince him is pointless. We need to find the anchor of those spells and destroy it."

Ida thought about the missing tower, the pedestal Vegard had almost died on. The way the room had felt like magic, even in the memory.

"But the tower is gone. It's been destroyed . . . or it never existed."

Vegard shook his head. "Something like Asteria wouldn't have been built with just one anchor," he said. "*I* wouldn't have built the castle with only one anchor. The tower was a convenient place to anchor the castle's magic because it was central, but it wouldn't have been the only place anchoring the spells. If I were building the castle now, from scratch, I would create a mirror anchor, a second identical anchor that would resonate with the first. It would ensure that the entire system was stable, and would allow the castle's magic to continue working even if something happened to the other anchor."

"There's a second anchor somewhere?"

"There has to be," Vegard said. "Without it, this castle would have collapsed a long time ago. And I think I know where it is."

He took the canteen of water, pouring it into the air to create a castle out of ice, the same model he had once made in Ida's workshop an age ago, the Asteria of their lost memories. Vegard pointed at the tower that had been destroyed, the one that led out of his chambers. He looked ready to explain, but Ida was a step ahead of him. Her eyes traced a line from the top of the tower straight down to the castle's base, to the ground in the center of the castle.

Magic liked symmetry.

It liked equivalence, the linking together of two distinct forces, the binding of opposites.

Ida had never worked magic on the scale of the castle, but she knew what she would have done if she had to choose two points to anchor something so massive. She knew where the second anchor was.

"It's here, isn't it?" she asked Vegard. "In the Subterrane."

Vegard stopped, looking up at Ida from over the castle's crystal spires. He looked surprised for only a moment. It was a surprise she recognized—the magical were used to having to explain themselves. And it had been a while since the three of them had worked magic together.

"Yes," Vegard said, letting the castle crumble to fine dust. "Yes, exactly."

"Can you find it?"

Vegard shook his head. "Not fast enough. There are hundreds of rooms in the Subterrane, and the anchor is probably hidden. We wouldn't have placed it where anyone could stumble upon it."

We.

Ida understood suddenly, with terrible clarity, exactly what role she was supposed to play.

Vegard had powered the spells that gave Asteria its magic, but he hadn't been their architect. Somewhere in the Subterrane, there was one last remnant of her father's power, one last item he had created, and Ida needed to find it.

Only she could do it, because her magic was the same as her father's.

Grief settled over her like a heavy shroud, pressing cold pinpricks into her skin. She remembered the visions her nightflower candle had shown her and wondered if she would ever be like that Ida in another world, smiling, reading a book, living without feeling like there was a weight on her chest and over her heart.

But that would have to come later. She needed to break the king's spell, not just so that she could leave, but so that she could take Vegard and Lenore with her. Ida needed them by her side, needed them to leave with her, so that they could figure all this out together.

"I need my tools," she said, getting to her feet. "Did Sabine take everything from the workshop to Feld?"

Sabine hadn't. She'd had the presence of mind to leave Vegard with some of Ida's latest creations, the ones she had been working on before her imprisonment. The burned-out candle she, Vegard, and Lenore had used to discover the truth; the golden candle from the garden she had created on the night King Aurel approached her; and the candles she had made for her forays into the king's dreams.

She set aside the others, picking up the votive candles that she'd made to shatter unwillingness and pretension and give her greater access to King Aurel's mind. The candles she had burned on that night had been destroyed by the guards, but she rarely ever made just one. Those, she set out on the floor, one to her left and one to her right.

Neither she nor Vegard could produce fire. But she took Vegard's hands and let him channel his magic down into her candles, and she hoped that using him as a conduit would be enough.

There were so many ways Ida wished she could do this better.

She would have lit the candles herself. She would have had three of them, at least, enough to surround herself with so that she could be fully immersed. She would have used her father's firestrike, the feel of which always helped her sink into her magic. But her hand was a stinging mess, covered in burns, her father's firestrike was slag on the floor of the king's dungeons, and Sabine had only managed to save two of her candles before they were destroyed.

In the past, that would have been enough to stop her from trying.

Now, Ida closed her eyes and sank into the magic.

This time, there wasn't a mind to attach herself to. She didn't have a sleeper willing to allow her to float over the outskirts of his consciousness. This time, she sank into Asteria.

In the library, on the night of the Mythic Revel, Ida had encountered a being she had thought was the will of the castle. A living creature so much larger than she was, woven together from a hundred spells, a thousand, given meaning by the magic that had given it life. Now, Ida could see the spells that made up that will, shining threads of magic that held Asteria together. Each thread was a spell placed there over time, gleaming and tied to the mage or spirit or creature that had cast it. She could see her own threads, golden like the sun, could see Vegard's silver and Lenore's winding vines. She saw the airy traces left by Gloam and their kind, the glittering lights of the faeries in the courtyard, the beams of moonlight the starborn left in their wake, the musical echoes of the sirens in the Grotto.

The fabric of the castle was made of ten thousand threads, each woven tightly to the others, held in place so that they could never escape.

Faced with a myriad, Ida searched for one.

She searched for the thread that called to her heart, the one that felt like home, the one that all the others were anchored to. And as she searched, something happened. The threads of magic drew aside, parting for her. It was as if Asteria could feel her searching, as if it was inviting her in. It made her wonder if she had misunderstood the castle before, in the library. If the castle wasn't preventing her from finding the truth, wasn't trying to harm her. After all, after her first encounter with the hounds, she hadn't been attacked, had she?

Had it understood something about her, after that? Had Asteria truly only wanted to speak with her?

Had it decided to help her?

She felt its touch as she faded down into its heart, feather-light against her consciousness. It wasn't a confirmation, not exactly. It felt like an acknowledgment of who she was, what she was here for.

And then, at the castle's core, she found the thread she was seeking. It rang like a plucked string, its magic an echo of her own.

Chapter 33

SEA AND SKY

"I know where it is," Ida said when she opened her eyes. She was startled to find wetness on her cheek and wiped away the tear with one hand. "I don't know how to get to it, though."

Vegard nodded. "It's probably locked away. We wouldn't have placed it in a room any Reveler could have entered."

"Can you remember anything at all?"

"Unfortunately not. But if you can get me as close as possible, I might be able to figure something out."

Ida nodded, getting to her feet. She extinguished the candles and gathered them up, wishing she could do something about the scent that lingered in the air. She had to hope that it would dissipate before anyone thought to search the Subterrane, had to hope that they were gone and away from the castle long before that would be a problem.

The two of them listened at the door for a moment, only leaving when they heard no sounds in the hallway. The Subterrane was still silent, empty except for the two of them, but they moved furtively along the halls, stopping at each intersection to watch for pursuers. The quiet unnerved Ida. She wanted to know what was happening aboveground, whether they had begun to search for her yet. She wanted to know what Lenore was doing, in her confrontation with her father.

She glanced at Vegard as they walked. Vegard's expression was focused, eyes fixed ahead of him in determination. She reached up with one hand, fingers closing around the locket that hung around her neck, but although the metal felt cold to the touch, it wasn't fluctuating as much as she had come to expect.

Vegard was steadier now, whether because he had some of his memories back or because he had finally found a goal he cared about, Ida didn't know. It looked good on him, the steadiness, but she mourned the fact that she hadn't been there to watch him change, to watch it happen fully.

If she survived this, she told herself, she was going to value her friends more. She was going to be part of their lives. She wasn't going to go off on her own, abandoning them to their fates.

If. If, if . . .

The thread from her memory ended, plunging into an empty patch of wall at the end of a corridor.

Ida placed her hand on the cold stone, feeling the echoing thrum of her father's magic, a note as familiar as the lullabies that had once sung her to sleep. She closed her eyes, savoring the feel of it, and then nodded at Vegard.

"Through here," she told him.

Vegard stepped forward, and Ida moved aside to give him room. He reached out and touched the tips of his fingers to the stone, then moved them deliberately across the surface in sweeping patterns Ida couldn't grasp. The air prickled with magic, but it wasn't the blizzard she had become used to thinking of as Vegard's power. This was far more subtle than that. A creeping frost rather than an avalanche. It dried out her mouth and made her fingertips tingle.

Then, he jabbed his fingertips *into* the wall.

The wall melted around his hand.

Stone turned into dark liquid, dripping down his arm as the wall engulfed his hand to the wrist. Vegard's expression never changed, his eyes glowing like silver beacons in the dim light of the Subterrane. A ripple exuded outward from his hand, traveling through the wall.

There was a flash of light, and Ida tasted ice on her tongue. With a rush of air, the entire wall lifted off its moorings, rushing toward them like water. The stone splintered into a thousand tiny motes of ice, a flurry of snowflakes that dissolved in the wind and left pinpricks of cold against Ida's skin.

She shivered as she saw what Vegard's magic had revealed.

It wasn't a door, but an archway set into the wall, its frame gilded in an elaborate design. Through the arch lay only shadows, and at its feet, closest to the floor, silver whorls formed themselves into the outline of waves, an ocean tossed by the breeze. Sea spray snaked upward to form the sides of the archway, gradually melting into clouds as they reached the top. To the left of the door, a stylized fisherman standing in a boat hurled a net upward, toward the top of the arch, where a full moon glowed in all its beauty.

A man trying to capture the moon.

Ida placed her hand on the metal of the frame. It was cold to the touch, but the second her fingers made contact with it, warmth bloomed in her heart, in her chest, across her body. Tears pricked at her eyes.

She would know this anywhere. This was her father's magic.

She wondered if the depiction had been how he felt, standing here in Asteria, crafting the spells that would turn this place into the fabled court of the Night King. Like he was a mortal reaching up to the heavens, grasping at the divine.

"Ida," Vegard said gently.

Ida pulled herself out of her reverie, lowering her hand to her side. "This is it," she said, "I can feel it."

Vegard nodded at the archway, stepping back. "After you."

Ida swallowed, wiping her cold hands off on her trousers. In all honesty, Vegard should have gone first. This was his magic, as surely as it was her father's, the two working in concert. But she couldn't bring herself to deny him. At the end of the day, she *wanted* to see what was behind this arch, wanted the first eyes to see her father's creation to be hers.

She nodded at Vegard and stepped into the darkness.

It was bitingly cold.

Ida had walked through a lot of illusions since arriving in Asteria, many of them ones she had crafted herself. She was used to the way they altered her perception, distorting her feelings of distance and space and time. She had fallen through the fabric of the world in those illusions, shattered to a million pieces, been impaled by a thousand shards of glass.

But this *wasn't* an illusion, and a part of her mind screamed at her in warning. This was her real body, shivering, her real heart pumping frantically in her chest, her real hands clutching Vegard's locket tight as if a single drop of blood would be enough to protect her, her real breath freezing in her lungs.

This was real—and if she'd made a horrible mistake, she was about to pay the price.

But then she took another step, and the cold vanished, leaving her standing alone in the center of a room.

Unlike the rest of the Subterrane, this room had a tiled floor, the ceramic a light blue green that reminded Ida of water. The walls were dark, the room curving upward into a dome, from which hung a silvery globe, casting the room in a pale white light.

The moon.

Ahead of her, the floor rose into a circular dais. And on that dais was a stone pedestal. It would have reminded Ida of the pedestal she had seen in Vegard's memories, except while that one had been starkly unadorned, this one was carved to look like a wave, rising up from the ocean. On the dais was a censer, a metal orb decorated with the fisherman in his boat, casting his net upward, the waves tossing his boat beneath him as he hung suspended between sea and sky. The faint scent of salt exuded from the censer, tickling Ida's nose—the incense inside was still burning slowly, its magic saturating the air she breathed.

She understood, in a way, why the two rooms were so different, why they had been designed this way.

The pedestal at the top of the tower, the one in Vegard's room, was meant to represent the sky. And if Ida were trying to craft an enormous spell, like the one that powered Asteria, she would have set two opposing anchors, would have made them to encapsulate earth and sky, to show that her magic meant to encompass everything in between.

But her father hadn't used the earth. He'd used the sea.

The Niressians were islands, a fact that Ida knew in her head but had never lived. And her father's magic worked the way hers did, in thoughts and suggestions and emotional associations. This was the one he had reached for, to convey infinity. Her heart ached for the memory of her father, for the fact that she hadn't known him long enough for him to teach her what it meant to look at all the world, all the mountains and lakes and glaciers of Arred, and think that they were nothing in the face of the sea.

Another ripple passed through the world, and Vegard stepped through the arch behind her. He looked mildly surprised, as if he hadn't been sure what to expect, but found it more pleasant than he imagined. He turned and raised his hand, and the stone walls of the chamber grew once more to cover the archway, erasing it from sight until it seemed like there was no entrance or exit from this chamber at all.

Ida walked over to him, watching as he studied the walls, the room they were standing in.

"We're below the castle," he said.

Ida nodded. It was highly likely they had passed through a portal, and that the room they were standing in now was not physically connected to the Subterrane. "We're probably in the mountain somewhere."

"Most likely," Vegard said. "It's hard to tell. I wish I had my memories in full. I'd say we're below the castle's foundations."

Ida felt the claustrophobia of that statement, couldn't help but imagine the mountain pressing in, crushing them like an egg. The room had stayed intact for nearly a decade, Ida reminded herself. It probably wasn't going to collapse now. She shook off the mild panic, looking back at Vegard.

"The entrance is sealed?"

"I don't think anyone will be coming after us here. They'd have to know this place existed in the first place, and not even the king knows that. We're safe for now, but we obviously can't stay here forever."

Ida nodded, turning her eyes back to the censer on the pedestal, the currents of magic that radiated from it. She had no doubt that this was what they had come here to find. She stepped forward, climbing up onto the dais.

From here, the feeling of magic at work was much stronger, a pressure against her chest that made it hard to breathe. She looked back over her shoulder at Vegard, who was still watching her. His eyes met hers, cool and clear, and she knew she had done the right thing. Because this was her father's magic, a magic they shared. Vegard might have given the spell fuel, but he couldn't take that power back—once given, it existed until it finished running its course. But Ida could alter the spell. Maybe. Probably.

If she couldn't, at least, she didn't think there was anyone who could.

"I'll try to get it to release us," she said. "Maybe there's a way to undo what the king's done. But this might take a while—I've never done anything like this before."

"I'll keep watch," Vegard said. "Don't worry."

Don't worry.

There was so much to be worried about, so many unanswered questions, so many things to fear.

But at the end of the day, it didn't matter. She wasn't leaving without setting things right.

She reached out and grabbed hold of the censer with both hands.

When her skin touched metal, Ida recoiled. The magic ripped through her like a hurricane, a wave of blistering cold fueled by Vegard's power, and she sucked in a breath as she felt the locket around her neck grow colder and colder, a nexus of winter centered between her collarbones. She forced herself to breathe deep, to lean into the sensation, and to search past the chill, past Vegard's power. To search for the very foundation of the spell.

Finding it was like breaking into a summer day.

Warmth washed over her, easing into her frozen limbs. The echo of her father's magic, now a symphony as it played across her mind, so that for a moment she was standing in the full embrace of the sun, watching as the structure of the spell unfolded around her. The lines and whorls and threads of the spell expanded outward, projecting on the walls and floor around her, so that Ida stood at the heart of a world of glittering stars, and when she heard Vegard take in a breath, she knew that Vegard could see it too.

It wasn't perfect. There was a dark line through the heart of the spell, pulsing with its own life as it smothered the golden threads woven around it. And there were parts of the spell that were patchy or had gone dark, elements that her father would have likely come back to repair if he had been around. If he had known—if *anyone* had known what was needed. It was also unbalanced, missing its counterweight, the piece that had once been at the center of Vegard's tower.

But it was still more intricate than anything Ida had seen before. And she knew, holding on to the censer with wonder, that *this* was Asteria. This was the true magic of the court of the Night King.

That line, that dark void that cut through the wall across from her, eating into the golden light and pulsating like a thing alive. That had to be it—King Aurel's blight, the change he had wrought in the spell on that day. Looking at it now, Ida could see that it was growing, that if left unchecked it would swallow the whole castle, maybe all of Arred.

That was what she would have to cut out, if they were to have any hope of escaping.

She reached for it, brushing against it with her mind, and the world vanished as Ida sank into the depths of the castle.

Chapter 34

FATHER AND CHILD

Asteria spread out before her, a gleaming chasm of darkness and light. With her mind attuned to the censer's magic, Ida could see everything in the castle, all the movement of its inhabitants, all the flashes of magic lighting up different areas of the Night King's Court. She saw the Revel, pinpricks of power and light in the castle's main courtyard, fully unaware of the world crashing down around them as the members of the court celebrated the simple joy of being alive. She saw the kitchens where the palace's staff, both human and nonhuman, worked tirelessly to provide the experience of magic for each member of the court, bustling along service corridors and going to elaborate lengths to ensure that none of the highborn guests ever thought about where their meals were coming from. She saw the guards carefully searching each level of the castle, trying to find her and Vegard without disturbing the guests. And in the heart of the castle, she saw Lenore and her father, the two of them locked in a battle of wills, Lenore trying to sustain her own glimmer of light against the pulse of darkness that Ida now saw was tied, fully and irrevocably, to the king.

It was this last that Ida focused on, because this was the heart of everything she sought. The dark void that warped her father's magic, the chains that bound Ida, Vegard, Lenore, and every other member of the King's Collection within its walls, the shadows that lay at the heart of Asteria.

It was all within King Aurel.

A pillar of darkness emanating from him, tangling and swallowing the gold threads her father had so carefully woven. She reached for it, trying to pull her father's golden threads out of that dark heart, to untangle the mess his legacy had become. As soon as she touched the threads, she shrank back as if burned, hissing through her teeth. The magic had sent a shock throughout her entire body, like Ida had tried to grasp lightning. Through her closed eyes, she heard Vegard speak up.

"Ida? Are you all right?"

It took effort to open her mouth and answer. It felt like she was in two places at once. Part of her was still standing in the hidden chamber with Vegard, her hands pressed to the sides of her father's censer, her eyes closed. The rest of her was floating in the liminal spaces of Asteria, staring futilely at the snarled threads of magic that surrounded the king.

"Fine," she ground out, trying to keep her mind in one place, her body in another. "This is harder than I thought."

"Can I help?"

"Not unless you can figure out how to untangle the magic from around the king," Ida said. She tugged at his power, a beacon of white light beside her, and fed a small amount of it into her perception so that he could see what she did. She heard him let out a breath beside her and knew that the problem looked exactly as complex to him as it did to her.

"I don't know which thread to pull," she confessed. "I don't even know where to start."

"If I touch this, there's no telling what it will do," Vegard said. "To me, or Asteria."

Ida nodded. She'd already guessed as much. The situation was far too volatile. In terms of magic, Vegard was a hammer, useful only when the solution was complete destruction. She sank back into the image, trying to tug free some of the smaller threads from the writhing mass that surrounded the king. This time, she succeeded, gritting past the pain and numbness that spread from the tips of her fingers up into her arms as she pulled two handfuls of golden threads out of the void. But their cut edges writhed uselessly in the space as Ida pulled them away, their magic already consumed. She couldn't figure out how to put them back together, how to recreate the spells that formed Asteria without them.

And they were only a small, small part of the tangle of magic that surrounded King Aurel.

Ida could have sobbed in frustration and despair. She kept hold of the censer, but only just, her head dipping and shoulders slumping forward as she tried to keep herself upright. Her father had been brilliant, and he'd had years to put these spells together from scratch. If she had a hundred years, she wouldn't be able to fix this.

"I can't do it," Ida said. "It's too much."

"Lenore," Vegard whispered, and she felt his presence retreat from her mind. "She shares blood with the king. She might be able to help you."

The last thing Ida wanted to do was distract Lenore when she was clearly doing everything in her power to keep the king from leaving his rooms. She could see Lenore's magic sparking around her, holding back waves of compulsion, keeping the doors shut, ensuring that no one outside the chamber could hear the king's shouts. She must know that her magic was limited, that there would be no going back from here.

But Vegard was right. If he couldn't help her, maybe Lenore could.

Ida took a breath and touched Lenore's consciousness, the knot of power buried deep within her.

Lenore, she whispered.

And Lenore answered.

Lenore's magic was the magic of living things, of the life that grew boundlessly through the forest or hid in secluded mossy caverns in the mountains. When Ida touched the thread of her power, it was like stepping into the heart of an unfurling flower. Lenore's defenses parted around her, soft and gentle, so that for one moment Ida was with her in her mind, seeing out of her eyes, hearing out of her ears. She could see King Aurel standing before her, looking absurd in his nightgown, his face contorted with rage. Could feel her connection to the woody vines that crisscrossed behind Lenore, holding the door shut from all angles. Could sense the strain in Lenore's magic, in her mind, as King Aurel looked at her and yelled: "You will *not disobey me*!"

I'm a little busy right now, Ida, Lenore thought, and it echoed in Ida's mind as clearly as if Lenore had been standing next to her, speaking into her ear.

I need you to take a look at something, Ida said, and then because there was no way to soften the blow, no way to prepare Lenore for what Ida wanted her to see, she drew Lenore's consciousness out of her protective shell, exposing her to the network of spells that surrounded Asteria. Showing her the dark heart centered over the presence of the king.

Ida felt Lenore's surprise, registered it as an echo against her own mind. She could sense Lenore's shock as she took in the scope of the distortion, the way it warped and drew in the spells that powered Asteria.

What is this?

I think this is what's keeping the Collection from leaving.

It's more than that . . . Lenore said, after a moment of studying the distortion. *I think . . . this is what's tying us to this reality. What's keeping people from remembering your father, or my mother, or anything from that other timeline. Look, it's tied to everything.*

Ida looked, and with Lenore accompanying her, it was easy to see what she had missed. The roots that spread from the heart of the distortion, burrowing past the castle's walls and into reality itself. It was more than just a warping of her father's spells, of the vision that surrounded the castle. It was a key, binding them to this altered reality.

Ida's heart sank.

"This is hopeless," she groaned, out loud and in her mind. She felt her body curl inward as she slumped over the censer.

"Ida?" Vegard asked.

"It's too much," Ida said. Now that her vision had been expanded, now that she could see the whole of what she was facing, she understood. There was no way to simply untangle her father's spells from King Aurel. No way to remove the king's influence from the castle, not when the king had a hold of reality itself. There was no way to do any of that and keep everything else intact.

The only way they would be able to break this spell, the only way they would be able to change things, would be to destroy it. The magic of Asteria, the last remnant of her father's work, the last thing holding this reality in place.

All of it.

A vision passed through her, an image of something she had seen once, when using her nightflower candle. Of that other reality. The woman in royal robes, a crown on her head, standing in front of a coffin. The image of Asteria in ruins behind her.

If things had taken their natural course, the Witch of Callania's spell would have achieved its intended end.

Asteria's magic would disappear, and the Night King's Court would never have existed.

And King Aurel would have died.

The thought cut through Ida's mind like a knife, and Ida felt Lenore flinch away from it instinctively. Currents of grief begin to swirl through Lenore, and Ida ached in sympathy for her. Because King Aurel was a horrible person, and Ida hated him for what he had done to her family, but he was still Lenore's father. There was only one solution that made any sense. But could she claim to be Lenore's friend and ask this of her? In what world was this their only choice, the only thing that was right?

It's fine, Lenore said. *Do it.*

Lenore, I'm sorry. I'm not strong enough . . .

You are, Ida. Lenore's magic surged through her, a rush of warmth like an embrace. It wrapped tightly around Ida, pulling her close, so that for a moment all that Ida knew was the sensation of Lenore all around her, magic like a caress against her skin. She could feel the pressure of Lenore's fingers on her back, had the sense that Lenore was holding her close in this space between their minds. She almost felt like Lenore was pulling back, looking her in the eye.

Lenore's words washed over her, ringing in her mind. There was no doubt in Lenore's voice, no hesitation, no fear. Lenore spoke the words like she was speaking only fact, like anyone on earth would obviously see what she saw. They rang like a bell in Ida's mind, cutting through her own doubts.

Lenore's presence surged forward, and Ida felt pressure on her lips, there for a moment and gone again, a flash of lightning that rooted her to the ground as Lenore said, *You ARE strong enough.*

Lenore, I . . .

The enormity of it was difficult to grasp, the consequences of this choice. Ida's mind reached for any other solution, but her thoughts were sliding away from her like water through a sieve. The magic of Asteria pulsed around her, beautiful and horrible and hopelessly tangled, and she could feel the censer vibrating under her touch, a fragile sheet of metal between her and the last pieces of her father's magic, and she knew that it was always easier to destroy than to repair.

Her mouth was dry, her heart pounding in her chest.

They would lose so much, *so much*, if she did this.

She couldn't help but ask, *Are you sure?*

Lenore faltered. And then she flinched back into her reality, at the feeling of hands clutching her arms, her father's face filling up her vision, his eyes full of rage and hatred and greed.

"How dare you *ignore me*?" King Aurel roared. He shook Lenore hard enough to hurt, hard enough that Ida could feel it, hard enough to make Lenore let out a yelp that echoed in the high room.

Lenore's answer rang in her mind, sharp and frightened.

I'm sure, Ida. Do it. Do it now!

And then Ida was being shoved out of Lenore's mind, pushed away from her as if by physical force, and the last thing Ida saw was Lenore blinking tears out of her eyes, stretching a hand out toward her father. The vines that held the door in place surged up to form a wall between them, a physical barrier between the king and Lenore, and she could feel Lenore curling inward, all her power coming into herself.

Then Ida crashed back into her own body, into the secret room that waited deep beneath Asteria, the space she shared with Vegard.

Ida sucked in a pained breath, her fingers pressing so tightly into the censer that she could feel the engravings leaving indentations in her fingertips. Her burnt hand, the left one, pulsed with a numb throbbing that she knew couldn't mean anything good, but she was so far removed from the sensation that she didn't care. She squeezed her eyes shut, doubling over the censer so that the scent of the sea filled her nose, until she was adrift in it. The vision of the castle never returned, but she clung to the censer anyway. Being surrounded by the aura of her father's magic felt like being in the same room as him, felt like having him there with her.

This did nothing to make her decision any easier.

If she destroyed it, what would be left?

If she destroyed this, what would become of the three of them? Of her? Of her memories from the past few years that had never truly existed?

What would be left of her father?

"Ida?" She felt Vegard ascend the dais, coming to stand next to her. He was the eye of a winter storm, but she was so wrapped up in the magic of Asteria that she could barely feel the cold, barely feel anything but a gentle pressure as his hand came to settle on her shoulders. "Ida, what's wrong?"

She wished that she could freeze time. That she was strong enough to hold on to a moment and never let it go. If she had enough time to think, maybe she could come up with a better solution.

But no.

Lenore had already told her what she wanted done. Lenore, who had more to lose than Ida had. Ida had left her once. She wouldn't leave her again.

She straightened up, loosening her grip on the censer, and looked over her shoulder at Vegard.

"Lenore says we should destroy this."

Vegard saw all the implications of that statement at once. She could see it in the way his eyes widened in slight surprise, calculation as his gaze drifted from the left to the right, acceptance as his eyes found hers. He squeezed her shoulder, and the gesture, from someone who had once been so reluctant to touch her, nearly undid her.

"And?" he asked. "What do you say?"

Leaving the decision up to her was a cruel sort of kindness. Ida cast a helpless glance at the wall, where the diagram of her father's final magic was still projected, King Aurel's dark scar swirling at its heart.

Did she have a choice either way?

Yes.

She knew that she did, felt it in the power that ran through her veins, the same magic that had designed Asteria. She didn't have Vegard's raw power, didn't have Lenore's experience. But this magic sang to her heart, to her blood. She had a choice. There had always been a choice.

She could do what King Aurel did. Take Vegard's power from him and use it to rewrite reality. Maybe she could even design a sufficiently convincing illusion, one that made her believe her father was still alive.

She could become Asteria's dark heart.

But she already knew she wouldn't do that. She swallowed past the knot in her throat.

Her father was dead. He was never coming back.

Ida *had* to let him go.

"There's no other way," she said. "And Lenore won't last much longer. I need you to help me."

Vegard's eyes were on hers. There was a pause, a held breath before they flashed silver, a brilliant light searing impressions onto her eyelids.

And then his magic flowed through her, and Ida could do anything.

Chapter 35

REALITY

Power flowed through her, a heady sensation that left Ida's mind spinning, her senses struggling to expand to contain it. The magic held between her hands, the spells contained in her father's censer, which at first seemed so vast that Ida could barely comprehend it, now felt fragile, a creation made of spun sugar. Vegard's magic was a wild animal inside her, rattling against the cage made of her skin, and it was so tempting to let it tear out of her and wreak havoc.

She reined it in, keeping the magic at bay as it wrapped around the censer. Frost coated the metal exterior, freezing her fingers to the surface. When she exhaled, she breathed out mist, air condensing from the ice in her lungs. The world froze, and it felt to Ida like she was suspended in time, hovering once more in that space between moments. She was aware, once again, of that presence she had glimpsed in the library, the all-consuming will of Asteria. Except now, with Vegard's power running through her, she no longer saw that figure as a solid mass of energy. She saw the gaps that ran through it, the dark portions that had rotted and fallen away.

She saw where she could strike.

The figure didn't move to stop her. It only watched her, as if waiting to see what she would do. It seemed so unconcerned about its demise.

If she waited too much longer, the power would consume her.

Ida wasn't used to having what she thought of as real power, the power to alter the physical world. But in some ways, using Vegard's power was like crafting an illusion. A beautiful lie, that the power belonged to her, that she was able to channel and control it as she wished. She imagined shards of ice gathered around the censer, around her hands, each shard of power lovingly crafted into a blade. She remembered the glass mirrors of her dream and the way they had torn through her, and thought of this as a fitting end.

Her skin vibrated with the urge to let the power loose.

It wouldn't take long. A thought, a whisper, and then it would be done. Her swords would slice through the spells' weaknesses, and it would all fall apart.

It would be so easy.

But still, Ida hesitated.

Even corrupted, the spell was so beautiful. It had brought magic and light and life to so many. How could Ida take that away?

She thought of her father, the way he had smiled as he talked about designing the spell. And she thought about the look on his face, the utter betrayal and despair as Aurel turned on him, as Aurel prepared to kill to keep the power he had.

She thought of her father's masterpiece in King Aurel's hands forever.

Enough. Ida held the power within her like a breath, and then, her rage crystallizing inside her heart, she breathed out and let it go. Her blades pierced through the figure in her mind, the laden and beleaguered will of Asteria, slicing through its weak points like paper. She saw it tremble, doubling over, before the magic that composed it began to uncoil. In its last moments, it raised its head to look at Ida. It let out a shuddering breath, laced with something that felt almost like relief, and then it began to fade away.

The spells gave way next. Ida felt their destruction like physical blows, felt their resistance and weight as the shards of Vegard's power ripped out of her and into them. They tore and recoiled and were sliced apart by the blows, all while goose bumps erupted on Ida's skin and she felt the strength leave her muscles with the power's release. One by one, the golden threads that filled the air around them snapped apart and went dark, their magic winking out of existence with them. Then the censer cracked, a great, jagged tear opening in it from top to bottom, splitting apart the image of the fisherman in the boat, the net cast upward to the moon. And as the censer crumbled, the last remnants of Tomas Rosales's magic exploded outward, a blast that took Ida's consciousness, took her mind, and threatened to tear it right out of her body.

She held on, grounding herself in the sensations. The weakness of her limbs, the feeling of the cold metal beneath her hands, Vegard's grip tight on her shoulder to keep her from falling. The taste of blood from where she had bitten her lip, the ground beneath her feet, the scent of the air.

It all kept her grounded, kept her within herself.

And it let her feel the moment the explosion ended, and the magic began to curl into itself like a dying flame.

It made her feel . . .

A warmth, blossoming in her heart. The touch of a hand on her face, warm and familiar. The scent of smoke and incense and home. A feeling, deep down inside her bones, that felt almost like pride.

Pride and love and so much grief, like a piece of her father's magic knew her, recognized her, and knew what she had done.

Her father's magic had always been part of the will of Asteria.

Ida tasted salt and realized she was crying.

The magic curled in on itself, a snuffed candle. And then the last of the gold threads vanished, the room going dark around them.

Ida sagged forward, releasing her hold on the broken censer. She would have hit the ground if Vegard hadn't quickly wrapped his arms around her, pulling her away from the pedestal. In the darkness, Ida heard only their labored breathing, felt only the last vestiges of her father's magic slip away.

And then, without the magic, the roots anchoring reality began to slip, tethers breaking one by one.

Ida opened her eyes and lifted her head, feeling the ground rumble beneath her feet. The last of the supports broke, King Aurel's darkness slipping through the cracks without her father's magic to brace it.

That was when the world fell apart.

Up until that point, most of what happened had been on a separate plane, a battle for the magic within the hidden spaces between thought and reality. But this unraveling was very real. Ida felt the shock of it ripple through the floors beneath their feet, then the walls, the roof over their heads, until the entire chamber was trembling. When a deafening snap split the air around them and a crack appeared in the stone wall across from them, Ida knew time was running out.

"We need to go," Vegard said. He tightened his grip on her, and before she could do anything, could ask any more questions, a dome of ice formed over their heads. Ida gasped as the ceiling began to cave in, a chunk of stone striking the surface of the shield with enough force to crack the ice and make Vegard suck in a breath.

"What's happening?" Ida asked.

Vegard's answer made the bottom drop out of her stomach.

"The castle is collapsing. We have to leave. Now."

"How do we—?" Ida began, but that was all she could get out before light erupted from Vegard, a rush of power twining around the two of them. It swept her up off her feet, shoving them back out through the arch as the chamber collapsed around them. Ida screamed, her stomach lurching as they appeared back in the bowels of the Subterrane.

Into an Asteria that was tearing apart.

The two of them landed on the floor in a tangle of limbs, and Ida pushed herself up off of Vegard's chest, her eyes wide as she saw what was happening to the silver arch on the wall. It had broken in two, snapped cleanly down the middle, and as Ida watched, was already beginning to tarnish and decay. Black rot spread from the bottom of the arch upward, tainting the image of the man on his boat, the ocean, the moon.

The tremor had started underground. Beneath the earth. But as Ida lay there, she could feel the floor of the Subterrane beginning to shift and tremble too. Vegard was right. The whole castle was collapsing.

"We need to get outside," Ida said.

From the ground, Vegard coughed, pushing himself up. His eyes were still silver, his face pale. One of his hands clutched his chest, where Ida knew the scar from his encounter with the king was hidden. His fingers dug into his clothes and she held her breath, hoping against hope that Vegard wasn't about to have an episode right now.

But then he pushed himself up to his feet, pulling Ida up with him.

"We need to find a window," he said instead, drawing something from his pocket. A whistle, thin and silver and gleaming like a shard of moonlight.

"What's that?" Ida asked.

"It calls the starborn."

The starborn. The white horses that could race through the skies.

"There's a small window by the entrance. Near the stairs."

Vegard nodded and they ran. As they sprinted through the corridors, the shaking around Asteria worsened, the ground bucking and heaving beneath their feet. Ida was already drained from exertion, but she ran as fast as she could, her lungs burning, a stitch stabbing into her side.

She nearly sobbed in relief when she saw the window.

It wasn't truly a window, but rather a narrow rectangular slit cut into the space between wall and ceiling, covered by a thin metal screen. It was meant for ventilation more than anything else, a window at ground level to keep the Subterrane from being suffocating. Vegard extended a hand, and a blast of ice slammed into the delicate screen, blasting it off the side of the mountain. He all but threw her up through the gap, following her out into the winter air as she scrambled onto the rocky ledge outside the window.

By the time they were outside, the castle was shaking like a tree in a storm, blocks of white stone raining down around them. Lights flickered uncertainly in its windows. Ida heard distant cries and felt a flash of fear.

The window had never been meant for people to climb through.

There was no path that led away from the patch of ground they were standing on, nothing but a falling castle above them and a sheer drop off the mountain.

Vegard raised the whistle to his lips, blowing three times. The notes rang high and clear, vibrating through the air, and then the starborn answered.

Two of them, sleek white horses rushing from the top of Asteria's highest tower. Vegard shoved her toward one as they came to a stop in front of them, and Ida didn't need telling twice. She moved, hauling herself onto the horse's back, and held tight to its neck as it took to the air. The bottom of Ida's stomach dropped away as they gained altitude. Ida shivered against the winter breeze, unaware up until that moment that she could still feel cold, and held on until the two of them were in the night sky, away from Asteria.

Away from the collapsing castle, the last moments of the Night King's Court.

Now that she was safe, Ida turned back to look at the castle with a cold realization. There were still so many people within its walls. Celeste, the Revelers, *Lenore*. She turned her horse toward the castle, swallowing against the tightness in her throat. One of the castle's highest towers broke off, crashing against the ground, and Ida prayed no one had been in it or under it.

"We need to get them out!" she said.

"How?" Vegard asked.

Ida didn't know, but she had to do *something*. She couldn't just sit and watch this happen.

She nudged her horse around, toward the collapsing castle, the shattering remnants of King Aurel's dreams. Ida was fully prepared to charge in. She didn't know what she would be able to do, but she had a vision of herself swooping into the remnants of the castle, through the king's chambers. She saw herself taking Lenore by the arm and hauling her out, putting her on the starborn's back and searching the wreckage for Celeste and the others. She saw herself rescuing as many people as she could. Even as she considered it, she knew it was hopeless—there weren't enough starborn, not for everyone in the court—but she had to *try*. She would never be able to forgive herself if she ran away without doing *anything*.

She kneed her horse in the side. The starborn charged forward and would have carried out Ida's will if it wasn't for the rush of cold air that suddenly appeared in front of her, ice crystals blocking her path. Her horse reared at the sudden obstacle, and Ida's stomach lurched as she threw both her arms around the starborn's neck, fighting to keep her seat.

Vegard rode up beside her just as Ida got her horse to settle, her heartbeat calming as she began to feel a little more stable. He reached out, grabbing her by the arm to keep her in place.

"Wait," he told her.

Ida stared at him helplessly. How could he tell her to *wait*?

"What about *Lenore*? She's still in there!"

Vegard's response was to tip his head back toward the castle. Ida followed his gaze, her lip trembling. She kept a tight, two-handed grip on the starborn's mane.

At first, she had no idea what he was talking about. Her eyes were filled with the crumbling castle, the falling stones, and Ida was overwhelmed with the sudden terrible certainty that no one in the castle would make it out alive.

She felt it before she saw it.

A rumble of magic, coming up from the ground. It was a massive tremor, coming out of the bones of the mountain itself. For a moment, Ida couldn't place it. It felt like an earthquake, an avalanche. But then the magic reached up into Asteria itself, into the castle's rotting foundations, and Ida sensed it: trees and plants and growing things. She had only a moment to register it as Lenore's magic before a massive tree ripped out of the mountaintop, its trunk piercing the heart of Asteria as it continued to grow. Its branches wrapped around the falling castle, holding walls in place, bolstering floors and keeping the structure from falling apart.

At the top of the castle, where the towers had once been, the tree burst upward, its branches crowning themselves with green leaves despite the winter chill. As Ida watched, the leaves shimmered and shifted, going from a deep summer green to the glowing reds of autumn before withering into brown and falling away entirely. When there was nothing more of the leaves but bare branches, the trembling stopped.

Asteria remained upright, part of the tree. It was a thing half-formed, all sagging walls and cracks and pieces barely held together by wood, but it was upright. And already, Ida could see people running out of the castle, making their way out of the courtyards and onto the path that led down from the mountain. She breathed deep, feeling something in her chest uncoil. There had to have been injuries—there had been too much destruction for there not to be. But this was so much better than it could have been. The members of the court would survive.

Vegard waited a moment longer, until it was certain that the castle was stable. Then, he released her arm.

"Come," he told her, nudging his own starborn toward what was left of the castle. "Let's find Lenore."

Chapter 36

THE END AND THE BEGINNING

The king's chambers stood in the heart of the castle. During the collapse, they had cracked open to the sky, so it wasn't hard for Ida to guide her starborn through the gaps between the tree's massive branches and into the king's rooms themselves. The magic had stopped for now, the wild rebound that Ida had felt when she destroyed the spell settling to a background hum. The world had stopped changing, but in Ida's mind, it still felt like the world was ending.

The sudden calm was playing havoc with her nerves. She knew she would only be able to relax when she saw Lenore.

Ida felt a sense of foreboding in her gut as she and Vegard flew through the canopy of branches. Lenore had used so much magic here, more than Ida had ever seen anyone use at one time. She must have had to draw deep to create a tree like this, and channeling that much power had consequences.

She didn't know what she and Vegard would find.

As they ducked down through the branches, the pieces of Asteria began to replace the tree's structure, stones and tapestries interspersed throughout the wood. The smell of lamp oil filled the air, although the structure remained dark. Ida winced—the whole place was a fire hazard. If it wasn't already being evacuated, everyone needed to leave. She was about to say as much to Vegard when she caught sight of a flicker in the air in front of her, motes of light that swirled around her head before settling in front of her face.

A weak voice spoke. "Miss Ida . . ."

"Gloam!" Ida said. Her voice echoed in the high chamber, but she didn't care. She was so relieved to find them alive. "Gloam, are you hurt? Are you okay?"

Gloam's lights flickered weakly, and their voice was soft, but clear. "I . . . will survive, Miss Ida. We lent our power to . . . Lady Lenore. You must help Lady Lenore . . ."

Ida's heart seized.

"Take us to her, Gloam," Ida said. "Please."

Gloam flickered once in affirmation and streamed off, a line of faint glittering motes, into the dark. Ida followed them, her starborn trailing moonlight as they pushed through the tangle of branches that made up the space. As Ida hurried to catch up, her heart pounding noisily in her chest, she was reminded of her early days in Asteria. Of the way Gloam had led her to the Revel, that first night in the palace when King Aurel's court had seemed so magical.

With the castle's interior exposed, with the last traces of her father's magic fading from Ida's mind, Asteria no longer looked like a place of magic. It looked like what it was—the bones of a beautiful lie. But Ida dealt with illusions, and she couldn't help but feel, somehow, that this was the castle's truest state. The beauty of the castle's magic had never been in the illusion, it had been in the making. In the fact that her father had seen stone and wood and glass and dreamed what the castle could be.

Such a waste, that it had never reached its true potential.

There would never be a place like this again.

The starborn's hooves touched the ground, and Ida leaped off the horse's back, scrambling after Gloam. The wreckage of the king's bedchamber was almost unrecognizable, but Ida could make out the enormous canopied bed where King Aurel slept and the wooden desk she had used to set up her candles before everything went wrong. She ducked under what was left of a fallen wardrobe, following Gloam to the side of the room nearest what was once the main door of the king's quarters.

There were two bundles of cloth on the ground, barely illuminated by Gloam's dim light. Neither were moving.

Ida let out a ragged gasp. She ran to the first, turning it over, and nearly screamed when she saw that it was full of bones. An eyeless skull was staring up at her, reflected in Gloam's eerie light, jaw fixed in a permanent grin. Only the rich clothes that encased the skeleton and the signet ring on one ivory finger told her this was all that was left of the king.

Ida pushed the bones away from her, startled. They rattled as they hit the ground. She stepped back, heart pounding.

How long had her father been missing? Seven years, almost eight? King Aurel's stolen magic had allowed him to stay alive for far longer than he should have. Now, the magic had rebounded on him, revealing him for what he really was. Bones and dust.

She shuddered, rising, and fought down her revulsion as she ran toward the other figure on the ground.

Lenore, thankfully, was flesh and blood. She lay on her side, Gloam swirling around her in concern, but her limbs were so cold, her face so pale. One of her hands rested on the wooden surface of the tree, a nest of branches that bound the door shut, and Ida realized that this was where it had started, the spell that held up Asteria.

She crouched down beside Lenore, pulling her gently onto her back and resting Lenore's head on her lap. Ida had never been so relieved to see Lenore's chest rise and fall with her breath. She let out a hitching sob, one that echoed in the darkness of the king's bedchamber.

Footsteps from behind her told her that Vegard had arrived. He came up to Ida and Lenore, crouching down beside her. Ida doubled over Lenore, tightening her grip, and couldn't stop the sobs from escaping her, the tears from rolling down her face. She felt Vegard's hand on her trembling back and cried harder, keeping her hold on Lenore.

She had been such a fool. She should never have pushed these people away, should never have let her friends go. If Lenore had died—

"How is she?" Vegard asked.

Ida realized she was clutching Lenore too tightly. She pulled back, giving her more air. In the firelight, Lenore looked pallid, but her eyes twitched at the light and she was breathing. That was enough. Gods, it would have to be enough.

"She's alive," Ida said. She sniffed, wiped at her eyes and nose with her hand, and struggled to regain her composure. "What do we do now?"

"We get Lenore out," he said. "And from there, on to Feld. I don't think we want to be caught in here with the body of the king."

"We'll meet up with Sabine," Ida said, the pieces of the plan coming together. "If we hurry, we can fly the starborn to Feld before word spreads. We can pick Sabine up and find somewhere to wait this out."

"Where do we go?" Vegard asked.

In Ida's mind, she was already mapping out the route. Past Trissaire, in the sky, northward into the hills. To a small town where barely anyone lived, where Ida would find her mother and the rest of her family. She had so much to say to her mother.

But before she could go home, there were things she needed to take care of.

"Gloam," Ida said, speaking into the emptiness. "What do you want to do?"

"I will be leaving soon, Mistress Ida," they responded. Their voice was even softer now than it had been. "Many of the Collection . . . wish to return to their homes. I will go with them. And then I may . . . return. To look after the Lady Lenore."

Ida nodded. Gloam had been by Lenore's side for a long time. It said a lot, that they still wanted to be with her. "Can I ask you for one last favor?" she asked. "I know I've asked you for a lot."

"It is . . . my pleasure."

"On your way out, could you find Celeste Valois, and make sure she gets out of the castle? Could you tell her . . . could you tell her I'm alive, and that I haven't forgotten my promise? Could you ask her where I can find her, when this is all done? And when you come back to Lenore, could you give me her answer?"

"I can do that for you, Miss Ida."

"Good," said Ida. She sighed, her heart heavy, and looked at Vegard. "Do you have your memories back?" she asked him, because that was what had started all of this. Because now, at the end of all things, a part of her still wanted to know if they had won.

"Some . . ." he admitted. "I think some are simply gone."

"Are we going to forget the last few years?"

Vegard shook his head. "I don't think so. We've lived too much, done too much. For better or for worse, for the last seven years, *this* timeline was our reality. It's more likely that the two realities will merge. That what results will borrow from both timelines, while being something all its own."

Ida nodded, understanding. Just as the alternate timeline had left her with her memories intact, because she had to exist somehow, the world that had been when she erased the king's magic couldn't simply disappear. Too many people had lived in that world, too many lives, too many marks. Instead, they'd rewritten history.

Or . . . if time was a river, then the king's command had stopped its flow for some time. But now that they'd taken that command away, water was rushing through, carving new channels and charging along old ones, creating something that looked a lot like it had been before but was still indelibly altered.

There was no telling what the future would look like, what the world would look like after this.

But she knew where she had to go next. She looked up at Vegard.

"Come home with me," she said. "We'll wait things out there."

EPILOGUE

A grave was too small to contain a life.

Ida felt emptiness echoing around her as she stood beside her mother on a chilly spring morning, dressed in black, her hands clasped in front of her as she looked down at the stone. Tomas Rosales, beloved husband and father, the date of his birth and the date of his death. It seemed like too little to say, because how could a single stone contain all Ida's feelings?

The grief that welled up inside of her as soon as she and her mother were alone, the storm that had crystallized over the long winter, becoming a shard of ice she could still feel tucked in her chest when she breathed. The relief, as terrible as it was, of holding her mother close while the two of them cried, knowing that a wound that had been open for so long could finally begin to heal. The guilt—both at the fact that she had gone all the way to Asteria, pulled the place up by its roots, and still had not been able to come up with a better answer than this, and at the knowledge that tore at her every day she woke up in her attic bedroom in her grandmother's farmhouse feeling like she was too large for her skin. The knowledge that she couldn't stay here. That as much as she loved her mother, as much as she loved her family, she had never belonged here.

Her friends stood a respectful distance away, watching the proceedings. Ida could sense their eyes on her back, the steady push and pull of Vegard's and Lenore's magic—Vegard's waning now that the air was warming, Lenore's growing at pace with the shift of the earth beneath them.

They were both leaving. Ida knew that in her heart. They had stayed with her throughout the winter, on and off, shuffled between various houses and barns and wearing her grandmother's patience thin to the bone, but they had other things to do.

Lenore needed to return to Callania. She had fulfilled all her responsibilities here, had gone back to Trissaire after her recovery to tell her half siblings, the princes and princesses, what had happened to their father. She'd cleared Ida's name of all suspicion, saying only that the king had been using magic to prolong his life and that it had finally backfired on him. Her siblings had never trusted Asteria, had been hungry for the throne, and it hadn't taken much convincing on Lenore's part to get them to accept her version of events. According to Lenore, who returned to Ida's village shortly after, they hadn't even fought to keep her there. In fact, they were relieved to see her go. They'd given her a stipend fit for the child of a king, under the implied condition that she refrained from drawing too much attention to herself and stayed out of their way. She hadn't even been invited to the queen's coronation.

Vegard would go back to the north. He'd stayed all through the winter as Ida grieved, as Lenore recuperated, as Arred recovered from the shock of losing its monarch and its magic at the same time.

But she could see the longing in his eyes, the way he looked northward when he thought she wasn't looking. He had the patience of someone who knew they would live for centuries, but he was still young. He wanted to go home.

And Ida . . .

Ida wanted to go too. She didn't know *where* she wanted to go, but she wanted to leave. It was a thought she couldn't shake, that maybe . . . maybe she could accompany Lenore to Callania. Callania was a difficult country for Niressos, in a lot of ways, but those were ways that Ida needed to face for herself. She couldn't keep telling herself that she was Arreden.

Or no . . . she couldn't keep telling herself that she was *only* Arreden. She was both Arreden and Niresso, and she couldn't keep looking away from that other half of herself.

And if she was being honest, she *wanted* to spend more time with Lenore.

She knew, standing there on that cold day, looking at her father's tombstone, that she couldn't stay here. She didn't *want* to live out the rest of her days in obscurity, with only a quiet grave to mark her passing. Her time at the court had changed her, had taught her what she was capable of.

Her heart had outgrown this town.

"Do you know," her mother said, startling Ida out of her reverie, "for the longest time after you left, I struggled to understand why. Why you would leave me and go chasing after someone I thought had left us."

The words stabbed at Ida's heart like ice, bringing up a fresh wave of guilt. She didn't respond, didn't know how to tell her mother how it had felt to have half of herself missing, to sit in this home in this village where everyone was *the same*, and to be different and not know why. But she didn't need to, because her mother sighed and looked at Ida, and Ida got the sense that maybe, just maybe, her mother was starting to understand.

"I realized it when you came back. When you told me what happened to Tomas. I see it every day, with you and your friends. You're a different person with them, Ida. Someone . . . whole. I haven't seen you like that since Trissaire."

Her mother looked at Ida and then looked away, her gaze on the grave in front of them. "I was never happy in Trissaire. I loved you, and I loved your father, but the city was too big, too crowded. The world was too full, and our place in it was so small. I knew why we had to live there—it made the most sense for your father's career. But the longer we stayed in Trissaire and the less we saw him, the more I wanted to go home. I thought it would be the best thing for me, and it was, but I made a mistake because I thought going home would be the best thing for you too."

"Mother . . ." Ida began.

"Let me finish." Gisela's eyes flashed, and Ida, obeying an instinct honed in childhood, stopped talking. "I should have known you were your father's daughter. And he could never have been happy here. How could someone who had seen the world, who created magic and spoke to kings and crossed oceans, be happy in this little mountain town? He would always want to leave. And I . . . I understand if you want to go too."

There were so many things Ida wanted to say. The words bubbled up in her throat, new and half-formed. She didn't know how to start, and felt that by saying any one of those words out loud, they would drag the rest up with them, until she was speaking without meaning, trying to craft a feeling the same way she crafted one of her illusions. So instead, she sucked in a breath, lowering her eyes to the ground.

"I don't want to hurt you . . ." she said. "I know I did, by leaving, and I'm sorry about that. I don't want to hurt you anymore."

"Ida . . ."

Her mother's voice was so gentle, softer than Ida remembered hearing in years. She felt a hand on her shoulder, and her breath hitched as she tried not to cry.

"Ida, you could never hurt me by being who you *are*," Gisela said. "You're a child of two worlds. You were always made for more than this. And in fact, there's something that I want you to do for me." Her mother's eyes moved away from Ida, resting once more on the grave. "Tomas deserves more than this too. He has family in the Niressians. *You* have family there. And they need to know what happened to him." She squeezed Ida's shoulder tightly, as if trying to commit the feel of her to memory, as if trying to make sure that Ida would never forget about her or about home. "I think you should go."

Ida exhaled, feeling as if her whole world had upended itself in a single breath. The Niressians—the islands on the other side of the world. Her father had once told her the journey there took months. Fear pulsed through her veins at the thought of going so far away from home, but there was another feeling right there with it, racing through her veins and setting every nerve alight.

Excitement. Anticipation.

The possibility of an adventure.

"It's so far away," she said. "I don't know how long I'd be gone."

"You should see the world while you're young," her mother said, nodding to herself as if this was an argument she'd been having in her own mind for a long time. "And you don't need to worry about me, Ida. All I ask is that you write, and that you come home."

"The Niressians?" Lenore asked, a note of surprise in her voice as she watched Ida go through her things.

Ida nodded. She still felt like a wrung-out towel, her heart aching with the memory of her mother's face as they spoke, her mother's arms around her next to her father's grave. The tears had burst out of her then, raw and ugly, and in their passing she felt like her soul had been scoured. She busied herself with looking through her clothes, making sure she had any good enough for a long journey, because she didn't know if she would be able to talk to Lenore about this without keeping her hands busy.

She'd already decided that she wanted to go. To see the Niressians—her father's homeland—for herself. But it was harder than she thought to tell the others she was leaving them behind. To tell Lenore she was leaving her behind.

"Mother wants me to go abroad," she said. "To . . . visit my father's side of the family. She thinks I should get to know them, learn about where he came from. And . . . she wants me to tell them he's gone."

"Do you know where they are?" Vegard asked. "Your father's been gone from home for a long time, by human reckoning. They may have moved."

"She gave me a notebook he showed her once, when they were first courting." Ida rested her hand over the cloth-wrapped bundle on her bed, feeling the outline of the book beneath her fingers. She wasn't sure how she felt about it, both to have something so personal in her possession and to know there was anything left of her father that her mother had never shown her. "It's an address book, for his friends and family in the Niressians. I should be able to find *somebody.*"

"And how will you cross the sea?" asked Vegard.

That was the most difficult part. Ida had once imagined herself making the trip to the islands to visit her father's family, had often imagined her father's voyage across the world. But the reality of it was daunting. She'd have to find a ship to take her, and she'd have to find the money to pay her way. Her magic made things easier, but . . .

"You should go to Callania," Lenore said. "Ships travel from there to the Niressians all the time. It would be the best place to start."

Ida winced. That would have been her first thought. Except . . .

"Callish ships are expensive. I've been thinking about working for passage, but I haven't heard the best things about how Niresso sailors are treated."

The other two exchanged looks of confusion. Ida inhaled, suddenly afraid that she was going to have to explain Niresso history to them, going to have to talk about Callish colonization when to be honest, she knew *embarrassingly* little about everything to do with her heritage, only what she had read in the papers and what her cousins in their crueler moments had seen fit to throw in her face.

But Vegard only said, "You haven't told her yet?"

"What?" Ida asked, when Lenore and Vegard looked sheepish. "Told me what?"

Lenore cleared her throat. "Um. During my trip to Trissaire, I met with Steward Dallenbach. It took some convincing, but we . . . managed to get him to release the money he's been holding in trust for you."

Ida gaped at her.

"Your salary," Lenore clarified. "For your time as Court Luminaire. You were the king's personal mage for almost half a year, and you hardly spent anything. You have enough money to see yourself to the Niressians and back, depending on how you spend it."

Her pay. She hadn't even thought of her salary, with everything that had happened, but she *had* been earning a salary, hadn't she?

And as Celeste had been quick to point out, royal patronage paid well.

"I suppose," Lenore added, with the air of someone who was continuing a conversation that had been discussed long ago, "we could seek passage in southern Callania, after finding my mother."

Ida stopped what she was doing, raising her head and turning to stare at Lenore.

"We?"

Lenore's smile, half-hidden, grew, until it seemed too big for her face to contain. There was so much light in her eyes, it was like the sun shining through the trees, so that for a moment it felt like the two of them were the only ones in the room.

"*We,*" Lenore repeated.

"We were hoping to give you a moment to grieve before we spoke to you," Vegard added. "But this information greatly speeds up our timeline."

Lenore's eyes slid away from Ida to exchange a glance with Vegard. Ida looked between the two of them, suddenly aware that they had made plans without her.

"Someone needs to start explaining things," she said, folding her arms. "Otherwise I'm going to be mad."

"You know we've been meaning to leave," Lenore said gently.

Ida nodded. It was part of the ache she'd had to swallow down every morning, when she looked at the two of them and wondered how many more days she would have of their friendship. When she looked at Lenore and wondered how much longer she would have in her company.

"We were thinking," said Lenore, "we could all go together."

That, Ida hadn't been expecting.

She stared at Lenore. "Together?"

"We'll travel to Callania first," Vegard said, "visit Lenore's mother, who lives in the north of the country. Then, I suppose, we can travel to the Niressians. See that side of the world."

"But what about you?" Ida asked Vegard. "Didn't you want to return home?"

Vegard smiled. "I do. But my time frame is quite a bit longer than yours. Before I head home, I'd like to do what I set out to in the first place. See the world."

"It seemed like the most effective way," said Lenore. "After all, in our own ways, we're all tired of being alone. We were hoping you would join us, Ida. So I suppose . . . in a way, this works out. We could go with you." She looked away as if self-conscious, tucking a strand of hair behind her ear. "If . . . that's all right with you."

All right?

There was something swelling in her chest, warm and golden. Happiness, spreading across her soul like honey, like molten sugar, like the first thaw of spring. She hadn't thought she would feel this for a long time, but her heart swelled at the thought. The three of them, traveling together. The three of them, heading off to parts unknown.

Ida no longer had to face the world alone.

This adventure didn't have to end.

Ida let out an excited shout, surging across the room. Before she fully grasped what she was doing, she had taken Lenore by the arms, had pulled her forward to press her lips to hers in a kiss. She felt Lenore's surprise, there and gone in an instant, felt Lenore relax against her, resting hands on her shoulders to keep her there before she could pull away.

Ida's heart skipped a beat. The moment was everything. Warm, and golden, and perfect.

The two of them pulled apart, laughing breathlessly, Lenore reaching up to untangle a lock of her hair that had gotten caught up in Ida's. Ida was out of breath, and Lenore's face was flushed, and Ida couldn't remember the last time she had felt like this, like she had captured lightning.

"So—" Ida began. She couldn't stop smiling. "Um—"

Mischief glittered in Lenore's eyes. They slid toward Vegard, who Ida had just remembered was there, and who was politely examining her bedroom wall with great interest. Lenore laughed, taking Ida by the hand.

"So," said Lenore. "I take it you're coming with us."

"I need to do one thing," Ida said. She drew away from Lenore, crouching down to pull something out from under her bed. A candle in a black box, one that she had finished, finally, just at the cusp of the change in seasons, during winter's last gasp before it shifted to spring. The candle inside was silver and white, shaped like a castle, like the Asteria that should have been. At its base, she'd recreated the engraving from her father's censer, the man in his boat looking up at the moon, but above the castle, she'd put in stars, and three figures on starborn horses flying away.

"This needs to go to Celeste," said Ida. "I made a promise."

"I'm sure that can be arranged," said Lenore.

When Celeste burned the candle, she would find herself back in her own Asteria, her workshop and her rooms and all the magic and all the revelry, except this time, it would be *right.* Asteria as it was meant to be, without King Aurel. The Asteria Ida would have made, if she could.

"*Are* you coming with us?" Lenore asked again.

She stared at Ida as if she held her heart in her hands. Ida set the box on the bed, rested her fingers against it, and imagined she could feel the magic seeping through its lid as she took Lenore's hand and said:

"Yes. Oh gods, *yes*. I would love nothing more."

ACKNOWLEDGMENTS

This book came into my head like a storm, and swept through an incredibly eventful season of my life. I would not have been able to get to this point without the support of a lot of people, who Ida and I both owe so much to. That includes my amazing agents, Natalie Lakosil and Antoinette van Sluytman; my incredible editor, Clare Vaughn, whose passion for Ida's story really helped it shine; and my cover illustrator, Maxine Vee, who brought Ida's world to life. I also have to thank my production editors, Jessica Berg and Mary Magrisso; my marketing director Shannon Cox; my production managers, Kristen Eckhardt and James Neel; my designers Alison Klapthor, Jessie Gang, Catherine Lee, and Alice Wang; my publicist Lindsey Triebel; and everyone else at HarperCollins who helped get this book out the door. Your hard work made *The Night King's Court* possible, and I am sincerely grateful for everything you've done.

Since books take a while to come out and a lot of work often happens after these acknowledgments are written, I'd also like to take the time to thank everyone who helped me with *Lovely Dark and Deep's* release, especially the members of my street team. Special thanks go to my Red Stripe, August Cooper. Thank you so much for your help. I also couldn't have done it without everyone else on the team, including Aleksander E. Petit, Erin Gibson (@readingwithwrin), Caitlyn DeRouin, Justine Korson, Krys, Luke, Thya Leger, Chai, and Fatima Grace. Thank you for your support.

The idea for this book came on a family vacation through Munich, Salzburg, and Vienna. Thank you, Mom, for putting up with me on that trip. I might have derailed it a little by getting too excited about my new idea, but I hope this book makes up for it.

To Rob, thank you for always being there to support me when times get tough, and for keeping me sane while I tried to get this book, and all my other books, out into the world. I'm so happy to have you by my side.

To Abuelita, rest in peace. We are so blessed to have had you in our lives.

To Dante, my little ray of sunshine. I love you so very much, and I can't wait to see who you become.